THE FOUR Day FAKEOUT

HANNAH SHIELD

Cover photography: Wander Aguiar

Cover design: Angela Haddon

Produced by:

Diana Road Books

Edgewater, Colorado

THE FOUR Day FAKEOUT

PROLOGUE

Fourteen Years Ago

I was one-quarter awake and dreaming. One of those dreams that seems like it could be real, yet you know it's not. I was throwing the ninth inning of a no-hitter against West Oaks Prep. My hands were tacky with rosin, and the dust and grass were thick in my nostrils.

The catcher signaled for a back-foot slider. A tough pitch even for a pro. For me? Pretty much impossible. But this wasn't real anyway. So I wound up, pronating my wrist just-so on the release.

The ball slammed into the catcher's mitt, barely missing the foot of the left-handed batter.

Out.

And there was the game.

The catcher stood, a hand reaching up to tug off his mask. Instead of my pock-marked teammate's face, a pair of plush, feminine lips smiled at me. Long auburn hair tumbled down around her face.

But that dark and hungry glint in her eyes? That wasn't the way my best friend usually looked at me.

Hey, army, Harper said. *You didn't choke.*

I strode toward her, giving her my cockiest grin. I was in desert camo, complete with body armor and an M4 slung across my chest, which was weird. But Harper wore my jersey and nothing else, which was very much okay.

A bumblebee flew past my ear, and I shooed it away. The crowd was still roaring, but I didn't care about the win. Just the girl in front of me.

You thought I'd blow that pitch?

No, I figured you could handle it. I had faith in you. She put her hand on my chest, gazing up at me. My rifle had disappeared. *Why haven't we ever done this before?*

Done what? I asked. *Played ball together? You hate it. You never even come to my games.*

No, not that, she said. Her hand moved down along my stomach. Then kept going, dipping inside my waistband.

Oh, *that.* Fuck.

This dream was turning into a best-friends-to-something-more porno, and I was absolutely down for it.

The bumblebee did a fly-by again. I brushed at my ear. But the buzzing didn't stop.

No, I thought. Come on. I really wanted this dream to play out. Because this scenario between Harper and me was never going to happen in real life.

I opened one eye. The light on my nightstand was on, and a green dot flashed on my phone. I grabbed the device and flipped it open.

Harper: Shelborne, are you up?
I see a light on in your room. Would you fucking write me back?
I need a ride. It's an emergency.

The words swam in front of my eyes. It was—jeez, two in the morning? Then, a final message that really told me this was serious.

PLEASE.

I snapped to full alertness. I still had half a hard-on, but it was fading fast. My thumbs jotted out a response over the keys.

Me: I was asleep. Where are you?
Harper: Outside. My front yard. Code Red.
Me: omw

I swung my legs down and almost stepped on my little sister Madison. My toes nudged her before I cursed and pulled back. She cracked an eye.

"Hi," Madison whispered. She was hugging her stuffed green dinosaur, and she'd made a nest beside my bed with her My Little Pony sleeping bag and LA Dodgers pillow. One of my hand-me-downs. "What're you doing?" she asked.

"What're *you* doing?"

"I was scared."

"Because you watched *The Shining* with Aiden on TV. After I told you not to."

"He dared me!"

"Because he's a little shit."

I didn't have to look to know that my brother was asleep in his bed across the room. Fourteen years old, and the kid snored worse than our dad.

Madison was eleven. Despite our age difference, I got along with her far better than I did with our other siblings. But maybe that was unfair. The twins were only seven.

As the oldest, I was supposed to wrangle my siblings and keep them in line. But that was like herding chipmunks.

"Don't tell Aiden I got scared of the dark," Madison whispered. "He'll make fun of me."

"I won't tell him if you'll cover for me." I stepped over her and grabbed my jeans from the back of a chair, followed by my wallet and truck keys.

"Where are you going?"

"Harper's."

"Are you going over there to kiss her?"

"What? *No*." Scenes from my dream surfaced in my mind, and I shoved them back down. "She's upset about something. She needs my help."

"What's wrong?"

Madison's voice was getting louder, and I had to put a finger over my lips and shush her. "Don't worry about it. Just cover for me if Aiden wakes up and sees I'm not here. Or if Mom…" We both knew how our mom would react if she realized I'd snuck out. It wasn't the kind of thing I usually did. Mom would demand to know all.

Madison nodded. "I can handle it. If you pay me twenty bucks."

"Ouch." I ruffled her pale blond hair. "Yeah, fine. You drive a hard bargain."

I climbed out the window of my bathroom onto the porch roof, then into the huge elm growing in my family's front yard. I jumped down from the tree onto the lawn, landing in a crouch. Then I stood, brushing my hands on my West Oaks High Baseball hoodie.

A silhouette emerged from the shadows across the street and ran toward me. She wore boots, ripped jeans, and a tank top. Her hair glowed under the streetlight, turning strands of copper and bronze and gold. She was breathing heavily, and her eyes looked rounder and wilder than I'd ever seen before.

Most of the time, Harper wore a sardonic expression, unfazed by just about everything. Like she'd already seen enough in her eighteen years that she could no longer be surprised.

"What's the emergency?" I asked.

"Wren's gone."

Harper's little sister. Wren was a freshman. A bit unpredictable, even more than Harper.

"Where'd she go?"

"Marc Landley's house. She called me half an hour ago saying she wanted to leave, but the call cut off and now she won't answer. I was just about to call a cab and go there myself."

I flattened my lips together. Shit. I grabbed my keys from the pocket of my hoodie and nodded toward my F150.

"Now you see the urgency, army?" she asked. "I said Code Red, and I meant fucking Code Red."

"Yeah. I get it now. Let's go."

TWO YEARS AGO, HARPER KENDRICK AND HER family had moved into the house across the street. In some ways, she and I were unlikely friends. I was the good boy, class president, starting pitcher on the varsity team even then. I'd known since I was in elementary that the US Armed Forces were my future. I took my Eagle Scout project and the Pledge of Allegiance very seriously. But I also couldn't wait to kick some bad guys in the ass.

Harper had that rebel artist vibe going. Paint-spattered shirts, cut-offs and combat boots. At school, she carried a battered leather messenger bag that was stuffed with sketchbooks and art supplies instead of her textbooks. The Monday after her family moved to West Oaks, she appeared in the back of my bio class, slouching in her seat and doodling in her notebook like she'd rather be anywhere else.

My parents invited her family over for dinner on a Saturday night. After dinner, while the younger kids were getting boisterous playing board games and our parents were getting drunk on white wine in the kitchen, I saw Harper sneak away.

I found her in the backyard, sitting in the grass and reading a dogeared copy of *The Gunslinger* by Stephen King. A pair of headphones covered her ears. I'm sure she saw me there, but she ignored me.

I nudged her black leather boot with my Nike. "Good book," I said. "Have you read the rest of the series?"

She frowned and looked up, edging one of her headphones ever so slightly off her ear. "You like The Dark Tower series?" I heard the skepticism in her tone. As if a jock like me couldn't possibly enjoy the same things she did.

"Sure, it's great. Crazy how the final book ends though. I still haven't decided how I feel about it."

Her eyes changed focus, like she was really looking at me for the first time. "I know, right?"

I sat down beside her in the grass, and she slid off her headphones, hanging them around her neck. "What's with the shirt?" She nodded at my chest, where the word ARMY was emblazoned in all caps.

"I've wanted to enlist since forever. But my parents want me to get a degree, so first I'll go to an ROTC program for college."

"So the shirt isn't, like, ironic or anything?"

"Nope. The United States Army is no laughing matter and has no sense of humor that they're aware of."

She snorted, and my deadpan expression cracked.

"So, Mr. Golden Boy All-American," she said. "You want to save the world?"

"Something like that." I believed most people out there had good intentions. But some just wanted to prey on the others, and I couldn't wait to smack down those assholes.

"You enjoy getting up early and running around doing what other people tell you?"

"Most people in the world end up doing what other people tell them. At least I'll be doing it for a cause I believe in."

She seemed to consider this, and a sad look passed through her eyes, almost too fast for me to see it. "Okay, army. Tell me what other books you've read. We'll see if they pass muster."

WE WERE HEADING TOWARD MARC LANDLEY'S house. I roughly remembered his address from a pool party he hosted back in middle school.

"Thank you for doing this," Harper said. "I'm sorry."

"Don't be. You know I'd do anything you needed." I wasn't exaggerating.

"Kill somebody?"

I looked at her. "Depends on the reason. You have a target in mind?"

She huffed a small laugh. "Not yet."

I gunned my truck. "Why is Wren hanging out with someone like Landley?" He was your typical high school jackass. Senior tight end on the football team, notorious for drugs, parties, and sex. Very much not the type a freshman girl like Wren should mess with.

"I dunno. She was in a rebellious mood tonight, I guess."

"Why? Did something happen?"

Harper stared out the passenger window, brows tightening.

After two years of friendship, I knew Harper didn't answer questions unless she wanted to. She was still mysterious to me. Maybe that's what drew me in. Sometimes, it seemed like she had the weight of big secrets on her shoulders. She'd open her mouth, and I could feel her longing to say whatever she was keeping inside. But she never did.

Streetlights flashed across her face as we drove.

"Jake, you're a really good person. The best."

I glanced at her again. This sudden burst of sincerity worried me more than her usual deflections. "I know I'm the best. You don't have to say that."

"Or maybe I do. Because at some point, I won't have the chance."

"You're freaking me out, Harper. What's this about?"

She wiped a hand over her face. "I'm just nervous about Wren."

I knew she was lying to me. But I didn't press.

Why didn't I push for a real answer? I've asked myself that question so many times in the years since. Would it have made a difference?

It was 2:30 a.m. when we pulled up in front of Landley's house. I had to park behind a huge line of cars. Music spilled out onto the street, voices shouting. Every light in the house blazed.

Harper reached the door first. It was unlocked, and we barged inside. A couple guys from the soccer team were passing by, holding red Solo cups of punch. Their eyes widened when they saw me. "Hey, Shelborne," one said warily. Like he thought I was here to start trouble. Well, he was right. Teachers and parents thought I was an angel, but I once knocked out a dude in the guys' restroom for getting handsy with one of my female friends.

I was six-two and almost two hundred pounds of muscle, and Harper wasn't the only person who called me "army."

"Where's Landley?" I asked.

The soccer players snickered nervously. "Uh oh, what did he do?"

"Jake!" Harper called from another room. "Over here!"

Wren was sitting by herself in the dining room, resting her head on the table with her eyes closed. Harper knelt beside her. "Wren? Are you okay?"

Wren mumbled something. Harper turned around, fixing me with a panicked gaze.

I went over and lifted Wren out of the chair, cradling her like a baby. She stirred, blinking her eyes. "What? Jake? What're you doing here?"

"We're here to take you home."

Her sister came in close, grabbing Wren's chin. "Have you been drinking? Did you take something?"

"I had one beer. I'm just tired. I was waiting for you to get here."

"Do you have any idea how scared I was?" Harper asked. "What the hell were you thinking?"

"I guess I wasn't."

I was studying her clothes. She didn't look disheveled, but it was hard to tell. "Did anybody mess with you?" I asked. "Landley?"

"No," Wren said sharply. "Please. Let's just go."

I carried her out to the truck. Halfway there, Wren insisted on walking by herself. Harper helped her into the back seat.

"I'll be right back," I said to them, handing Harper my keys so she could get the engine started. "Just need to do something real quick."

"Jake, don't do anything stupid."

"Who, *me*?" I flashed her a grin, and she shook her head.

I made a circuit of the house until I found Marc Landley. He was outside on a patio lounger with some girl on his lap. Marc sneered when he saw me. "What are you doing here, Shelborne? I didn't invite the class narc."

"I'd like a word about Wren Kendrick."

"Who?"

"Harper's little sister. Did you lay a hand on her?"

He laughed and grinned at his friends, who were watching but wary of me. "You talk like you're from the fucking 1950s. I wouldn't lay a hand or anything else on anybody related to Harpy Kendrick. She's a frigid bitch."

I advanced on him. The girl in his lap scampered away. Marc shot up, standing toe to toe with me. He was as tall as me, not so wide in the shoulders. He sucked in a breath, probably ready to add another insult to the list.

I didn't give him the chance.

I wound my arm up and punched him in the face. My own personal knuckle ball. Cartilage and bone crunched under my fist.

Someone screamed. Marc fell backward onto the lounger, blood spurting from his nose. He was up in half a second, bellowing and running for me like a left tackle.

I sidestepped, pushing him with the tips of my fingers right into the pool.

Splash.

Marc surfaced, sputtering and coughing on pool water and blood.

"Somebody get him out of there before he drowns," I said. If Landley wanted to tattle on me, then I'd make sure everybody knew about the underage girls at his party.

The other guys stared in shock. Nobody said a word to me.

On my way out, I met Harper in the doorway of the house. "What were you doing?" she asked.

"Making my opinion known. Now we can go."

Wren nodded off on the drive back. We got her up the stairs and into her bed. It was not a quiet process, especially with her muttering in her sleep.

"How are your parents sleeping through this?" I asked when we were out in the hall.

"Ambien and martinis." Harper noticed my hand. My knuckles were swollen and split, oozing blood. "Shit, that looks awful."

"It's fine."

"Not, it's not." She tugged me into the hall bathroom and rinsed off the blood. "Making your opinion known, huh?"

I shrugged. "I have strong opinions."

She snorted. Her fingers moved gently over my hand as she placed a bandage over the broken skin. "You're something else, army. I've never met anybody like you. So...*noble*."

"When you say it, it sounds bad."

I expected a comeback. A protest about how pigheaded I could be. How she didn't need me to defend her or Wren's honor. But when her hazel eyes lifted, they were soft. "Wait here. I'll get an ice pack."

"I could get one at home."

"Jake, please," she whispered. "Just stay here."

"Stay until you get the ice pack? Or..."

"Stay the night."

My heart and my lungs weren't working right anymore. Everything was pumping too fast.

"Will you?" she asked. "I don't want to be alone."

"Yeah. If you need me, then of course I'll stay. Always."

Harper closed her eyes and frowned, as if my answer disappointed her. I wanted to ask why, but she was out the door and heading downstairs.

She brought the ice pack, and we went into her bedroom. I'd been here a million times, but never at night. I took off my jeans. Harper did the same, facing away from me. She did that weird thing girls do where they take off their bra under their shirt and then pull it out through a sleeve.

We both slid under the covers, lying on our backs and staring at the ceiling. The sound of our breathing filled the silence.

I was concentrating very intently on not getting hard.

It was not working.

"Jake?"

"Yeah?"

"There are things you don't know about my family. About me."

"Okay…"

She didn't go on, so I prompted, "Like what?"

"I can't tell you."

This was ringing all kinds of alarm bells in my brain. Waking up the fury and indignation that seemed to live just under the surface of my skin at all times. I usually hid it well. But when I needed that anger? Boom. It was there.

"Did someone in your family hurt you?"

"Not like that. Not what you're thinking." She rolled to her side to face me. "I just want you to know that you mean a lot to me, and if I could tell anyone the truth, it would be you. I wish nothing had to change between us, but it will. I won't always have you."

"Do you mean after we graduate? That's months away."

Her eyes were full of an intensity I couldn't interpret.

"Will you kiss me?" she asked.

That question was like a bomb in the center of my thoughts. Everything scattered.

I should've kept asking for explanations. Shouldn't have let her distract me. But once she made that request, there was only one possible thing I could do.

I leaned across the pillow and kissed her.

Harper's mouth was so soft, softer than I would've imagined from all the shit she'd given me over the past two years.

My best friend. Probably my favorite person in the world.

I pulled her against me. Fitted her to my chest and stomach, my arms going tight around her. Her bare thigh pressed to my crotch and moved, rubbing against my stiff cock through my boxer briefs.

She opened up to my tongue like she would give me everything if I asked. And I wanted it. God, did I want it.

And that's what made me stop. I didn't understand what was going on with her, but she wasn't herself tonight. I didn't want to do anything that would hurt her or jeopardize our friendship.

I pulled my hips back, softened my kisses. Ran my fingers gently through her hair. I didn't let go of her, but I turned the heat way, way down.

"You don't want to?" she asked.

"I really want to. But you have to think about it and be sure."

"Such a fucking hero."

Harper buried her face against my neck, and I held her until she fell asleep.

THAT WASN'T THE LAST TIME I KISSED HER. BUT A few weeks later, there was a for-sale sign in Harper's yard, and her family was gone.

A month later, I got a single postcard showing the Chicago skyline. No return address.

Had to move. I'll miss you, army. Be careful out there saving the world.

And then, silence.

1

Jake

I dump my suitcase by the door, praying my kids don't have anything else to add when they arrive. Four stuffed animals have got to be enough.

Buster, our golden retriever, wags his tail and looks at me expectantly. Like he's asking, *When are we leaving? Is it now?*

I rub his ears, thinking, *I know, buddy, I'm anxious to blow this pop stand too.*

"Let's shop for groceries when we get there," I say.

Madison scoffs. "On Catalina Island? Do you know how expensive that will be? Nash, back me up here."

My sister's boyfriend looks up from the toast he's buttering. "What are you two arguing about?"

"They're talking about groceries, Dad," his teenage daughter Emma says. "Keep up. I agree with Madison. The selection at whatever market they have on the island could be terrible."

"But if we try to hit the mega store with Riley and Hudson, it'll take all day," I point out. "I want to get on the road."

This will be the first vacation I've had in almost a year.

First one that hasn't been canceled because of work, anyway. I want to get out there before my boss can somehow ruin it. Once we're on the ferry, I can pretend I don't have cell reception.

Nash glances around his great room. "Speaking of your children, where are they?"

"Adrienne's on her way with them. I told her I'd pick them up myself, but she wanted to take them out to breakfast."

"She's brave," Madison mutters.

"And you're not?" I ask. My sister is a cop with West Oaks PD. Nash is a SWAT tactical sergeant. It's how he and Madison met. They've been dating for six months, and Nash and Emma are already an integral part of our big, messy family.

"Brave enough to take your five-year-olds to a restaurant?" Madison says. "I'm still traumatized after the last time we tried that."

"It wasn't that bad."

"They tripped the hostess and asked her so many questions that she quit her job and walked out," Emma reminds me.

"That's an exaggeration. The hostess tripped on her shoelace."

Madison and Emma crack up. The doorbell rings, and I flip them both off on my way to answer it. I hear Nash grumbling about my use of rude gestures in front of his daughter, but he doesn't mean it. He loves me.

More importantly, Nash and I get each other. We're both ex-military, both in law enforcement, and we're divorced dads doing our best not to mess up our kids. Only, Nash has found his perfect partner in my sister.

I don't have time for a hook-up, much less a love connection. I might be jealous if I wasn't so thrilled for them.

I hear Riley and Hudson on Nash's porch, bickering as usual. "No," Riley yells, "Owelette is way better than Catboy!"

Madison does have a point. My kids have the combined energy of a category-five hurricane, and they never stop storming.

I throw open the door. "Hey! My favorite people!"

"Daddy!" They both drop their tiny backpacks and rush me, hugging me and pushing at each other at the same time.

I look up at Adrienne, my ex-wife. She's calm and put-together, not a hair out of place. I stand and give her a kiss on the cheek.

"You ready for a week of bliss?" I ask.

She moans. "I've been fantasizing about this spa retreat since I read about it. I can almost smell the lavender and patchouli."

Riley and Hudson tear past me, racing into the house in search of Emma. "When's your flight?" I ask.

"Three hours."

"Jeez, you'd better get moving."

"I know. But I wanted to make sure nothing unexpected had come up. After last time…"

"I still feel awful about that."

"Not blaming you. There's always somebody who needs rescue. Bad guys to thwart. Justice never sleeps. Etcetera." She's teasing, but I can tell she's bracing herself for bad news.

Earlier this year, Adrienne was supposed to take a girls' weekend, but she had to bail when I couldn't get out of work and none of my family members could take the kids. And that's after the Disney World trip I had to cancel.

I might not be the *worst* ex-husband and co-parent, but I must be up there.

"For the next week, I'm officially out of the hero business. Nothing is going to come up. I swear."

She exhales. "Good, because I *really* need this trip. The kids packed their own bags, so they're full of fruit snacks and bath toys."

"That's okay. I've got the essentials covered."

Madison pokes her head out. "Adrienne! Hey!" My sister and my ex hug, gushing about our respective vacations. They get along great. Adrienne's always fit in well with my family. Even though she realized she didn't fit so well with *me*.

"Riley and Hudson are going to have so much fun," Madison says. "Emma has games and coloring supplies lined up for the drive."

"She's the best." Adrienne beams. "Wish I could stay and visit, but I gotta run. Thanks, Jake. Love you, okay?"

There's a pang in my chest. "Yep. Love you, too."

I watch her dash to her car and drive away, a huge smile on her face.

When we got married, I meant forever. But things don't always work out that way.

"You okay?" Madison asks softly.

I glance over at her. She's got similar features to mine, though hers are softened with femininity. Her blond hair is pale as cornsilk, while mine is a dirtier shade. Where she's polished, I'm rough and hardened.

She's got some gnarly scars from gunshot wounds. Me, I've got my share of scars too. But I've never been seriously wounded, despite tours in war zones and years as a Federal Drug Enforcement Agent.

Most of *my* scars are on the inside.

"Couldn't be better," I say, flashing a grin. But I know exactly what she means. Madison is one of the few people in the world who knows the story behind my divorce.

Adrienne and I met just before my second deployment,

and I was head over heels. She was almost done with her psychology degree. I asked her to build a life with me. She said yes. So far, so good.

There was a hiccup when she got pregnant with twins just a few months into our marriage. I was overseas at the time, and I freaked out a little. Not because I wasn't happy about the news, but because I couldn't get my head around how much my life was about to change.

It turned out that having two squalling newborns wasn't the hardest part. Not by a long shot. That was when my wife opened up to me and said that she didn't want to be married anymore.

By then, I had known for a while that something wasn't right in my marriage. We'd fallen in love fast, and we hadn't gotten intimate until after our wedding. Adrienne had said she wanted to wait. I was nowhere near a virgin, but I was completely on board and respected her wishes. I loved her enough that I would've done anything. And patience? I've always had that in spades.

I didn't realize she was waiting for a spark of physical desire that never arrived.

She tried. And so did I. After she told me she didn't want to have sex—as in *ever again*—we went to couple's therapy for an entire year. She realized that she just wasn't wired for physical intimacy. It's nothing that I blame her for. Sometimes, you discover things about yourself when you're ready, not when it's convenient.

I would've stuck it out through anything. I wanted our family to work. I'd seen terrible things in the army, so much that was wrong with the world, and I clung to the purity of what I had with Adrienne, even if neither of us was happy.

But Adrienne could see the truth I wasn't ready to admit —that we were simply incompatible at a fundamental level.

And we could still be a loving family even if we weren't married.

We've been divorced for two years now. I can say that it's for the best. We live five minutes away from each other, and the kids transition effortlessly between us. We could probably still live together if Adrienne wasn't so insistent that she wants me to find someone new. Though I don't have much more sex now than I did while I was married. And the frustration, that *need* is...hmmm. Intense sometimes.

But any spare moment that I'm not with my family, I'm working. Otherwise, I'm living that dad life. Wiping butts, comforting scared kids after nightmares, and playing the bouncer to two tiny wrecking balls.

In almost every aspect of my life, I've hit the jackpot. So what if a small piece here and there is missing?

Madison and I head inside. I breathe a sigh of relief when I see Nash swinging Hudson around and Emma braiding Riley's hair. Buster bounces around excitedly, tail whipping back and forth. Thank God for my family.

This week on Catalina Island is going to rock. I'll even play along and buy the groceries wherever Madison wants.

I'm feeling so mellow and optimistic that I let my guard down. That's the only explanation. Because when my phone rings, I answer without thinking.

"Jake here," I say.

"Shelborne. It's Agent Reyes. Did I catch you before you left town?"

My eyes sink closed. Fuck, no. Why?

Why?

"Um." I chew my lip, seriously considering lying to my boss. But he's probably tracking my phone location right now. Wouldn't put it past him. "We're just about to head out. Packing up the kids into the car. Pool floaties, sunscreen, boogie boards. For the vacation that I scheduled months ago. Remember that one?"

Reyes is unmoved. "I remember it, yeah. But I just got off the phone with a nurse at UCLA Medical Center. It's Kevin Eisenhower. He was hit by a car on his morning jog."

"Oh, no. Is he all right? What's the damage?"

"They don't know yet. But it's looking like a head injury."

I glance at my kids, who are smiling in their summer shorts and sun hats. Madison and Nash have gone watchful and quiet.

"Was he targeted?" I ask. Kevin is a good guy, and I'm feeling sick thinking of what this could mean for him and his family.

But I also know Kevin's been focused on some big project. Something so sensitive that I'm not aware of the details. It's need-to-know, and I haven't had a need. I don't *want* to have a need.

"As far as we can tell, it was just shitty luck," Reyes tells me. "A little old lady slammed into him going around a blind corner the wrong way. She was injured in the crash too. Might not survive. It's terrible, but we have no reason to suspect it was intentional."

"Should I go to the hospital? Does his wife need anything?"

Reyes clears his throat. "We've got people taking care of Kevin's family. What I have for you is a bigger ask. It's about the op he's been working on. Everything is set up, and Kevin going MIA? It's going to be hell on our plans. We've already got people in motion."

"Then abort the op."

"This isn't the kind of op we can just scrap and try again later."

"You can't seriously expect me to—"

"Shelborne, we need to discuss this in person. When you hear what's going on, you'll understand. Okay?"

When I end the call, I lower my phone, squeezing the plastic hard enough to make it creak. Madison's hand rests on my shoulder.

I try to smile as I edge away from her. Comfort is not what I want right now. I want to fucking break something. Preferably some drug kingpin's face for ruining my attempt at family time.

One week. Was that really so much to fucking ask?

Hudson gasps. "Daddy, you said a bad word!"

Oops. Guess that was out loud.

Buster noses my hand, and my kids are frowning at me. Even Madison looks concerned. The tension beneath the silence runs ocean-deep.

With my family, I try my best to be super dad. But at work, I deal with assholes and scum on a daily basis. You can't show a single moment of weakness, and sometimes, I don't like this side of myself. The parts that are hard. Even cruel. That's not who I want to be with my kids.

I worry that someday, I won't be able to turn it off anymore.

"Sorry, guys. I have to go see my boss. But I'll be back soon."

"Daddy, no!" Riley flops onto the ground. Hudson has tears in his eyes.

Nash sticks his hands in the pockets of his board shorts. "Of course. If you have to work, you have to work. Duty calls, right?"

I stand up, tucking my phone away. "I'm going to sort this out, and then we'll go on our trip. Together. I just need a couple hours."

"We'll get the groceries," Madison says.

"And I can watch a movie with Riley and Hudson," Emma volunteers.

Nash walks me to the door. "We've got this. Take all the time you need."

"Thanks, man."

I haven't spoken to Nash in detail about my job. There are parts of it I don't discuss with anyone. But I'm sure he knows. Nash is an ex-Navy SEAL, and he understands what men like us are sometimes called upon to do. He's found a way to straddle both worlds. The warrior and the family man. He's found his equilibrium, and he knows how to keep his priorities straight.

And when he books a vacation, he gets to take the fucking vacation.

But it's not even the trip that's bothering me, deep down. The real issue is, I feel the darkness bleeding into the daylight. It's getting harder to banish it when I go home at night.

I have to keep that stuff away from my family. I won't ever allow it to touch them.

Especially not the cruel, battle-scarred parts of *me*.

2

Jake

*D*etective Angela Murphy from West Oaks PD is already waiting when I arrive. She's perched on top of a picnic table, wearing suit pants and a button-down shirt that hugs her curves. The tiny braids of her hair are pulled into an elegant twist behind her head. A tad over-dressed for the beach, but she must've come here straight from the station.

I'm guessing Reyes, my boss, made sure that Murphy got here first. He knows I'll react better to her. Partly because she's stunning, and partly because she's a tough badass, and I've gotta respect that in a woman. She's not interested in softening herself to make others comfortable.

If I was up for dating, Murphy would be high on my list of prospects. But who knows, maybe I'm not her type.

She tugs down her sunglasses as I pad across the sand and shakes her head at me. "Shelborne, a frown like that should be illegal on a day like today."

I'm wearing my swim trunks and a ratty t-shirt. With my messy dirty-blond hair, I've got the surfer look down. But she's right. The scowl ruins the effect.

"I'm pissed at Agent Reyes," I say. "Not you."

"I wasn't taking it personally anyway." She brushes sand from the cuffs of her pants. Her heels are off, cast aside on the picnic bench.

I work undercover a lot, and that means I keep a low profile. Hence this beachside meeting. Detective Murphy is a member of the regional drug and organized crime task force. It's made up of state, federal, and local officials. We work together across jurisdictions to fight the drug trade. Though I live in West Oaks, my work often takes me to nearby Los Angeles.

Murphy's presence here tells me this assignment will be closer to home. Not sure how I feel about that.

I'm known for handling difficult undercover cases. The kind that involve some of the most vicious, violent mobsters and gangsters. I have a knack for making them believe I'm one of them. It's not a talent I'd brag about. Just a fact.

Finally, Agent Reyes makes an appearance. He has fed written all over him. Sunglasses, clean-cut style. At least he didn't wear his DEA windbreaker.

"What was Kevin Eisenhower working on?" I ask without preamble.

Reyes takes a seat and gestures for Murphy to go ahead. "How much do you know about the Caldwell crime family?" she asks.

"I know they're originally from Chicago. They provide logistics and transport for moving illegal drugs into the middle of the country."

A man named Amos Caldwell is their figurehead. His two sons, Tristan and Roman, run the high-level operations of the organization from their base in Illinois. At least that's what I've heard. I haven't dealt with anything touching the Caldwells myself.

Murphy nods. "They've been building up their presence

and foothold here in Southern California, particularly in their shipping operations. They partner with a company called SunSpeed, based right here in SoCal, and we've suspected for years that it's a front."

"Right, I've heard of it. But we've never been able to prove anything."

"SunSpeed has legit clients, and they hide drugs in the shipments. The Caldwells have spent over a decade putting pieces into place, building their operation. And now, with the collapse of the Silverlake Syndicate in the last year or two, there's room for the Caldwells to make an even bigger move in this region."

She glances at Reyes, and he takes over the narrative.

"Just recently, a contact from within the Caldwell organization got in touch with us. An extended family member. Said she wanted to become a confidential informant."

I take off my sunglasses and turn to face my boss. "From within the organization? And Kevin Eisenhower was working with this CI?"

"That's right," Agent Reyes says. "It was a joint effort between our offices in LA and Chicago. The Caldwells have spent months planning a meeting with potential investors here in West Oaks."

"Investors?" I snort, but not because it's funny. Because it's so disgusting and so predictable. "Guys with the big bucks are looking for new ways to diversify their portfolios? Figures."

"So you can see why this is important." Murphy's smooth skin doesn't have a trace of sweat, despite the sun. "The Caldwells will be wooing and entertaining their investors at a West Oaks resort over the next four days. Kevin was supposed to go undercover, posing as our CI's boyfriend. He was tasked with identifying these investors. From there, we'll roll out the wiretaps, get search warrants, start flipping witnesses. We want to bring the Caldwells down. And then, maybe the cartels they're working with."

I want to help. I do. But there's always *something*, just like Adrienne said. There's always a bad guy. Sometimes, I feel like I'm giving more of my life to the criminals than to my loved ones.

"I understand how important this is," I say. "It was bad luck that Kevin got hurt. But some ops don't work out. This time, I can't charge in and save the day."

Murphy and Reyes exchange another tense look. They're up to something. And I really don't like it.

"What?" I ask.

"There's another aspect to the situation," Murphy says. "A personal connection."

"Personal? Personal to what?" I'm getting impatient. I feel like they're stringing me along, doling out information bit by bit. I just want to know what the hell is really going on.

"A personal connection to *you*."

She produces a piece of paper from her blazer and sets it on the picnic table. A breeze ruffles the edge of the page. I reach for it, but she keeps her hand in place. "You grew up here in West Oaks, right?"

"Yes. You know that." My sister is West Oaks PD. Not only that, Murphy and I have bonded over late night coffee breaks and task force Zoom calls.

And she should know me well enough to realize this slow-rolling of information is pissing me off.

"Well, our CI spent some time in West Oaks too," she says. "We've been aware of this connection and chose to keep it quiet."

Agent Reyes must see the fury in my expression because he dives in, trying to explain. "We were worried you wouldn't be able to stay objective. But now that Kevin is out of commission? You're the only person who might be able to step in."

"I'm not smart enough to figure out what the hell you're talking about," I snap. "So just spell it out for me."

Murphy lifts her hand from the piece of paper, and I snatch it up. But when I see the face there, the name, my whole world—everything that made sense a moment ago—tilts on its head.

I'm looking at my former best friend. The girl who meant the world to me when I was eighteen years old and still had a sheen of innocence in my eyes.

Harper.

3

Harper

"We're now beginning our descent," the pilot says over the loudspeaker.

I lift my tray table and put away my laptop. I wasn't looking at those budget spreadsheets anyway. I've been too nervous, my mind bouncing from one thing to the next.

Beside me, my father snores, his mouth hanging open. He couldn't always sleep this soundly at the drop of a hat. When I was younger, Mom and Dad both needed pills and alcohol to get through the night. Now, my mother needs those things to get through the *day*.

But my father's better off. For one, he's divorced from my mom and happier for it. Plus, in the last decade or so, Dad's gotten more skilled at tuning out the distractions of the rest of the world. In other words, all the realities that he'd rather forget.

Sometimes, I wish I had that particular talent.

I push Dad's tray table up into place, then drop a kiss onto his cheek. Good thing he's resting now. I don't know how much sleep we'll get over the next several days.

The plane starts to descend, and I raise my window shade

to watch. At first, it's just white out there. The occasional teasing glimpse of blue peeking between the clouds.

And then, finally, there it is. The deep blue of the Pacific Ocean. I inhale deeply, imagining the salt-kissed air. The whisper of freedom.

I was sure to pick a seat on this side of the plane so I wouldn't miss it as we landed.

Dad and I make the trip to Los Angeles every month or two, and I never miss this view. It's why I rented an apartment with a lake view in Chicago. Seeing the water every day calms me. Makes the tasks ahead not seem so intolerable. And I can look out at the waves and pretend the whitecaps inside my soul are the same as those on the water. Just a tumult on the surface, but serene underneath. A wide-open horizon, even if freedom has just been an illusion for most of my life.

When I'm staring at the water, it feels like all that potential is within my reach.

Today, it might really be true. I want to believe this trip is different. Because *I'm* different. I'm taking a step I've never been brave enough to make before.

In the past, I told myself that I wasn't ready, that I needed more time. More information and more prep. But I think it was really fear.

Because once you're out on the open water, who knows what might happen. If you mess up, all that vastness could swallow you whole.

My dad snorts, sitting up. He wipes the line of drool from his chin. "We landing soon?" he asks.

"Yep. Maybe twenty minutes."

He nods, like this is any other visit to the LA basin. Like this trip isn't going to change our lives forever. For better, or maybe for worse.

I focus on the ocean again. My fingers twitch, and I wish

that I had my charcoal pencil. I imagine the shadows I'd make, the smudges and cross-hatches. With water, it's all about the way the light hits. The reflections of the sky and sun, the hints of depth underneath. But that's what I love about drawing with charcoal. You shade in the darkness in order to reveal the light.

Too soon, the view of the water disappears. We land hard on the concrete runway. My hands grip the armrests. The plane shakes, speeding toward an unseen finish line. But my mind is still out there with the ocean.

I imagine the coast. Venice Beach, Santa Monica, Malibu. The twists and turns of the rocky edge of California.

West Oaks.

When I come to LA by myself, I like to book a hotel with a beach view. But in the fourteen years since I left West Oaks, I've never made it to that particular town. I've told myself I didn't want to deal with the traffic, even though a few hours spent driving the PCH is high on my list of favorite things to do. The truth is, I couldn't bring myself to go back to the place where I was the happiest in my life.

The two best years, when my name was Kendrick instead of Caldwell.

Acid rises in my stomach like a storm surge. I'll be returning to West Oaks for this trip, and I don't think I'm ready for it. But everything is riding on what happens in the next four days.

My future. My family.

So I'd better shove aside all these sentimental thoughts. Memories of a life I wish that I'd never had to leave.

A handsome golden-haired boy who, for a little while, played my hero.

When it's our turn to leave the plane, I grab my carry-on from the overhead bin and then my dad's. "Thanks," he mumbles. He's not as strong as he used to be, even though he tries not to show it.

But that's how things are in my family. We've each found our way to survive, and we don't let the pain show.

I walk on autopilot through the terminal. Once we leave the secure area, there's a man in a suit with the name Caldwell on the sign. Our usual driver, though he works for my family, not truly for me.

"Hey, Jimmy," I say.

He nods. "Miss Caldwell. Mr. Caldwell. How was the flight?"

We make polite conversation on the way outside. The sun is baking the pavement, but at least it's not the Chicago humidity. I breathe in, imagining I can smell a hint of salt underneath that aroma of car exhaust. My heels click, and the wheels on my bag whir. I force everything else out of my mind. Everything I'll have to do, the insane risk that I'm taking.

What am I thinking? How the hell is this going to work?

I've imagined every way that this plan could go wrong. Usually, it plays out film-noir style. The black and white aesthetic hides the gaudy red of the blood spatter. The spreading pool beneath the head of someone I love.

Stop.

I shove all those doubts and fears down beneath the beating of my heart and the honking that I can already hear from the freeway a few miles away.

I guess that's why I don't notice the car at first. Jimmy's usual ride is a black town car. Understated, elegant. Always waxed to a shiny black gleam. But when Jimmy opens the back door of the vehicle, we're standing at a limo.

I open my mouth, starting to ask what's going on.

Then a pair of big hands presses on my shoulders, shocking me with their iron grip. I smell cherry cough drops.

Lars. My cousin's personal bodyguard. He's massive, with long curly hair and a messy beard. Like a Viking straight out of medieval times and just as friendly.

"Let go of me," I say through gritted teeth.

"Get in."

The more rational part of me knows that it's better to accept what's happening. But instead, I stomp my heel into the toe of his shoe. He grunts as I try to wriggle free. "Let go!" I shout.

"Harper, enough," says a voice from the back of the limo. The muffin I ate that morning burns on its way back up my throat.

They know. Somehow, my family knows what I've done.

Lars pushes me into the back of the limo.

"Roman," I choke out.

"Is there some reason you don't want to see me, Harper?" my cousin asks from the seat beside me.

I brush off my clothes. "I don't appreciate being manhandled. You could've asked." Bravado masks my fear. My heart's buzzing like a wind-up toy. "It's disrespectful."

"Didn't realize you were so concerned about respect." Roman's wearing a suit that probably cost five thousand dollars, though he's paired it with a black T-shirt like he's some TV gangster. He's a lot of things, but he's never been very original.

The door slams closed. I glance at the window. Jimmy's got an arm on my father, keeping him in place. Lars gets into the driver's seat of the limo, and the whole thing rocks beneath us.

Shit. Are they taking me to the LA River to dump my body? That would be the perfect cliché, wouldn't it?

But Lars doesn't start the engine. We stay in the parking lot.

Roman crosses his legs. "Can I offer you a drink?"

I don't answer, and he pours a finger of some brown liquor from a crystal decanter. He hands me the glass. I take it, my knuckles turning white as I grip it.

"What are you doing here?" I ask.

I'm playing dumb. Yep, that's all I've got.

"I heard you were arriving a day early. But you're not coming out to the resort until tomorrow. Why is that?"

I shrug, forcing my eyes to meet his. I'm so keyed up I want to scream. "We're taking some business meetings today before we head to West Oaks. In fact, you're going to make us late."

"Business meetings." Roman nods, as if he has any idea. While most of the Caldwells live in Chicago, Roman lives here in LA. But he's more muscle than brains. I try to avoid him as much as possible.

It's been a long time since I harbored any illusions about my family. And it's taken far too long for me to work up the courage to betray them. I guess you'd call us organized crime. Drugs, guns, protection rackets. Though the drugs have taken center stage in our income stream in recent years, in large part because of SunSpeed, the shipping company that Dad and I run out of California.

I detest this life. Hate it with every fiber of my being. I want *out*. For me and those I love.

But that's much easier dreamed than done.

"I just wanted to check in on you," Roman says. "Where's the boyfriend I've heard so much about? I thought he'd be here."

"He's meeting us later in Beverly Hills. Not that it's your business."

My "boyfriend" is really an agent with the DEA. I've been planting the seeds of Kevin's backstory for months. His fake name will be "Jake Worthington," something I pulled out of my brain at random. Supposedly, he's one of SunSpeed's legitimate clients. He captured my heart, and now he wants to officially join the Caldwell clan. I've sought permission to introduce him to the family.

If my Uncle Amos—our current patriarch, and Roman's father—approves of him, my "boyfriend" will ask me to marry him.

Obviously, I have other plans.

"We're staying at a hotel on the west side overnight," I say, "and he'll be at the resort tomorrow to meet Uncle Amos."

Roman pours his own glass of liquor. "We've already told you what we need from you over the next several days. If you screw this up, my father is not going to be forgiving."

"I have no doubt of that."

Roman's eyes move over my body, and I cross my arms over my suit.

He's never touched me. Roman is all about power. Intimidation.

That's what I keep telling myself.

"So compliant all of a sudden," he says.

"Hardly. I'm just doing my part for the family. Doing my *job*. But I don't have to take your shit." This is a more grownup version of *you're not the boss of me*, something I've been saying to Roman since we were kids in Illinois. But still true.

He leans in. "You don't think so?"

I'm so close to losing it already. If I wasn't used to living with an insane amount of stress hormones in my body, I'd probably be catatonic right now. I want to dig my fingers into my hair and scratch at my scalp, but that's my tell. A sure sign I'm anxious.

"My father is still Amos's brother," I say. "Your uncle."

"And Mason's in any state to protect you?"

"I can protect myself."

Roman grabs my wrist, and I don't think. I throw the

liquid from my glass into his face. For a split second, he's shocked. Liquor drips down over his lips and into the scruff on his chin.

Then Roman lunges, grabbing me around the throat. He forces me back against the seat, looming over me. He brings his lips right up against my ear. I smell his sweat, sharp and acidic. His goatee tickles my cheek.

I cringe away, but I can't move. I can barely even breathe.

"There's my girl," he murmurs. "That spitfire I know and love. You can never keep her caged for long. But you know what will happen if you fuck up this meeting for us. If it goes well, you and your parents and Wren are set. And your boyfriend too, because that's who we are. The Caldwells are generous."

I squeak. He squeezes my throat. I can't breathe. I claw at his chest, and his grip just gets tighter. "But if anything goes wrong?" he asks.

He doesn't have to say it. When you're a Caldwell, you know what'll happen if you step out of line. But then he fills in the blanks, just in case I'm suffering from a lack of imagination.

"It won't just be you and Mason who are punished. It'll be your sister. You will never see her again. But I'll send you a recording of her screams. You get it?"

I nod. My vision is starting to blur.

He lets go of my throat, and I gasp and cough.

It hurts, but I already know it won't bruise. Roman has a sixth sense for how to cause pain without leaving any marks. Practice, I figure.

"Get out," he says, turning away.

I push out of the limo, stumbling over the concrete. My father rushes to my side. "Harper?" Dad asks, voice trembling. "Are you all right?"

We're huddled together. Jimmy watches, waiting beside the town car to drive us into West LA.

I whisper, "You see why we have to go through with it? We can't back out."

My father hesitates. Then he mutters, "I know. I'll do whatever you ask."

"You swear?"

"I promise, sweetheart. I will."

My throat is on fire. But elation fills my body.

I had to bring my father in on the DEA's undercover operation. It wasn't easy to convince him. He was terrified at first, even though Dad wants to get out from under Amos's thumb as much as I do.

I needed Dad to vouch for "Jake Worthington" as a SunSpeed client and potential son-in-law. Without my father, we won't be able to pull this off. But Dad is falling in line. He's far from perfect, but he'll do what he has to.

And most importantly? Roman doesn't know what I really have planned. If he did, he wouldn't have let me go.

I would already be dead.

4

Jake

It takes the full two-hour drive into LA to dampen my shock.

When I reach the hotel, I find a parking space a couple of blocks off—*not* an easy feat—and walk the rest of the way. I slip into a service entrance at the rear of the hotel and find the nearest storage closet, which has a stack of spare uniforms and the rest of the props that I'll need. Thank you, LAPD. They've already paved the way for me.

Once I'm in costume, I walk down the hallway that leads past the laundry room and kitchens, carrying my toolbox and whistling quietly under my breath. Heat and the smells of detergent and garlic fill the air. I nod at a guy in a bellhop uniform who's carrying a pack of cigarettes. He nods back with barely a glance.

Just your regular, everyday maintenance guy here. Nothing to see.

This is one thing I've gotten pretty good at. Blending in. Becoming what's expected. That's how I waltz into one of the fanciest hotels in Beverly Hills and find an alcove to kill time in, waiting for the word that I'm cleared to head upstairs.

Through my earpiece, I hear the two undercover LAPD officers in the lobby bantering back and forth. They don't know exactly who I am or what I'm really doing here, but they're keeping an eye out for certain faces associated with the Caldwell family. A lot of thought and care has gone into the prep for this operation.

And Murphy and Reyes expect me to just step into Kevin's place?

I told them it was far too risky. If it hadn't been Harper's face on that piece of paper, I would've kept on refusing.

To me, she was Harper Kendrick. But apparently, that wasn't her real name. She's part of the Caldwell crime family.

Just how many lies did she tell me?

All the times I sensed that Harper was hiding things from me... The way her family appeared so suddenly in West Oaks, then disappeared without any warning. That aura of something *not right* in their house.

I should've found some way to...I don't know. Save her.

The officers in the lobby start bantering about the latest trades the Dodgers made, which is my signal. Harper has arrived, and I'm cleared to go upstairs.

I grab my toolbox and head out into the hall, making a beeline for the service elevator.

As the elevator takes me to the third floor, my nerves settle. I can almost pretend I'm just here to do a job. That I'm not full up with a million questions clamoring for an answer.

I'm going to see Harper again. But I'm not the same boy I was back when we used to know each other. And there's no way she's the same person either.

What's she going to think of me?

I reach the correct room number and knock, my heart thundering in my ears. "Maintenance," I announce. I drum my heels against the carpet, my fingers fidgeting on the toolbox.

Some defiant part of my brain is still hoping this is a mistake. Another woman is going to open that door, and it's not going to be my Harper at all. Or it will be her, and we'll laugh about how the federal government seems to think she's an accomplice to drug dealers and murderers.

The seconds tick by, and I just want *something* to happen. Because I can't fucking breathe.

Finally, the door opens.

The woman standing there has long, dark auburn hair. Large hazel eyes. I tower over her, just like I used to, and I can't help but remember how she felt in my arms, fitted right against my side.

Those eyes widen, and her mouth opens. "*Jake?*"

"Hey, Harper." I take a tentative step forward.

And the door slams into my face.

It's as if a clenched fist just landed smack on my nose, and the sudden burst of pain brings tears to my eyes.

"Fuck!" I drop the toolbox to the carpet with a clatter. I have a high tolerance for discomfort, but jeez. Couldn't a guy get some warning before being sucker punched?

The door flies open again. Harper gasps. "Oh, crap. Are you okay?"

I've got my hand clasped over my face, wiggling my nose to see if it's broken. My teeth clench on a moan. "I'm *great*. Thanks."

She reaches for me, then pulls back. "Are you bleeding?"

"Don't think so." Hurts, but I'm pretty sure there's no lasting damage. Except to my ego, maybe. "I'm a friend of Kevin's," I grind out. That's what I was *supposed* to say when she opened the door.

"Kevin?" she asks breathlessly. "I...uh..."

"I suggest you let me in? So we can talk about it?"

She continues to stammer.

I walk forward, and she backs up at the same time. I

nudge the toolbox in after me with my boot, then shut the door.

"I'm so sorry." Her skin has gone too pale. She keeps touching her mouth. "Um, you looked like...I thought..."

"Harper."

"Which would've been impossible, because there's no way..."

"*Harper.*"

Panic fills her eyes. "Ice! I'll go get ice." She grabs the plastic bucket from the dresser.

My hand closes around her slender bicep before she can charge out of the room. I take the ice bucket from her grip and set it aside.

"It's really me," I murmur. "It's Jake. You used to call me 'army'?"

She goes still.

Suddenly, it's like none of what Agent Reyes or Detective Murphy told me matters. This is *Harper.* My best friend who disappeared from my life and who once meant everything to me. I push an auburn strand from her face, tucking it behind her ear.

And fuck, it's all I can do not to kiss her.

"*Jake,*" she whispers.

I open my arms, and she folds into me. We hold each other tight.

Scientists say that time travel isn't real, but I would beg to differ. Because I'd swear that we're right back in high school, and the rest of my life was the dream I just woke up from.

I never, *ever*, thought I'd be standing here.

"How is this possible?" She's shaking. Her head rests below my chin, and I breathe her in. Vanilla and coffee, ink and graphite. She sniffles, but when she looks up at me, her eyes are dry.

She looks good. Really good. Her hair's a little shorter than before, but it still cascades down her back. I want to run my fingers through its softness.

Her curves are accentuated, her hips and chest rounder, which only makes her waist look narrower by contrast. I saw Harper in all her luscious glory only once, and I'd bet she's even more unforgettable now.

Do her moans of pleasure still sound the same?

Reality smacks into me as hard as Harper's hotel room door. I'm thirty-two, not eighteen.

I let go of her, though I keep a hand resting on her arm to steady her. Just like I've done for other witnesses who needed grounding. Because that's who she is. A witness. A CI.

Right. With other CIs, I don't feel like I'm being zapped by a live wire when I touch their skin.

"How are you here?" she asks. "Why?"

"I'm an agent with the DEA. There's been an accident. Kevin's out of commission. Just bad luck, no reason to think it's tied to your case."

"I got an encrypted text a few minutes ago saying Kevin wasn't coming. That something happened, and they were sending someone else. But...the universe must have one twisted sense of humor, because this is extreme." She backs up until she sits down on the bed, and her hand rubs at her chest. "I feel like I'm going to have a heart attack."

"Don't do that. Wouldn't look too good on my next annual review. Losing confidential informants is frowned upon."

She twists her lips, not quite a smile. "Is Kevin going to be all right?"

"Sounds that way. He's at the hospital getting fixed up. Head injury, but from what I heard, it could've been much worse. He's stubborn. He'll bounce back."

"Ugh, I'd send him flowers, but that's probably a bad

idea." She bites her lip. "I don't understand. How are you a DEA agent? What about the army?"

"I served. Put in my time, and when I was ready to leave, I didn't re-up. Sent out my résumé, and it was the feds who gave me the best offer." That's the two-second version, anyway.

"I guess I shouldn't be surprised. You always had that hero complex."

I shift my weight, unsure of what to do. Then I decide, to hell with it. I sit on the bed beside her.

"Marc Landley and his football friends wouldn't be surprised either. He used to call me a narc. Now it's really true."

That coaxes a smile from her. "I used to wonder how you were doing. If you were overseas, if you were okay."

"Two tours in Afghanistan. I used to wonder about you too. After that postcard, I hoped I'd hear from you. My parents still live in the same house."

You could've written again, I think. *Given me your address. But you didn't.*

Silence falls and hangs between us, growing more meaningful with each passing second.

"Jake, I'm sorry..."

There are a million and ten different things we need to say to each other. But with a list like that, we'll have to prioritize. "Let's worry about the past later. We need to talk about what's going on right now."

She flinches. "So you know. I guess you must."

"I had no clue until this morning. My bosses figured out I was connected to you, and they tried to keep me out of it. If Kevin hadn't gone and played chicken with a car, I never would've known."

"I'm not sure if that would've been better or worse."

I'm not either. It's probably too soon to tell.

"I want to hear it from you," I say. "You're part of the Caldwell family?"

"It's true," she whispers.

"You knew back then?"

There are things you don't know about my family. About me.

She's looking anywhere except into my eyes. "Yes."

"You almost told me that night. Didn't you?"

She nods. "I wanted to. I'd found out that day that we had to go back to Chicago. That's why Wren took off and went to Marc Landley's party. Those two years in West Oaks, we'd been happy. Wren and I started to believe we'd never have to go home. But that life we'd built...they were taking it away, and there was nothing I could do to stop it."

"Who is 'they'? Your parents?"

"No." Her voice has gone flat and distant. "My parents had no more control than I did. Back then, it was my grandfather in charge. He's the one who sent us to West Oaks in the first place. My dad was supposed to start a shipping company."

"SunSpeed?" I remember now that Harper's dad was in shipping. As a DEA agent all these years later, I never made the connection. "Does your father know what you're planning now?"

"Yes. My dad wants to get out, too, but he's followed orders for so long, his confidence is shot. Dad needed me to come up with the strategy."

I cross my arms over my chest. "My boss told me about the investor meeting in West Oaks. Kevin was supposed to pose as your boyfriend to get access."

"I told my uncle I was in love and my boyfriend wanted to ask formal permission to join the family. All the Caldwells will be in West Oaks for this investor thing, so it was the perfect way to get Kevin in."

I shake my head. "Your plan is shit."

Her eyes narrow. "Wow, thanks. How would you have done it better, army?"

"I would've found some way to get you to safety instead of walking with you into the lion's den."

"Well, next time I'm planning to betray my family, I'll get your advice first. This is the plan I've got, and I can hold up my end of it. Honestly, I was a little worried that Kevin was the weaker link and wouldn't be able to pull it off. Maybe it's better that you're stepping in." She forces a laugh. "You even have the right name."

"What do you mean?"

"*Jake.* That's my fake boyfriend's name." Her face is turning crimson. "Jake Worthington."

"Jake Worthington," I repeat.

"I needed a name to give my uncle, and that's what popped into my head. Weird coincidence."

"*Coincidence?*"

"You're not the only guy in the world named Jake! It's a common, generic name. Boring, frankly."

"Sure. Keep telling yourself that."

"Dork." Harper punches my shoulder. I grab her hand when she tries to retreat, and her eyes widen when I don't let go.

Another whiff of vanilla hits me.

My thumb brushes up and down the soft skin of her hand. Harper inhales, then sighs. I want to tug her closer again. Hold her and travel back in time once more.

I want you to kiss me, she said that night. I remember her mouth on mine. Her thigh pressed into my erection.

I loosen my grip, allowing her to slide her fingers away.

"Just as cocky as you used to be," she says. "That hasn't changed."

"Guilty as charged."

She's the one who used my first name for this "boyfriend"

character. The weaker parts of my ego want to be flattered that I was on her mind, even if it was her subconscious.

But that glow of hope in her eyes, that rise of color in her cheeks. It just makes the pit of my stomach drop deeper and deeper.

She's not going to like what I have to say.

"Harper, I'm sorry. I'm not here to play your fake boyfriend. I'm here to talk you out of it."

5

Harper

"*T*alk me out of it?" I say. "Your agency is pulling their involvement? Their support? That isn't fair."

The DEA made promises to me. Like immunity. Protection. And now they want out of the deal?

"Not my agency. This is coming from *me*. I can't let you go through with this ridiculous plan of yours."

"Do you know how arrogant you sound?"

"Doesn't mean I'm wrong."

A little while ago, I slammed the door in Jake's face. And I apologized for that. It was...gah, it was dumb. I was just shocked to see him there. I couldn't deal.

But this, what he's doing to me? It's so much worse.

He's harder than I remembered. Angular, even though he's added more bulk to his large frame. He's even more handsome, which is saying a lot. But that hardness is inside of him, too. It's in his eyes. The line of his mouth. Like he's seen terrible things, and that's what he sees when he looks at me.

Like I'm some kind of monster.

This is why I never told him the truth. Because it would've been impossible for him to understand.

"The DEA and the task force want to go forward with this," he says. "They think the info you're providing them is important. They'd be pretty fucking pissed if they heard what I'm saying now. But I'm not just talking to you as an agent. I'm talking to you as your *friend*. Or at least, a guy who used to be your friend."

"Doesn't feel like you're being my friend. You're abandoning me."

His mouth presses into a thin line. *Like you abandoned me?* I know that's what he's thinking. At least he doesn't say it out loud.

"Harper, I can't condone you walking into such a dangerous situation."

When we were younger, Jake had so much righteous indignation inside him. He believed in right and wrong, like those are two opposites and not a vast spectrum of gray.

If I'd told him that I came from a family of criminals? That my dad probably bought that house with dirty money? Jake would've had every reason to hate me. I couldn't bear the thought of that.

But now, he knows. And he doesn't want to help me. I can't even blame him for it.

All I can do is stand my ground. There's no backing out. Not for me.

"You think I don't know this is dangerous? I'm a Caldwell. I've *seen* what happens to betrayers. I've been in it for my entire life. So you can stand there and judge me if you want, but—"

"This isn't about judging you. It's about what's going to keep you safe. Feed the DEA information some other way. We'll make another arrangement, and I will make sure you're protected."

"That won't work."

"Why does it have to be *this* meeting in West Oaks? The investor angle isn't enough for so much urgency. What else are you not telling me?"

My throat tightens. "Nothing."

"Harper." He takes gentle hold of my chin, forcing me to look at him. "I could always tell when you were hiding things. I let it slide when I was a kid, but not anymore."

I feel my skin burning. I'm a decent liar. I have to be. But I was never great at lying to Jake.

I look into his eyes. Dark green, like the forest at night. Darker than they used to be.

"I'll go without the DEA's support if that's what it takes. I've been making it on my own for the last fourteen years, and I'll keep on doing it if I have to."

The muscle in his jaw pulses. "So that's it then? There's no way I can talk you out of this?"

"If you're not willing to help me, then you should leave," I say. "It's been nice to see you again. But I'm sure there's someplace else you'd rather be."

He stands there, radiating disapproval. "Fair enough." A curtain seems to go down over his eyes. Closing me out.

I can hardly look at him as I open the door. He picks up the toolbox and steps into the hallway. "Harper…"

"Goodbye, Jake."

I shut the door and lean against it.

So. That's that.

I'm not angry with him. Just disappointed. Fourteen years apart, and we only had a few minutes together. I practically pushed him out the door.

I wish I could've run into him randomly at some restaurant or coffee shop and spent an hour hearing about *him*. Not talking about my screwed-up family.

I barely know anything about his life now, aside from the

DEA. Is Jake married? Is he with someone, in love? He must be, because how could someone like him not be taken?

And what about his parents and siblings? Madison and Aiden and the littler ones. They all must be grown up by now. Why didn't I ask about them?

I want to know if Jake is happy. At least one of us should be.

I slide down to the floor and sit with my knees to my chest. The past wells up inside me, just like the tears that're threatening to overflow.

There's a sharp knock at the door. My heart rate spikes, and I jump up. "Who's there?" I ask. It's too early for my dad to be back from his meetings.

"Maintenance."

I throw the door open. Jake stands there, hands in his pockets, that toolbox down at his feet. Exactly how I left him a few minutes ago. As if he hasn't moved an inch.

"You're not going to slam the door on me this time, are you?" he asks.

"What are you doing?"

"Something stupid." He shrugs. "But I tried to leave, and it didn't take."

I hold my breath until he's back inside the room.

"If you're going to be in danger anyway," he says, "then I'd be an asshole to let you do it alone. But you have to do *exactly* as I say. I need your word on that. I am in charge of this operation, not you."

I know this isn't the time to argue, not when he's just agreed to help me. But I wasn't a pushover when we were kids, and I'm even less of one now. "I'm the one who knows my family. Kevin said that I'd get to—"

"I'm not him," Jake growls.

He advances on me, and I back up against the wall. His

hands land palms-down to either side of me, caging me in. His nostrils flare.

"I'm not coming with you because I'm trying to save the world, Harper. Don't get me wrong, I want to take down the Caldwell family. Make no mistake about that. But I'm playing along with this particular plan because I intend to protect you. Do you have a problem with that?"

"No," I breathe.

"Good. Now, this will only work if we can agree on how it will go down. *I* am the one in charge. I need to hear you say it."

The intensity in his eyes, the possessiveness in his stance and in his tone, it all makes my blood rush and my heart thump and my panties go damp.

He's not the boy I remember. Not at all.

But what really pisses me off? He turns me on even more.

"Okay, army," I say. "You're in charge. For the next four days."

He holds my gaze for another beat, almost like he's challenging me to look away. To prove my submission completely. But I don't.

He finally lowers his arms and takes a step back. "Don't make me regret this."

"I was going to say the same thing."

6

Jake

I do my best to battle through LA traffic, but it's early afternoon by the time I get back to Nash and Madison's house. And then I'm standing on the porch, staring at their front door.

Much like I was doing to Harper's hotel room earlier.

I tried to walk away from her. It's not like me to change my mind. Once I make a decision, I usually stick with it because I know that I haven't taken it lightly in the first place.

But I never could say no to Harper.

I still think this undercover plan is a terrible idea. I should've had months to research and nail down every small detail, and I just don't trust Kevin or Agent Reyes's work like I would my own. If Detective Murphy had set it up, I might have more confidence, but she's only smoothing over the jurisdictional issues. Making sure that West Oaks PD responds if things really go south.

The DEA must've been salivating over the idea of taking down the Caldwells. They might've been willing to cut corners in ways that could jeopardize Harper. I don't have time to study Kevin's preparations, much less make my own.

Yet I'm about to step into Kevin's shoes because Harper's determined to put herself in danger. She doesn't have anyone else to watch out for her.

Guess it'll have to be me.

My sister must spot me through a window because the door opens, and she steps out. "You're looking very broody out here."

"Feeling it, too."

Despite our seven years of difference in age, Madison and I have always been able to read one another. So she already knows the score.

"It's okay," she says. "The kids will be fine. You are the one I feel sorry for because we're going to have an amazing time without you."

I rub my chin. "But I can't believe I'm doing this again. After I said I wouldn't."

"And you're a guy who keeps his promises. We all know that. But you can't be everywhere at once. You're great at your job, so it's no surprise to me that your boss called you in. But if you agreed to the assignment, then it must be important."

"I know the CI. She's a friend. I'd tell you more if I could." Madison knew Harper too, though she was still pretty young when Harper left town. "All I can say is she's in danger."

"And you'd feel terrible if you left her hanging. I get it." She squints at me. "Your nose looks a little red."

"It's nothing." I rub the sore spot. At least it isn't swelling. "The assignment lasts four days. I'll try to make it back for the tail end of the stay in Catalina. But…"

She rolls her eyes at me. "This is what family is for,

dumbass. Now come inside and tell your kids. That's the only part of this I'm not doing for you." She lowers her voice to a whisper. "If I'm the messenger, Riley will be grumpy at me the whole rest of the day. She's vindictive like that."

"I don't know where she gets it."

"Certainly wasn't Adrienne," Madison says under her breath.

I follow Madison inside. The kids come running, and I kneel in front of them, gathering one in each arm. "Hey, squirts. I have something to tell you."

"What is it, Daddy?" Hudson is still beaming. He's like a baby polar bear, burly and blond and full of innocence. But Riley is my natural born cynic.

My daughter scowls. "He's not coming with us on the trip."

How do the women in my life read me like a freaking book?

"I am really, really sorry. I wanted more than anything in the world to come with you. But sometimes, work needs me even when it's not the best time."

"But you *don't* want to come with us more than anything, because if you did, then you would!" Riley wriggles out of my grasp and stomps over to the couch.

Hudson's eyes are shining and his lower lip trembles. But then, a small miracle happens. Hudson takes a deep breath and walks over to his sister. "Riley, you can't be mad at Daddy. He fights bad guys and saves people at his job. He's a superhero like on PJ Mask."

"But I don't want him to be a superhero!" Riley shouts back. "I just want my dad!"

Jeez, these kids. They break my heart and put it back together every damn day.

Hudson takes his sister's hand. I go over to Riley and

kneel in front of her. Her little legs are dangling off the couch, and she won't look at me.

"Hey, I can't go with you to Catalina, but how about this? I'll leave something really important with you. Something that's almost as good as having me there."

Riley eyes me skeptically. "Your credit card?"

I laugh. "Yeah, for sure. I'll leave that in Aunt Madison's capable hands. But I'm talking about a different thing. Even better than a credit card."

Hudson perks up. "Is it for me too?"

"Of course." I draw a heart shape on Riley's palm, then one on Hudson's. "Now, I'm trusting you both with this. Right? You'll take good care of my heart while I'm gone?"

"Yes, Daddy," Hudson says.

"But we can't both have it," Riley protests. "You only have one heart."

"Nope, that's the amazing thing about love. You never run out. No matter how much you give, you always have more."

Riley's frown is still firmly in place, but she closes her hand and clasps it against her stomach. Like she's holding something precious, and she won't let it go.

I plant a kiss on each of their foreheads. "You'll need to listen to Aunt Madison and Uncle Nash. And Emma, too. I'm sure she can't wait to hang out with you guys, and she's probably glad I won't be there hogging your attention."

I'm resorting to blatant manipulation at this point, because I know how much they love Emma. But I'm not above it.

"Is Emma our cousin?" Hudson says.

"Yeah. She's just like a cousin." And judging by the way Nash adores my sister, Emma will become Riley and Hudson's official cousin before too much longer. I'd bet cash money that he pops the question before this year is out.

"Emma loves you both. Family is a lot more than blood or last names."

And now I'm thinking of Harper again, a ball of unease gathering in my stomach as I wonder what she's been through in the last fourteen years, surrounded by the Caldwells.

Has Harper had anyone she could truly trust? Anyone who loved her as much as she deserves?

"I love you, Daddy." Riley puts her little arms around me. Hudson crowds in beside her.

"I love you too." I put as much affection into my hug as possible. It'll have to last us the next four days.

I HAVE FIVE HOURS UNTIL I NEED TO BE BACK AT Harper's hotel, ready to play the role of her boyfriend. Tonight will be about settling any final details with Harper and her father. Making sure we have our stories straight, and I have all of my logistical ducks in a row. As much as I can manage in one night, anyway.

After I see my family off on their way, I head home. My first stop is my closet. I strip out of my beach wear and stand there in the buff, considering what I should pack.

Luckily, I've got a bizarrely diverse wardrobe after several years of working undercover. Ratty stuff I never wash for playing strung-out drug addicts. Biker-style leather jackets. Business suits for guys from all walks of life, from middle management to rich executives.

"What kind of asshole is Jake Worthington?" I ask my closet.

Kevin wrote up a whole description of the cover story for the file. I'm not just playing Harper's boyfriend. I supposedly work for one of SunSpeed's clients. "Jake Worthington" is a vice president for a medical device company called HealthTec. With Harper's help, the DEA snagged HealthTec for allowing the Caldwells to stash drugs in their medical device shipments. HealthTec then flipped in exchange for immunity. They set up Jake Worthington's paper trail as a supposed executive.

Worthington has the hots for Harper, and I can't blame him for that. But he's arrogant enough to think joining a crime family is an attractive opportunity. If he really loved Harper, he'd want to take her away from all that, not push her in even deeper.

Fuck Jake Worthington.

But he's the kind of sleazeball that the Caldwells would expect. He's someone who smells money. Better yet, he's probably someone who already comes from money and wants more.

I shift hangers aside until I find the suits I'm looking for. *Perfect.*

After I've dressed and tucked enough clothes into my suitcase for a long weekend, I rifle through my other gear. I'll need weapons and a way to keep in touch with my task force contacts. But, without a doubt, my bags will be searched.

Good thing this isn't my first rodeo.

When I'm nearly finished, I call Detective Murphy.

"Hey, Shelborne. Reyes told me you're on board?"

"I am. Against my better judgment."

She sighs into the phone. "Look, I wouldn't have blamed you for refusing. It wasn't my place to say this earlier in front of your agent in charge, but I've thought from the beginning that this op was a shitshow in the making."

I toss my toothbrush and toothpaste into my toiletry bag. "*Now* you tell me."

"You knew it from minute one. But I'm just representing the locals. The DEA doesn't care what I think."

"I do."

"And that's why I like you, Shelborne. Why'd you change your mind about taking Kevin's place? Your personal connection to the CI?"

"Perfect thing for you and Agent Reyes to use against me."

She grumbles. "I know. I'm sorry about that."

"Make it up to me. I need a clean vehicle. Something flashy."

"We've got a few things in impound. I'll arrange it. I'll even drop it off at a parking lot near your house with the keys under the seat."

"Have I told you lately that I love you?"

She's rolling her eyes so hard I can hear it through the phone. "Just come back from this op in one piece."

"Planning to. Hey, there's one more thing I need."

I describe what I have in mind, and she laughs.

"Sure. I think I can rustle up one of those. I'll leave it in the glove compartment. But I'll need it back, okay? I'll never hear the end of it if I don't return it to evidence."

I end the call and set my bags by the front door.

There's one last thing I need to do before I go.

I return to my closet, but this time I grab a shoebox that I keep on a high shelf. It's full of mementos, photos, keepsakes from my marriage and my kids. Hand-drawn Father's Day cards. My wedding ring. My dog tags. It's a little like a sedimentary rock formation, the layers getting older the deeper you go.

I find the scrap of paper I'm looking for and tug it out.

It's a selfie of me and Harper from senior year. I've got my arm around her, and she's sticking out her tongue because she hated being photographed. I printed this one on my parents' color inkjet, and it's all faded and creased.

Could I have saved her back then? Maybe not. But I can be here for her now.

As I stare at that photo of us, the memories come into clearer focus. Like how warm she was up against me the first time we kissed. How hungry her mouth was, how she melted against me like my kiss was all she needed in the world.

And a few days later. How she looked bathed in afternoon sunlight in my bed, all her smooth skin bared for me to see. My hands moving over her, dipping between her legs... I didn't get to find out how it felt to be inside her. One of my few regrets.

Fuck, if I keep thinking about that, I'm going to bust the seam of these tailored pants.

Seeing Harper again, knowing how much she's struggled to survive all these years—it's making my protective side come roaring to the forefront. And defending a beautiful woman, especially a strong, gutsy woman like Harper, has always riled me up in the worst way. My dick is predictable like that.

Doesn't help that she's even more stunning now. Her long legs and ample curves. The waves of her dark red hair that perfectly frame her face. Those lips that purse when she's being defiant.

I had harsh words for her earlier in her hotel room. But honestly? She impresses the hell out of me. Harper came to the DEA on her own. She wants to protect those she loves, make things right. And she's ready to risk her life to do it.

Harper. *My* Harper.

But I can't think of her that way. Not now.

I force myself to put the photo back in the shoebox and return it to the shelf.

I have to put away my old feelings for her. This affection and attraction. This fucking craving that's as consuming and undeniable today as it was when I was eighteen. With

Harper, I have to keep my distance. If I don't, I could wind up getting us both killed.

I'll let my sharp edges rise to the surface. Even my cruelty. I don't want to be that man with Harper, but I've got no choice.

That's the only thing that'll keep her safe.

7

Harper

I spend the rest of the afternoon questioning my own sanity.

Did Jake Shelborne really show up at my hotel room? Did that actually happen?

When I try to explain it to my father, he certainly doesn't believe it. "Jake? That boy from across the street? Are you sure?"

"Yes, Dad. He's taking over for Kevin."

Jake is supposed to meet us tonight. I've already changed my outfit three times, and then I got undressed again and shaved my legs, which is ridiculous. Jake is not going to care whether I've shaved my legs. He's my fake boyfriend, not my real one.

Although we'll be sharing a room when we're in West Oaks.

Sharing a *bed*.

That didn't seem like a big deal when it was Kevin. Kevin is married, and he never acted the slightest bit interested in me. He was completely professional. But Jake and I have already been in bed together in the past, and things did not stay in the friend zone.

Oh, God. Is Jake married?

"Jake will meet us here tonight," I remind my father. "We're having dinner. You'll have to get used to him, because he's supposed to be one of SunSpeed's clients. Remember?"

"I remember. I'm not feeble-minded yet, my dear."

He slumps into the chair by my bedside. We're in my hotel room, which adjoins with his. Dad's looking pale. He's lost at least ten pounds since I told him my plan to get us out of the family business. But his decline didn't start then. He hasn't been well for at least a year.

Every time I ask him how he's doing, he denies there's anything wrong. But it's obvious that his health has taken a turn for the worse. The only question is how bad it really is.

"You feel okay, Dad? You can skip dinner if you want."

"Harper, I'm fine. I'm strong enough." His throat works like he's swallowing. "Perhaps not strong enough to take this burden from you like I should've, but I won't let you down."

"You've done the best you could." Not everyone is built with the amount of courage that they need. My dad could've used a bit more, but I don't think that was his fault. He was born a gentle soul in harsh surroundings.

Dad lifts his eyes. "Jake was good to you when we lived in West Oaks, wasn't he? A real friend."

"He was. The best."

"And the Shelbornes were fine people. I'm glad we got to know them. Those were good days." He nods, like he's settling something in his own head. "I'm pleased Jake will be there through this."

"Me too, Dad. Jake is...a good man." He might have changed, but I still believe that.

After checking my hair and makeup a couple times, no more than three times, we head down to the lobby. It's a buzz of activity, which makes sense for a swanky place in Beverly Hills. A jazz band plays over in the bar, and I think I spot a celebrity couple strolling by, drinking glasses of champagne.

I chose this hotel because I wanted to blend into the background for this fake boyfriend meetup. I'd spoken to Kevin in person before, but this would've been our debut as a couple.

Now that it's going to be Jake instead? I'm wondering if I should've chosen a quieter spot. The fancy decor, the designer outfits, the pomp and the snobbery in this room— it's not Jake. At all. He's going to hate it.

My father taps me on the shoulder. "Harper? That's him, isn't it?"

I turn toward the revolving doors. Half a dozen female heads turn with me, along with some of the men.

Jake just walked in, and that sultry jazz melody creates the perfect soundtrack.

The maintenance jumpsuit from earlier is gone. His hair is styled and slicked back, though he's left the stubble on his face. He's wearing a dark blue suit that's tailored to within an inch of its life. The wool is snug against his broad shoulders and endless legs, skimming his biceps like he might hulk out of that jacket if he flexes.

If I thought we'd go unnoticed here amidst the celebrities and jetsetters, I was definitely wrong.

Jake gives his suitcase to a bellhop, along with a folded stack of bills. He glances casually at his watch as he struts across the open space, as if he's oblivious to the attention.

Then his eyes lift, and they go straight to me.

His emerald eyes take me in, and a cocky smile grows on his face. My heart is fluttering like it's being pulled in an ocean current toward somewhere dark and dangerous. But I have no desire to get away. I'm more than willing to go wherever this man wants to take me.

Then I force myself to snap out of those thoughts.

Get a grip, Harper.

Jake has certainly got the dashing secret-agent routine down, and that just reminds me that I hardly know the man he's become. Jake is playing a role, and hell, so am I.

He's not mine anymore. If he ever was.

"Hello, beautiful." His voice dips, and he kisses my cheek, squeezing my arm gently as he leans in. He smells like leather and expensive cologne. "That dress doesn't do you justice."

"Um, thank…you?" I'm not sure that was a compliment. I glance down at myself, wondering if I should've picked the first dress instead.

Jake stretches his hand out to my father. "Sir. Great to see you."

My dad stands a bit taller. "You too. How's your family?"

"No complaints. Were your business meetings fruitful this afternoon?"

"Indeed. Yes. They—"

"Could I get anyone a drink?" Jake interrupts. "Harper, a dirty martini?"

I blink at him before I remember telling Kevin my favorite drink. Jake simply read my DEA file.

This isn't real, I scold myself. *None of it.*

Besides, I prefer him in his army T-shirt and jeans. But he *does* look like he could play the next James Bond. Can you blame a girl for swooning a little? When a man looks this sexy, it's practically an instinctual response.

Though his attitude isn't nearly so attractive. Jake is snapping his fingers at a waiter in the bar, trying to wave the guy over here.

"Actually," I say, "I'd rather head to the restaurant. If that's all right?"

He holds out his arm to me. "Whatever you want, darling."

I grit my teeth and slide my hand around his elbow. Jake steers me toward the exit. My father brings up the rear.

"You look dashing in that suit," I say under my breath. "I'll give you that. But you might want to tone it down before I throw up in my mouth. You're way over the top."

He grins breezily. "We'll see."

We walk to a nearby restaurant, where I've made a reservation for three. Along the way, he chats with my dad about SunSpeed's clients, and I've got to hand it to him. It sounds like he's been doing his homework. Either that, or Jake is a better bullshitter than I ever imagined.

"Right this way," the hostess says.

But when she shows us our table, Jake scoffs. "No. This table won't work."

The girl blanches. "Why?"

"I can see into the kitchen and bathrooms from here." He scans the dining room and his gaze falls on a table by a large window. "That one," he says.

"I'm sorry, sir. But that table—"

"Is where we're sitting. My future fiancée deserves the best." Jake grabs my hand and drags me toward the nicer table. People are staring at us again, and I hear my father apologizing to the poor hostess.

"Jake," I hiss. "What was that?"

All I get is another cocky grin. He pulls out my chair and almost shoves me into it. Then he grabs my napkin, unfolds it, and sticks it in my lap. "No woman of mine should have to lift a finger. Don't you think so, Mason?" He turns to my dad.

"Well...um..."

"The lady will have a dirty martini," Jake tells the hostess. "Top shelf gin, not the trash from the well." He sits, leaning back in his chair like he's holding court. His hand grips my knee under the table like I'm his princess in captivity.

What the heck is going on here?

Ten minutes later, I've downed my first martini without even tasting it. Jake's deep in a discussion of the financial markets with my father, who's on his second gin and tonic. Aside from ordering my food for me, Jake has basically ignored me.

I don't have a clue what Jake thinks he's doing. Is he trying to piss me off? Is he trying to sabotage this arrangement before we even get started?

"Another martini, darling?" he asks.

"Actually, could I speak to you alone for a minute, *sweetums*?" I ask.

His lips move like he's trying not to laugh. The asshole. "I'm sure whatever you need to say, you can say in front of your father. Right, Mason?"

My father looks down at his plate. He doesn't know what to do with Jake, either.

I stand up. "Now." I stride toward the bathrooms, expecting him to follow.

I push into one of the single occupancy restrooms. Jake sweeps in behind me, a heated wall of muscle right at my back.

He shoves the door closed and locks it behind us.

"What are you doing?" I ask.

"You called this meeting, not me."

"I mean, out there. Ordering my drinks and food for me? Treating servers like crap? *Insulting* me? I would never date a guy like that." *No matter how hot he is*, I add silently.

"News flash, you're not really dating me."

"Good thing, because if I were, I would dump you."

He leans against the door, crossing his arms and tilting his head sardonically. "Did you forget who I'm supposed to be? I'm Jake Worthington, the douchebag who wants to kiss up to the Caldwell crime family and join their ranks. Did you think I'd be sensitive and enjoy hearing women's opinions?"

"Well, Jake Worthington is a dick."

"Thank you. That's what I'm going for."

"This is hard enough without you...*showboating*." I turn to face the mirror, running my fingers through my hair. The problem with dragging Jake into this bathroom is that now, I can't escape. He's blocking the door, and this place is tiny.

At least it smells like cinnamon candles. It overwhelms the enticing, spicy aroma of Jake's cologne.

He's watching me in the mirror.

"Harper, this isn't supposed to be fun. We're not two friends catching up on old times. When you look at me, you can't see Jake Shelborne. I need to know that you and your father can hold this cover story together for the next four days."

"We will. But couldn't you be a little less repugnant? I wouldn't date a guy just because he's handsome. And I don't want to be treated like a sheltered princess."

"You think I'm handsome?"

I make an exasperated sound. My fingers dig into my scalp, and my hair is sticking out all over the place. "On second thought, I can't do this."

"Nope, that won't work. It's too late to back out."

"For me, it is. But I could break up with you. My family isn't going to believe I'd put up with this nonsense. I'm not known for being passive and submissive."

"I'm glad to hear *that* much hasn't changed."

"You're not helping." I scratch at the skin along my hairline.

"You still do that? It's a bad habit." He steps away from the door, taking my hands by the wrists. We're facing the mirror, and Jake is right behind me, his chest and stomach to my back. He rubs his thumbs over my palms, and it's like he's pressed some secret button inside me, forcing me to relax.

He puts his mouth beside my ear, and when he speaks, I can feel the vibrations of his Adam's apple.

"Tell me what kinds of men you're usually with."

My eyes fly to his in the mirror. A more pleasurable cocktail of chemicals is speeding through my veins, quickly replacing the frustration.

"I don't have a lot of examples. I don't date very much."

"No?" he asks softly. "Why not?"

"Just hasn't worked out. I travel a lot between LA and Chicago. And...I guess it's hard to trust people given my family background."

He's still rubbing my palms with his thumbs. "But if a guy wanted to make you fall for him, what would he have to do?"

My rebellious brain conjures up Jake in high school. His sweet smile. His intense focus when he pitched a game, how he moved his body. He thought I didn't go to his baseball games, but I did sometimes. It was like window shopping. Admiring what I couldn't have, not the way I wanted. My secrets always stood in the way.

"He would be kind and thoughtful. Listen to me. Make me feel..."

"Safe?"

"Not exactly. I was going to say, understood." Make me feel like I'm not judged. Not alone.

His brow creases like this wasn't what he expected. "That's asking a lot."

"Maybe that's why I haven't found him yet."

Someone knocks on the bathroom door, and I startle. "Just a sec," I call out.

Jake doesn't let me go yet. "If we're going to make it

through the next few days, you'll have to toughen up. I can't play your dream guy. This is life or death stuff, Harper, and we're not kids anymore."

"I know." I yank my hands from his grip. "Back then, you used to be a lot nicer."

"You think? Marc Landley would disagree. The night we got Wren from his house, I broke his nose and knocked out two of his teeth."

"Then I stand corrected. You were always an alphahole, and I was the idiot who idolized you." I unlock the door and throw it open. The woman who's waiting gives us a *look* when she sees Jake emerge along with me.

Jake wraps his arm around my waist. "Sorry, this one couldn't wait until we got home. She's insatiable."

I glare at him over my shoulder.

We walk back to the dining room together. Not like I have any choice, because Jake keeps his hands on me. He's taking this *I'm-in-charge* thing very seriously.

If this is what it takes to get free of my family, then I shouldn't care. I should jump through whatever hoops that Jake sets up for me and thank him.

I made it fourteen years without Jake Shelborne in my life. Why does it bother me so much that he's being infuriating now?

Jake stops me halfway across the dining room, holding me closer. "Who's our guest?" he murmurs in my ear.

I've been so distracted I didn't notice the new addition to our table.

Shit.

"My cousin Roman."

He's sitting next to my father. My heart takes off like a frightened rabbit. Without my permission, my hand goes to my neck.

But a slow smirk grows on Jake's face. Then he surprises me yet again.

He grabs my chin, turns my head. His other arm circles my waist, drawing me so close he must feel my heartbeat and the tightening of my nipples.

Then he captures my lips with his own. Like he's trying to set the entire restaurant on fire with the heat between us.

8

Jake

I know I must've had a good reason for kissing Harper. But the moment my lips hit hers, I can't remember it for the life of me.

The scent of vanilla fills my nose, as familiar as home, yet rich and transporting at the same time.

My lips move over hers, and the tension in her body starts to unravel. Her fingers grasp at the back of my neck. When I run my tongue teasingly at the seam of her mouth, her moan sends shivers of desire racing through me.

Then a throat clears at a nearby table, and I come back to reality. I break the kiss, and she actually whimpers, her hazel eyes glazed like she can't remember where she is either.

Might've gotten slightly carried away there.

"You okay?" I ask.

She looks dazed. "I'm...um...yep."

I take her hand and turn toward our table. But as we approach, a tremor passes through her. I slow down and lean over again. "What is it?"

She shakes her head. "Let's just go. Roman's waiting."

I don't like the hint of fear that suffuses her voice. The Harper I know isn't scared of anyone.

Already, I'm not a fan of this cousin of hers.

I plaster a smarmy grin on my face, the kind Jake Worthington would wear. Even though I'd prefer to grab hold of Roman, drag him outside, and demand to know why Harper is so unnerved by him.

When we reach the table, I pull Harper's chair out. She sits, and I gently push her forward. Once she's securely in place, I kiss her cheek.

Only then do I finally lock eyes with Roman.

His hair is dark, with just a hint of copper. He's got a thin goatee, beady eyes. There's strength to his frame, the kind that comes from a gym and not practical living. He sits with his spine straight, a confident set to his shoulders.

"Jake Worthington," I say. I stick out my hand, deliberately crossing into his personal space. "Such a pleasure to meet Harper's cousin. Ryan, was it?"

I'm not surprised when he just glares. His eyes are ice cold. I pass behind his chair on the way to my own, and as I do, I grip Roman's shoulder and squeeze.

"It's Roman, actually." He knocks my hand from his shoulder.

Mason's eyes are panicked, and Harper doesn't look amused.

I just snicker, like it's all in good fun.

I settle into my seat, shaking out my napkin and sitting back. I got a little thrill out of pissing Roman off, but I also know his type. He's predisposed not to like me. If he senses any weakness from me, he won't let up.

Over the next several days, I'll need room to operate. I can't do that with Roman breathing down my neck. So, it's convenient that Jake Worthington is a class-A asshole and doesn't mess around.

Not all that different from Jake Shelborne, now that I think of it. When I'm working, at least.

"Roman, I don't remember inviting you to dinner tonight," Harper says.

"Wanted to meet the newest potential addition to the family. Everyone's dying to see the guy who tamed Harper."

I reach over and pat her on the thigh. "Tamed her? I don't know about that." I wink at Harper, and she sends back a begrudging, closed-mouth smile. I pick up the glass in front of me and sip my old-fashioned.

Our server comes over to take Roman's order. He picks the most expensive steak on the menu, and I have no doubt he's going to leave me with the bill. This meal is going to stretch my daily stipend as a government employee.

"I'm curious. What kind of guy gets Harper to finally settle down?" Roman says.

"My company HealthTec is a client of SunSpeed's. The moment I met Harper, I knew I'd never go with another shipping company."

Harper coughs. "*Gag*," she says with a hand over her mouth.

I drape my arm around her. "It took me a while and a lot of persistence, but finally she agreed to have dinner with me. I took her to Mastro's. You can guess the rest."

"And now you want my father's blessing?" Roman closes his lips on a sneer.

"I'd like to earn that privilege, yes."

He swigs his drink, his eyes saying, *Not if I have anything to do with it.*

Yep. Roman is definitely going to be a problem.

I'd better nip this in the bud. Right fucking now.

I take a cigar case from the inside pocket of my jacket. "Roman, would you join me for a smoke break?"

He sighs and pushes back from the table.

When we get outside, I open the case and hold it out. "We've just met, but I'm getting the impression that you don't like me."

He selects a Cuban. "Then congrats. You're not a complete idiot. I'm head of security for my family, and I did a background check on you. I didn't like what I saw."

"No?" I play nonchalant, but I'm cursing Agent Reyes. If they fucked up my cover story...

He snips the end of the cigar using the trimmer from inside the case. When he's done, I snap the case closed without taking a cigar myself.

Roman uses his own lighter to ignite the end. "You're from a family with a little money, fancy school, fancy car, and you think you can play with the big boys. But you're out of your league."

"Am I?"

He blows smoke into my face. "Harper might be a Caldwell, but you can't waltz in and demand a place at the table."

Wow, this guy needs some new metaphors. "Shouldn't your father be the judge of that?"

His sneer turns sour. I think I'm onto something. I'd bet Roman's influence with Amos Caldwell isn't what he'd like it to be.

"Just stay in your lane, Worthington."

I shake my head. "You know, I don't think I will. I think a better option is for you to go fuck yourself."

A crease appears between his eyebrows. Then he does exactly what I expect. He lunges, shoving me against the brick wall. "You might think Harper is your ticket in to my family, but you've got nothing. We already own her, and she does what we say, not the other way around."

I grab hold of him and spin him around. Roman slams into the brick so hard his head bounces. The cigar falls from his lips.

Leaning in, I lower my voice and whisper into his ear. "Harper doesn't belong to anyone. But if she *did?*" I slow down so even this dumbass can get the message. "She'd. Belong. To. *Me.*"

Roman tries to shove me back, but I won't move. "That cocky attitude isn't going to work with my father," he spits out. "You want my family's approval, you're shit out of luck. Because I'm going to fuck you over before you even get there."

"We'll see. But I appreciate the heads up. Sweet of you." I pat his cheek, and he bares his teeth like he might bite me.

Time to back off.

I retreat, putting a couple feet between us. And the guy reaches into his jacket. So fucking predictable. He can't hide the shock on his face.

"Looking for this?" A gun dangles from my finger. I snuck it out of his pocket when he was roughing me up. I figured he'd be carrying.

"Give me that."

"Nope, I'll hold on to it for now." I pop out the magazine, stowing it in my pants pocket separately from the weapon. "If you behave, you'll get your toy back."

He glares murder at me.

"I don't have a problem with you," I say. "I'd suggest you let go of your problem with me. Harper's mine. If you aim your bad breath in her direction, you'll have to answer to me."

"This isn't over." Roman spits at my feet and storms off. Guess he's not hungry for that steak he ordered.

Something tells me I haven't made a new friend.

～

Back at the hotel after dinner, Harper pulls me into her room. We haven't discussed where I'll be staying tonight. For now, the bellhop brought my suitcase here. It's sitting next to Harper's in the corner.

She looks sexy in the dress she's wearing. When I said it didn't do her justice, that was a bald-faced lie. And she's even better when she's fired up.

All things I shouldn't be noticing.

"What were you and Roman doing outside the restaurant?" she asks. "Pissing on each other? Proving who's the alpha?"

Her cousin didn't return to the table after our confrontation. I sent his steak to the kitchen with my compliments. Hopefully the staff enjoyed eating it.

"That would've been silly. Between me and Roman, I'm obviously the dominant one."

"Provoking Roman is a bad idea."

"I tried to play nice. He's the one who wouldn't behave, so I had to correct certain assumptions of his. Such as thinking he owns you. I was getting some creepy, pervy vibes. Anything I need to know there?"

Harper kicks off her heels, turning away from me. "He's never touched me like *that*. If that's what you mean."

"Has he touched you some other way?"

Her hand rubs at her throat. "Roman likes to intimidate me. Makes him feel important. In my family, everyone bows to the patriarch, and at the moment that's my Uncle Amos. Roman's dad. Roman is the younger son, so he thinks he has something to prove."

"But Amos makes the decisions."

"Yes. He took over when my grandfather died. My dad is Amos's younger brother."

"Right. How does Amos feel about you?"

She crosses one arm over her middle. "My uncle can be

cruel when he wants to be, but he's always been easier on me. Hell if I know why. Maybe because he has a soft spot for my dad. My father's never tried to challenge him."

"Then why did you contact the DEA?" I ask. "What's changed?"

Harper walks over to the window. The sheer is pulled across the glass, and she puts her palm over the fabric, pressing into it like she wishes she could escape this room.

"It started out as a fantasy. An idea that got me through the days. I made anonymous tips to police whenever I could. Sabotaged deals. As long as I was sure it wouldn't lead back to me. But as I got older, *stronger*, I started planning my escape for real. I had to find a way to get my parents and Wren out without getting killed in the process. I don't even care what happens to me anymore, but I'm tired of…"

"What?"

"Everything."

"What will you do after this is finished?"

"Start over, I guess. Someplace far away. But we'll be free."

I have an urge to touch her. Comfort her. Instead, I sit on the bed, clasping my hands between my knees. "Tell me more about your family members. Their dynamics."

"Well, Amos's eldest son is Tristan. He's the dealmaker. Tristan has made new contacts within the cartels and has expanded the Caldwell Enterprises market share. Roman is the enforcer, head of security but with less of a say in how things are run. And their sister Mia is younger. In college. She's been studying to get a social work degree, and she's the wild card. I'm not sure how much she's involved in the family business."

I slot this information away in my mind. Amos, Tristan, Roman and Mia. Harper's father Mason. Harper's sister Wren.

"Is Wren going to be there in West Oaks?" I ask.

Harper looks at the carpet. "I doubt it." She shrugs. "You remember Wren. She gets into messes."

"And you used to drag her out of them."

"Well, not lately." Harper bites her lip. "Jake, around my family, you should be careful and tread lightly. Pissing them off is dangerous."

"You worried about me getting hurt?"

"I'd rather avoid it if possible. You must have people waiting for you to come home. A wife?"

"Fishing for information?"

She huffs. "With the way you kissed me earlier? I'd like to know if I made out with another woman's husband."

I glance down at the rug. "I'm not attached."

"I'm not either. But I guess that's obvious." She sits beside me on the bed, though she leaves as much space as possible between us. "Fourteen years is a long time. You know my secrets now, but I know nothing about you."

Part of me wants to tell her about my life. About Riley and Hudson, how cute and rambunctious my kids are. About Madison and Nash and Aiden and everyone else in my family.

But Harper is my assignment.

I get up from the bed. "It's better if you and I keep our distance. My personal life is none of your concern."

Her eyes widen with shock and hurt.

I cross the room and grab my suitcase. "I'm going to sleep in your father's room tonight. I'll see you in the morning."

"*Fine*. You do that."

I go through the door connecting the two rooms. Harper doesn't say goodnight. She's pissed at me, which of course I deserve. But it'll be easier to keep things professional if she thinks I'm a jerk.

Mason looks up when I come into his room.

"Mind if I bunk with you?" I ask.

"Oh. No, not at all." He clears off his things from the other side of the bed. It's just one king, so we'll have to share.

I carefully take off my suit and hang it up. It feels like I'm taking off a costume. I change into my sweats and tee and feel much more at home.

While Mason is in the bathroom, I sit in a chair and flip through the cable channels. But really, I'm thinking about my kids.

I've got so many stories about them that I could share with Harper. I'd tell her about the time we took a family cooking class, and…

I squeeze my eyes closed. No. I can't think of Harper like she's my old friend. Way too easy to slip into that.

I don't even have any pictures of Riley or Hudson to look at, much less show off. I left my personal phone at home. I've stripped myself of anything that could identify me as Jake Shelborne. I've got some government gear secreted away in a compartment of my suitcase, stuff that could get me killed if the wrong Caldwell finds it. But nothing to tie me to my real identity.

It's always like this when I go undercover. It's a matter of safety. Yet it leaves me feeling adrift. As if the kind, sensitive parts of me are sailing further and further away.

But right now, with Harper, that's for the best. I can't allow myself to get too close to her. Far too much is at stake.

Mason emerges from the bathroom. He's wearing a pair of flannel pajamas. "Jake. I wanted to thank you for doing this. Helping us."

I nod. But I need him to know why I'm here. "Mr. Caldwell—"

"Mason."

"Mason. All due respect, I'm not doing it for you."

"You're doing your job."

"Yes, but to be honest, I'm here in spite of my better judgment. If I had it my way, Harper wouldn't have anything to do with this plan. Or the Caldwell family."

The implication of what I'm saying is obvious. *You're her father. You didn't take care of her.*

"You can't begin to understand what living in a family like ours is like," Mason says.

My parents taught me to respect my elders, and once upon a time, I would never have talked back to a man like Mason. But those days are long gone.

"Maybe you're right, and I can't understand. But from where I'm sitting, it sounds like you're just trying to justify your actions to yourself. To pretend that you're not responsible for the choices you've made."

"Jake, my health isn't good. I haven't told Harper the extent of it, but—"

"Then stop right there. Please. Because I don't want to lie to her." Not any more than I already have to.

I grab my toiletry bag, ready to head in to the bathroom to brush my teeth. But then I turn back. "Look. I respect that you're making the right decision now. But don't make me your confessor. I can't give you forgiveness."

"I'm not asking for your forgiveness or even your mercy. If you can help Harper, I'll do anything you need."

"Good. Then you and I will get along just fine." I head into the bathroom and close the door.

Inside, I stare into the mirror. Wondering who exactly it is looking back.

9

Harper

My personal life is none of your concern.

I cannot believe Jake said that to me.

I should be getting ready for bed, but instead I'm pacing back and forth in front of the connecting door to my dad's hotel room.

"None of my concern?" I repeat. "Really? Why did you agree to help me at all if you were going to be so...*shitty* about it?"

Of course, Jake doesn't answer. Because he can't hear me through the door.

I feel an urge to throw the nearest chair at the wall, but I can keep my temper better than that. Instead of giving in to my rage at Jake, I flop onto the mattress and stare at the ceiling.

He wants to treat me like he doesn't even know me. But that's such bullshit. He was my best friend for two years.

I almost lost my virginity to that man. *Almost.*

I groan, my hands covering my face. I shouldn't let those memories unfold in my mind. I shouldn't let myself remember what his mouth tasted like, how his skin felt...

Whelp, it seems I'm already doing it.

It happened the day before I left West Oaks. A week after the night we got Wren from Marc Landley's house and we first kissed. There was a neighborhood block party going on, and our families were down in the street hanging out.

Jake was outside in front of his house serving pizza to the little kids. I pulled him aside and asked, "Can we talk? Alone?"

I knew it was my last day. Tomorrow, I would be going back to Chicago—to Uncle Amos, the terrible truth of my family—and there was no way out. But I wanted a few moments with Jake. A chance to show him how much he meant.

To say goodbye.

We went to his house. His room. Closed the door. And there was no talking at all.

I just kissed him.

Jake didn't complain. Nope. Instead, he kissed me back like it was his personal mission. Like satisfying me was his community service project. He tasted like Mountain Dew mixed with our neighbor's pomegranate punch, and his tongue was so eager and energetic.

We stripped each other's clothes, leaving more kisses as each part of us was uncovered. We stretched out on his bed. Jake was gorgeous. Tan, smooth skin, muscles toned by his position on the varsity baseball team. Not much hair on his body. The skin of his stomach was baby soft, with hard ridges of muscle underneath.

And his cock. Ughn, I can still picture it. Long and hard and weeping against his stomach. Have I ever wanted a man that much?

I was just about to scoot downward and acquaint my mouth with those glorious eight-plus inches when the door opened.

And his mother walked in.

There was a lot of yelling and grabbing of clothes. Awkward is an understatement.

He ended up walking me home, his face burning crimson, apologizing up and down. "I'm sorry. Next time."

There wasn't going to be a next time for us. Jake was never going to be my first. But I didn't tell him. I was too much of a coward back then.

I had feelings for him, even if I couldn't admit them to his face. And I guess I never will. I'm a far braver woman now, but about Jake, I'm still a coward.

Wow. I *really* need to stop feeling sorry for myself. I need something to take up this Jake-sized hole in my brain.

I force myself up to standing. My hands won't stay still, so I grab my sketchbook and dig out my pencil case from the bottom of my bag. I sit at the hotel desk and move the pencil over a blank sheet.

Instantly, the dry sound and the friction calm me.

I trace curves, not even sure what I'm drawing yet. Shape and structure appear out of nothing. It only takes a minute or two before I realize what I'm drawing. My hand stills on the paper.

It's Jake. *Of course* it's him. But it's Jake how he looks now. The slope of his nose, the bow of his lips. His cheekbones, which are more defined than they were when we were teenagers. There's not much softness to him now. At least, not what I could see.

What's he thinking right now? What does he think of *me*?

My fist tightens on the charcoal pencil, and I draw a harsh black line across my sketch, ruining it.

This is a waste of time. I'd be better off getting some sleep.

If I'm going to make it through the next few days, I have to keep my mind off the man who's staying in the next room.

And who, tomorrow, will be sharing my bed.

IN THE MORNING, WE PACK UP AND HEAD downstairs. The valet pulls around Jake's car, a white Porsche 911.

I whistle. "Nice ride."

"Jake Worthington travels in style." He's wearing another pair of tailored wool pants and a slim fit button-down, open at the collar. His cuffs are rolled up over his forearms, showing off a sleeve of tattoos I hadn't seen before on his right arm.

Yet another surprise. The ink gives a sexy edge to his preppy outfit.

"Mason, why don't you take shotgun?" Jake asks. He opens the driver's side door and folds over the seat. He gestures for me to get in. He doesn't ask me if I want to sit here, but whatever.

As I climb in, Jake gives me a sweet smile and a soft kiss on the cheek, which I guess is a peace offering. At least he's not being a *complete* asshole like he was last night. Just a partial one.

I don't know if he's going to be less infuriating today or what. All I can do is sit back and roll with it.

Maybe that was Jake's plan all along. There's not any question right now of who is in charge. I'm letting him take the driver's seat in more ways than one. But I intend to make him work for it. And if I have a problem with an order he gives me, I'm not about to follow it.

He's the former army grunt. Not me.

Once we're all seated, Jake adjusts the rearview mirror. "Sleep well?"

"Well enough."

He tunes the radio to classic rock as we head out of Beverly Hills. But he doesn't take the entrance to the interstate. Instead, he drives down Wilshire to Santa Monica, and we turn onto the Pacific Coast Highway.

"Thought we'd take the scenic route." His eyes catch mine in the mirror.

Definitely a peace offering. He remembers how much I love the water. I just shrug, like it makes no difference to me.

The three of us are silent as Jake drives. I can't tear my eyes away from the window. The glittering ocean, dotted with boats and swimmers.

Back when we were in high school, we'd sometimes head to the beach after school instead of going home. Jake tried to teach me to surf a few times, and I was terrible at it. I've never had good balance. But Jake could jump onto the surfboard and ride the waves like he was born there. He was all golden hair, golden muscles, swim trunks riding low on his hips. I loved those afternoons.

I haven't thought of those days in so long.

I wonder if he's thinking of those memories too. Probably not. He said last night we had to be distant. But I can't turn off my feelings the way he can.

After a while, we reach West Oaks and Jake exits the freeway. We drive down Ocean Lane, past shops and the ice cream parlor we used to like. Wren's favorite was mint chocolate chip. Jake liked chocolate, preferably layered with fudge and chocolate chips.

When I glance forward, Jake is watching me again in the rearview mirror.

"Aren't you supposed to have eyes on the road?" I ask.

"I'm a multitasker."

My dad's being way too quiet, and I think he's fallen asleep. But then I notice he's staring at the windshield with a glazed expression. "Dad? You okay?"

He startles, his hand grasping for the dash. "Yes, Harper. Just fine."

Jake must have the directions memorized because he turns onto a road leading into the West Oaks hills. We follow the twists and turns as we climb, and the ocean falls away, spreading out beneath us like it could cover every inch of the world.

My uncle Amos has rented out an entire golf resort for this event. A fancy gatehouse appears, and Jake stops to give my father's name.

The security guard notes down the license plate, then walks a slow circuit around the car. "Open your trunk please, sir?" the guard calls out.

I whisper a curse.

"I'm sure it's just routine," Jake mutters.

Or it's Roman's doing.

Jake pops the trunk. The guard pokes around. I don't take another breath until he closes the trunk and nods for us to drive forward.

But Jake leans out of the open window. "Almost forgot. I have something for the lost and found. Mind if I leave it here?" He hands the guard a paper shopping bag. Then he smiles and puts the car in gear like he doesn't have a care in the world, but my heart is rattling my rib cage.

"What was that?" I ask.

"Something Roman left behind yesterday. Don't worry about it."

I'm sure it's nothing good if it came from Roman.

Suddenly, I want to tell Jake to turn the car around. Just get out of here, run. I never should've pulled him into my mess. If he gets hurt because of me…

But this is Jake's job, and it's too late for those doubts now.

We're in. I'm really doing this. I hope I'm ready.

10

Harper

We follow the driveway until a massive building appears. It looks like a castle set on the coast of the Mediterranean. Beige stucco, blue accents, a tiled roof. The grounds are manicured, full of winding stone paths and fountains.

The parking lot is mostly empty. The investors will arrive tomorrow, but tonight it's just the Caldwell family.

Oh, joy.

Jake pulls beneath the porte-cochère and stops the car. A welcoming party steps outside through the glass lobby doors. Roman, his bodyguard Lars, and Jimmy.

Jake gets out first, then folds over the seat and helps me out. He doesn't let go of my hand. Jimmy, my driver from the airport, heads over to intercept us while Roman looks on.

"Do you know this guy who's coming our way?" Jake asks quietly.

"Jimmy. He's usually our driver when we're in the LA area."

"You like him?"

"I did," I mutter. "But I'm not so sure."

I know Jake wants to ask more, but Jimmy's within earshot now. Jake tosses Jimmy the keys to the Porsche. "Watch the paint job, man. Thanks."

A porter hurries over to get our bags. Roman just glowers with his arms crossed over his linen shirt.

Jake starts toward Roman, but Jimmy stops him. "One moment please, Mr. Worthington. I'll need to search you before you go in."

"What?" I ask. "Why are you searching Jake? First the inspection at the gatehouse, now this?"

"Mr. Caldwell's orders." Jimmy nods at Roman.

There are way too many "Mr. Caldwells" around here. I might laugh if I didn't feel like puking.

"That's all right. I have nothing to hide." Jake holds out his arms at his sides. Jimmy pats him down. "Looking for something in particular?"

"Yeah, asshole," Roman barks. "My gun."

My eyes fly to Jake. Gun? What gun?

"Oh, you still wanted that? I left it at the gatehouse."

Roman screws up his mouth to say something else, but my cousin Mia—his sister—steps through the automatic glass doors.

"Enough," she says. "Let Harper's boyfriend come inside. Quit being a dick."

I haven't seen Mia much the past few years while she's been in school. She's got the Caldwell red-toned hair, though hers is strawberry blond. She's wearing cutoff shorts and a cropped T-shirt, far more informal than anyone else I've seen here so far.

Roman frowns at his sister and sweeps back into the hotel without another word. Lars follows.

Mia rolls her eyes. "Sorry about him. He's had his panties in a twist all morning. But that's typical for Roman." She grins. "Hey, Uncle Mason. Harper. And you must be the boyfriend?" she asks Jake.

"That's me."

"Welcome to our fucked up family." She coughs. "Sorry, Uncle Mason."

My father laughs. "I've heard worse."

We follow Mia inside, and she shows us around. The lobby is elegant, with white marble, plush rugs, and art déco touches. We stop by the front desk, where a staff member hands us our keycards.

Jake's fingers skim my arm or lower back at all times. It's reassuring, actually. Knowing he's there without needing to look. I'm surrounded by people who might wish me harm, but I'm glad he's here with me, even if he's made it clear we're not friends anymore.

Mia keeps sneaking peeks at Jake and giving me thumbs up, showing her approval. She's being so goofy I can't help but smile.

"Ballroom is down there, and the pool is that way," Mia says. "I'm happy to take you to your rooms. You're all staying in the north wing. Same as me. Far away from my brothers." She gives me a wink. "I can show you the rest of the resort this afternoon, if you feel like it. I don't mind playing tour guide. I'm bored out of my gourd, so you'd be doing me a favor."

"I might take you up on that," I say cautiously. "We should catch up."

She walks us to our rooms. My dad's is first. He stifles a yawn, even though it's still mid-morning. "I think I'll lie down for a bit."

"Sure, Uncle Mason," Mia says. "Lunch is in the sun room."

I watch him shuffle through his door.

The room I'm sharing with Jake is down the hall, just

across from Mia's. Perfect for her to keep an eye on us. Jake taps his keycard and heads into the room.

Mia winks at me. "Just let me know about that tour. If not, dinner's at six."

"Thanks."

She lowers her voice. "And nice work on the boy toy. Is he always that quiet?"

"Sadly, no."

She frowns. "Too bad. I think sexy and silent is the ideal man. Well, I'll catch you later."

I wave goodbye, and she heads into her own room. I'm left alone in the hall. But as soon as I step through that door, it'll just be me and Jake.

Buck up, I tell myself. *You have dealt with worse than Jake Shelborne. Or Worthington. Or…jeez, whatever.*

I sigh. It's going to be a long four days.

IN THE ROOM, JAKE IS WALKING AROUND LIKE HE'S trying to study every single detail.

I set down my purse and kick off my shoes. My eyes land on the bed. He won't be able to escape to my father's room tonight. But Jake could sleep on the floor. Seems like the kind of thing he'd do.

"I'm guessing our bags are being searched right now," I say.

"I'm in no rush for more clothes." Jake comes over to me and puts his finger to my lips. There's flirtatiousness in the gesture, but he's also clearly telling me to be quiet.

What? I mouth.

He crowds me against the window, and he laces our fingers together. His eyes are too bright, sending me a message. *Just wait.*

He thinks we're being watched. From the golf course? From *inside* the room? Would my family stoop that low?

Wait. Roman is head of security. I know the answer to that.

Jake kisses my forehead, then resumes his perusal of every inch of the room. After a few minutes, a porter delivers our bags. Jake tips the guy, thanks him, and shuts the door.

Then he tugs the curtains closed.

It seems like he's satisfied with whatever he saw while he was examining our room. With a focused expression, he sets his suitcase on the bed, opens it up, and removes several stacks of clothes. I hover behind his shoulder. He slides his fingers around the inner edges of the suitcase, and suddenly, a panel snaps open.

A secret compartment.

It holds a bunch of items nestled into foam. Including a handgun. The sight of it sends a cold fingernail down my back.

Jake ignores the gun and instead takes out a rectangular plastic device. He moves with confidence as he sweeps it over the room. He knows exactly what he's doing.

A light flashes on Jake's rectangular device when he goes near the bedside lamp. He examines the shade. Then he waves me over and points. There's a tiny metal circle hidden on the inside of the lampshade. It's almost impossible to notice.

He puts his finger over his lips again. *Quiet.* He doesn't touch the metal circle. Instead, he replaces his plastic device in his suitcase compartment and waves me toward the bathroom.

"How about a shower? I'm *dying* to get you naked."

I nearly choke on my tongue.

He tugs me inside the tiny room, closes the door, and starts the water.

"Um, *what?*" I force out. My heart rate has just taken off and my blood is pumping heat to all my extremities.

Jake pulls me close and drops his voice to a whisper. "They won't be able to hear us now. If we need to talk, we can do it in here. I'd rather leave their bug in place. It's audio only, no visual."

My skin flushes. "Okay."

What did I think? That he really wanted to jump in the shower with me? This role play isn't going that far.

But for a second there, did I want it to?

Distance, I remind myself. Jake has the right idea.

"I should check Mason's room for bugs as well," he says. "And I need to make contact with Agent Reyes."

I'm not sure how Jake will handle that, but I'm sure he's got it covered with his compartment full of spy gear. "I'll go on a tour with Mia. I'd like to see the grounds." I have more than one reason for that, but I don't share it with Jake.

The water is turning hot. Steam billows into the room, blurring over the mirror. I'm way too conscious of him. His broad shoulders, his height. The new-to-me tattoos winding up his arm.

I remember the way he wrapped me up yesterday when we kissed at the restaurant.

Ugh, everything's getting turned around in my head. The boy who was my friend. The man who's playing my hero.

"On the drive up here..." Why am I even mentioning this? I shouldn't. Yet I keep talking. "I was thinking of the times we went surfing back in high school. You always popped right up, and I crashed and burned every time."

Jake's face is impassive.

What was I expecting? That he'd want to reminisce?

"Never mind," I mutter. "Just...be careful contacting Reyes. Don't get caught."

"I won't. Not the first time I've been undercover."

"Yeah. I've got it. You've worked with lots of informants, and I'm just the latest." Maybe he kissed those other informants too.

He stares, betraying nothing. He'll flirt with me and touch me when we're playing our roles, but he doesn't want our friendship back. He doesn't want anything from me.

I spin around and open the door, desperate to get out of there.

11

Jake

While Harper goes on a tour of the grounds with her cousin Mia, I grab my bug detector and go to Mason's room. Part of me wanted to follow Harper, to never leave her alone around these people. But I needed some space.

Having an excuse to kiss her and touch her? It's a little too tempting. A little too easy to forget that she's not mine.

But I've turned down the obnoxiousness, as she requested. Jake Worthington is still a douche, but I'm trying to be the type of guy who'd win her heart. That'll be far more believable, even though I do enjoy how cute she is when she scowls at me.

I half expect Mason to be napping, but he answers my knock right away. He watches me in silence while I run another sweep for listening devices. I don't find any. Apparently, the room I'm sharing with Harper is a more attractive place for eavesdropping. But that's why I came prepared. The compartment in my suitcase has special shielding to prevent the contents from being detected, even with the most sophisticated tools.

I also brought along a tactical knife, my Sig Sauer P365, and plenty of ammo. For now, my weapons are staying in my suitcase. But I'll have easy access if I need them.

I leave Mason's room, change into running clothes, and take my own personal tour of the golf resort.

I studied the maps of this place yesterday while I was reviewing Kevin's notes. The main hotel itself has fifty rooms. It was built in the 1920s as the playground of some Hollywood producer. Archways lead into small courtyards and sitting areas. I stroll down the hallways, acting like I'm admiring the artwork. But really, I'm spotting the cameras. I make a mental note of their placement and their blind spots.

I pass by the ballroom, where staff is setting up tables with delicate china and expensive linens. I'm guessing this is the venue for when the investors arrive tomorrow. The Cald-wells are throwing a big shindig to wine and dine their potential business partners.

I move on before anybody notices me and head outside.

The hotel is situated right on the golf course. Rolling hills and decorative ponds expand all the way to the coastline. It looks like the beach is about a ten-minute walk down a paved path and several sets of stairs along the cliffside.

I jog toward the ocean, keeping an eye out for anyone following me. Once I'm completely sure I'm alone, I take my encrypted burner phone from my pocket. I plug another plastic device into the charging port. This gadget will allow me to contact Agent Reyes without being tracked, and once I unplug the device, the phone won't show any record of this call being made.

"Hey, boss."

"Agent. What's your status?"

I give him an update of what's happened so far: that we're in West Oaks and I'm pretty well set up here. "The rest of the Caldwells should arrive shortly. The investors will show tomorrow. How's Kevin doing?"

Reyes says my fellow agent is recovering nicely, though he's still in the hospital.

"We've located an extraction point for you on the northwest side of the resort," he says, "should it become necessary. I'm sending the coordinates to you now. We delivered some supplies last night. If things get too hairy, you can head there and set up an emergency beacon."

"Understood."

After I end the call, I follow the coordinates to the extraction point. It's hidden below a rocky cliff in an area overgrown with brush. I find a dry bag with an inflatable raft, a motor, emergency supplies, and a radio. Then I repack it all, making sure it'll stay out of the tide.

Finally, I jog back toward the hotel. I follow the paths for a while to keep up the pretense that I'm out for some exercise.

I'm dripping with sweat by the time I walk past the golf course. In the distance, I spot Harper walking with her cousin Mia. The two women are laughing.

I realize how little I've seen Harper smile since she opened the door of her hotel room yesterday. Part of the reason is me. I haven't been easy on her, which is necessary. But I do miss her smile.

I was such a dick in the bathroom a little while ago. Pretending I didn't remember those surfing lessons. The afternoons we spent at the beach. God, I remember it all. She looked so damn sexy in her bikini, soaking wet with her breasts bouncing in those tiny triangles of fabric. You can bet I memorized that image and replayed it while I stroked myself later. I mean, come on, I was a teenage kid.

But it was her laugh that I lived for. The snarky comments

she'd throw at me. The deep conversations we got into about movies or books.

"I know that look," someone says.

I turn, instinctively adopting a defensive stance. A guy in preppy shorts and a polo stands a few feet away on the putting green. He's in his late thirties, with Harper's dark auburn hair and Roman's sharp features. A couple of large gold rings stand out on his fingers. There's a keenness to his gaze that makes my spine prickle with caution.

"You must be Harper's boyfriend. I'm Tristan."

Harper hasn't told me much about Tristan. She doesn't dislike him as much as she does Roman, but that's not saying a lot.

"Jake Worthington." I shake his hand.

He's wearing slip-on shoes that look like they belong on a yacht. "Harper's never brought a boyfriend to meet the family," he says matter-of-factly. "She must think you're something special." His voice is friendly, but his eyes are shrewd, studying me. A warning, I think. But what kind? The don't-mess-with-my-cousin kind? Or something else?

I shrug. "If she thinks so, that's all that matters to me."

I'm still trying to figure out how to play this. Acting like a cocky asshole won't work with Tristan. For one, because I'm sure Tristan has his father's ear in a way that Roman doesn't.

"I've been hearing your name more and more in the last few months," Tristan says. "Yet we haven't met until now. I wondered why Uncle Mason and Harper were keeping you under wraps."

"Not under wraps. I've just been busy getting on Mason's good side. I wanted to make sure I had his approval before I took on her entire family."

"You were intimidated by us?"

"I wouldn't say intimidated." I incline my head. "Respectful."

"That's wise. My father appreciates respect. So do I. Roman..." He shakes his head. "He doesn't make friends easily. He doesn't think much of you."

"I'm sorry to hear that."

Tristan smiles, revealing the toothy grin of a crocodile. "No you're not."

I shrug again.

"I'm glad Harper's here." He says this like she had a choice in the matter. "I've wondered lately about her commitment to the family. She has a rebellious streak. I remember one time I asked to see SunSpeed's financials, and she told me to take a long walk off the skydeck at Willis Tower."

"Sounds like something she'd say." I glance over in her direction. She and Mia are heading back toward the hotel. "That's what attracted me to her. She keeps things interesting."

"I'll bet. And yet you work for a medical device company. HealthTec? Not the most exciting industry."

So he's done his homework. I channel Jake Worthington, arrogant executive.

"It's business. I like the challenge of being the best. There are plenty of ways to stay entertained in the process."

He nods slowly. "Especially if you're willing to bend a few rules."

I return his gaze, trying to show that I understand exactly what he means, and I'm on board. He holds out his hand, and we shake again. But this time, I think there's a deeper understanding there.

Either that, or he's drawing me in so he can figure out where to stick the knife later.

Guess I'll find out.

～

WHEN I GET BACK TO OUR ROOM, I JUMP IN THE shower. I hear the outer door open and close while I'm drying off.

I come out in a towel, and Harper zips past me into the bathroom, not sparing me a glance. She's carrying her clothes and toiletries in her arms.

Okay, then. We're skipping the small talk.

While she gets cleaned up, I throw on my boxers and sit on the bed to gather my thoughts. The players are starting to take shape, but I still can't tell where the greatest danger will come from. Roman? Tristan?

A lot will depend on our meeting with Amos tonight.

I dress in another tailored suit, this one in a pinstripe pattern. I fix my cufflinks into place and smooth down my jacket in the mirror, assessing. Not bad. In fact, I look pretty damn good, even if this outfit isn't really me.

Does Harper like me better in a suit, I wonder? Or in my ratty jeans and a tee?

I try not to imagine her naked right now, water pouring over her body. But that makes me think of her in a bikini again.

Which I was also doing in the shower a short while ago. Scandalous of me. I need to get a grip on myself, but not *that* kind of grip.

I rub my hands over my face. *Come on, Shelborne. Snap out of it*.

The water stops. I hear her opening and closing bottles on the counter. Then there's a thump, followed by a curse.

I get up and go to the door. "Everything okay in there?"

The door flies open. Harper's hair is damp, and her dress is falling off her shoulders. My eyes trace down her neckline just as one strap falls even lower, revealing another inch of luscious cleavage spilling from the cups of a black bra.

"I can't get the zipper. Could you help me?"

She turns around. And now, the stunning expanse of her back is exposed to view, crossed by her bra and ending at the satin trim of her panties. I reach for the zipper and drag it up, my fingers brushing each knob of her vertebrae on the way. *Damn.* My body lights up like a sparkler.

On my best behavior, I have the patience of a saint. I can ignore temptations. But this? It's a lot.

She shivers, but she doesn't turn around.

"Okay, thanks," she says. "You can go now. *Honey.*"

I want to kiss her shoulder. Inhale the sweet scent of her body wash and lotion. "Happy to help. I'm good at unzipping, too."

Fuck. Did I just say that?

I snap my mouth shut and back away. I'm not supposed to be flirting with her. I'm supposed to be stiff and professional.

Oh, you were getting stiff all right, a naughty voice says in my head.

This is not going well.

When Harper finally emerges from the bathroom, we're only five minutes from the start of dinner. But when I get a good look at her, I forget how to fucking speak.

She's arranged her hair in soft waves like a classic movie star. Eyeliner makes her eyes even larger than usual, and her lips are a pouty bright red. Her black dress skims over the lines of her body, ending just below her knees. Every gorgeous detail of her is accentuated.

Harper tucks her feet into a pair of sky-high black stilettos. "Ready to go?" she asks. Then she notices me staring. "What?"

"You just… You look incredible."

Her eyes flick over to where the listening device is hidden in her bedside lamp and frowns.

"You don't look so bad yourself," she says. But she's not smiling.

I want to take her into the bathroom and tell her I meant it. I wasn't just flirting for whoever might be listening.

But we're out of time.

We head out into the hall. When she slides her hand along my forearm, my cock does an excited shimmy in my pants, like it thinks this is really a date. I am *this close* to losing my composure after one day with Harper. That's not a good place to be.

Can I behave myself for an entire night of sharing a bed with her?

I need to sort this shit out *now*. Before the rest of me forgets what the hell I'm doing.

12

Harper

*A*s we walk down the hallway, I try not to notice how handsome Jake looks in yet another suit. Or think about the view when he walked past me in a towel.

Don't you dare think about it.

The veins on his biceps, the hair on his muscular pecs, the happy trail leading downward. The blue and green ink on his arm that snaked its way up to his shoulder…

I clear my throat. "How was your afternoon?"

"Not bad. Productive. I met your cousin Tristan." Jake smirks. "I don't think he hates me yet."

"Then you're behind schedule. Don't worry, there's still time to get him on your bad side."

"Relax. Your family is going to love me. *Darling.*"

"Could you do me a favor and stop calling me that?" I whisper.

He turns thoughtful. "No, don't think that's possible."

There could be cameras watching, so I keep my expression placid. But it's a challenge.

A moment ago in the room, I didn't miss the way his eyes

moved over every inch of my body. When he complimented me, he might've been performing for Roman's security guards who were listening in. But they couldn't see the look on Jake's face.

Which makes me think he was actually appreciating the view, like I was of him.

I can't figure the man out. He was the one who said we needed distance. Even friendship is too much for him. Yet ogling me is within bounds? That seems like hypocrisy. But I'm not the fancy federal agent with a closet full of custom-tailored suits. This dress is off the rack.

We reach the courtyard where tonight's dinner will be held, and my heel catches on the stone pavers. I stumble, but Jake's arm shoots out, steadying me.

"Careful," Mia says, coming over to greet us. She's wearing a silky emerald dress. "You'd better keep your bearings around here," she says with a wink.

"That's why she brought me," Jake says.

She laughs. "It's good you know your purpose. We could all be so lucky."

"You didn't bring a date?" I ask.

"I'm not as brave as you."

This afternoon, I enjoyed catching up with Mia. She's in her last year of her social work degree at Cal Berkeley. On the surface, Mia resembles the girl I knew when she was younger. She used to volunteer at a clinic for victims of domestic violence and wanted to start a charity. I donate both money and time as much as I can, but Mia actually wanted to make nonprofit work her life. And it seemed like Uncle Amos was going to let her.

Now? Her sarcasm matches mine. She's going to finish her degree, but she deflected when I asked about her plans for after graduation.

I wonder if she'll get sucked into the family business like I did. Maybe it's already happened. There's no escape. Not unless you do something drastic.

Would Mia want to help me if she knew? Would she want a way out?

It's too risky for me to test that theory. I can't trust anyone here except my dad and Jake.

And even *they* don't know everything.

Jake keeps a hand on my back as we grab drinks at the bar. Rows of lights are strung overhead, and a water feature babbles gently in the background. There's a long table in the center of the courtyard decked out with shiny dishes and candles. My father appears, followed by Tristan and Roman. Extended family members trickle in, and they make the rounds, kissing me on the cheek and asking how I've been. There are curious glances and polite handshakes with Jake, but everyone seems to know his status isn't determined yet.

There's an air of anticipation. We're all waiting for my uncle to arrive.

I know the exact minute he steps into the courtyard. Every head turns, and conversation halts. It's a little like when Jake strutted into that Beverly Hills hotel, except fear is what my uncle uses to command attention, not just good looks.

Amos is tall and slender, his thick salt-and-pepper hair swooping across his forehead. He has a tiny, twenty-something blond on his arm. By appearance, my uncle reminds me of George Clooney, a man who somehow only gets better looking as the years pass. Totally not fair. But while George seems like a nice enough guy, my uncle has a heart of stone underneath that amiable exterior.

Everyone wants to pay their respects to him. But it's *me* his eyes fix upon. His mouth curls smugly. He knows I'll be asking a favor, and he waits for me to come to him.

What if my uncle sees through me? What if this is a terrible mistake?

Jake's arm tightens at my hip.

Amos greets our other family members as Jake, my father, and I make our way to him. We wait our turn as my stomach contorts. The smell of dinner wafting from the kitchens makes me want to gag.

And then, finally, Amos turns to us. He shakes Dad's hand first. But he's quick to move onto me. "Harper," my uncle purrs. "Such a pleasure to see you. It's been a year at least."

"Has it?"

"It has. Long enough to think you've been avoiding me."

"Not on purpose. I've just been busy." I hold my breath as I kiss Amos on the cheek.

"With SunSpeed, I know. I really should get out to California more. West Oaks is particularly beautiful, but you already knew that, didn't you?" Amos glances slyly at my dad. "Mason, you used to tell me how much the girls enjoyed their high school years here."

His words are innocuous. But he's saying so much more.

"They did," Dad agrees.

"Especially Wren," Amos adds.

Jake's brow tenses in confusion. He doesn't understand this exchange. But I do. This is why Uncle Amos chose to host this event in West Oaks. It was a signal. A taunt. My heart tries to shrivel up and run.

I know the things this man has done to the people I care about.

Specifically, to my father's best friend just before my dad moved us out here to West Oaks.

Nobody else in the courtyard is speaking. Even Amos's date for the night—he divorced my aunt ages ago—has stepped aside. The lights are too bright. My head is pounding. Jake's palm presses into my back, holding me upright.

Amos's gaze moves to the man next to me. "And you must be Jake. I've heard a lot about you."

"Thank you for letting me be here, sir. It's an honor."

Uncle Amos takes Jake's hand in both of his. "You've only known Harper a few months from what Mason tells me. A whirlwind courtship."

Jake looks over at me, and I can't swallow around the lump of dread in my throat. He's turned away from my uncle.

No one does that.

"I've loved Harper since the moment I saw her." Jake speaks softly, but there's an underlying thread of steel in his voice. "I would do anything she needed."

"Anything?"

"Yes, sir." Jake's eyes haven't left mine.

The moment hangs for too long. My heart thrums so hard that everyone in this courtyard must hear it.

But finally, a slow smile appears on Amos's regal face. "A romantic. I can respect that." He lets go of Jake's hand. Claps Jake on the shoulder. "I hope you and Harper enjoy my hospitality."

"We intend to," Jake says with a grin, and my uncle barks a laugh.

I exhale. Sweat runs down the sides of my black dress.

I think we passed the first test. Good thing Jake is a hell of an actor.

AFTER DINNER, JAKE PULLS ME THROUGH AN EXIT door. "Let's take a walk."

I can guess why. He wants to talk freely, and that's hard to do in our hotel room.

We stroll along the path toward the ocean, hand in hand. I breathe deeply, letting relief flood into me. I've been wound tighter than a spring tonight.

The rest of dinner went well. Uncle Amos seemed to be in a great mood, and even my dad perked up, smiling and chatting with his relatives. Everyone was buzzing about the investors arriving tomorrow.

Jake stayed stuck to my side the entire evening. If anything, he was a little *too* touchy-feely. Twirling the ends of my hair around his fingers, nudging his leg to mine beneath the table, even though nobody else would be able to see. Every few minutes, he'd lean over and press his lips to my hairline. His kisses went to my head faster than my martini.

If I didn't know better, I'd say Jake was enjoying this.

But my family is full of liars and murderers, and Jake is a federal agent. Not exactly an idyllic date night.

At least Roman kept to his side of the courtyard. He was too busy avoiding his siblings to bother me. He, Mia, and Tristan moved inside their own bubbles, rarely overlapping.

Thank God it's over.

Outside, it's a beautiful night. The moon is half full, and in the distance, the water shimmers with moonlight. Jake leads me down the winding staircases along the cliffside to the beach.

"Did you notice we have a shadow?" he murmurs.

"What?"

"Don't turn around. It's Jimmy. The guy who searched me when we arrived this morning?"

"Yeah."

"He's staying back. No reason for concern. But I wanted you to know."

When we reach the sand, we leave our shoes behind and walk to the edge of the crashing surf. Jake pulls me closer, standing behind me, warm against my back.

"Are we still safe to talk with Jimmy trailing us?" I ask.

"Even if they have a mike aimed at us, they won't get anything over the waves. I came down here earlier this afternoon, but nobody followed me then. Guess we warrant more attention now?"

I wonder who ordered Jimmy to trail us. Roman? Or Amos?

"On my jog earlier, I made contact with Agent Reyes," Jake goes on. "He said if we need to get out fast, we have an extraction point. It's down the coast, at that spot where the rocks jut out at the base of the cliff." Jake doesn't point, but he turns my head gently, kissing the side of my neck to cover the movement. Tingles spread across my skin. I wonder if he can feel my pulse speeding up.

"Got it," I say. "Hopefully that won't be necessary."

"Hopefully. Do you know much about the investors coming tomorrow?" His nose drags along the skin behind my ear, the stubble on his cheek scratching gently.

A small moan falls from my lips, totally outside my control. I can't help but angle my head to give him better access. The wet sand is cool beneath by feet, but the rest of me is burning up.

"SunSpeed is the heart of my uncle's plan to expand the Caldwells' operations nationwide. My dad's the CEO, but I'm the head of operations and the one who really runs the company. Tristan is bringing people from hedge funds and venture capitalist firms to consider investing in SunSpeed. Dad and I will make a presentation on Sunday about the company. That's the big pitch."

"Which is why your uncle was so adamant about you and your father being here? The pitch meeting?"

"Exactly." Without SunSpeed's shipping ability and our legitimate clients to provide cover, this whole expansion will fall apart.

But even these thoughts are a struggle to keep in my head. Because Jake keeps peppering me with kisses, rubbing my bare arms.

"Is this okay?" His thumb strokes down along the zipper of my dress. His head dips lower to kiss the spot where my neck curves into my shoulder.

"It's…"

His tongue darts out, tasting. Holy moly. And then his lips close and he *sucks on my skin*. It's like a lightning bolt through my insides, an injection of liquid desire.

Jake's going above and beyond the call of duty here.

I gasp, pulling away from him. "What are you doing?"

The heat in his eyes sears me. "I don't know. Something I shouldn't."

"Then *stop*."

"You really want me to?"

Whatever's going on here, I can't handle it.

I dash into the icy surf. The frigid water swallows my ankles, snapping me out of my reverie. I tug my dress higher on my legs so it doesn't get wet.

Jake's ever-present touch, his mouth on my skin, the intensity of his words…

I've loved her since the moment I saw her.

A cold bath is exactly what I need. I have to focus on what I'm here to do. It's not just meeting the investors or delivering info about them to the DEA.

I'm here to save my family. The parts worth saving, anyway. And I can't forget that.

I wade out deeper. The dark waves knock into my legs, one after the other. I lose my balance, and the current pulls at my feet. I'm about to go under.

I'm shocked when a strong arm hooks me by the waist and keeps me above the surface. "You shouldn't be out this far when it's dark."

I look over my shoulder at him. I didn't expect Jake to follow me into the water in his fancy clothes. "You're going to ruin your suit!"

He lifts me up again when the next wave hits. The force pushes me against him, my back to his chest, my ass to his crotch.

And I can feel a *lot* of him. The cold water doesn't seem to be causing a shrinkage issue.

"Jake, *please* let go of me," I say through gritted teeth. "You've done enough to convince Jimmy that we're having a romantic moment."

"I thought you didn't mind me touching you."

Which is exactly the problem. I like it too much. "Let go," I say again.

His arms and his warmth disappear as he retreats. Then a massive wave picks that very moment to charge. I curse, trying to escape, and Jake scoops me up, cradling me sideways against him.

The wave hits us, and Jake is like an anchor. He barely moves.

The blood in my veins, though? Oh, that's moving.

I look up at him. His green irises are bright with moonlight, like the ocean, with equally wild depths beneath. His gaze travels to my lips and stays. I feel every single one of his fingers where he's holding me.

"I'd rather you didn't look at me like that," I say.

"Like what?"

"Like you want me. I've had enough pretend for one day."

Jake carries me back to the sand and sets me down. I tug my damp dress lower on my legs. "We should go back."

I turn toward the stairs, but Jake grasps my elbow. "Wait. Harper."

And that's it. I can't take any more.

"Just *stop*. Please. Don't you see how difficult this is for me?"

Does this man truly have no idea how important his friendship was to me? How much I longed for him to be more?

"I'm still attracted to you," I say, "and I can't just flip a switch in my brain to turn that on and off like you can."

"You think I'm faking my attraction to you?"

"I'm so confused! You made clear this is just professional, but then you look at me like you just did. One minute you're pushing me away, and then the next you're—"

My words cut off when his mouth crashes down on mine.

This isn't the way he kissed me in the restaurant in front of Roman. Or even the teasing way he kissed me earlier today with the eyes of my family on us.

This kiss is aggressive. A barely contained whirlwind of need. His tongue strokes into my mouth, his teeth nipping at my lips. His fingers wind into my hair and tug at the roots. This kiss aches with longing. Begs me not to go.

It takes me back fourteen years. To the boy I wanted to be my first.

Then he stops, chest heaving, and rests his forehead against mine. He takes my hand and guides it to the bulge in his pants. I gasp.

His erection strains at the fabric. It's hot and hard beneath my palm. And as I touch him, his cock responds by swelling even more against the layer of wool. I can feel the blood coursing with need beneath his skin.

This is nowhere near professional. But I don't pull my hand away. Instead I rub him, and he groans.

"*This* is what you do to me. I'm not faking that," he says. "I wanted you, dreamed about you back when we were eighteen, and I know this is a bad fucking idea but I can't stop wanting you. I *can't*."

After that flood of words, he takes another long pull from my lips, sucking the lower one.

"I've had constant blue balls since I laid eyes on you again. If you're not interested, then I'll back the hell off and keep my distance. But if this chemistry is just as distracting to you as it is to me..."

I almost say yes. Almost unzip his pants and push up my dress so we can both find release. But for the two happiest years of my life, he was my best friend.

What am I to him now?

I drop my hand from his hard-on. "Do you just want me to get you off? Like it doesn't mean anything?"

He has the courtesy to look guilty.

"You won't tell me about your life," I say. "You won't let me get close because I'm not the girl you thought I was. And I can understand that. I'm not..." I swallow hard because I will *not* cry. "I'm not your friend anymore. But I can't have sex with you and pretend I don't care about you."

He exhales slowly, closing his eyes. Clears his throat.

And then, nothing. He has nothing to say.

Which is basically an admission that I was right. It would've meant exactly *nothing* to him. And that really stings.

Way to make a girl feel special.

Jake takes off his jacket and drapes it around my shoulders, but we don't touch on the walk back. I don't even see Jimmy.

When we're almost to the hotel, Jake pulls me off the path. "I need to say something before we go in there."

"You've said enough."

"No, I haven't. I've done a shitty job of explaining myself. There's something I should've said fourteen years ago, but I was a stupid kid. I don't have any excuse now."

I turn slowly to face him, not meeting his eyes.

"I'm trying to stay distant to keep you safe. Trying and

fucking failing. But I have always cared about you. That hasn't changed. When we were kids..." He shakes his head, not finishing that sentence.

"It doesn't matter."

"It does. I don't have to fake having feelings for you. Because I know *exactly* what that's like. Would you look at me? Please?"

He waits until I lift my eyes.

"You meant everything to me. *Everything*. And when you left? You broke my fucking heart."

I can't move. Can't speak.

"It's been a long time since then," he says. "But you could never mean *nothing*."

Jake heads back to the path and waits for me to catch up with him.

He opens the door to the hotel for me. Takes my hand once we're inside. But there's a barrier up between us again. It's the separation between the past and the present.

Between the naive kids we used to be, and who we are now.

13

Harper

*W*hen we get to the room, Jake disappears into the bathroom.

I sit on the bed. Without realizing it, I take off Jake's suit jacket and hold the collar to my nose. There's the expensive, spicy cologne he's been wearing, yes, but underneath it's just him. Masculine. Familiar. The scent I wished I could wrap myself up inside when we were younger. The scent of goodness and comfort and safety.

My best friend. My Jake.

You broke my fucking heart.

That long-ago afternoon that we almost had sex, before his mother interrupted us, I already knew I was leaving West Oaks. I knew, and I hated the idea of never showing Jake what he meant to me. Jake had had girlfriends during our friendship, and I knew he wasn't a virgin like I was. But I wanted him to be my first. I wanted to give that to him.

Even if I only felt him inside of me once, I thought it would be worth it. To finally feel like I was *his*, even if it wasn't going to last.

Back then, I knew I was important to him. But this?

You broke my heart.

I had so many secrets, and one of them was that I loved him.

We couldn't be together then. Now, the idea is ludicrous. We've just reunited. We don't know each other and we're not even friends. Not to mention the fact that I'll end up somewhere far away once this is over, maybe with a new identity.

There's no future for us. All we have left are memories.

Unfinished business.

And it *is* pretty damn distracting.

What if that's what we need? To just get this out of our systems so we can focus on what we're here to do?

I torture myself for another five minutes. Then I go to the bathroom and knock.

"Jake?"

There's a pause, and he opens up. He's still dressed in his salt-stained pants and shirt. The top few buttons are undone, and his tie hangs loose at the collar. As if he's just been standing in here, his head full of as many confused thoughts as my own.

"Could you unzip me?"

I turn around, lifting my hair. His fingers close around the pull, and he slides the zipper down along its teeth. When it reaches the bottom, I shrug the straps of my dress off my shoulders and let it fall to the tile floor. I hear a small intake of breath behind me.

I turn, wearing nothing but a black silk bra and matching panties.

Nothing good in my life has ever lasted. So…why not take what Jake is offering me? Even if it's just one perfect night in the midst of so much else that's wrong?

Jake's eyes devour me, taking their fill. "Harper…"

I reach for his tie. It slides against his collar and drops to the ground. My fingers shake as I unbutton his shirt. Untuck it. The crisp white fabric pushes past his shoulders and down his arms. He takes over, tugging off his undershirt.

And finally, his upper body is on glorious display. I had a preview earlier when he walked past me, but now I get to look all I want.

He's bulkier than he used to be, more hair. His skin is rougher. Marked with his tattoos and some raised areas that must be scars. I touch his Adam's apple, and it bobs as he swallows. My fingers trace the hollow at the base of his neck and the deep channel between his pecs. His abs aren't as defined as when he was eighteen, not such a perfect six pack, but he's somehow more solid. His muscles radiate with coiled strength under my palms.

His nipples bead beneath my touch. I see the long outline of his cock rising in his pants.

"Harper, I could use some clarity. Earlier, I thought you said no to me. I'm getting mixed signals here."

"I want you."

And that's all it takes.

Jake grasps my face and pulls me to him. Overwhelms me with his kisses, his mouth dipping to mine again and again as he walks us backward into the bedroom.

We're picking up right where we left off on the beach, like there was no pause at all. His tongue ravages my mouth, drawing my tongue out and sucking it deep.

He lifts me up and dumps me onto the mattress. Once I stop bouncing, I prop myself onto my elbows, watching as he yanks off his belt and undoes his fly.

He shoves his pants down and toes off his socks, though he leaves his boxer briefs. His erection makes a prominent bulge in the fabric. It's huge, leaking against the cotton. It's a good thing I'm not standing because my whole body goes weak. My clit throbs and my panties dampen as all my nerve endings shout *yes*. It's like this desire has lived inside me for all these years, and it's just as intense now as when I was eighteen.

He kneels on the mattress and lowers himself on top of me, covering me with all that manly muscle. His pupils are dilated. Feral with lust.

"Harper," he groans, staring down at me with those darkened green eyes.

We're both still in our underwear, but he spreads my legs and thrusts his hard shaft against me, right over my clit as he kisses me. Like a preview of how he'll fuck me once we're naked.

His mouth moves down to my collarbones, licking and sucking at my skin. His big hands knead my breasts, thumbs flicking at my nipples through the fabric of my bra.

And it's *Jake* doing all this to me.

It feels so incredible that my head spins. I bite down on my lip to cover the sound of my gasps, then give up.

I have no idea who's listening to this. But there's no question of stopping or even trying to keep quiet. My orgasm is already cresting toward me, getting closer with each vigorous thrust of his cock against me.

It hasn't been more than a minute and I sail right over the edge. I buck my hips and cry out. My body shudders and convulses as pleasure chemicals ignite my bloodstream. His eyes lock with mine, and he gives me a wicked smile.

Oh, *wow*.

Guess I was a little worked up. That's what a fourteen-year cockblock and two days of nonstop sexual tension do to me. Plus…you know. Jake. Just, *all* of him.

"Loved the sound of that," Jake says.

I'm struggling to catch my breath. "I don't usually, uh, go off so fast."

"I just regret I didn't have my tongue in you while you came. But I can fix that for round two."

He kisses his way down my body. When he reaches my panties, he slides them off. He trails soft kisses along my belly and my thighs. His whiskers leave a delicious burn.

Then he guides my knees apart and dips his mouth between my legs.

"*Oh.*" It seems round two has already started.

His tongue dances over my clit, gently at first. But apparently my body is already raring to go again. I can't stop my hips from moving against his face. My thighs close on his head and he shoves them open again.

He smiles up at me and pushes his tongue into me. I make some incoherent noise, the consonants of his name but mixed up in the wrong order.

Both of my hands fly to the top of his head and tangle in his unruly dirty-blond hair, making the strands even messier.

While his tongue slides in and out of my pussy, his thumb finds my clit. He rubs circles into the sensitive nub, using the wetness his mouth left there.

And it's just too much.

I shake with another orgasm. When it subsides, he backs off a little, massaging my thighs in his strong grip.

But Jake still isn't done yet.

He returns his fingers to my center and pushes them inside me. He fucks me with two of them while his lips close around my clit and *suck*. I throw my head back and shout as he wrings yet another climax out of me.

Then I'm just riding on a pleasure-soaked wave, at the mercy of Jake's fingers and tongue for I don't know how long before I slump against the mattress, completely spent.

Holy shit.

He crawls up my body and slides his arms around me, nestling me into his side. Jake turns my head to kiss me. But this time it's sweeter. Soothing. I lick my own arousal from his lips.

He trails the backs of his fingers along my cheek. "Was that worth the wait?"

"I'm not complaining."

Would it have been this hot when we were eighteen? Is that possible? Who the hell knows, but this man was made for sex. I'm about to say something to that effect.

I remember just in time that this isn't a completely private space. And Jake's statement makes it sound like we haven't done any of this before.

"Fourteen—" he starts to say.

"*Jake*," I hiss. I nod at the lamp. *Careful*, I mouth silently.

He blinks in confusion, then in realization.

Did he forget about the bug in the lamp? The fact that the security guards can hear what we've been up to and what we say?

At least I know none of his passion was for show. Jake was very much in the moment.

But now, he's got a pissed-off scowl. He rubs a hand over his face.

His cock is still standing at attention in his underwear, but he scoots off the mattress and heads for the bathroom.

I get up to follow him, wearing just my bra. He starts the water in the shower. I shut the door so we won't be overheard.

He casts a glower over his shoulder at me. "I fucked up."

"But I stopped you before you said anything too bad."

"Which is a position you shouldn't have been in."

"Can't say I minded the position I was just in." I haven't been this sexually satisfied in…ever. I reach for the waistband of his boxer briefs. "They can't hear us now. I'd like to return the favor."

"Not necessary. I'm good."

"You're—wait, what?"

He strips off his underwear. I get a glimpse of his cock

bobbing, huge and tantalizing and very hard, before he steps behind the shower curtain and tugs it closed.

The man gave me *three* orgasms and then didn't want one for himself?

I'm good?

What the actual fuck?

Oh my God. I've been dismissed.

I leave the bathroom and go back to the bedroom, grabbing a sleep shirt along the way.

I don't even know what just happened.

No, I guess I do. When it comes to Jake and me, there's always an interruption. An outside world forcing us apart.

Whatever he once felt for me, those emotions live in the past. We were acting out a fantasy just now. Weaving a moment out of dreams and memories. But then Jake came to his senses and realized too much has changed. Reality smacked us both in the face.

Because I'm not Harper, the girl across the street. I'm Harper *Caldwell*. He doesn't want me after all.

And you know what? I can't forget who I am either.

Or what I'm really here to do.

14

Jake

I am an idiot. Both for forgetting we had an audience, and for thinking I could fool around with Harper at all.

She looked beyond stunning tonight, and that was part of it. But seeing her with her family and knowing how much they've hurt her made me want to hold her and shield her.

Kiss her. Touch her.

I'm never the guy who can't keep it in his pants. But Harper looks at me, and that carefully honed control goes up in flames.

At dinner, I wasn't playing her fake boyfriend. I was just being *me*, the guy who's wanted her since she was the mysterious, wonderful girl across the street.

When we walked down to the beach, I knew I was crossing all kinds of lines. Pushing. Hoping she'd sail right past those boundaries with me, even when she kept warning me to stop. *Just stop.*

I meant to. I tried.

But then she accused me of feeling nothing for her. Harper deserves all the happiness and pleasure in the world.

A lifetime of it. I guess that's how I justified my actions. I thought if I could give her even a few minutes of goodtime feelings, then I'd be an asshole to withhold it.

Which my horny brain then interpreted as, *give her as many orgasms as I can fit into a half-hour period.*

I let my baser urges take over, and you know what? It was way too easy. By letting my dick make the decisions, I put Harper at risk. Because we weren't truly alone, and I fucking forgot about it.

I jump under the spray of the shower and turn it up hot enough to scald. I drop my head. The water pounds into my neck. I was complaining about blue balls earlier—upstanding behavior there, nice one, Jake—and now I'm in a worse state than ever. She still would've gotten me off, too, if I'd let her. Probably would have gone down on her knees right here in the bathroom. Wrapped her soft lips around my shaft. Sucked on my tip, running her tongue around it...

Jesus. That would've made me hate myself even more. I don't regret making her feel good, but she doesn't owe me a damn thing.

However. I need to do something about this erection before the lack of blood in my brain hobbles me any further.

I jack my cock hard and fast. My grip is tight. Brutal. Like I'm punishing my dick for its naughty, naughty ways. But in his defense, I haven't been around a woman as tempting as Harper since...well, since Harper back when we were younger.

My balls are tight. Achingly full. I'm already turned all the way up from feasting on Harper's most private parts. My tongue rolls in my mouth, chasing after the taste of her. She was better than I ever could've imagined. I was so eager to make her moan, get her ready for my cock. I wanted to bury myself balls-deep inside her. Fuck her until I had her screaming.

I come with a shout, spattering my hand with my release. "*Fuck*." My cock spurts again, this time hitting the shower wall. My hand braces against the tile and I gasp the humid air as the water washes away the evidence.

I'm relieved that I didn't say anything too stupid where Roman's security could hear. But honestly, the part that makes my blood boil even more? The fact that those assholes now know what she sounds like when she comes. The noises she made should've belonged to *me*. And if I ever do sink my cock into her? I don't intend to share that. I don't want an audience.

Not that it's going to happen. I need to resist those urges or I might lose my head again and mess up a lot worse.

Harper's safety depends on it.

When I finally emerge from the bathroom and go to tug on my sweats, Harper's pretending she's asleep. I get it. I ruined the moment between us. I ruined any hope of us resuming our friendship either.

If she doesn't want to face me, that's probably for the best.

Sharing a bed with her is easier if she's mad at me. But there's no way she's as angry as I am with myself.

After my time in the army, years as an undercover operative, and as a father of twins, I'm a light sleeper. You never know when shit's going to go down at a moment's notice.

So when Harper sits up next to me in bed a couple hours later, my eyes immediately open.

It's dark in the room, but enough moonlight bleeds through the curtains to see her. She gets up and hurries to her suitcase like a woman on a mission. She takes off her sleep shirt. Pulls on a dark sweatshirt and black leggings, then a pair of sneakers.

What is she up to?

I expect Harper to open the door to the hall and slip through. Where else could she be heading? But instead, she goes into the bathroom. I hear the window slide open. Then the tiniest thud.

Unbelievable. I think she just jumped out the window.

We're on the first floor, but come on. Why is she being so stealthy? And why didn't she tell me? Is it because of the awkwardness between us tonight, or has she been planning this excursion for longer?

I have to know where she's headed.

I jump out of bed and throw on a T-shirt over my sweats, shoving my feet into my jogging shoes without bothering with socks. In seconds, I push the window open again and jump through.

Harper's silhouette dashes away, hair flowing behind her.

I follow.

She's going toward the golf course. I spot a couple of guards making their rounds with flashlights, but they're easy to avoid.

Harper stops and looks behind her, and I have to dip back into the shadows. She clearly doesn't want anyone to see what she's doing. The more cynical part of me wonders just how much she's hiding. If this could be some sort of double-cross.

But I can't believe Harper capable of that. No, whatever this is, she has a reason for it. And a reason for keeping it a secret from me. Even if I can't imagine what it could be.

She reaches a row of small buildings. They're surrounded by manicured flowerbeds and fountains. These look like guest lodgings rather than staff or functional areas. There's a swimming pool, smaller than the one at the main hotel, with a cover over it.

I pass a sign, which identifies these guest rooms as *The Villas*. But who could be staying out here? I thought her family was in the main hotel.

Harper vanishes along the side of one of the buildings.

I approach silently behind her. She's peering into a darkened window. Then she tries to open it.

"I wouldn't do that," I say. "Looks like it has an alarm."

She jumps, closing her mouth on a scream as she whirls around. "Jake. What are you doing here?"

"Stopping you from whatever trouble you're trying to get into."

"Go back to our room." She moves on to another of the villas, cupping her hands at the next window to peer inside. Then she curses under her breath, moving on to another. The curtains on all of these windows are up, showing dark, unoccupied rooms. "I thought for sure she'd be in one of these units." Harper is muttering to herself, not talking to me. "But if it's not here, then where?"

She digs her fingers into her scalp, and I grab her hands. "You need to explain."

Her expression is wild and defiant. "Do I? Like you've told me about your life? You went down on me, you told me I broke your heart, and you're still holding the important stuff back."

I flinch, because she's right. "My life isn't relevant. What are you doing out here? Whatever it is, you've been keeping it a secret, and I want to know why."

"Because I knew the DEA wouldn't be interested in helping me. Not with this. It's my job to look out for her, and that's what I intend to do."

Suddenly, it dawns on me. "You're looking for Wren."

Harper doesn't say anything, but the desperation in her

eyes confirms it. "They've got her," she whispers, tears filling her eyes. "This is why I couldn't back out and had to make my move *now*. Because they took Wren, and she's here somewhere, and I have to get her free."

"Why didn't you tell me?"

"I was afraid the DEA would refuse to help me."

"But you still wanted the benefit of the agency's resources?"

"Fuck you, Shelborne. I was doing what I had to do." She starts to walk away from me.

"No." I grab her wrists and push her up against the stucco wall of the villa. "No, you're going to explain yourself." She wriggles in my grasp, so I hold her in place with my body. "How long have you known that Wren would be here?"

"Months."

I curse. She's been lying to my agency, lying to me from minute one.

Just like when we were teenagers.

"This is why you contacted the DEA to inform on your family. Not because you wanted to do the right thing. And we fell for it."

"Saving my sister isn't the right thing?"

I close my eyes. "Let's back up. Wren was kidnapped? Is that what you're telling me?"

"It's not that simple." Her eyes beg me to understand. "I don't know for sure how it happened. All I know is my uncle has been keeping her close. Roman promised I'd get to see her after I performed in their little dog-and-pony show for the investors. Which means she has to be here. Amos would want her right under his thumb. But I thought...if the government was already involved...you'd help me get her out if I couldn't manage it myself."

"Because we'd be in so deep by then, we wouldn't have a

choice." The more I hear, the worse it gets. "You were using us." Using *me*.

Her breasts heave as she breathes. I feel every beat of her heart, every tremble as she's pressed up against me. "*I knew* how you people would see it. Even if everything else I've told you is true. You don't understand. You never have, and you never will."

Her words are as harsh as a slap in the face. "I know Wren. I care about her, too. Hell, at least I could've prepared better if you'd told me the truth."

"And you would've kept it from your bosses?"

"I might have."

"Bullshit. They would've told you to stay out of it. That saving Wren wasn't part of your mission."

I open my mouth to disagree. But I can't.

This isn't a kidnapping with a ransom note where the FBI rolls in. For all I know, Wren went with her uncle voluntarily. This could get messy. And that isn't the kind of thing the DEA wants to get involved in.

They want intel to bring down drug rings. Not complicated problems that will be risky and delicate to solve.

"Harper, if you had just trusted me…"

I trail off, listening.

The hairs on my arms raise.

"You would've what?" she asks.

"Shhh."

I swivel my head, my eyes scanning the darkness. Still holding onto Harper with one hand, I peer around the side of the building.

There's a figure walking down the path past the villas, his back toward us. He's heading away from the hotel.

"It's Tristan," I whisper to Harper. "Any idea what your cousin is doing out here this late?"

"No. We should go after him."

"*We?*"

"Jake, come on. What if this is important? What if he could lead us to Wren?"

I should tell her no, that we need to head back to the hotel. That this isn't part of the op I signed up for.

But I know Harper. She'll just go on without me, and unless I want to pick her up and carry her back, I can't stop her. I'd rather stick by her.

The same way I've always felt about her, for better or worse.

"All right. We'll follow him. But you need to stay with me. Do *not* take off without me."

She smirks. "Because you're in charge?"

"Exactly," I mutter.

We tail her cousin, staying on a parallel path. I hold tight to Harper's hand. No way am I letting her get away from me this time.

She sends a scowl over her shoulder and pulls me along faster.

The path takes us uphill, into the higher cliffs to the north of the golf resort. I saw this part of the coast from the beach today, out where the sand disappears and it gets rocky and treacherous. It's not far from the emergency extraction point Agent Reyes set up for us.

Then Tristan disappears around a curve in the path and is swallowed up by densely growing trees.

"Come on, we're losing him," Harper says.

We speed up and make it around the curve. But there's no sign of Tristan. I don't see where he might've gone.

All I hear is the crash of waves against the cliffs.

Then I feel a sharp poke in my lower back.

"Don't move," Roman says. "I've got you now, you arrogant fuck."

15

Harper

I try to run, but two beefy arms close around me like a steel trap. I smell artificial cherry. It's Lars, Roman's personal bodyguard. *Crap.*

I kick and elbow him, but the man doesn't even seem to feel it.

Roman stands behind Jake, looking smug and triumphant. "Hands up." He jabs Jake in the back—I think with a gun, though I can't see it—and Jake slowly raises his hands.

"Roman, *stop*," I yell. "Leave him alone!"

Jake is far calmer than me. "Let Harper go. I'm the one you have a problem with."

"I don't agree." My cousin sneers. "You two are out late. I want to know why."

"None of your business," Jake says smoothly.

I know the look in Roman's eyes. He's going to lash out. "We were just taking a nighttime stroll. That's of no concern to you."

"I don't believe that for a second. You two are up to something." He pushes Jake again. Jake's mouth tightens. "Which means you're even dumber than I thought, Worthington."

"Can't say your low opinion is going to keep me up at night," Jake deadpans.

"No, I already know what keeps you up at night." Roman moans in a falsetto.

Lars snickers in my ear, his hand sneaking down to pinch my ass.

Then Jake moves so fast I can barely follow what's happening. In half a second, he's spun behind Roman. He's got one of Roman's arms bent in a way that makes my cousin's face twist.

And Jake now holds the gun to Roman's head.

How did he *do* that?

Lars fits a meaty hand around my throat and squeezes. I whimper as the breath leaves my throat. Lars lifts me up, and I go onto my tiptoes.

"Back off or Lars will snap her neck," Roman chokes out.

"If he hurts Harper, I'll kill you and Lars both."

Jake doesn't sound like he's bluffing. Nobody moves.

Roman blinks first. "Enough. I don't have time for this." He nods at Lars, who releases me.

I rub my throat and gasp for breath. Jake shoves Roman away.

Then he throws the gun in a wide arc. It sails right over the cliff and hits the water with a faint splash.

"*Asshole*," Roman screeches.

Jake tsks. "You should keep better track of your belongings. Wasn't that the gun I just returned to you this morning?"

My cousin's fists clench and unclench. But he doesn't make a move toward Jake, and neither does Lars.

"I'm keeping my eye on you, Worthington."

"I have no doubt."

Roman's beady eyes dart to me. "Hope you know what

you're doing with him, Harper. At some point, my father won't let you get away with your shit anymore."

He and his bodyguard stalk away.

Jake pulls me into his arms, and I tuck my face against his shoulder. The temperature has dropped enough to feel the chill coming from the ocean. But the warmth of him blazes through his T-shirt.

Just a few minutes ago, we were furious with one another. But I wouldn't trust anyone more than Jake to keep me safe.

He gently touches my throat. "You okay?"

I nod. "He just scared me, that's all."

"They're both going to fucking pay for that. You sure you're all right?"

"Yeah. I am."

We head back to the hotel. I wish I'd been able to find out where Tristan was going, but he's long gone.

Jake has returned his hand to my back. A reassuring pressure. He's letting me know that, no matter what happened between us earlier, he's on my side. I did keep the secret about Wren, but only because I didn't trust that the DEA would care about rescuing her.

Maybe I should've expected better from Jake. But I was just trying to do what he wanted. Not get too deeply involved. I was trying to keep him out of it.

Now, that's no longer an option. If he's willing to help me, I'm grateful. But we've crossed so many lines already. Hooking up earlier, and now this.

"We need to talk," he says.

"I know." I need to tell him the rest. I need to tell Jake things that I've been keeping secret since I was a teenager.

More than anything, I want his friendship back. I want to trust him this time. *Really* trust him. But only if he's willing to listen.

We find a secluded place to sit on the golf course. I lie

back on the grass and look up at the stars in the sky. Jake lies beside me, his arm and hip pressed against mine.

I swallow down my dread and force the next sentence out. "Wren isn't really my sister."

Jake doesn't move. Doesn't even blink as I tell the story.

Wren was the daughter of my dad's best friend, a lieutenant in the Caldwell organization. Wren and I were close, and our families did everything together. That was before I understood what business the Caldwells were in. Our parents warned us about strangers and drugs. I didn't know that members of my family supplied those dealers with their product.

But that double life wore on Wren's father. He hadn't been born into it like my father, and he wanted out. Wren's dad went to my grandpa, offered to buy his way free. Anything to get his wife and daughter out of that life.

Amos was the enforcer back then, and my grandfather gave him the order. Death for their betrayal.

Wren's parents ended up in Lake Michigan.

I'm staring up into the night sky. At stars and satellites, a few pricks of light in a vast blanket of dark. "The car slid out on an icy road. The police ruled it an accident."

"Amos did this? And Mason knew?"

"Yeah. There's nothing my dad could've done to stop it. If he'd spoken up, Amos would've punished us too. After that, Dad was sent to California to start SunSpeed. Wren came to live with us, and my parents adopted her. She became my sister."

"That happened right before I met you?" Jake asks.

I nod. "Before then, I'd been an only child. After she became my sister, I would've done anything to protect her. I knew how much she'd already been through."

Wren was so messed up after losing her parents. I tried to be there for her, even when she didn't want me hovering.

Jake was a bright spot in my life, as warm as the sun shining down from the Southern California sky. I knew I could count on him the way I couldn't count on anyone else. My golden boy.

I loved him for that.

But I also knew I couldn't tell him where my family had really come from. Who Wren really was. Because then, all the rest of it would come out.

"What's going on with Wren now?"

"She's gotten into trouble in the past. Lowlife boyfriends, mostly. I always managed to bail her out. But she started avoiding me about six months ago. I knew something was wrong, and she refused to talk to me. Then she disappeared. I was frantic until Roman said they were 'protecting' her for her own good. Keeping her prisoner, more like."

"Are you sure?"

"Why else haven't I heard from her in so long? They've let her call my dad, and because of that he has no clue how bad things really are. Roman has sent me a couple of videos of her. She looked so sad. Like she didn't care about anything because they've taken too much from her."

A single tear slides down the side of my face. We're still lying on the grass. Jake has his head turned to watch me, and he brushes the tear away with his thumb.

I finally look at him. "Can you forgive me?"

This is what I've always been afraid of. Jake's judgment. His rejection. When we were kids, he viewed things in black and white, right and wrong.

"You need to forgive yourself," he says.

"But I kept the truth from you. And I didn't protect Wren. I stayed with my family. Did what my uncle said." I dreamed of finding a way out, but it took me fourteen years.

"I don't blame you for any of it." He pushes a strand of

hair from my cheek. "I cared about you then, and I still do. That hasn't changed."

There's a decade's worth of tears lodged in my throat trying to get free. I breathe through it. Jake runs his fingertips over my hair, my chin, my arm.

"I have two kids," he says suddenly.

"You…" I shake my head at the subject change. "You have kids?"

"Twins. Riley and Hudson. They're five."

My face burns. "But you're not with—"

"Their mother? No. I told you I'm not attached. Otherwise, I wouldn't have done what we did earlier."

"No. I know you wouldn't." I exhale. "Wow. *Twins*. Like your siblings."

"Yeah, but fraternal twins come from the mother's side. Adrienne's mom was a twin, too. Our family events are crowded."

"But much less problematic than mine, I'm sure."

"There's that."

Jake must be a wonderful dad. Kind and loving and a lot of fun, too.

Did I take him away from them? What's he sacrificing to be here helping me? *It's his job*, I remind myself. But he's gone above and beyond for me.

I want to protect him from danger the way he's protecting me. But that's never been my strong suit.

"I thought you wanted to keep your personal life private," I say.

"You opened up to me. I should do the same. I want to."

"Why?"

He sighs. "Because you're you."

I'm not sure what that means. But if he's willing to let down his guard, I'm glad for it.

"I'll help you find Wren," he says.

"You will?"

"Yes." He says this without hesitation. "All you've ever had to do was ask. Sometimes I try to change your mind, but you know I come around in the end. You have that effect on me."

We smile at each other. I rest my hand on his cheek.

"Tell me about Riley and Hudson?"

It's almost sunrise by the time we climb through the bathroom window and go back to bed. I snuggle against him, using his chest as a pillow. Jake kisses me chastely on the forehead.

"Thank you," I whisper. "For everything."

"Night, Harper."

"Night."

I feel like I have my best friend back. Even if it's just for the next couple days, it's more than I ever expected. Or believed that I deserved.

16

Jake

In the morning, I don't get to linger over waking up next to Harper. When I open my eyes, she's already showered and dressed. I yawn and stretch as I kick the blankets aside.

I'm just wearing my sweatpants. Her gaze snags on my bare chest, then darts away.

"Get moving, lazy," she says. "Don't want to miss breakfast."

She's wearing a tiny athletic skirt, a pastel sleeveless sweater, and a pair of white sneakers with no socks. Every time she moves, her top rises up and plays peekaboo with her belly button.

"Do you have a tennis game to get to?" I ask.

She raises an eyebrow. "Didn't you read the agenda? Golf game this morning. I hope you can play."

"Shit, I forgot about that." One of those "mandatory fun" events that her family has scheduled. Jake Worthington would probably be a practiced golfer, but I've only played a couple of times in my life. Good thing I've always been athletic. Baseball players are naturals at golf.

"I can handle it." I sit up, moving to the edge of the bed. Before she can leave the room, I grab her hand. "Come here."

I wrap my arms around her waist. I'm trying not to picture her body splayed out on this bed last night. The taste of her. The way she moaned.

I cough. "Just wanted to see how you're doing." I try to put everything I mean into my expression, since I can't spell it out here. Who knows who might be listening.

It took Harper a lot of courage to tell me about Wren's history. After that, I had to open up to her about myself. And as soon as I started, I couldn't believe I'd held back. I loved sharing those parts of myself with her. I wish she could meet my kids and see Madison and how happy my sister is now. Maybe we'll get that chance someday. I hope so.

"I'm fine, *babe*," she says. "But thanks for asking." She drops a kiss onto my nose. "Now get moving. And try to behave yourself today. Will you?"

"*Me?*"

She puts her lips to my ear and whispers, "We can't afford any more trouble with Roman."

It's her cousin who keeps tensions high, not me. And if he messes with Harper, I'm going to retaliate.

"We'll see," I murmur.

She glares a warning, and I shrug.

I dress in a pair of khaki pants and an athletic polo, tidy myself up in the bathroom, then hurry out the door.

We get breakfast, and I fill my plate like I usually do. Pancakes, bacon, a blueberry muffin and coffee. A skill I learned in the army. You sleep when you can, eat when you can. Harper picks at a boiled egg and a slice of French toast.

We sit with her father, who looks tired but is trying to be chipper this morning. Harper's other family members watch us, even though they're trying to pretend to mind their own business.

Roman is at the other end of the table. I'm trying to keep my cool because my blood is still running hot about last night.

Roman's bodyguard put his hands on Harper, and I'm not about to let that go.

"Sleep well?" Mason asks Harper.

"Yep. Mostly." She glances at me, and I wish she wouldn't. I'd rather her dad didn't guess what we were up to last night. Either the orgasms or the tussle with her cousin.

"Did something keep you up?" Roman asks. Everyone turns to him.

I wipe my mouth with my napkin. "We decided to get out and explore the grounds. It's a beautiful resort. Except we ran into some local wildlife."

"Wildlife?" Mason says. "What kind?"

Harper is frowning at me. But I keep going.

"Just pests, really. But the gardeners might want to take care of it before they cause any damage to the golf course." I take a bite of bacon. "What about you, Roman? You were out last night too, weren't you?"

In fact, I've been wondering about that. How did Roman and Lars manage to catch us? They didn't follow us from the hotel. I'm sure of it. And I don't think any cameras spotted us either, unless it was one near the villas, and the timing doesn't add up. Roman and Lars caught up to us way too quickly. As if they were already out and about.

What were they really doing out there?

"I was supervising our security team," he says.

"In the middle of the night? That's dedication."

There's a smugness to the twist of Roman's mouth. I don't like it. I've embarrassed the guy twice now. Harper thinks I can defuse this situation, but it seems Roman is the type of guy who only escalates.

Our confrontation last night won't be the last.

HARPER AND I HEAD TO THE GOLF CLUBHOUSE. It looks like the younger sibling of the hotel. White stucco, blue trim. There's a courtyard in the center, where a bar is serving mimosas and tiny sandwiches for anyone who missed breakfast. Swanky digs.

Harper will be golfing with three other women, including her cousin Mia. I'll be in a foursome with Amos, Mason, and Roman. I'm not sure if it's a privilege or a punishment.

I didn't bring a set of golf clubs with me—like I own a fucking set of clubs—so I get a caddy's help with my equipment. Everyone else has already got their stuff ready to go.

Roman saunters over to sneer at me. "Do you think Mason would appreciate hearing the dirty details of what you and his daughter were doing in your room last night?"

The caddy's face turns red. He comes up with something important to do in the back room.

I pretend to be surprised. "How would you know?"

"I told you I've been watching you and Harper. My security team is passing around screenshots of her like trading cards. She takes it like a champ, doesn't she?"

I know he's lying. At most, he had audio. But my guts tighten. This guy is brazen, considering I've disarmed him twice without breaking a sweat. But his dad is a few yards away, so Roman knows I can't touch him. Not here.

A side effect of him overhearing our fun, though? He doesn't have a single doubt that I'm her boyfriend.

"You have an unhealthy fascination with your cousin. Would your family want to know about that?"

"I know you're up to something. I'm not letting up until I figure it out."

"If I were you, I'd be more concerned about my brother finding out I was following him last night."

Roman's sneer turns savage. There's a flicker of fear in his eyes. I've hit the nail on the head.

He was following Tristan. But why?

"Don't worry, I'm not going to tell. Yet." I wink at him, which makes his scowl deepen.

He's so thrown that he has to run to catch up to me.

I go to shake hands with his father. "Mr. Caldwell, my apologies for holding us up," I say.

"Think nothing of it. Beautiful day for a game, isn't it? Do you play much, Jake?"

"Not as much as I'd like."

Amos leads us outside. We've got a couple of carts. The caddies are loading them up with our golf bags. Roman hovers at his father's shoulder, and Amos says a few stiff words to him that I can't hear.

I walk beside Mason. Out in the sun, it's all the more obvious how pale he is.

He wasn't looking well at breakfast either.

"Are you sure you're up for this?" I ask him quietly.

"I might've eaten something that didn't agree with me. I'll be fine." He walks off, and I'm not convinced. But if he says he's okay, what can I do?

I look up and find Roman's eyes glued to me.

After hitting warm-up shots on the driving range for a while, we gather at the first hole. Amos swings first, the ball sailing in an arc all the way to the green. I'm not into golf, but even I can appreciate a shot like that. Elegant in its precision.

Yet I'm also thinking of what Harper confessed to me. That her uncle killed Wren's parents. That knowledge has terrified Harper for all these years, racked her with guilt. Amos deserves whatever vengeance is coming to him.

I sure as shit hope I get to deliver it. Preferably after Harper and Wren are both safe and sound.

The rest of us take our shots next, and I don't embarrass myself. Amos and Mason take one cart, which leaves me with Roman. I let him drive, and we zoom along the path in stony silence. I wonder if he's contemplating what I said before about Tristan.

But Roman isn't like his father. He's not careful or precise. Dangerous? Sure. But the guy is beyond predictable.

It doesn't take him long to start fucking with me. He messes around with my golf balls on the greens, knocking them into hazards when the other men aren't looking. "Accidentally" leaves me behind at the third hole, so I have to run until a caddy picks me up in a spare cart. But it's fine.

Roman is way out of his depth here.

"Very impressive swing," Amos says, after I hit another 275 yard drive.

"Thank you, sir."

"You must be a natural athlete." Amos leans on his driver. He's wearing a pair of golf gloves, one hand perched at his hip. "Have you been enjoying the resort, Jake? Making use of the facilities?"

I wonder what Roman's been telling him. But for some reason, Roman doesn't look so smug at the moment.

"I have," I say. "In fact, the strangest thing happened last night when Harper and I were taking a moonlight stroll to the beach."

Roman's head whips sharply in my direction, panic lancing across his features.

"Oh?" Amos says. "And what was that?"

I let the pause linger. Letting it really sink in for Roman. What I could do to him. I'm sure Roman knows every bit as well as Harper what his father is capable of. How harsh his judgment can be.

Of course, I'm bluffing. I don't have a clue why he was following Tristan or why he's hiding it from his dad. But he's giving so much away. There's something here worth finding out.

"I realized that, as beautiful as that view was, it didn't compare to Harper. Mr. Caldwell, I'd like to ask your niece to marry me." I nod at Mason. "And of course, I'd like Mason's permission as well. I don't want to let another day go by without showing her what she means to me."

Amos nods in approval. "If Mason is happy to have you as a son-in-law, then I don't have any objections. Make Harper happy. Why not?"

"Thank you, sir. My thoughts exactly." I look over at Roman. "I'll do anything to make her happy."

Roman's upper lip curls, and he looks away.

17

Harper

*W*e're on the green for the fifth hole, and Aunt Gretchen has spent the last five minutes lining up her putt. She's really a cousin of Amos and my father, but I can't remember exactly where she falls in the family tree.

Mia leans into me. "You'll have to bury me at the sixth hole. Because I will have died from extreme boredom."

I snicker.

Aunt Gretchen's putt goes askew, and she glares over her shoulder at us.

"Sorry," I mutter.

My uncle's date-of-the-moment stands off to one side, oblivious, scrolling her social feed with a long glittery nail. Gretchen finally gets the ball into the hole, then stomps over to her cart and shoves her putter into the bag.

"Ladies, you could at least make an effort."

She's the only one of us who seems to care about the game. My uncle's date, who's younger than Mia, keeps asking about the rules. The only part she has right is the outfit, though her golf skirt and top are covered in designer logos and would be more at home in a magazine spread than an actual golf course.

"I don't see the point," Mia says. "It's not like Dad can see us over here."

"*Mia*," Gretchen scolds.

"What? That's what you care about. Kissing his ass in every way possible."

That's more cynical than I would've expected from her. But it's true. "Isn't that what we're *all* doing?" I ask.

Gretchen looks scandalized and gets into her cart with my uncle's date. They take off down the path. Mia eyes me, and I wonder if I've said too much.

"You're right," she says. "We all run around in circles to impress him. My brothers are the worst of all. It's exhausting."

I shrug. These kinds of thoughts are dangerous to voice. But when Mia does it, it seems playful instead of treasonous.

She plops herself into the cart with a sigh. "Want to ditch? I'm dying for a cigarette."

"You don't think Gretchen will tell on us?" I speak flippantly, but I'm serious. I need to stay on my uncle's good side.

"Nah, we're fine. Let's go."

We drive the cart off the path and into a small garden. There are enough trees and bushes to shield us from view. Mia jumps out of the cart and pops down onto a rock, making herself at home. She's wearing a fanny pack, and she unzips it and pulls out a pack of cigarettes and a stainless steel flask.

She sticks a cigarette into her mouth, then offers one to me. I shake my head.

"Then at least have a drink. I can't be bad all by myself."

I take the flask, unscrew the top, and take a sniff. "Bourbon?"

"Kentucky's finest."

I take a tentative sip.

"It's been a while since we hung out, hasn't it? Before this trip, I mean." Mia takes a long drag, then exhales the smoke through her nose. "You seem different."

"So do you."

"Because I'm not all bright-eyed and bushy-tailed anymore? I'll have to graduate soon and leave school. Take my rightful place as a Caldwell daughter." She rolls her eyes. "I guess you know how that goes."

Be careful, I tell myself.

"We all have our responsibilities," I say.

"Is that why you're so eager to settle down all of a sudden? This Jake guy, sweeping you off your feet."

I don't have to fake my smile. "He took me by surprise."

She takes another drag, staring into me. "But this romantic fairytale of yours? I don't buy it."

A chill speeds through me. I take another swig of bourbon to hide my nerves. "What?"

"If you weren't taking shots right now, I'd think you were pregnant. You're *not*, right?"

I sputter, almost choking on the whiskey. "No! Definitely not."

"Then what's the truth?"

"We're in love," I insist.

"I believe that he could be, from the way he looks at you." She leans closer, lowering her voice. "But you? With our family, where we come from? True love isn't meant for people like us."

I hate that I agree with her. "That's a depressing thought."

"Take my brothers, for example. They're so busy competing with each other for my father's affection that they hardly have time for anything else."

"Competing? I thought Tristan was going to take over since he's older."

"You'd think." She blows smoke up into the sky. "But sometimes, I suspect Roman has other ideas. He's always plotting things. Roman thinks he's so subtle, but I see a lot more than he realizes." Her shrewd gaze moves back to me. "Like the way he's been antagonizing your boyfriend. Roman feels threatened. He thinks Jake could be a new competitor in the Caldwell family hierarchy."

Which is exactly why Jake should be steering clear of Roman instead of constantly pushing his buttons. I'm thankful Jake was with me last night, but now that Roman suspects us, we need to lie low. How am I supposed to find Wren if Roman is watching my every step?

"Jake isn't trying to compete with Tristan or Roman," I say. "If you think that's why he's involved with me—"

"Jake can do what he likes. Does it matter who's in charge? Tristan or Roman or whoever, I can't imagine it would make a difference." She takes another long drag. "Do you ever just want to say, fuck it, and disappear? Leave all of this mess behind and just go?"

The whiskey must be going to my head. It sounds an awful lot like Mia wants to escape from our family, too.

Is she looking for an ally?

Can I possibly trust her?

"I'm sure everyone feels that sometimes," I say.

"What about Wren? She's not showing her face at this reunion. Wonder what she's up to?"

My insides turn to jelly.

Is this some kind of message? She knows about Wren?

I chew the inside of my lip. "I can't speak for my sister."

Mia smiles sardonically. She knows I'm trying to deflect. "Don't worry. I'm not going to tell on you if you admit you're not perfectly happy as a Caldwell." Mia stabs out her cigarette on the grass. "You want to know the truth? None of us is."

She holds my gaze like she's waiting for me to respond. But I don't, and she gets up with a disappointed frown.

Mia drives us back toward the clubhouse. I don't know what to make of her ramblings. Did she want me to agree that I'm unhappy? That I want out?

Could it have been a trap?

Except for my dad and Jake, I have no idea who to trust.

As we're crossing the eighteenth hole, we hear shouts. Mia speeds up the cart. We crest a hill, and we see a cluster of people outside the clubhouse.

Someone's lying on the grass. And then I realize who it is.

"Mia, stop. It's my dad!"

She punches the brakes, and I jump out, already running.

Jake kneels over my father, checking his vitals. Dad looks lifeless. Like he's not breathing.

"What's going on?" I demand.

"He just collapsed," Jake says. "His heartbeat is faint. He's breathing, but just barely."

"Oh my God."

Uncle Amos puts a hand on my arm, drawing me back. "Give him room. Roman went to call an ambulance." My uncle's fingers dig into my skin. I want to shake him off, but I don't dare.

It's only a couple of minutes later when I hear sirens. Jake hasn't left my father's side for a moment, but the paramedics take over, swarming all around. Over Amos's shoulder, I see Mia standing by the cart, along with staff and some of our extended family members.

"I don't understand," I say. "What happened?"

Uncle Amos hasn't released his grip on my arm. "Mason looked ill since this morning. He's been lagging behind. Has he been unwell?"

"I don't know." I've suspected it, but I won't tell Amos that. "I should talk to the paramedics."

My uncle pulls me back again. "I want your word you'll be at the gala tonight for the investors."

"The *investors*? That's your concern right now?"

"And the pitch meeting tomorrow. I'm counting on you, Harper. I hope you'll repay my confidence in you."

I want to spit in his face. Not just for the callousness he's showing toward my dad, his own brother, but for what he's done to the rest of my family.

"Do I have to remind you what's at stake?" Amos asks.

Jake appears at my side. "Harper? I didn't know you were here." His eyes ask if I'm all right. I give the slightest shake of my head.

My uncle's smile flickers at Jake's interruption, and he lets go of my arm. "How's Mason?"

"The medics are giving him oxygen, and they said his blood pressure is low. He's refused to go to the hospital. But Harper, he was asking for you."

My heart lurches. "I should talk to him. Try to convince him to go get checked out properly. If I go with him—"

Amos cuts me off. "No," he says sharply. "I can arrange for a doctor to come. You won't be going anywhere."

Jake steps in closer to me, angling his shoulder protectively. "I hope you're not saying that Harper isn't allowed to leave." He's kept his voice neutral, but this is way too close to a challenge of my uncle.

In a single moment, Jake is trashing any goodwill he might've had.

Amos stares at him. "And if I was? Is that your concern?"

"All due respect, I think it is," Jake says softly. "Sir."

I'm afraid of what Jake might do if this keeps going. This is the worst possible time for Jake's overprotective streak to rear its head. I have to defuse this situation.

"A doctor would be great. Thank you, Uncle Amos. And I'll be there tonight at the gala. Jake, we should go check on Dad."

Amos holds Jake's gaze for another moment, and then he watches us walk away.

18

Jake

We get Mason settled into bed in his room. I really don't know what happened. One moment he seemed fine, chatting with Amos. The next, Mason's eyes had rolled back in his head and he was lying on the grass.

I'd suspect Roman, mostly because I think he's capable of anything, but Roman wasn't anywhere near the man. And I remember what Mason hinted when we shared that hotel room in Beverly Hills. That he's sick and that Harper doesn't know. She has so few people in her life that she loves and trusts. If she loses her dad, it's going to devastate her.

Harper sits by his bedside, holding his hand. "What do you need?" she asks.

Mason's eyes are sunken. He looks like he's lost five pounds just since we arrived here. "I've been overtaxing myself. Not eating enough. Probably a cold I caught on the plane."

"Dad, I know it's more than that. Tell me what's really wrong. *Please*."

I'm standing at the foot of the bed, my arms crossed. I

already scanned this room for bugs yesterday, so we can speak relatively freely. But will Mason tell Harper the truth?

He opens his mouth, and a coughing fit steals his voice, shaking his gaunt frame. I get him a glass of water from the bathroom sink. He takes it in shaking hands, and Harper steadies him, helping him get a few sips down.

"Is this because of the stress?" she asks. "Did I push you too hard? If you don't think you can do this…"

"I have to do this. For you. For Wren."

"What have you heard about Wren?"

His expression is grave. Heartbroken. "I know Amos has her secreted away somewhere. I've overheard enough to put things together. This is why you were so adamant about your plan. You think you have to save her because no one else will, and you're right. I couldn't protect her on my own. I'm not strong enough."

I see his struggle in every part of his body. Like he wants to hold the rest inside but knows he can't.

Should I leave them alone for this conversation? I'm not family. I have no right to be here to witness it. But I also don't want to abandon Harper if she needs me.

"I'm sick," Mason says.

"*Dad.*" Harper takes his hand. "How bad is it?"

"I have acute monocytic leukemia. The prognosis for me isn't good. I've declined treatment. It's…the survival rate is very low given my circumstances."

She goes still, her face turning to stone. "No. That's ridiculous."

"I might be able to delay the inevitable, but by months, not years. I would've preferred not telling you at all. I don't want you to worry."

For a moment, she doesn't move. Then Harper storms into the bathroom and slams the door.

Mason sighs, sinking into the pillows.

I'm still standing by the end of the bed. "I'm sorry. Is there anything I can do for you?"

Mason regards me with his shadow-ringed eyes. "I think Harper meant something to you once. You were a good friend to her."

I glance over at the closed bathroom door. "I tried to be."

"I know it's a lot to ask, but I hope you'll take care of her. Protect her. Even…after."

"I intend to." In whatever way I can.

After the doctor arrives and takes over, Harper and I step out into the hall. She hasn't said much since her dad's confession. I put a hand in the middle of her shoulders.

"Do you want to talk about it?" I ask quietly, aware of the hallway cameras.

She's got her head down. "No. I'd rather be alone for a while."

"If you want to lie down, I could go for a jog." I'll take the opportunity to check in with Agent Reyes, let him know the latest developments.

But will that include Harper's intention to rescue her sister? I haven't decided yet. Reyes isn't going to like it.

Harper nods. "Yeah, that sounds—" Her eyes widen. She's looking at something behind me. "Our door's open."

I turn around. The door to our room is cracked, but I definitely locked it when we left this morning.

We hurry down the hall. The hinges creak when I push the door open.

Oh, hell.

Harper gasps behind me. "What on *earth*?"

The place is trashed. But only half of it. My half, to be exact. Harper's clothes are still hanging in the closet. But mine are strewn everywhere, cut into tatters.

I step through the mess, picking up pieces of blue and black wool. The remains of my suits and my tux. My green silk tie has been carved up like a sushi roll. My Italian leather belt is sliced in half, and a knife has made mincemeat of my dress shoes.

I put my hands on my hips, turning in a circle. Everywhere I look, there's more devastation. My toiletry bag has been upended, toothpaste squished out of the tube, my cologne bottle smashed.

I know exactly who did this. One of Roman's henchmen, probably Lars, on Roman's orders. He must've been at it while most of the family was playing golf. Were they just sending a message? Or were they looking for something?

My suitcase.

"Shut the door," I say. Harper seems like she wants to ask a question, but I shake my head.

I rush to grab my bag from the closet and flip it open. My heart is in my throat until I confirm that the secret compartment hasn't been touched. Thank God. That would've been bad.

"I cannot believe—"

I hold up my finger to my mouth before Harper can finish that sentence. I point at the lamp, which got toppled on its side in the commotion. There's no way I'm going to forget about that listening device again.

But this mess could be the perfect opportunity.

"Looks like we have some tidying up to do," I say. "Not the end of the world. A little mess never hurt anybody."

She looks at me like I've lost it. "A *little* mess?"

I grab the lamp and lift it up in the air. Then I send it smashing down onto the tile floor. Harper gasps, hands flying to her mouth.

"Oops, slipped right out of my fingers. Well, just one more thing to sweep up." I bring my heel down on the listening device and crush it.

No more spying.

I grab the bug detector from my suitcase and run another sweep just in case, but Lars didn't plant anything else. "We can say whatever we want now. Well, as long as we keep our voices down. But they'd have to eavesdrop the old-fashioned way. From outside the door. They did us a favor."

"Really? You're enjoying this?"

"If Roman keeps his mind games focused on me instead of you, I'm all for it. Though it might be awkward when I have to wear a pair of boxers to the gala instead of black tie."

"This isn't funny, Jake."

"In a certain light, it is."

She's digging at her scalp, pacing the clothing-strewn floor. "This wouldn't have happened if you'd backed off. But no, you have to keep on poking at him. Even at breakfast this morning."

"Whoa. This is my fault now? Blaming the victim?"

"You should leave him alone. He suspects us already."

"Maybe, but he doesn't know what we're really up to. That's clear." I brush off a chair and sit down. When Harper paces by me, I hook an arm around her and pull her into my lap.

"Jake, don't." Her heart's beating like a caged bird. I feel it through her back against my chest.

"I want you to listen to what I'm saying. How do you think Roman found us last night? It was by accident. He was following *Tristan*. And he doesn't want Amos to know about it."

"Mia mentioned that Roman and Tristan are competing for Amos's attention. Everyone assumes Tristan will take over for his father, and maybe Roman doesn't like that."

"Can't imagine he would. Is he looking for an angle to use against his brother?" More importantly, how can Harper and I use this to our advantage?

"Mia hinted that she feels trapped too. I think she's looking for a way out. And she mentioned Wren."

"Do you think you can trust Mia?"

"I'm really not sure." Harper relaxes against me. "I hate this. The lies, the plotting. And now my dad." Her voice cracks. "I can't take it anymore, Jake. I *can't*."

It's enough to make me wish I could get Harper and Mason out of here right now. But even if we wanted to leave, I'm sure her Uncle Amos wouldn't let her. Unless we call in the task force, we're stuck here, trapped from all sides.

Harper turns her face toward me. She's way too wound up, trying desperately to keep her heart together. We're so close that all I smell is vanilla, all I see are hazel eyes and long eyelashes and the tiny freckles by her hairline.

Then calm washes over her features, as if she's packing away all those hurts someplace deep.

She gets up from my lap. "I need to find you some new clothes. Luckily, I run a shipping company, and I have more than a few contacts. A friend in the LA Fashion District can probably hook us up with a last minute wardrobe. Give me your measurements, and I'll get it taken care of."

"I'd appreciate it."

While Harper makes the call, I swing by the hotel's kitchen to get trash bags and a pair of rubber gloves to clean up our room. I ask a cook to wrap up some sandwiches for us as well, since I doubt Harper will feel like eating in the dining room with her family.

On my way back, I pop in to check on her dad again. Mason is resting, and his vitals have improved. He's going to skip the gala for the investors tonight.

We stuff the trash bags full of ruined clothes. But the carpet will need a vacuum to pick up the stray threads, which have gone *everywhere*. After that, we sit and eat our club sandwiches in silence. Harper seems to be eating mechanically and only manages half of it. She offers the rest to me. I argue that she needs her strength, but finally I eat her leftovers, not wanting it to go to waste. My stomach is pretty much bottomless.

"Do you still need some time alone?" I ask. "It's okay if you do. I won't go far."

Her nail scratches at her hairline. "I didn't mean it. Stay?"

"Of course." I'll update Agent Reyes later.

I'm not avoiding my boss. Not me. No way.

Harper lies down to rest, and I watch over her from the chair by the bed. It's the first opportunity I've had, in well over a decade, anyway, to just observe her for as long as I want. The afternoon sun filters softly through the curtain, kissing her hair and skin with light. I can see the holes in her ear cartilage from the rings she used to wear. Was that just a teenage thing? Something she outgrew? Or did she remove them in an effort to meet her uncle's expectations while she's here?

What does Harper do for fun now? What clothes does she wear on lazy weekends? What are her favorite TV shows? Has she kept up with her art?

I want to know everything. But I doubt I'll get the chance to find out. We have two more days here at the resort unless we make our escape before that. And then? Where will Harper end up?

There's no way it'll be West Oaks.

After a while, I use my burner phone to study the map of the resort. There's the gatehouse, the main hotel building, the golf clubhouse. The villas, which seem to cater to families that want a rental with a kitchen and space for kids to run around. Explains why they're empty during the Caldwells' event. No kids invited.

If Amos is keeping Wren close, as Harper thinks, where is she? In one of the rooms in the main hotel? That's hard to imagine. Too much scrutiny by staff and other family members.

I'm pondering the possibilities when Harper opens her eyes. "Hey," she says. She's curled on her side on top of the blankets. "What're you doing?"

I go over and sit down beside her. "Trying to puzzle out where they're keeping Wren," I murmur. The listening device is gone, but for this conversation, we still need to be careful. If the wrong person walks by and catches the wrong word, it could mean disaster.

I'll have to sit extra close to her. Murmur in her ear. A hardship, I know.

I stretch out next to her and show her the maps I was studying on my phone. We talk it through for a while. "I want to check the golf clubhouse," she says. "I tried when I was there this morning, but it was too busy."

"Hmmm. Maybe they've got a random storage room that could hide her. It's nowhere obvious, that's for sure."

Harper's eyes are shining with intensity. "Will you go with me to the clubhouse tonight? After the gala?"

I nod. "Sure. If you're there, I'm there."

She gives me a tentative smile. So sweet and hopeful it echoes against my heart.

"We'll find her," I say.

She sighs and nods.

I run a fingertip down her cheek. It's difficult for me to have Harper this close and not touch her. We were always affectionate as friends. I'm not sure what we are now, but I hope she still considers me a friend. I have the feeling she needs more of those. Harper has been through more than most people have to deal with in a lifetime.

"When this is over and you're free," I whisper, "what'll you do? Start a new shipping company?"

"Ugh, no. I think..." Her eyelashes flutter. "I have this

idea about being an art teacher? I'd have to go back to school. I have a business degree, but I'd need education courses. And more art credits, I guess. I've never looked at the requirements. It just seemed…impossible. Before."

"What age of students?"

"Little kids. Art was my escape, my therapy. It still is. I like the idea of doing that for other kids who're struggling."

I touch her fingertips. Her nails have traces of charcoal on them, just like when we were teenagers. "I remember you used to draw and paint with watercolors and all that stuff. You're very talented."

"I don't know about that."

"I do. I've got tons of artistic knowledge. Major cred in the art world."

She snickers. "Do you?"

"I'm basically an expert."

"You haven't seen any of my art in fourteen years."

"Then show me. Do you have any with you?"

She grimaces. "I'm not showing you."

"C'mon. Please?"

"No. Enough about me. I want to hear more about you."

I drone about my life, my family. She closes her eyes as she listens, a little smile on her lips, asking questions occasionally.

I'm not sure if I move or if she does. But as we speak, we keep inching closer and closer together. Until our lips almost brush with every word. Until I can't focus on what I'm saying anymore.

I want to line up our bodies, feel her against every inch of me, as if we can share what we're thinking through contact alone.

"You're making it difficult for me to resist you," I murmur.

Her eyes pop open. "I'm not doing anything."

"You don't have to." I twirl a lock of her hair around my finger. "I want to kiss you. Tell me not to."

She shakes her head.

I cross those last few millimeters and press my lips to hers. I keep it soft and light. No demands. Today's been too rough on her, and I need to be gentle.

After a few more kisses, I say, "Tell me what I can do for you."

The waver in her breathing is the only hint of the distress she's keeping inside. "Hold me?"

She rolls so her back is to me. I pull her against my chest, positioning my legs and arms to cradle her while we're on our sides. Two spoons fitted perfectly together.

Her ass slots right up against my crotch. She's still wearing her tiny golf skirt, and somehow it gets pushed up so only her panties and my clothes separate us.

My cock fills. She inhales slowly, and I know she feels it. My growing length presses into her ass cheek. Insistent about what it wants. I'm here being chaste and polite, and my dick is being…well, a fucking dick.

"Sorry," I mutter.

"I don't mind." Harper turns her head to look at me. Reaches up to cup my face.

There's so much shit going on around us. But *this*, this magnetic pull between us, this chemistry. No matter how much I try to downplay it or push it aside, it keeps charging back to the surface. She is so damn brave. So beautiful. She could break my heart a few more times, and I'd still come back for more. It just might be worth it.

I'm trying to be good, but damn. My body doesn't want to let me.

"I thought," she says, "after last night, you weren't interested in that. With me."

"Are you kidding?"

"I offered to make you come, and you turned me down."

I close my mouth on a growl. "Not because I didn't want you. I was mad at myself for forgetting that anyone was listening, and I had no intention of sharing you." I drop a kiss on her temple. Her nose. "I can't stop thinking about how sweet you tasted. I want to take care of you. I want my cock in you, making you feel good."

She hums appreciatively and rolls her hips against my erection.

"But I have to make sure we're both clear about what we're doing," I say. "When I'm distracted, I fuck up. I'd be risking your safety."

"Still playing my hero. Still looking out for me, even when I don't want you to."

"Careful what you wish for."

"Why? What else will you do to me, Shelborne?"

I stifle a groan. What I want to do isn't heroic. Or G-rated.

I *should* be looking out for her. But Harper is waking up parts of me I haven't let out in a long time. Parts of me I've tried to bury and quiet and civilize.

My voice is deep when I speak, rumbling out of my chest.

"If I make love to you, I won't want to be rushed. I'll need to know I have you all to myself." I rub my stubbled cheek against her soft one, and she trembles. "I want to touch you and explore you in every way I can think of. And I'll need to know you're on board with me taking control so I can give you the pleasure you deserve."

"That's not a surprise. You like being in charge."

I catch her chin with my fingers. "But I also let you get away with a hell of a lot. In bed, I'm more demanding." I lean in. "While I'm inside you, I own you."

Harper's whole body shivers. "Is that Jake Worthington talking?"

"Nope," I whisper. "It's all me." I plant another kiss on her cheek. "But now, I need to shower. I'd invite you to join me, but we have dinner soon. Can't be late." We have to be ready to deal with douchebag investors *and* her family.

She makes a frustrated sound. "You're the worst kind of tease."

"True." But she wasn't thinking dark, painful thoughts for a while. That makes me smile.

With half an hour to spare, a clothing delivery arrives. I'm impressed. I doubt the army could've air-dropped these supplies any faster.

Harper unpacks the garments, laying them out on the bed. There's a tux for tonight, complete with shoes. Business casual clothes for the rest of the trip. Athletic wear. Even new boxer briefs, though in a skimpier cut and in brighter colors than I'm usually rocking. I've already showered, so I drop my towel and slide on a pair, feeling like hot stuff.

"How do I look?" I ask.

She gives me a once over. "Like trouble."

I grin.

Harper frowns at the tux lying on the bed. "Wish I had time to have the jacket steamed. But this will do."

"Thank you for taking care of me. Even though I prefer things the other way around."

She sticks out her tongue, and I kiss the top of her head.

19

Harper

I need a cold shower after Jake got me all riled up. But there isn't time. Jake hogged the bathroom, so I have to settle for a change of panties.

That man…

It's hard to imagine us finding the perfect moment to finally enjoy each other as much as we want. It didn't happen when we were teenagers, despite trying. And right now? Not the ideal circumstances. In a couple more days, this undercover op will be over and we'll part ways again. Once I've satisfied my side of the deal with the DEA, I want to get Dad and Wren as far from the rest of the Caldwells as I can.

But a girl can dream.

Jake is shaving in the bathroom. I slip into my dress, a floor-length silver gown. It flares out at the waist with gathers of fabric, and the top has a plunging neckline that shows off my cleavage.

I take a deep breath as I swipe on my makeup. All the investors will be at the dinner tonight. We'll be able to get info on each one of them. And the tumult of today, with Mia's hints and my dad's illness, I'm feeling much steadier. I credit Jake for that. He got me smiling even though part of me still wants to scream and run.

I have no idea what I'd do if Jake wasn't here. The other agent, Kevin, seemed like a nice guy and all, but he didn't inspire anywhere near this much confidence.

If anyone can help me get through the rest of this, it's Jake. With luck, we'll find Wren tonight and I can plan out the final details of our escape. Then I'll figure out a treatment plan for my father. It's one thing at a time.

Jake comes out with his stubble touched up and trimmed, though I'm glad he hasn't shaved it entirely. I like this rugged version of him. Especially in those sexy-as-hell briefs. He looks like an underwear model. I don't tell him, though. He's cocky enough.

"Zip me up?" I ask.

He swaggers over and takes way too long working my zipper up, his thumbs rubbing my backbone in the process. Then he drops a kiss to the bare part of my shoulder. "Every time I think you can't look better, you prove me wrong," he says.

"Stop making those eyes at me, or we'll never make it to the event tonight at all. And then we'll really be in hot water."

He puts his hands on my arms and squeezes gently. "You've got this. Everything will go according to plan."

I nod. "Right. We're just gathering intel on the investors. No big deal."

My eyes try to wander over him again to the bulge in his briefs. So I force myself to reorganize my clothing in the closet. Can't have my mind on *that* right now.

When I turn back around, he's got his pants on, and he's buttoning up his white dress shirt. His bowtie hangs loose around his collar. "We're going to need a few more accessories tonight."

"Didn't know that word was in your vocabulary."

"I have a daughter, and she's a girly-girl. 'Accessories' is definitely in my vocabulary." Jake goes to his suitcase and gets two tiny squares of plastic, as well as a sleeve of sewing needles and a spool of thread. "These will catch every conversation with the investors tonight. But they record only, they don't transmit, so they're much harder to detect."

He sews one bug inside the neckline of my dress, and another beneath the lapel of his jacket. Next, Jake takes a small but vicious-looking knife out of his suitcase. "Given what we're doing tonight, I want you to be armed. Just in case things go south."

My stomach churns. I point at my gown. "I don't have any pockets. Where am I supposed to put a weapon?"

"Thought of that, too." He grabs a black strap from the secret compartment. "It's an adjustable holster."

I lift up my skirt, and Jake fits the strap around my thigh like a wedding garter. He carefully slides the knife into place in the holster. When I let my skirt fall, the fabric conceals the weapon entirely.

I feel like a badass, actually. A super-spy.

"I'm not an expert in hand-to-hand combat," I warn him.

"You don't have to be. If you get into a bad situation, just hold the guy off until I can get there." Jake puts on a holster of his own, this one concealing a gun at his lower back. "But if you can, run. Head for the extraction point I showed you and activate the beacon. Don't wait for me. I'll catch up. Got it?"

I nod, my throat too tight to speak.

Jake ties his bowtie and slides on his jacket. Then he holds out his hand. "Let's go."

∼

We walk arm and arm to the ballroom. The entire place sparkles like it was sprinkled with fairy dust. The linens and decor are in white, gray and black with accents of silver. My dress fits right in.

A jazz ensemble plays soft music, and investors and their dates mingle while snacking on passed hors d'oeuvres.

When a waiter walks by with a tray of champagne, Jake and I each take a glass. I'm not planning to drink much. I sobered up quick this afternoon after Mia's shots of bourbon, but I need to stay alert.

I spot Mia herself across the ballroom, downing her glass of bubbly before grabbing another. She raises her glass to me, but then turns and heads the other way instead of coming over.

"Is she avoiding you?" Jake asks in my ear.

"I don't know. Maybe it's you."

"She doesn't like me?"

"I can't begin to figure Mia out."

Tristan is chatting with a group of investors. He sees me and waves me over. "Gentlemen, may I introduce my cousin Harper, the chief operating officer of SunSpeed shipping."

Jake smiles placidly while I chat with the investors. He doesn't budge from my side, only edging closer. He's got the possessive boyfriend routine down.

All I can think about are the listening devices in our clothes, recording every word. Their names, their companies. I've never made such a blatant move against my family, not even getting the DEA involved in the first place. If I'm searched and that tiny square of plastic is found, there will be no question in my uncle's eyes about what I've done.

The investors are clearly enjoying my uncle's hospitality. I spot tan lines where wedding rings should be, and a lot of them have college-aged women on their arms. I wouldn't be surprised if Tristan had these women brought in from an escort service. Hell, maybe Tristan is gathering potential blackmail fodder. That's the kind of thing my uncle would approve of.

One investor in particular seems determined to get me away from Jake. He keeps standing in Jake's way and staring at my cleavage instead of my eyes.

"Does SunSpeed have its headquarters in LA?" the guy asks me. "I'd love to get a tour of your *facilities*."

Jake taps the guy on the shoulder. "I'm a VP for a SunSpeed client. HealthTec. I'm happy to answer your questions."

"Oh. I'd rather hear about it from her."

"I'm also her boyfriend," Jake growls.

The guy looks at Jake fully for the first time. "HealthTec. I've invested with them, and I know a couple board members. What was your name again? Worthington? I don't remember hearing of you before."

I take a swallow of champagne, my eyes darting around in the hopes of finding an exit from this conversation. But I've got nothing.

"I prefer to stay out of the limelight," Jake says. "I'm a behind-the-scenes, workaholic type."

"That's odd if you're in a sales industry. Isn't it?"

The guy won't let up. I'm starting to get nervous. And Tristan is coming over.

Suddenly, Jake grabs a fork and hits it against his champagne glass. The crowd quiets, glancing over to see what's going on.

"If I could interrupt for a moment?" Jake says, "I have an announcement to make."

Tristan stops a few yards away, staring. Roman does the same. Uncle Amos smiles knowingly. And Jake digs into the breast pocket of his jacket.

He gets down on one knee.

My chest clenches as I suck in a breath. Between Jake's fingers, a huge diamond glints in the low light of the ballroom. My shock is very much the real deal.

Where on earth did he get a rock like that?

"Harper Caldwell, I adore you. You've changed my life in every way possible, and I can't make it a single day more without knowing that you're mine. Will you marry me?"

I grit my teeth. "Yes. Now would you get up off the floor?"

I know he's trying to cause a distraction, but I don't love having this kind of spotlight on me.

Jake stands and pulls me into a kiss, then fits the ring on my finger. "You're making me a very happy man."

"Nice save, by the way," I whisper. It freaks me out how close that investor was getting to calling out Jake's cover story.

The suspicious investor gets pushed aside as my family descends, congratulating us. Uncle Amos comes over, shaking Jake's hand and giving me a kiss on the cheek. "It's a shame that your father isn't here tonight."

"Or Wren," Tristan adds.

My guts twist. What did he mean by that? But Tristan moves away as other well-wishers take his place.

"Good luck," Mia murmurs to Jake. "Around here, you're going to need it."

That's for sure.

I'm breathless when Jake pulls me out onto the dance floor. I rest my head against his shoulder and sink into him. My heart is beating a mile a minute.

I'm supposed to be experiencing one of the happiest moments of my life. But instead, I'm fraying at the edges.

"How are you holding up?" Jake asks.

"Ask me when this is over." I move my hand, and the bling on my finger nearly blinds me. While the diamond seems authentic, this ring is as fake as the well wishes from my family. Yet Jake's arms feel so solid around me. And when he dips down to kiss me, the sudden longing in my blood is real too.

I want to burrow into Jake's arms. I need him to hold me so that one small piece of my life has substance. Jake's touch makes me feel alive. Like I'm more than just a pawn being used by forces outside my control.

Somehow, I get through dinner. But Jake's distraction worked. Nobody else questions his cover story. All anybody talks about is our engagement.

My uncle drags me around to meet the last couple of investors I missed. There are ten of them in total, eight men and two women. I imagine the bug in my dress recording every name, every ingratiating statement.

Finally, Jake and I get back to our table. I grab the small clutch that I brought here, which holds my phone. My lips are chapped from so much talking, so I open up the clasp to get my lip balm.

My pulse spikes. There's a tiny piece of paper inside my clutch. But I don't dare unfold it here. "I'm going to stop by the restroom."

Jake holds out his arm. "Happy to escort you."

He waits outside the door while I go in. The moment the door clicks shut, I open my clutch and unfold the piece of paper.

If you want to see your sister, meet me at unit 3 in the villas at midnight. I know where she is.

The writing is feminine. There's no signature on the note. But I think it must be from Mia. Who else could it be? Even if it's not, this is the first clue I've had about Wren since I arrived.

Fear and excitement war within me.

I open the door to the bathroom and pull Jake inside.

He smirks. "We're playing the newly engaged couple, but your uncle might draw the line at a bathroom tryst."

I show him the note.

"Shit. Midnight is in twenty minutes."

"We have to go," I say. "If there's a chance I could figure out where Wren is, I have to take it."

"This could be a trick to lure us out."

"But if it's not?"

"You're going anyway, aren't you?"

"You know the answer to that."

We slip out through a side door into the night.

WE HEAD DOWN THE PAVED PATH TOWARD THE villas, just like last night. I've always hated the feeling of déjà vu.

There's no time to stop and change our clothes, so I'm in my silver gown and Jake is in his tux. We don't bother to sneak around this time. We're far too noticeable. But our engagement gives us the perfect excuse to be out wandering. If anyone asks, we're in search of a romantic spot to be alone.

Some party guests are already outside, taking in the views. They barely glance at us. I see Roman among them, talking to a pretty brunette, and he doesn't notice us pass. At least, I don't think so.

Jake tangles our fingers together. The moonlight is catching the golden strands of his hair, and my eyes can't help lingering on him in that tux.

My skirts swish around my legs. I feel the knife's weight against my thigh with every step. I could be a Bond girl, out on an adventure with my sexy spy boyfriend. If only this situation was fun and exciting instead of dire.

If I don't find Wren before this trip is over, my uncle could spirit her away again. I'm running out of time.

We keep going, leaving the partygoers behind. I hear waves crash in the distance. Jake's head is on a swivel, watching all sides of us. "I haven't seen a single guard in five minutes," he says. "I would expect them to be out in force patrolling tonight."

"Maybe they're staying closer to the hotel."

"Could be. Some of those investors were partying hard, and they showed no signs of stopping when we left. I'm sure security's going to be keeping an eye on that. But I don't know. My gut doesn't like this, Harper. It's too quiet."

"Or we're finally catching a break."

Wren won't believe that Jake's here. We have so much to catch up on. I want to see my sister *so badly*.

Forget the careful planning. When we find her, I'll tell Jake to get Wren out of here *tonight*, even if they have to call in the DEA or the FBI or the freaking air force to do it.

Just as long as I know she's safe from my family. So that I've finally done something right.

The villas appear up ahead. There's no sign of anyone inside, no lights, much like the night before. We reach unit number three, and when Jake tries the front door, it opens onto a shadowed hallway.

"Stay behind me," he murmurs.

He reaches beneath his jacket and draws his gun. I think about grabbing my knife, but my hands are shaking.

We sneak into the unit. Everything is silent. There's a sleek, modern kitchen off to one side and a living room filled with minimalist furniture. A sharp contrast to the more ornate style of the main hotel.

The floor of the hallway creaks beneath our feet. Jake keeps his gun pointed at an angle in front of him, aiming at the floor. He checks each doorway and room as we pass.

There's a bedroom. A bathroom. All dark, filled with tidy furniture. Ready for future guests.

But just as he's about to reach the next doorway, I hear a voice coming from the darkness. It's desperate and scared.

"*Harper?*"

My heart is trying to leap out of my chest. "Wren?" I call out. I'm about to run forward, but Jake holds me back.

"Let me go first."

That's when two men lunge out of the shadows of the doorway. Their silhouettes are massive. I recognize Lars, Roman's bodyguard. He slams Jake into a wall.

Jimmy is the other attacker. He grabs me and drags me into the bedroom, then slams the door shut, trapping me.

In the hallway, a gun goes off.

"*Jake,*" I scream.

Jimmy throws me onto the bed facedown. He's trying to get my hands behind my back. I roll and bring my knee up hard into Jimmy's crotch. He grunts, and I kick at him while I reach beneath the folds of my skirt for the knife. I tear it out of the holster, slicing a long tear through my dress.

Jimmy reaches for me again, and I swipe the knife across the palm of his hand. "Dammit," he yells.

"Where's my sister? *Where is she?*"

He cradles his bleeding hand. "I don't know. I'm just supposed to bring you back!"

This was a trap, like Jake thought. They faked Wren's voice somehow. And I walked us right into it.

"Miss Caldwell, this'll be easier if you calm down and—"

I slash Jimmy a second time, catching him across the face. He bear-hugs me, trying to get the knife, and that's a big mistake. Because I feel a gun in the back of his waistband. I grab hold of it.

Jimmy takes the knife from my other hand, but who needs a knife?

I push away and point the gun at him.

He didn't expect this much trouble from me. I've usually been composed around him, but not anymore. I see the moment that he's had enough. He's done trying to deal with me.

Jimmy ducks out of the way. He throws open the door and rushes into the hall.

The door slams, and I hear a latch slot into place on the outside. I wiggle the handle, then try kicking the door, but I'm locked in here.

I could try shooting the lock, but what if I hit Jake? He's out there with Lars and Jimmy both. They got us separated like that was the plan from the start.

I finally get it. This wasn't a trap for me. It was a trap for *Jake*.

They're going to kill him.

20

Jake

This asshole is not going down easy.

Right out of the gate, Lars rushes me like a charging bull. He knocks me back against the opposite wall of the hallway. I barely keep hold of my weapon. Lars has a gun of his own and tries to aim it at me. I grab his wrist. We grapple with each other.

Jimmy takes Harper into the bedroom and slams the door shut. Roaring, I try to get past Lars. I have to reach Harper. But Lars goes for my weapon and twists. My finger slips from the guard onto the trigger. The gun goes off.

I slam him with my shoulder and force him back. But Lars aims his gun at me. We glare at one other, facing off, the barrels of our weapons almost touching, his massive and mine deceptively undersized by comparison. But you know what they say. It's not the size that counts.

"Roman sent you," I say.

"You're a troublemaker. You signed your own death warrant."

"Did Amos give the order?"

A muscle near his eye twitches. No, Roman's acting

alone. Interesting. But not surprising. "And what about Harper?"

"She won't be hurt if you give yourself up. You'll be saving her. Not a bad way to go out."

I tend to agree. But I'm not going to lay down my weapon and give in. This guy doesn't know me, but he should've guessed that much already.

"No," I growl. "You give up. And *maybe* I'll let you live."

Lars feints to one side. I match his movement. In the bedroom behind him, I hear Harper screaming and shouting. My skin crawls with the need to get to her. But between these two fuckers, Jimmy seems like the more reasonable one. I believe Lars about Harper not being harmed. That's the only thing keeping me in place right now instead of charging through Lars and risking a gunshot in the process.

The muscles in my body sing with energy. Rage pumps through my veins.

Then the door behind Lars bursts open. Jimmy dashes out, spinning around to close the door. I catch a glimpse of Harper, her lips pulled back in a snarl. She's holding a gun. Jimmy's got a bloody slash across his face.

That's my girl.

"I can't deal with her," Jimmy says. "She took my weapon!"

Lars curses, and his gaze flickers away from me for a split second. Big mistake.

I shoot him in the thigh.

Lars screams and fires. The shot goes wide, hitting the wall. Lars grabs Jimmy and pulls him in between us. He's using Jimmy as a human shield. But if Lars thinks this new move is going to make me hesitate, he's wrong.

Jimmy knows it too. He gets a good look at me, really *looks*, and whatever he sees in my face fucking terrifies him. "Shoot him, Lars, shoot—" He raises the knife he's holding, as if that'll help him. Lars is trying to get his gun up, too. All this happens in less than a second.

But my finger's already squeezing the trigger.

I double-tap Jimmy in the chest. The rounds go straight through him and into Lars.

They both fall in a heap onto the rug.

I step forward and stomp on Lars's wrist, then I pull the gun from his grasp. Either one of them would've dumped my body into the ocean if they'd had the chance. And both men were rough with Harper. So I can't feel too bad about taking them out.

Okay, I don't feel bad at all.

"Jake?" Harper calls from the bedroom. She pounds on the door. *"Jake!"*

"Just a sec."

I stoop to check the men's vitals. Dead. They're taking up most of the hallway, so I have to jump over them to reach the bedroom door. I open the slide lock, newly installed by the looks of it, and open the door.

"Jake. Oh my God." She drops the gun she's holding. Her arms squeeze around my neck so tightly I can hardly breathe.

"Did you think they got me?" I manage to ask.

She burrows against my chest, and I kiss her temple.

"I was worried. But I knew you'd figure it out." She looks past my shoulder at the gore-splattered hallway. Not a pretty sight. But my Harper is strong. If anything, her voice is even harder when she speaks again. "What now?"

"We get this cleaned up before anybody else comes around looking."

First, I empty their pockets. Lars has some goodies that I save for later. Harper takes down the shower curtains from the bathrooms, and I haul Jimmy and Lars onto the plastic and wrap them up like the worst party favors ever.

This is every bit as awful as it sounds.

Once I've got them each gift-wrapped, I fireman-carry them one at a time outside to the pool and dump them beneath the pool cover. Harper keeps watch. The dark water swallows them up.

When that's over with, I wash my hands in the nearest bathroom. My tux is a disaster. I trash my button-down, leaving my undershirt. It's still dotted with red, but my jacket will cover most of it. I seem to be going through clothing at a record rate on this trip.

When I come out, Harper's laid a couple of mats over the bloodstains on the hall carpet. It'll only fool someone who glances in, not if they actually come down the hall. But it's the best we can do.

It's hard enough dealing with all this while keeping the overhead lights off.

Then we sit in the living room of unit 3, and I spread out the contents of the men's pockets on the coffee table. Harper holds up Jimmy's phone as a light.

There's a keycard for the resort that I suspect is a master. It'll unlock any unit. That would explain how someone, probably Lars, got access to our room earlier to trash my clothes. And how Lars got into this unit of the villas.

There's also a tiny voice recorder and player. I press the button, and Wren's voice speaks.

Harper covers her mouth with her hand. "That's her. She sounds so afraid."

"We don't know when or where this was recorded."

She swallows, nodding. "What's this other thing?" She points at a device with a video screen. I'm pretty sure I know what it is. I turn it on. A menu comes up, and I click through it.

Video feeds around the resort show up.

This thing connects to the resort's security system. I play around with it and realize I can switch cameras around the hotel on and off. This could come in *very* handy. I confirm that all the cameras with a view of the villas are currently switched off. Makes sense, given the fact that Lars planned to kill me.

"Does it have footage recorded?" Harper asks. "Maybe we can find out where they're hiding Wren."

I poke around a bit longer, but it looks like the feeds are live only. No recordings are accessible from this device.

"Won't be that easy," I say. "Sorry."

"You think *any* of this is easy? You were almost murdered!"

"Not the first time that's happened." I shrug. "Roman ordered them here. But I think Roman was acting without your uncle's permission. He figured he could get rid of me and ask forgiveness, just so long as he didn't hurt you."

Shredding my clothes earlier was a shot across the bow. Roman decided he'd had enough.

"He knows how desperate I am to find Wren. I did exactly what he wanted."

"Because you love your sister. That's hardly a character flaw."

She's chewing her lip so hard the skin's ragged. "You think I shouldn't let them use her against me."

"Not what I said. If it were one of my sisters, I'd do the same. This isn't your fault. If it wasn't tonight, Roman would've gotten to me someplace else. This was about me more than it was about you."

"Revenge for pissing him off?"

"No," I say tightly. I don't want to argue about that subject again. I'd earned a beating, maybe. Execution? Roman was taking a risk by going outside Amos's authority, and he knew it. "I bet Roman wanted me dead so I wouldn't reveal that he followed Tristan last night."

"It's that important?"

"Must be."

Either way, there's a lot more going on here than we realized. Fault lines in the Caldwell family. Dangers that we can't even see.

"Are we heading back to the hotel?" Harper asks.

"Unless you want to stay here in the villas."

"God, no. I never want to see this place again. But I'd wanted to check the clubhouse for Wren, and now..."

We need to get out of the open. Find a safe place. I put my arm around her shoulder. "Come on. We'll check the club-house tomorrow once we've regrouped. Let's get you back."

I lock up on the way out. Hopefully, it'll be a few days before anyone else ventures inside unit 3. With nobody staying here, the staff has no reason to clean. Or to peek beneath that pool cover.

Harper and I don't speak on our way out. But as we walk across the golf course, I notice she's limping.

I stop. "Are you hurt?"

"Just these damn heels. I'll take them off. I'm..." She rubs her eyes. "I can hardly think."

I'm feeling the opposite. So much adrenaline is coursing through my body that I'm hyperaware. I can see the tiny hairs on Harper's arms. The scent of her is so strong it makes my chest ache.

"I'll carry you." This sounds selfless, but it's not. I want my hands on her. I need to know, at a physical, visceral level, that no one else will touch her.

In fact, I'm struggling to keep my calm right now. Killing makes me feel...not myself.

Or maybe *too much* like myself. Like the man I am deep inside, but don't want to be.

"Wait," she says. "We can't go back to our room. What if Roman's waiting there? Or if he sends someone else?"

Then I'll end him too, that feral part of me says.

"I don't think he will. We finally have an advantage. We can black out the cameras and go into the hotel unnoticed."

I'm guessing that nobody except Roman knows that Lars and Jimmy went to kill us. He might figure out pretty quick that things went sideways. But I doubt even Roman knows what his next move will be.

"You trust me?" I ask.

She nods.

"Then hop on. Let's go."

She hikes up her dress and climbs onto my back.

If Roman wants to track us down and finish the job, I'll be ready. It would be unwise to test me. Because right now, I'd do pretty much *anything* to keep Harper protected. Anything to keep her close to me.

IT'S LATE WHEN WE REACH THE HOTEL. A FEW partiers are still wandering the halls, but they're too drunk to notice the blood on our clothes or the wariness in our expressions. We look partied-out ourselves, with us both disheveled and Harper riding piggyback and carrying her heels.

I switch off enough cameras to confuse anyone who's watching. I've now got three guns stuck in various pockets of my tux, along with the tactical knife. But I'm slightly less keyed up. As in, I might not kill the first guy who looks at us wrong. Best to get Harper to a secure location so I don't have to test that theory.

Once we pass through the lobby, I let her down. Harper grabs my arm, eyes filled with panic again. "My dad. I need to check on him."

"Don't worry. I was planning on it."

We use the master keycard to unlock Mason's room. He's sleeping soundly in bed, snoring.

I'm holding Harper's hand, and I can feel her relief like her thoughts are beaming into mine.

Our next stop is our room. "Wait here," I whisper. I draw my gun and check for intruders, but the room is dark and quiet.

Harper throws a few things into my suitcase. We get out of there as fast as possible.

I take her to a room down the hall from ours. It's unoccupied, and it's close enough we'll be able to keep an eye on her father. And we'll know if anyone goes to our assigned hotel room.

It's not the safe house I would've preferred. No place in this resort is completely safe. But this will have to do.

Inside the room, Harper sinks into a chair while I run a quick sweep. No bugs here.

My brain ticks off each of my remaining tasks as I complete it. Engage the safety bar. Check. Close the curtains. Check. Arrange the weapons in various spots around the room, within easy reach. Check.

Finally, I go to Harper and stand her up. She's dazed, but after I unzip her, she manages to undress. I free the recording devices from the seams of our clothes, placing them inside the secret compartment of my suitcase, and then pile up my ruined tux and her gown in a corner.

We're down to our underwear, but there's no modesty left between us. We both need a shower. But instead, I sit on a chair and pull Harper onto my lap. She has her legs sideways, her cheek tucked against my shoulder. Her breasts are pushed up, rounding over the cups of her bra. Her arms and legs fidget, and her skin seems to jump beneath my hands. Like she's as restless with energy as I am.

"I can't figure out what to do next," she says. "I thought I had this planned out, but it's all gone wrong. How am I supposed to find Wren?"

"We'll talk it through in the morning. I promise."

"You're trying to comfort me."

"So?"

"I don't need it."

"Maybe *I* need comfort."

She lifts her head. "Do you, army?"

I need a lot of things right now. Too much. "I need to know you're all right."

"How could I be?" she whispers. "Nothing is all right."

"What can I do?"

"*Talk* to me. Tell me what you're planning, because I know it's something."

"You won't like what I say."

"Then you'd better fucking tell me *now*."

I sigh. "Whatever's going on here, we're caught in the middle of it. And I've just realized it's too big for us to handle."

"What does that mean?"

"It means I'll let you stay here one more day. But if we can't find Wren by tomorrow evening, we're leaving. You're not spending another night here after this."

"You'll *let me*?" She puts her hands on my shoulders and sits back, looking at me incredulously. "I'm not going anywhere until I find my sister."

"My priority is your safety, not your fantasies about running away with your happy family intact. You don't even know if Wren is here at the resort. Or whether she wants to be saved."

Harper doesn't say anything for a moment. Her mouth is open, stunned.

Then she moves fast. She pushes out of my lap. She yanks at the diamond ring she's been wearing since the gala and throws it at me. The ring bounces off my chest and to the carpet.

"Fuck you, Jake."

I get up and follow her across the room. "The truth is hard to hear. But you can't wish it away or hide from it. I was willing to help with your rescue mission, but now—"

Harper spins around and shoves me. I shuffle back a couple steps, only because I don't want her to hurt herself while she's taking out her anger on me.

"Then leave," she says. "Take what we've gotten on the investors to your agency, and *go*. I'll do the rest on my own. I don't need you."

"I'm not finished," I say.

"Yes, you are."

Harper goes into the bathroom. I slap my hand on the door before she can shut it. She gasps, eyes wide.

"I'm not leaving you in danger."

"You said it yourself, Jake. Roman won't really hurt me."

"But that could change. We don't understand what's really happening, and if you keep digging, something will eventually bite back. Whether it's Roman or your uncle or Tristan. They'll decide it's *you* who's the real problem, not me, and I'm worried I won't be able to shield you."

She's going to do something reckless in the name of saving Wren, and I won't let her. I can't.

"Are you listening?" I ask.

She refuses to look at me. I take Harper by the wrists. She struggles, so I press her up against the wall. She's panting, her breasts lifting and falling with each breath. Her eyes are dark, her pupils nearly swallowing up the hazel. Her nostrils flare defiantly.

"Take your hands off me."

"No."

"So you're like *them* now? Like Roman and his thugs? I don't know you anymore."

"But you need me," I growl. "You need someone who's as

ruthless as they are. You know it, and I know it. So just admit it."

I hold her gaze. There's barely room for both of us in the small space of the bathroom. My heart's racing, pumping so much adrenaline I feel high from it. I feel *wild*. But all that energy focuses on a single intent. I *will* keep her safe. Whether she likes it or not.

"Fine. I need you."

A fresh thrill of arousal—of something dark and possessive—floods my veins. It pools in my chest. Makes me lightheaded. "Then stop fighting me. You promised when this began that I'd be in charge. Now it's time to act like it."

Harper lifts her chin. "Are *you* going to act like it?"

"What do you think I've been doing?"

"See, that's where you've got it wrong." The fury in her tone is an exact answer to mine. "I need you. I can admit that. But I don't like your version of control. I don't want to be treated like a helpless child who needs protecting. You're not my babysitter."

"You don't need protecting? I disagree. You're terrified of your family. And you know I can keep you safe. Tonight, you witnessed me *kill* men for you."

"That wasn't for me."

I move in even closer and lower my voice so much I hardly recognize it. "Like hell it wasn't."

My eyes trace downward. Her bra is made of some translucent fabric. Pretty much see-through. Her tits are perfect. Round and supple, her nipples dark pink, jutting out in two needy little points. I smell vanilla but something headier, too, more primal, exuding from her skin.

I glare down at her in a dominant stance. Her fists clench. The cords in her neck stand out. Her teeth bare like she might bite me or spit at me.

Instead, Harper runs the tip of her tongue across my lower lip.

Fuuuck.

My half-hard cock swells so fast, I feel the rush like a fucking drug.

"You really think *I'm* the one who's fighting this?" she asks.

We're not talking about the escape plan anymore.

There's a rumble in my chest. A growl trying to get out. I'm still holding Harper's wrists against the wall, but I'm fighting myself too. Every sinew of me is taut with holding back the tsunami inside me.

"I want you, Jake. But I need you to be *a man* with me. I want everything you've got, and I won't settle for the scraps you've been throwing me." She cranes her head back. Returning my stare and then some. "If you're in charge, then *prove it*."

What am I supposed to say to that?

Our mouths collide. Tongues pushing, teeth scraping. Rough and hungry. Her hands run over my chest. Her nails drag down my abs, leaving trails behind in my skin. I try to pull her against me, but she pushes even as she keeps devouring my mouth.

And I know exactly what she's doing.

She's defying me, even now. Making me force her to submit.

She wants the darkest parts of me. The sides that aren't gentle or civilized or sweet.

And it's like something breaks open inside me. Cracks in the dam that finally can't hold any longer and give way. The most feral, instinctual parts of me surge forward into the breach. Refusing to be denied.

I break the kiss and my hand cups her throat, pushing her back to the wall.

I'm not pressing hard enough to hurt her. I would never hurt her. But it's enough to keep her from speaking. Enough to show her exactly what's happening here.

I am in control.

Her eyes are like fireworks, bright and dazzling.

"I'll give you what you need," I say. "But at *my* pace. In whatever way I decide. Are you listening?"

Slowly, she nods.

"Good. Then get naked."

21

Harper

Jake has his hand at my throat, and I feel my pulse rabbiting against his palm. His touch is gentle yet firm, like a collar at my neck. A reassuring declaration.

You're mine.

And it's *exactly* what I want from him.

With trembling hands—shaking with need, with anticipation—I unhook my bra and let it slide down my body. My thumbs hook my panties and drag them down.

Jake doesn't move. Just watches me. But his cock twitches in his briefs. "Stay."

He releases me and reaches into the shower to twist the knob. I stay there leaning against the wall. My legs are squeezed together, my clit throbbing. Aching with want.

He's right. I'm scared of the worst tendencies in my family, uncertain what to do. I have to be strong enough to save my sister, but I've never been able to do that on my own. I need Jake by my side. And this connection between us? It has never been simple, and it's *never* just been platonic. Denying that would be denying who we are to each other.

But if he expects me to take a backseat and follow him, trust him, then I want *all* of him. I can't do this in fits and starts anymore. It's all or nothing.

I'll give myself to him, but only if he gives himself to me in return.

Jake leaves the bathroom and returns a moment later. He's got a gun and the surveillance system controller that he took from Lars. "If we're doing this," he says, "I want to make sure we won't be interrupted."

The water heats while he checks the video feeds. Then he sets the small screen on the counter. "Looks like everybody's finally settled down after the gala. All I see are security guards sitting around. Nobody's on alert."

"That's good. So they have no idea about Jimmy or Lars yet."

Jake turns to me. His green eyes blaze. "You don't need to worry."

"I'm trying not to." I imagine those thoughts and images washing away down the shower drain.

Jake kisses my temple, the pressure so light compared to the dominance he was just showing. "Focus on me. I'm going to take care of you."

If I trust him enough, maybe it'll be true.

I've so rarely had a moment like this in my life, when I get to have what I want, and I really freaking hope we don't have to stop this time. Jake accused me of living in a fantasy, and I guess I'm guilty. I have to believe in a happy ending because everything else has been so damn bleak.

I need this with Jake. The strong, golden-haired boy who once made me believe that things would be okay. That he could make the world better for me just because he thought I deserved it.

He doesn't take his eyes off me as he slides his briefs down and steps out of them. His cock pops up. The head is shiny, nearly purple, and precome wells at his slit, so much it'll drip to the floor any second.

I lick my lips. I want to catch that drop on my tongue and taste him. Make him say my name like I said his when his tongue was inside me. Was that just last night? It feels like ages.

He must guess what I'm thinking, because Jake seizes my chin in his hand. "Nope. That's not where I want you. Get under the water."

He nudges me toward the shower. I step under the spray. The heat instantly soothes me, and I close my eyes.

Jake's arms close around me, his chest to my shoulders. His cock nestles against my lower back. He kisses my neck while his hands wander. Caressing my stomach, thighs, hips. I lay my head against him, letting him support my weight when my knees go weak.

He lathers body wash in his hands and follows the same path again on my body, cleaning me. Next is the shampoo, and he massages my scalp for so long I'm ready to melt into a puddle and seep down the drain.

I'm not a submissive person, and I've given Jake plenty of trouble the last few days. But right now? I'd give him anything he asked. That's how much of a relief this is.

After the suds are rinsed away, he moves to stand in front of me, keeping one arm around my waist. His mouth latches onto mine, drawing my tongue into his mouth. Then his fingers finally move downward and push between my legs, and I whimper against his lips. My clit is swollen and achy. Insanely responsive to his touch.

His fingers slide over my sensitive spot. Faster. Rougher. He's got me completely under his sway.

"Come for me," he whispers, and God, I do. I climax with his fingers still working fast over my clit.

He keeps murmuring dirty things in my ear. "You love that, don't you? Being so good for me."

"*Yes.*" I grab onto his shoulders and hold on, chanting his name until the ripples of pleasure subside.

When I'm able to stand unaided again, Jake measures out a dime-sized amount of body wash into my hand. "Wash me," he says.

I grin. This, I'm going to enjoy. *Like you weren't enjoying yourself already*, I think.

I start with his gorgeous pecs. His chest hair is the same dirty-blond shade as his head and his stubble that's not quite a beard. His pubic hair is a little darker, neatly trimmed. His nipples harden as I smooth my thumbs around them in circles.

"I'm pretty sure that area is clean now," he says sardonically.

"Just making sure."

I move to his arms next. That sexy sleeve of tattoos on the right side. Dragons and scaly sea creatures. His left arm has a few scars that I hadn't noticed before. I'm surprised he hasn't covered them with more tattoos the way some people do. "What are these from?" I ask. "These scars?"

I'm expecting an adventure story from the army or his undercover work. But he surprises me.

"I was riding bikes with Madison during summer break when I was in college. My sister was...hmm. Thirteen, I think? A car pulled out, headed right for us, and I swerved in front of her."

"Did it hit you?"

"Yep. Knocked me off the bike. I skidded across the road, right on my arm. That's what the scars are from."

"Jeez." I can't imagine how badly that must've hurt. "Very heroic of you. Saving your little sister like that." I raise my eyebrows, giving him a pointed look.

"Harper, I never said I don't sympathize with you wanting to help Wren."

I kiss his shoulder. "But we're not talking about that right now. I'm getting you clean, like you asked. I'm being good."

My fingers close around his erection. He groans. "*Very* good."

I stroke him until he tugs my hand away.

"That's enough. I'm not ready to come yet."

"You've given me four orgasms now, and you won't let me give you one?"

"I haven't been counting."

He must get off on delayed gratification. I've been edging this man for fourteen years.

"I'm starting to take this personally."

He gives me a smoldering look. "I know how I want you to get me off, and it's not in the shower."

"Oh. That sounds promising."

"Let's finish what we're doing in here, and then I'll show you."

I shampoo Jake's head and wash his hairy armpits, which is actually kind of hot. His masculinity makes me wild for him, all the ways we're different. We kiss some more under the water. Jake alternates between gentle, teasing kisses and deeper, more sensual ones. And he has this way of wrapping himself around me, making me feel like he's holding me up.

The man has me struggling to remember my own name, much less all of my fears.

Those are still there, of course. But I'm safe here with him. I can squint and pretend there's nothing to concern me except this minute and the next several to follow.

He told me not to worry, and I'm doing my best to listen.

Jake shuts off the water and we get out. He starts to towel me off, but we get distracted by more kissing. Soon he's nudging me out of the bathroom and toward the bed. He presses my shoulders until I sit on the mattress. Tucks wet strands of my hair behind my ears and out of the way.

Then he lays me back and, once again, trails his tongue down my body.

"If you don't let me give you an orgasm," I say, "I'm going to think something weird is going on. Like, maybe you're a sex robot who took Jake's place."

He's grinning as he swirls his tongue in my belly button. "Be patient. As patient as me."

"Show off," I mutter.

He playfully smacks my hip so I'll scoot into the center of the mattress. Then Jake crawls back up, stopping when he's straddling my upper body. He nestles a pillow underneath my head.

And his long, swollen cock is *right there* in front of my face.

I think I'm getting the idea.

Jake brushes his fingertips down my cheek. "This is where I want you. Splayed out underneath me. Taking what I give you."

"Mmmm," I hum.

"I'm going to fuck your mouth with my cock, and you're going to suck me and you're going to love it."

"Yes, please."

"That's just what I wanted to hear."

He pushes his hips forward. His cockhead drags over my lips and my whole body shudders. I reach for two handfuls of baseball player ass, still thick and toned all these years later, but he takes my wrists and places my arms over my head.

His tip breaks the seal of my lips. I open up to take him in. Salty warmth, smooth skin. My tongue laps at him. I close my mouth around him and suck, lifting my eyes to look at him.

His lips are slightly open, watching me with awe. And

there's a sweetness to his face. A kindness and care mixed with dark-eyed lust. Not too much of one or the other.

It's just like that for a while, that give and take, until Jake picks up the rhythm. My cheeks hollow and my tongue drags along the underside of his shaft. In this position, he can't go very deep, and I wonder if he chose that on purpose. So he could demand pleasure from me in this dominant way, yet not accidentally go farther than I can take.

Soon, I can't manage any coherent wonderings anymore. There's just his growls and moans, his hands holding mine in place, hips pumping, and his cock filling my mouth. My jaw aches and spit runs down my chin. And he's right. I *love it*.

"Harper." His voice is ragged. "I'm going to come. If you don't want..." He pulls out enough for me to speak if I need to. I wriggle my hands free of his grasp. My hands squeeze his ass again, guiding him forward. I suck him as deep as I can, and he goes off. His shaft swells in my mouth, pulses, and hot come lands on my tongue. I swallow it as another shot of his release coats my mouth and throat. There's so much I struggle to get it all down. Some sneaks out of the corner of my mouth.

Jake slides down my body. His thumb swipes over the come at my mouth. I lick it off. He's got a lazy smile, all blissed out. Jake smiles all the time, but not like this. A complete absence of tension or worry. I didn't even realize until it was missing.

I gave that to him, and I'm feeling the same thing.

"How'd I do?" I ask.

"Perfect." He wiggles the blanket out from beneath our bodies, then pulls it to cover us both. Jake drapes an arm and a leg over me too. Rests his forehead against mine. I'm pinned into place, and I just want to stay in this moment, live right here as if nothing else exists.

I trust you, I want to say. *Tell me what to do. Tell me how to fix my broken life and make it whole.*

He runs his fingertips over my arms and chest beneath the blanket.

My mind wanders to our past. I even doze a little. Jake has been checking the video feeds periodically, and the rest of the resort seems to be asleep. I haven't looked at the clock in a while, but it's somewhere after three in the morning.

"Tell me about Madison," I say. "What's she doing now?"

"My sister is still in West Oaks. She's a cop."

I turn my head on the pillow we're sharing. "Really?" I remember Madison being too smart and devious for the typical tween. She didn't strike me as such a rule follower. But she was tough. She's...wow, mid-twenties now? Makes me feel old, though I'm only thirty-two. Same as Jake.

"She's with a guy who's older than me," Jake says. "A former Navy SEAL on the West Oaks SWAT team. He's got a teenage daughter. Madison went from his student to living with him in, like, a day."

My eyebrows raise. "That's a story I'd like to hear."

"It's a long one. I'll let her tell it when you see her."

There's a discordant note in my heart. Jake must feel it too, because his smile falters. When am I ever going to see Madison? But neither of us comments on it.

"What about Aiden?" I ask. Jake used to complain constantly about his younger brother.

"He had a stint in the army like me. But he hated it. Now he's a chef for my parents' catering company."

"He works for your *parents*?" I'm not one to scoff at continuing the family business, but Aiden always chafed at being told what to do. Especially by his mom and dad.

"Yeah, he grew up and stopped being such a dick. Most of the time."

We laugh as Jake tells me about his army days, more

about his kids. He has endless stories about the twins. He's giving me small pieces of himself, and I know how precious this is, how much it means. But it's bittersweet, too. I wish I could be part of the life he's describing. These wonderful people who love Jake and each other, even if they don't always get along.

I know he can be dangerous. I saw what he did to Lars and Jimmy. Yet everything about Jake is so *good*. Even when he's being aggressive with me, the man is careful in the way he does it. Like kindness is ingrained within him. I'm getting to bask in a few rays of Jake's sunshine, and I'm grateful.

I've got too much on my mind to try to figure out what's happening between us. I can't imagine it will go beyond the next day or two. Jake's life, his children, are here in Southern California. I'm planning to end up somewhere far away. But maybe the memories of this time with him will sustain me for the next fourteen years, the way the last ones did.

If I can get Wren and my father and Jake safely away from the rest of the Caldwells, then I won't ask for anything more. I'll just be happy with the little bit of goodness that I got to have.

22

Jake

When Harper and I were kids, I couldn't imagine another girl being as gorgeous as her. That might still be accurate, but Harper as a grown woman knocks Harper the teenager out of the water.

We're talking and cuddling right now, but really? I want to run my hands all over her, kiss her and stroke her until she's moaning again. I want her panting *yes* to everything I do to her, everything I say.

I'm sporting a semi again already.

I won't tell her this because she'd take it the wrong way, but I am nowhere near satisfied. Getting to watch her with her lips stretched around my cock... *Ughn*. That was one for the record books. It took all my control to last as long as I did. Seeing the lust in her eyes, the way she kept licking my tip afterward to get every last drop, did all kinds of things to my insides. Left me wanting so much more.

But that's not what Harper needs from me right now. And I told her I'd give her what she needs, so that's what I intend to do.

I've been telling her more stories about my family. I think

of a funny one about my kids. "A couple months ago, I had my weekend free, so I took Riley and Hudson to the zoo in LA. They watched the monkeys for a solid hour. They insisted on speaking nothing but 'monkey' the rest of the day, just hooting and climbing on me. They had their own language going by the end of the day, with grammar and everything."

"That sounds fun."

"It was. Adrienne was a good sport about it too, but after the kids didn't stop for three days straight, she about wanted to kill me."

"You and Adrienne were married?"

I pause. Not because I don't want to share this part of myself with Harper. But because it's a sensitive subject for other reasons. "Yeah. We've been divorced for two years."

"Are you friends?"

"We are. Close friends. Adrienne's great."

Harper plays with my chest hair. I can feel her questions, though she doesn't ask. So I try to give her a little more.

"We weren't compatible. It was hard for me when our marriage ended. I would've stuck it out and kept trying, but Adrienne thought we were better apart."

Harper is studying me. "Would you get back together with her if you could?"

I rub my forehead, feeling sheepish. "I don't think so. She was right. We weren't meant to be." I don't want to get into our reasons for breaking up because it would divulge personal information about my ex. But I also don't want Harper to think I'm pining away for someone. "She's just a friend."

Harper rests her chin on her hands. "No offense to her, but I don't see how anyone could give you up. Not if they had a choice about it."

I laugh, though the levity sits strangely in my chest. Doesn't feel quite right. "You think very highly of me."

"Don't let it go to your head. But I've always thought highly of you. You know that."

"I'm not perfect, Harper. I would never claim to be."

"But you might be close," she says begrudgingly.

"I'm not," I say again, and she frowns.

Harper used to call me a hero when we were younger. She still does it, teasingly. And that's what my kids call me.

But that's because they don't know the other sides of me. The ugly things I've had to do.

Harper's been beating herself up about not getting away from her family sooner, not saving Wren. But she doesn't realize that everyone has to make compromises. I've seen the darker aspects of humanity too. Including within myself. I'm confident I was on the right side of things, but that doesn't mean I'm proud of all I had to do.

She asked me to show her who I am. *I want everything you've got.*

Does she truly want to know?

"While I was in the army, the CIA recruited me for a few covert ops. I saw some terrible shit. Had to dole it out myself. And I was *good* at it." I stare at the ceiling. My mouth is dry, and I swallow.

I've never even told Adrienne this. But I keep going.

"The CIA offered me a job. I turned them down because I didn't like what it did to me. I thought a job with the feds would be more stable. But with the DEA...I've played some nasty characters. Much worse than Jake Worthington. My bosses keep giving me those assignments, like they know..." Like they know that's what I'm best at. Even if that's not who I want to be. I push out a breath. "I don't talk about this much. Not with anyone."

"Why are you telling me?"

"Because I don't want you to think I'm more than I am. Or better than you somehow. I promise you, my hands are far from clean."

I rarely have nightmares, but when I do, that's what I see: my hands bloodied, my enemy's insides sprayed across a dirty stone wall.

My stomach lurches briefly, remembering what happened a few hours ago. Two gunshots. Two men dead. I have no regrets, but it's still ugly. Having to end another person's life.

My deepest, darkest secret is that, sometimes, *I enjoy it*.

I don't want my kids to ever know that about me. Adrienne only knows pieces. She only ever saw the gentler sides of me. Maybe that's another reason our marriage was never going to work.

"You did what you had to," Harper says.

"Like you did?"

She shrugs.

"You said I'm not as nice as I used to be. You were right. But maybe I never was. Maybe the nice guy was a disguise for what's really underneath."

Harper trails her fingers along my cheek, then my lower lip. "I don't want nice. Not if it's fake, or a role you feel you have to play. Not if it's a lie."

I can't hide my flinch.

Harper drops her hand and looks away. "I get it. I'm one to talk about lying. But—"

"No, I wasn't thinking about that." I slide my fingers into her hair. Turn her head to face me. "Harper, there are times I *like* hurting people."

Fuck, I shouldn't say this. I should stop my mouth from running.

But her eyes are open and curious. Not afraid.

"I don't know which is the real me, and that freaks me out. What if I'm really this twisted, violent person down deep and eventually, that's all I know how to be?" I half expect her to be horrified at this admission. I wouldn't blame her.

But she smiles instead. "I refuse to believe that."

"You refuse? You don't think I mean what I say?"

"Nope. I call bullshit. Not sure I believe in this dark, twisted Jake I've been hearing so much about. Not sure he's real."

"You don't think so?"

In a blink, I've got her on her back, hovering my body over hers. I look down at her naked underneath me. My dick, fully erect now, presses into her belly and leaves a smear of precome.

She raises her arms over her head without breaking eye contact. Her legs wrap around my hips. An invitation. Or maybe a dare.

She smirks. "I'm not denying that you're bossy as hell. But you haven't given me anything I can't handle. I know you wouldn't. Because I trust you."

Those words slide through me like a caress. "You do? You trust me?"

"Yes, so much it scares me. That's the *only* thing about you that scares me. Because I…I know I'd give you anything."

Damn. That is the sexiest thing she could say to me.

I dip my head to kiss her breasts. I start out slow, licking up and down her rounded flesh. Teasing. Forcing her to be patient. I pause to suck her left nipple, pulling a bit harder each time my lips close, taking her deeper into my mouth.

Then I sink my teeth into the swollen bud.

"*Jake.* Holy…"

I lick the pinked skin to soothe away the pain. "Still trust me?"

"I'm not going anywhere," she whispers.

I keep up my attention to her beautiful curves. Trailing licks and bites all over her breasts and then her stomach. I move down to her thighs, where I suck hickeys into the soft flesh. I can smell how wet she is.

"Can I fuck you without a condom?" I ask.

She whimpers. It's almost a greedy little whine. "I'm on the pill. I've never gone bare with anyone before."

"I haven't since I was married. Are you down for that?"

"With you? I'm down for anything."

That's what I thought, but I had to ask. Guess I'm not a total monster.

I groan and smooth my hands up and down her legs. "I used to dream about fucking you."

"Yeah?"

I trail my eyes over her body, laid out on display for me. Her legs splayed open. The marks left by my mouth.

"Night dreams, daydreams. I used to imagine you wearing my baseball jersey and nothing else." I kiss the inner edge of her knee. "I got myself off thinking about you for two years straight." And longer than that, if I'm being honest. It took me a while to stop hoping that I'd hear from her.

"I touched myself thinking about you, too."

Now that's an image that would've blown my eighteen-year-old mind.

"Show me how you touched yourself," I say.

Harper's fingers drag down her body to her center. She makes circles over her clit, her eyes falling closed as she moans. Her wetness glistens on her folds and soaks her fingers.

My breath quickens. My nostrils flare, inhaling her scent. I have to bite the inside of my cheek to keep myself from lunging at her.

"I was a virgin then," she says. "I wanted—*oh*—I wanted you to be my first."

I make a guttural sound. "You shouldn't tell me things like that."

"What would you have done?" She's panting. "If you'd been able to have me?"

What would it have been like if I'd had her when we were eighteen? If my cock was her first?

I've never put much stock in the virginity construct. Sex has whatever meaning you choose to give it, or none at all. But with Harper? It would've meant something profound to me. Probably more than I was ready for at that age.

I'm older now. I've been in and out of love. I know dreams aren't always what you imagine they'll be. But Harper? She's not just a dream girl. She's my friend. A brave woman who's still fighting despite all she's gone through. Someone who might be able to understand how my different pieces fit together and won't be afraid of what she sees.

I'm usually the king of patience, but not now. Not with her talking like that, pleasuring herself with her fingers.

I push her hand away and replace those fingers with my tongue. She grips my hair instead. *"Jake."*

I lick and suck and get her whimpering. Her taste coats my tongue. But it's not enough anymore. Not fucking enough. I can't wait any longer.

I need my cock in her. I need that connection, as close to her as I can get. I need it with a desperation that calls to the darkest reaches of me.

I get onto my knees, haul her toward me, and bury my cock to the hilt in her pussy.

She gasps and cries out, grabbing for the mattress and bunching the sheets. I'm still for a moment as she adjusts to me. A bead of sweat rolls down my stomach and onto hers.

My hands land to either side of her shoulders. My hips snap forward and thrust my shaft inside her. So wet, with just enough friction to get us both moaning incoherently.

I love seeing her like this. Smiling that euphoric smile, legs wrapped around my hips, her nails clawing at my biceps as she chants my name. I take what I want, driving into her hard and fast.

I press my hand to her chest, seeking out her heart. It's beating as quick as a hummingbird.

I hold her down just like that as I fuck her. And I'd swear that my heart is beating to the exact same rhythm, synchronized perfectly with hers.

Her thighs quake. Her back arches. I can feel how close she is.

But I want Harper to come when I'm ready for her.

I roll us both over so she's on top, legs spread with my cock deep inside her. She tries to take over and ride the hell out of me, but I grab her hips to keep her still. "Uh, uh," I say. "Patience."

"You're the worst."

"You said you trust me."

"Doesn't mean I always like it."

I cup her face, brushing my thumbs over her cheekbones. "Be good."

"I want to," she whispers. "Show me."

Our bodies are slick with sweat and arousal. A bonfire of heat where we're connected. I pull her down against me and kiss her. My hands trace up and down her back until she's melting.

When she looks at me, there's a different kind of vulnerability there. A question that she's asking.

This time, when I move my hips to pump into her, I keep it slow. Deep. Grinding our bodies together. I caress her breasts and stomach. Reach back to gently knead her ass. With every thrust of my cock, she relaxes more. Gives up another inch of control.

Her eyes flutter closed and her gasps speed up until she's babbling with need. "Jake...I can't...I want...Oh, please..."

She digs her fingers into her hair, elbows up, spine arched and breasts out. So beautiful.

"Now," I murmur, "right now."

Her thighs clench down on me. She cries out and shakes, and the sight and sensation of Harper trembling on my cock triggers my own orgasm. My balls draw up and I empty inside of her as pleasure zings to every last one of my nerve endings, whiting out my vision.

She falls forward onto me, utterly boneless. But I'm in no better state.

We cling to one another. I'm completely spent. Everything's wrung out of me. My aggression and lust and adrenaline, all burned up in my veins by a girl on fire.

I just want to hold on to her, feel her curled and purring on top of me, and never let her go.

Slowly, I come back to myself, but I'm mellowed. Tempered by the inferno between us.

If anyone's been subdued here, it's me.

My softened cock slips out of her. Harper drops kisses onto my face. "You okay?" she says.

"I'm supposed to be asking you that."

We trade lazy kisses. Our noses nuzzle together. I shift us again so she's beneath me, trapped under my weight. But she sighs as if it's a tremendous relief instead of a burden.

And it is for me too. Knowing she's with me, that she can take whatever I need to give her. That I've given her just what she needs in return.

23

Harper

I should be asleep right now.

But instead, I'm staring at Jake. Like a total creeper.

The sun's coming up, those first rays bleeding through the curtains and bathing his face in the most perfect light. It's Jake in all his messy-haired, sex-wrecked glory.

My sketch book. I need my sketch book.

I leave the warm cocoon of our blankets and tiptoe across the cold floor. I tucked my sketch book in with my clothes yesterday when we left our other room, along with my pencil case. I take both out now.

The charcoal darkens my fingertips as it flies across the page, shading in the shadows of Jake so the light can emerge. I get lost in the shapes and patterns of his tattoos. His muscles. The scruff on his face. And all the while, my heart is pitter-pattering. I spend forever trying to capture the exact shade of his hair in black and white.

When we made love last night, it was as if we were seeing inside of each other. The things he told me...both in words and through the movements of his body. I don't think anyone in my life has known me the way Jake does. And maybe it's the same for him.

My hand stops.

Look at me. I'm ridiculous. When did I become a sappy romantic cliché? A girl drawing the boy that she…

Oh, no. Do not finish that thought.

I want to tear out the page. Crumple it up and bury it so he'll never, ever see it. I need to shut out the beautiful fantasies that are cluttering my mind. The *maybes* and the *what ifs*.

But I just…can't.

Instead, I close the sketchbook, return it to the bottom of the suitcase, and wash my hands.

Rest. Focus on the day ahead. Those are the tasks I should be thinking about. Surviving my family and finding Wren. But as I snuggle into bed beside Jake again and close my eyes, those aren't the pictures that my mind weaves.

A LITTLE WHILE LATER, THERE'S POUNDING IN MY head. My brain is trying to drag me out of sleep, but I don't wanna go.

"*Shit.*"

I open my eyes. That was Jake's voice. He's getting out of bed. Bright, insistent sunlight now shines in the window.

Then I realize the source of the pounding. It's at the door.

Jake grabs a gun from the nightstand, then the controller for the surveillance system. He goes over beside the door to the hall. He's got his gun ready in one hand, checking the video system with the other.

He's also buck naked, which makes me want to laugh. Mostly out of nervousness.

I've been agonizing over what might come next. Seems I'm about to find out.

I jump up and throw on a pair of shorts and a tee, not bothering with a bra. Jake nods at me. "Take a look at this." He turns the screen so I can see it.

Mia is out in the hall. But she's banging on our assigned hotel room, not the one we're staying in right now.

She raises her fist and pounds again. Looks around frantically. Her lips move, muttering to herself.

"I have to talk to her," I say. "Before she recruits anyone else into breaking down that door."

Jake puts on his boxer briefs. "We should see what she wants. But I don't want you going out in the open unarmed." He holds out his gun to me, but I shake my head.

"She already looks upset. I don't want to make it any worse."

I have a lot of questions for my cousin. She's not going anywhere until I get some answers. But if I start waving around a weapon, she might take off.

I crack open the door. "*Mia*," I hiss.

She does a double take. Her hand rubs her chest like I gave her a shock. "Jeez, I was thinking some bad shit went down last night. Where have you been?"

"Bad shit? You could say that."

Glancing behind herself again, she walks over to me. I grab her hand, pull her inside, and shut the door.

"What's with all the—" Mia stops talking when she sees Jake standing there, still in nothing but his boxer briefs, the gun in his hand pointed at the floor. "Whoa, what the heck is going on here?"

"You first," I say. "Why were you banging on our door?"

She swallows, blinking fast. "You missed breakfast, and Roman's been acting strange all morning, and then he took off. Nobody has seen Lars or Jimmy. The other security guys are going around asking questions. And I thought…"

"What? That we were dead?"

"Well. This is our family we're talking about." Mia's eyes keep moving around the room, going to Jake, then to me.

But there's something more to her expression than just concern.

Guilt.

I shove her against the door. "Did you know? Did you have *anything* to do with what happened last night?"

Mia throws her hands up, palms out. "Relax, okay? All I knew was that Roman was plotting something, and that he's had it out for Jake. I was afraid Roman pulled a stupid stunt. It's happened before."

"And you didn't say anything to warn me?"

She fixes me with a glare. "I'm trying to make it through the day here, same as you. But it would help if your man could put on some clothes. Because him standing there in just his undies with a gun is weird. Weirdly hot, but still weird."

I arch my eyebrow.

"I don't *want* to be attracted to my cousin's fiancé. You're forcing it on me!"

I can't help it. I laugh. "All right. If Jake gets dressed, will you answer my questions?"

"I'll try." Mia stands with her back against the door, looking away from Jake. I grab the clutch I was carrying last night. It still has the note inside, the one used to lure me and Jake to the villas.

If you want to see your sister, meet me at unit 3 in the villas at midnight. I know where she is.

But when I close my clutch and turn to face my cousin again, her eyes dart guiltily away from Jake's butt. He's bending over to grab a pair of sweats and a shirt from the suitcase.

She shrugs helplessly. "I'm only human."

I know how she feels.

I unfold the note and hold it out to her. "Have you seen this before?"

She scans it. "No. Never. Did you do what it said? Go to the villas?"

Jake sits in a chair, gun resting on his knee. "Yeah. Jimmy and Lars were there. They tried to kill me."

Mia curses. "And I'm guessing, since you're here and they're missing, that it went badly?"

"Yeah," Jake says. "For them."

She exhales slowly. "And you thought I'd have anything to do with that? No way. I try to steer clear of my brothers and their machinations. *Both* of them." She points at the note. "But if this came from Roman, I'm surprised he mentioned Wren. Tristan's the one who was with her."

"What?" I say. "When was this?"

She holds up her hands again like she's warding me off. "Relax. I don't know much, but I'll tell you. I almost mentioned it yesterday at the golf game, but I didn't know what your deal was. I was feeling you out. Trying to decide if I could trust you."

"If *you* could trust *me*?"

"I hinted all over the place that I was looking for an ally against my dad and my brothers. Could I have been more obvious? I was afraid you were going to narc on me."

Jake coughs like he's hacking up a lung. "Sorry," he mutters. "Itch in my throat."

Subtle, I think.

But I doubt Mia's choice of words had any deeper subtext. She thinks I don't like how Caldwell Enterprises is being run, but that Jake is really my fiancé. This room certainly tells that story. The bed is destroyed. It looks like we were fucking in it for half the night.

Which is accurate.

"Tell me about Wren," I say.

Mia sits in the other chair. "I saw her the morning we arrived. My dad and siblings and I arrived separately because, well, that's how we do things. You've probably seen that already. I took a car from the airport and got to the resort earlier than expected. Tristan was already here. He was getting out of an SUV when my rideshare drove in, and it was only a glimpse, really. Wren was in the backseat with the window partway open. Tristan leaned in and said something to her. Then he noticed me, and the SUV took off. That was it."

"You're *sure* it was Wren?" I ask.

"Definitely."

I thought Roman was in charge of her. At least, he's been in charge of making threats against her and passing on video messages.

But Wren is *here*. Mia's confirmed it. That knowledge lifts my hope another level higher.

"You don't know where she is now?" I ask.

"No. I haven't seen her at all. Which is weird, right? Why isn't she attending this shindig with the rest of us? I got the sense there was a reason, and I shouldn't just go around blabbing my mouth about it. But I've been wondering."

Which is normal for the Caldwell clan. It can be dangerous to ask too many questions.

"Your father's been holding Wren and threatening to hurt her if my dad and I step out of line," I explain.

Mia pales. "Shit, I'm sorry. I had no idea, I swear."

"I believe you." It's still risky to trust Mia, but she's given every indication of honesty. She's been off in college, barely involved in the family at all the last few years.

"So, I'm guessing you're trying to find her?" Mia asks.

I share a glance with Jake. He nods his assent. I'm glad he's okay with this, but I was probably going to tell Mia anyway. I need all the help and allies I can get.

Sex with him has been incredible, but I'm not going to turn off my own brain and thoughtlessly follow his every command like Submissive Barbie.

I nod. "I'm here to find my sister and rescue her."

"Then I'm in. As long as you take me with you."

"Take you where?"

She rolls her eyes. "*Please*. You can't plan something like this without a permanent escape route. You and I both know how my dad will react, and you're not stupid. You've got a way to keep yourself and Wren safe. To get out, once and for all. That's what I want too."

What Mia is saying is treason. And if I agree, there's no going back. If this is a trap, I'm sunk. The tension in the room is like glass, so heavy and brittle that it's ready to crack.

She gets up and walks over to me. "My dad and brothers think I'm clueless," she murmurs. "But I see the fractures that have appeared in our family the last few years. I've been watching them. Tristan, Roman, my dad. They've been placing pawns around some invisible chess board. I don't want to be there when they make their final moves."

Mia's waiting for my response. Jake is too, which I'm grateful for. He's acknowledging that this particular call has to be mine.

"You're right," I say. "I have an exit plan. But I'm not going anywhere without Wren. If you'll help me find her, I'll take you with us when we leave."

Jake picks this moment to cut in. "Which has to be *today*, so we'd better get started."

My cousin looks to me for confirmation, but I don't say anything. I haven't made up my own mind about Jake's deadline yet. The best solution is to find her before then so it won't be an issue.

Jake takes the surveillance video controller from the table and hands it to Mia. "Do you know how this works?"

Mia switches it on. "I've seen Lars with it. Part of the security system, right?"

"Exactly," Jake says. "It connects to the hotel's cameras, but from what I can tell, there's no access to any recordings. We were hoping to check the footage to look for Wren."

Mia smiles. "Then you're lucky I'm on your side, because I can get into the database. You'll have to get into the main security room. It's near the hotel kitchen."

"How hard is it to get inside?" I ask.

She shrugs. "I've been in there before. We can manage it. Leave that part to me." Then she frowns. "Only problem is Roman. We'll need to be sure he stays away for a while."

Jake crosses his arms over his chest. "I'll handle Roman. He and I need to have a chat, anyway."

"Jake," I warn.

"I promise I'll behave. Just to make sure we're both on the same page. I think it's time to declare peace. If nothing else, it'll confuse the fuck out of him."

We plan to meet up in half an hour. Jake and I need time to get showered and properly dressed, and Mia wants to scope out the security room. With Lars and Jimmy down, we're hoping that Roman's team will be short-handed.

As Mia leaves, I see my dad in the hall, poking his head out of his doorway. And he looks very confused.

"Harper?" he says. "That's not your room. Is it?"

He starts toward me, saying hello to Mia when he passes her.

Shit. He's coming *here*. To the room Jake and I spent the night in. I don't care if Mia saw our clothes strewn everywhere, but my father? Ew.

I bar my arm over the entrance. "Dad! Hey."

"What's going on?"

"I can explain everything. But let's meet in your room. I'll be right there. Okay?"

"Okay…" He's wary, but he goes along with it.

I spin around, grab a sweatshirt, and throw it over my tee. Jake is already in the bathroom starting the shower.

Then I spot something else I need on the nightstand and scoop it up, sticking it in my sweatshirt pocket.

I pad down the hallway on my bare feet.

Once I'm in my father's hotel room, I shut the door and turn to him. "Sorry about that. There have been some…developments."

"I knocked on your place earlier," he says, "but you didn't answer. I wasn't sure if something was wrong, or… If you and Jake…" His face is turning red. Maybe dad suspects that my "relationship" with Jake isn't as fake as we've been claiming. My dad knows me well, and it's entirely possible that my attraction to Jake has been obvious.

But my father has never discussed my love life before, and I can't imagine he wants to start now.

"We had to relocate. Roman made a move last night."

"What's your cousin done now?"

I give him a summary, keeping the details as vague as possible. Meanwhile, I steer my father toward his bed so he'll sit. Now that I know how sick he really is, it's hard not to think about taking care of him. Getting him to a hospital and demanding that the doctors do *something*.

But we don't have time for that right now, and that isn't what my dad wants to hear.

"Don't worry about Roman," I say. "Jake and I dealt with it. Well, mostly Jake."

"He's looking out for you?"

I sit on the chair across from him. "Yeah, he is. You don't

have to worry. At least, not too much. Jake wants us to leave tonight."

I don't explain that Jake wants to leave whether or not we find Wren, but I'm tired of going around in circles about that subject. I don't intend to stress my father even more.

"Amos will expect us at the pitch meeting," Dad says.

"I'll cover it. Between the investor pitch and tracking down Wren, I've got my hands full today. You just rest and make sure you're ready. Speaking of ready—"

I reach into my sweatshirt pocket and pull out what I brought with me.

"*Harper,*" my dad gasps.

It's a pistol. The one that I stole from Jimmy last night.

Dad glares at it like it's a poisonous snake and he's afraid it'll strike. "Where did you get that?"

I bite back my annoyance. You'd think my father would be used to guns and violence by now. I wish I wasn't.

"Don't worry about it," I say again. "I want you to hold on to it. Just in case."

"If Amos finds out I have this…"

"Then make sure he doesn't." I put steel into my voice. I often use kid gloves with my father because I love him. I do. But right now, he needs to listen to me. "Dad, stay here and stay safe. Play up your illness if you have to. It's certainly bad enough. Just don't go anywhere until I'm back. And if anybody tries to make you do otherwise, protect yourself. I need to focus on finding Wren today, and I won't be able to if I'm stressed about you too. Can you do that for me?"

"Yes," he says hoarsely. "I can do that. I will."

"Thank you." I give him a hug.

After I'm finished with Dad, I return to my bedroom. It's not even ten yet, and I'm beyond exhausted. It's going to be a very long day.

But I perk up when Jake emerges from the bathroom, all tousled damp hair and spicy-smelling body wash.

He walks over and brushes his lips over mine. "How are you?"

"Hanging in."

"In eight hours, we'll be on our way out of here. And you'll be free."

As long as I've found Wren, I add silently.

He pulls back with a smile, then picks up a small object from the table. "You almost forgot this."

It's the diamond ring for our "engagement." I hold out my hand, and he slides it back on my finger. "Where's this from, anyway?"

"Evidence locker at West Oaks PD. So don't lose it. I'll be in deep shit." Jake dips his head for another kiss. As our lips meet, I brush my fingers over the short hair at the back of his neck. My stomach blooms with heat. If only we could go back to bed. Steal a few more moments.

"I wish we had more time," I say. More time for *everything*.

He gives me one more sultry kiss. "Once this is over, you'll have all the time in the world. You can be an art teacher or whatever else you decide. Your future will be yours."

But what about you? What if I want you in that future?

I keep those questions to myself. I've been doing enough wishful thinking.

24

Harper

I clean up quickly and dress in jeans and a silky top. My hair goes into a bun on top of my head because I don't want to waste time on blow-drying.

Mia knocks, and I smooth my hands down my shirt.

Let's do this.

She's leaning against the wall in the hallway when I open the door. "Is Jake gone?"

"Yeah. He found Roman on the cameras and is keeping an eye on him. If he comes our way, Jake will head him off."

Jake took the surveillance video controller. But I've got the master keycard. We figured that was an equitable division of our spoils. As for weapons, I've got my knife strapped to my thigh beneath my shorts, and I assume Jake has his gun with him. No messing around anymore.

But as we stroll down the hallway, I try to look like I'm just out for a casual walk with my cousin.

"I thought we'd stop by the kitchen first," Mia says. "Have you eaten?"

"No, but I'm not hungry." I'm way too nervous for that. "I'd rather go straight to the surveillance room."

"Patience, Harper. Kitchen first. It's part of my ingenious plan."

"Don't tell me to be patient," I grumble. "Jake does that."

She snorts. "I'll bet. Don't get me wrong, the guy's smoking. But are you completely sure you can trust him?"

"*Jake*? I trust him more than anybody. I'd trust him with my life."

"A guy you happened to meet because he works for a company that ships stuff?"

A couple of the investors step out into the hallway. We say a polite hello, then steer around them.

"I guess we just clicked," I say.

"Fine, don't tell me. But don't treat me like I'm stupid either."

I press my lips together.

As we wander through the kitchen, a cook eyes us warily. Steam hovers in the air, and pots clang.

Mia snags a freshly baked roll and hands it to me. It's warm, and my stomach makes an eager rumble. Maybe I was hungrier than I thought. Fighting thugs and then having hours of sex will do that to a girl. Even if Jake *did* insist on doing most of the work.

We stop in a quiet alcove beside a station no one's using. This side of the kitchen is quiet, far from the bustle of lunch preparation. I sink my teeth into the roll.

Then, to my horror, Mia ignites a gas burner and sticks a fabric napkin into the flame.

"*Mia*," I hiss. "What are you *doing*?"

Curls of black rise toward the ceiling, where a smoke detector waits. "Creating the diversion we needed. Come on!" She drags me through the rear exit and into a staff hallway. "Told you I had a plan."

My roll gets lost mid-escape. "A plan that involves

burning down the building? We have to go back there. Someone could get hurt!"

"It's fine. At the worst, the kitchen will have a little cosmetic damage."

"What if cameras recorded you setting that fire?"

"Then we *really* need to get access to the surveillance database. I'll delete the footage."

Right on cue, a shrill alarm rings out.

We reach a closed door with the words *No Admittance* emblazoned in red. Mia uses her fist to pound on the door. It cracks open, and a gruff face looks out. He has a huge handlebar mustache. Then the guy seems to recognize Mia. He straightens, his expression cycling through several kinds of panic.

"Miss Caldwell."

"Where is Lars?" Mia barks. "He's supposed to be on duty, and there's a fire alarm going off. Or did you not hear it?"

"I heard it, ma'am, but we're short-staffed and—"

"Then get your ass moving and do something about it! Do you have any idea what my father will do if he finds out about this?"

The guard dashes out. Behind him, I get a glimpse of a huge screen with multiple surveillance feeds. Nobody else is manning the room. *Perfect.*

But at the last moment, the guard reaches to slam the door closed. Then he jiggles the lock, just to make sure, before he runs down the hall toward the kitchen.

Mia curses under her breath. "Dang it, I couldn't move fast enough. We'll have to break the lock or something."

"Nope, I've got this." I pull out the master keycard we swiped from Lars last night. A wave, and we're in.

The moment the door's closed, I grab a chair and wedge it

beneath the knob. I don't want anyone bursting in here and surprising us.

Mia doesn't waste any time. She sits at the keyboard and starts tapping away. A new window appears on the wall screen. It's got a long list of file folders. She seems to know what she's doing.

"How do you know what to look for?" I ask.

She shrugs. "I hooked up with one of the security guards our first night here. I was bored. He showed me all the cool stuff."

"Seriously? Please say it wasn't Lars or Jimmy."

"God, no. He was an okay guy, but Roman found out and fired him. I felt like total shit."

"So Roman's protective of his sister? I wouldn't have expected that."

"Oh, that wasn't it. He was pissed off that the guy let me in here with the computers. Roman doesn't like to share his toys."

The camera recordings are organized by date and location. Mia opens one feed after another, filling the screen, and starts to run them all at the same time.

"This is the footage from the day the family arrived. I've got them playing back at super speed. Holler if you see Wren."

We watch for a little while. We see Tristan's SUV arrive, along with Mia's rideshare, but I can't tell who else was with Tristan.

"Can we see where the SUV went after this?" I ask.

We find the same vehicle driving along the private road that runs through the resort. But that's the last we see of it. The SUV doesn't pull up anywhere else. As if it left and didn't return, which could mean Wren is staying offsite.

The rest of the feeds run, but I don't see Wren. Some of the videos jump forward in time, seemingly at random. I'll bet that was Lars or Roman messing around with the cameras. But were they hiding footage of my sister?

I glance at the door to the security room. We've already spent a solid five minutes here and we haven't found much.

"Is there any way to download the videos?" I ask. "So we can go through them later?"

"That would be gigs upon gigs of data. Even if I had a portable hard drive, that would take a while to upload."

A bead of sweat rolls down my side. My skin crawls like it can feel the minutes ticking past. "Go to the footage from Friday night, the first night we were all here. Around one a.m."

"What are we looking for?"

"Tristan."

Jake and I were following Tristan that night before Roman caught up with us. We weren't able to go after Tristan then. But now, I can find out where he was going.

Mia speeds through the footage until her eldest brother crosses the lens, walking away from the main hotel.

"There he is," I say excitedly. "Where does he go next?"

Behind us, the doorknob rattles, but the chair keeps it from turning. "Hey, who's in there?"

Shit. The guard is back.

"*Hurry.*"

"I'm trying," Mia says through gritted teeth. She speeds even faster through the various camera feeds. The doorknob keeps rattling.

Come on, come on, I think.

I stab my finger at the screen. "Wait. *There.*"

Mia reverses the timestamp by a few seconds. We see Tristan walking along a path toward a cottage. This must be on the far outskirts of the resort, because the building doesn't look like the others here. It wasn't on the map that Jake was studying earlier.

Tristan goes to the cottage and knocks on the door. The door opens. There's only a glimpse of whoever's inside. I'm holding my breath.

Mia plays it again and freezes the video. She enlarges the image. A pale face. Long, dark hair.

"Do you know where this house is?" I ask.

Mia nods. "Yeah, I've seen it. It's just over the property line of the resort."

I pump my fist. We've got a location.

My cousin's fingers move across the keyboard. "Okay, one last thing. I need to delete the footage from the kitchen and the hallway outside this room. Roman doesn't need to know we were here."

"If you'd warned Jake, he could've switched off those cameras beforehand."

"And he'd have insisted on knowing my plan. You think Jake would've pre-approved me becoming an arsonist?"

Yeah, not so much. She's got a point.

Suddenly, the door bursts open. The security guard charges in, a stormy expression on his face. "What the hell is —" He stops mid-sentence when he sees me and Mia.

I glance at her and find the screen is black. She smiles lazily. "Oh, hey. Did you take care of that kitchen situation?"

The guard looks confused. "Yeah, it caused some mess, but it's handled. What are you doing in here?"

"Just waiting for you." Mia stands up and walks with me toward the door. She squeezes his bicep as she passes. "Wanted to make sure you were okay. That fire was scary. I was worried."

We hustle out of there while he's still giving her a flirtatious smile.

"Did you delete the footage of us breaking in?" I whisper once we're heading back to my room.

"Yep. All taken care of. And I disabled the cameras in the

hall so they wouldn't see us leaving, either. Unless Roman was watching the feed live, he wouldn't see it."

I exhale. "Good."

I just hope Jake isn't having any trouble with Roman. Or rather, starting trouble.

25

Jake

To one side of the hotel's main lobby, there's a deck where guests can take in the stunning views. That's where I park myself as I wait for Roman to show.

I track him on the cameras as he crosses the grounds. I wonder if he went to check the villas and if he found the remains of his henchmen. Even if he didn't, he would've realized something was up when he didn't hear back from them last night.

While I wait for Roman to turn up, I roll down the cuffs on my shirt, deciding to conceal my tats. People around here have seen them, but today I want to seem like nothing more than an upstanding businessman. As if the worst I got up to last night was boning my fiancée.

And there I go again, my brain grasping for any reason to turn back to Harper. I don't like that I'm not with her right now. But she's with Mia, who I am begrudgingly beginning to like. Harper also has the number to my burner phone. I'm close enough that I can come running if anything goes wrong.

I quickly switch the camera feed to the interior of the hotel, searching for Harper and Mia, and I'm relieved when I spot them walking down a corridor. No problems yet. But after a heated gun battle, even hotter sex, and too little sleep or food, I'm on edge.

It's a good thing I thrive under these conditions. The hairier things get, the more I can dial myself in and stay focused. Helps that Harper isn't in front of me right now, being all gorgeous as she tends to do.

I stand when I see Roman strutting toward the hotel entrance. But he's now with his father. Roman and Amos are talking, the younger man's head bent toward the older.

If they're talking about me, I'll find out in about one point four seconds.

I step into their path, though I leave a respectful distance between myself and Amos. I got a little close to challenging him yesterday after Mason collapsed, and I need to go back to the ingratiating future nephew-in-law.

"Mr. Caldwell, good morning."

Amos puts on a broad smile. I examine every twitch around his eyes, the tension of his mouth. Trying to read what he's thinking. But he genuinely seems pleased to see me. Which suggests that Roman wasn't telling him that I'm a loose cannon that needs to be dealt with.

They were conferencing about something else.

"Jake, how are you?" Amos asks. "Sleep well, I hope?"

My gaze cuts over to Roman, who stares back intently. I don't so much read his expression as absorb it. The guy is throwing death and destruction at me. His fists clench at his sides.

"I tried."

Amos chuckles. "You and Harper made quite the impression last night. Walk with me." He turns to take the path into a series of courtyards and gardens. The invitation didn't include his son, but Roman stays at my heels.

I feel the threats and the fury radiating from him.

"The investors have been talking about how charming a couple you are," Amos says. His tone has turned more serious. Getting down to business. "It's an excellent opportunity. Especially with Mason not being well enough to join us last night, and frankly, his lackluster charisma. I'd like it if you join Harper at the pitch meeting later today. The investors will appreciate seeing a man like you by her side. Is that something you'd be interested in?"

Of course he thinks that Harper can't hold her own. But I'm playing Jake Worthington, and this is exactly what he'd be eager to hear. He'd have no hesitation about hogging the spotlight, even if it means stepping over the woman he supposedly loves in the process.

"If you want me there, sir, then I'll be there. I've gotten to know SunSpeed's business. Both as a client, and from talking to Harper and Mason."

Amos puts a hand on my shoulder. "Excellent. You could be just what we need to close these deals. Are you aware of how important these investments are to our family enterprise?"

"I believe so, sir."

"Do you?" He focuses intently on me. It's the kind of look that tries to take the measure of a man.

No one has said anything in my hearing about the true business of Caldwell Enterprises. The deals with the cartels, the vicious foot soldiers who are out there defending the Caldwell market share against competing gangs. The distributions of deadly fentanyl and heroin and illegally manufactured opiates to the masses. The bloodshed.

The corner of my mouth inches up in a cocky smirk. "I'll do whatever you need me to do." *Give me a cut of that Caldwell money, a slice of your power, and I'm your man.*

Roman's panicked eyes dart back-and-forth between his

father and me. He doesn't dare interrupt. But this is pretty much his worst nightmare.

Amos pats my shoulder again. "Welcome to the family, Jake."

"Thank you, Mr. Caldwell. You don't know what that means to me."

Roman exhales through his nostrils like a dragon breathing smoke.

"Just Amos." The Caldwell patriarch resumes his walk, and I follow a deferential step behind. "It's Sunday. Relax and enjoy the day with Harper. Lounge by the pool, go for another nine holes. Whatever you like. I'll see you and Harper at the pitch meeting. Just don't be—"

A shrill alarm rings out. Amos and Roman both tense.

"What the hell is that?" Amos snaps, turning to his son.

Roman takes out his phone. "Just got a notification. Fire alarm. The kitchen."

I have no idea if Mia or Harper had anything to do with that, but I really hope they know what they're doing.

"See what's going on," Amos commands, "and resolve it. First you can't find your security guards, and now this?"

Roman glares at me. "I'll fix it," he tells his father.

"Don't tell me you will. Just do it."

Roman starts to go past me toward the hotel, and I fall into step beside him. He stops. "What the hell do you want, Worthington?"

I look back at Amos apologetically. "If it's all right with you, Mr. Caldwell, I'd like to lend a hand."

He waves us both off. "Go. Take care of it."

Roman storms away, and I catch up with him. As soon as we step into the hotel, I smell the faint aroma of smoke. But the alarm has stopped. A couple of staff members go running by.

"I hope it's not too bad," I say.

Roman's practically snarling.

We go toward the kitchen. But as soon as we're in a deserted hallway, he lunges at me, barring his arm across my chest and pushing me into the wall. I let him do it. He's not going to murder me in the middle of the hotel with his father's precious investors within earshot. Even if he's probably dreaming about it.

"I have had enough of you," he whispers harshly.

"I gathered that from the two goons you sent to kill me last night. That didn't go so well. For them, anyway."

He pushes back from me, and I realize that there's something new in his face this morning. Uncertainty. He didn't expect me to survive last night, and he doesn't know what to do with the fact that I did. I suspect that few things have failed to go Roman's way in his life. He has a powerful father, plenty of money. He's used to stomping around, intimidating people and getting his way.

He didn't count on me.

"I don't know what you're talking about," he says.

"Sure you don't. But you can relax. I'm not going to say anything."

His chin jerks. "Like anybody would believe your word over mine."

"They'd believe two dead bodies. But it's better for us both if this stays quiet."

If Roman reveals that I killed Lars and Jimmy, he'll also be revealing that he set up the situation. Or at least let it happen on his watch. And we both know how Amos would feel about it. Not so much because Amos views me as irreplaceable, but because Amos wouldn't like that Roman had put the image of their family at risk in front of the investors.

I relax against the wall, sliding my hands casually into my pockets. "There's plenty of room for both of us here," I say. "I'm not trying to compete with you."

Roman snorts.

"No, I mean it. I'm happy to focus on Harper and SunSpeed. So you let me do my thing, and I'll stay out of your way so you can do yours. If Caldwell Enterprises prospers under your father, everybody wins."

Roman looks at me for a long moment, pondering. Considering my offer.

Then he reluctantly gives me a single nod. "Fine."

He starts to walk away, and I think that's all he's going to say. He really should be getting to the kitchen to investigate that fire alarm. Roman needs to step up before he pisses off his father any further.

More importantly, my phone just buzzed in my pocket, which likely means Harper finished whatever she was doing. I check the notification lightning-quick. *We're out*, Harper just texted.

But Roman spins around, unable to resist having the last word. "You think you know what's what around here, but I can assure you, you don't. If you want to try navigating this family, go ahead. I'll be waiting and laughing when you drown."

He pivots on his heel and storms away.

26

Harper

There's a knock at the hotel room door. I confirm through the peephole that it's Jake, and then I open up. He slips inside. Mia waves from the chair she's sitting in.

"Was your mission successful?" Jake asks.

"We found her. She's close." I can't keep the excitement out of my voice. Grinning, Jake hugs me and swings me around, setting me down with a quick kiss to my lips.

"Now we just have to make contact," he says.

"Wait, I haven't even heard how you accomplished this." Jake slings an arm casually around my waist. "Were you two responsible for that fire alarm?"

I point at Mia. She doesn't bother to look guilty. "We needed a distraction. And the kitchen was only mildly singed. My father bought insurance for this event. It'll get paid for."

Jake looks at me like he's asking, *You sure this is who you want helping us?*

"Mia did a great job," I say.

She tips an invisible hat in my direction. "Thank you. Glad my skills are appreciated by someone around here."

"What about Roman?" I ask Jake. "How'd it go with him?"

"About as well as I could hope. But I ran into Amos too. He wants me at the pitch meeting this afternoon. To present with you."

I'm annoyed, even though I shouldn't care what my uncle thinks. "Because I need a man to make me look legitimate in front of the investors, and Dad won't be there?"

"Apparently, public opinion supports our engagement. He wants to keep those good vibes rolling."

"And you have a penis," I add dryly.

"Ah, you noticed."

"Don't take it personally, Harper," Mia says. "My father has never taken us girls seriously. Besides, it's sweet that the investors who were partying so hard with models and escorts last night are getting all romantic about you two. Not that I blame them. If you guys weren't together, I would totally ship you."

Jake grins smugly, and I roll my eyes. "Anyway, what else did Roman say?" I ask.

Jake sits on the bed. "He denied sending Jimmy and Lars to kill us, but he obviously doesn't want anyone to know what happened. We've mutually agreed to keep it quiet."

"Until the bodies start to stink?" Mia asks.

My stomach twists. I appreciate bluntness, but Mia takes it to extremes.

"Pretty much," Jake agrees, unfazed. "But we intend to be out of here before then."

Mia stretches her arms over her head. "I guarantee my brother's hatching his next plot as we speak. Hopefully it'll take him more than a day."

"Then we'd better get to Wren." I pace across the carpet. "Mia, what's our best way of approaching the cottage where Wren is staying?"

She taps a finger against her lip. "Here's a thought. Why don't you just march up to the door and knock on it?"

"But you can't hold somebody prisoner without a prison guard. They'll try to stop us."

"Then just say you're there to see your sister. My father is high on you both right now. He thinks you're in his pocket, so he'll let you get away with it. Ask forgiveness rather than permission." Mia shrugs. "You're a Caldwell, Harper. Maybe you should act the part."

I don't like that sentiment, but she's got a point.

Jake folds his arms below his chest, accentuating the muscles. "I like her plan."

I nod. It's the kind of brazen that just might work. "It's worth a try."

Jake claps his hands together. "Then we'd better get moving. Roman's busy here at the hotel. Amos told me we should enjoy ourselves today. Let's get out there and take him up on it."

Mia offers to stay at the hotel. She's going to keep an eye on my dad and will text Jake's burner if anything comes up. Unfortunately, our video surveillance controller isn't working anymore. I'm guessing Roman realized we had it and deactivated it remotely. So much for that advantage. But we got good use out of it while it lasted.

On our way out, we swing by the lunch spread. Jake's practically superhuman, but does need some fuel. I manage to get down a tomato and a piece of cheese. I'll need a hamburger and fries once this is over and I can stomach food again.

Within half an hour, Jake and I set out for Wren's cottage.

I'm practically vibrating with the need to see her. If she's hurt in any way, I'm going to make sure somebody pays for it. Probably Tristan. I'm still not so sure about my warrior skills, but I don't mind the reassuring pressure of my knife holster around my thigh.

But once I've hopefully confirmed that she's unharmed, I'm going to tell Wren our plan. We don't know yet how we'll get her to the extraction point, but I expect she'll have some ideas for that.

The hardest part will be leaving her while Jake and I take care of the investor meeting. But before dinner tonight, we intend to slip away and get the hell out of here.

Tristan is now the biggest obstacle in our way.

I've never felt like I knew Tristan well. He's about ten years older than me. When we were younger, he seemed aloof, too mature and interested in the adults to play around with us kids. After I left West Oaks and returned to Chicago, Tristan wasn't even in my sphere anymore.

But he was at Uncle Amos's right hand. Making his deals and serving his father with a cold expression and ruthless efficiency.

We'd all assumed that Tristan would someday take the reins. If something happened to Amos, it certainly wasn't going to be my father who became the patriarch.

Yet I never felt any particular threat from Tristan either. He was never cruel to me or Wren. It was more that we were beneath his notice.

So why on earth is he paying so much attention to my sister now? Is it simply that she's the bargaining chip that keeps me and my dad in line?

But if that's true, couldn't Roman have handled Wren? Why would Tristan take the time to go see her personally? And why was Roman following him that night?

I hold tight to Jake's hand as these thoughts swirl through

my mind. I'm afraid of what will happen when we get to the cottage door. What state Wren will be in.

And an even deeper fear. Will she be happy to see me? Will she blame me for whatever's going on? For her months of being held at the mercy of Amos and his sons?

The golf course is far behind us. The villas are out of sight. I can't even hear the crash of the ocean waves anymore. We're on the landlocked side of the property, way out in the boonies now. Here, the trees are thicker. The grass grows taller, wilder, not so carefully tended by the hotel's gardeners.

My heart thumps and my breath catches when I see the cottage up ahead.

Then Jake's hand tightens on mine. "Harper," he says sharply.

I hear the engines before I see them. An SUV is barreling toward us along the road that curves toward the cottage. Jake curses. He tugs me back in the other direction.

But there's another SUV, crossing right through the field of grass.

Two massive guys with military haircuts jump out. Both hold submachine guns. These aren't Roman's guards. These guys look a hell of a lot scarier and more proficient. Even worse than Lars.

Jake wraps his arm around me and pulls me close. He draws his gun.

Then Tristan steps out of the passenger side of the first SUV. His voice rings out. "Worthington, put the gun down. I'm only going to ask once."

"Do it," I whisper.

Another guard has joined Tristan, which puts three guys and three automatic weapons against Jake and his gun. I have a lot of faith in Jake's abilities, but this? We haven't got a chance. And I think Jake knows it too.

After a half second's hesitation, he lowers his gun to the ground. We both put our hands up.

The guards pull Jake and me apart, pat me down. One finds the knife strapped beneath my shorts and hands it to Tristan.

My cousin arches an eyebrow. "I've always known you were unpredictable, Harper. But this is something else."

My pulse is running wild. Jake's eyes find mine. Two of the guards hold weapons on him, but give him a wide berth. A muscle twitches in his jaw.

I only have one shred of hope, and that's to stick to the plan we made earlier. A plan that now seems ridiculous.

"I'm here to see Wren," I say defiantly. "I *demand* that you take me to her."

Tristan is still turning my knife over in his hands. "Should I be concerned about what you intend to do when you see her? You did bring weapons."

"Screw you, Tristan. You're the one who's holding her captive. I want to see her, right now, and she'd better be okay."

His icy gaze holds mine for another moment.

And then he actually grins.

"She'll be happy to see you. I'm here to escort you, nothing else. But with everything that's happening, I had to take some precautions."

"Everything that's happening? Do you mean kidnapping Wren? Or this investor meeting? Or just the general shit that our family gets up to?"

Tristan laughs. And then, to the surprise of everyone, me most of all, he hands me the knife, handle first.

"Why don't you come inside and talk to your sister," he says. "Then you can decide for yourself."

My mouth hangs open for a second. Then I recover. I

replace my knife in the holster. "I want Jake to come with me. And those assholes had better stop pointing guns at us."

Tristan signals, and the guards back off. "Fair enough. I'm sure Wren can't wait to meet your fiancé."

I can't tell if there's a hint of sarcasm in his tone or not.

Tristan gestures for me to go first, so I go up the steps to the front door of the cottage. The door opens as if on command. A fourth bodyguard opens the door and steps aside for us to come in.

We're in a cozy entryway. There are wood floors and hand-woven rugs. Old-fashioned landscape prints hang on the walls. This place looks like somebody's grandma's house. It has the feeling of a home that's been here a long time, probably before the resort was built.

I don't know if the hotel owns it, or if Tristan somehow commandeered it another way. But if I was imagining Wren in a dungeon, this certainly doesn't match that image.

A staircase with a spindly banister leads to the second floor.

Jake and Tristan come in behind me. "Wren is upstairs," Tristan says. "You can go on up." As if this is just a casual visit.

Jake crowds in right behind me. He leans forward to speak quietly in a murmur.

"Why don't you talk to Wren by yourself first? It might be a shock for her to see you. Tell her about me, and I can come when you're both ready."

I glance over my shoulder at him. He's got one of those intense Jake looks. The ones that say a lot more through his eyes than he's saying out loud.

He's thinking about the fact that Wren will recognize him. And if she blurts something where Tristan or a guard can hear it, it could be a serious problem. I should have realized that myself.

It's hard to imagine my sister doing anything that would put me in danger. She was always far more reckless with her own safety than with anyone else's. But Jake's right. I have no idea what state she'll be in. I can't make any assumptions.

I nod. "I'll call for you in a little while."

He reaches for my hand and squeezes it.

On my way up, I twist the diamond ring around and around on my finger. My stomach is doing the same thing inside of me.

There's a small landing at the top and a single door. I stop in front of it, unable to move, as if some part of me is afraid to find out what's behind it. But I've come this far.

I reach out and knock.

Wren's voice answers. "Come in."

I have a terrible flash of déjà vu. The hallway last night, hearing Wren's voice calling out to me, just before Jake and I were attacked.

But I force myself forward. I grip the doorknob, turn it, and step inside.

And there she is.

Thick wavy hair, more slender than me, her skin a deeper tan. Wren jumps up, smiling. Runs to me and hugs me.

"Oh my God, Harper. It's so good to see you."

I return her embrace, then hold her at arm's length to look at her. She looks better than I would've expected. Wren has always been beautiful in a waif-like, fragile kind of way. But she's filled out and healthy. Downright glowing.

At first, we're talking over each other. So many questions are flooding out of me. Where has she been all these months? Have they been treating her okay?

"I'm fine," she says. "I'm really well."

"You realize Uncle Amos has been threatening you?"

She grimaces. "I know that now. I'm sorry. But you shouldn't have worried."

"Are you *kidding*?" I swipe at my eyes. "You've been missing for months!"

"I can explain. Okay? Just sit down."

She's comforting *me*. As if I'm the one who's been kept prisoner and not her.

She takes me over to the little couch where she was sitting. There's an iPad with a TV show paused on it. I look around, wondering if they're listening to us. Watching us with cameras.

"Can they hear what we say?" I whisper.

Wren smiles, her lips closed. "It's not like that. It's not like anything you're thinking."

"Then what? Because I feel like I'm losing it. I had no idea what they were doing to you. And now…"

Wren holds my hands, her eyes bright. "I want to hear about you first. Tristan said you're engaged?" She looks down at my fingers and gasps. "Your ring is beautiful. Tell me about him. Tell me *everything*."

I can't get my brain to work. "He's great. Wonderful. But there are other things we need to discuss."

Wren plows right over me with another excited question. "And Dad? How is he?"

Maybe this subject will break through her cheerful attitude. Because she's freaking me out. "Dad isn't well. He's sick. *Really* sick. He didn't want to tell me for a long time. But I think it's the stress of being a Caldwell. It's been eating away at him for most of his life. Same thing it's doing to us all. Destroying us inside out."

Her face falls. "I wish I could see him."

"You will. Soon." I drop my voice to a whisper, just in case someone's listening at the door. "We're all going to leave with Jake. My fiancé."

Her grin returns. "Jake? Like that boy who lived across

the street from us in West Oaks? Of course you'd end up with a guy named Jake."

"Wren, *listen*. The four of us are leaving. *Tonight*."

Now Wren is the one who's confused. "What are you talking about?"

"That's why I came. To rescue you. I'm going to get you out of here."

27

Jake

I watch Harper go upstairs. The door at the top opens. She walks inside. The door closes again, and animated voices trail down from above, but Harper hasn't stormed out of there yet. I guess that's a good sign.

I want to know what's going on up there.

Tristan didn't seem too fazed by Harper's and my appearance here. As if he expected it. While he took my gun and hasn't returned it, he let Harper keep her knife and let us both keep our phones. Tristan dismissed the security guard with a wave of his hand, which means he and I are alone. But he's not bothering to hold a weapon on me.

Is that because his personal guards are nearby? They aren't from Roman's crew, by the way. These guys are commandos. Everything about them conveys that they don't mess around.

Or does Tristan simply not see me as a threat? Aside from the dramatic interception before we reached the cottage, Tristan has treated us with courtesy. As if we're guests.

My burner phone vibrates. I take it out of my pocket and see a text.

Mia: Mason is resting comfortably. Nothing interesting happening here. You and Harper having fun?
Me: So far.

"How is my sister doing?" Tristan asks.

I make the mistake of reacting, and Tristan smiles. I've just confirmed who I'm texting with.

"I know Mia's been palling around with Harper," he says. "I think it's good. Mia gets into trouble when she's bored."

"So you spy on her?"

"I watch out for her. And I keep tabs on Roman. Our father made him head of security to give him something important to do, but I prefer to handle things myself. What can I say? I'm a control freak."

"Then we have that much in common."

He looks away, a small smile on his lips. All smug and enigmatic. I'm not sure how to take it.

I lean against the wall and cross my arms, studying him. Today is the first time I've spoken to the guy since the day I arrived, and all I know about him comes from what Harper's told me. His clothes are upscale business casual, crisp with starch and expensive fabrics.

How much does he know about what's happened the past couple of days? What the heck is this guy's deal?

"It's rude to stare." He's examining his fingernails. "Some people might take it as an insult. If you want to ask something, do it."

"I'm just wondering what's going on here."

He shifts his weight, penny loafers squeaking. "Yet you're so eager to join our family. Here I was assuming you knew more than you let on."

That smells like a trap, so I stay quiet. Luckily, Tristan decides to keep talking on his own. "You've butted heads with my brother. That alone predisposes me to like you."

"If that's all it takes to get on your good side, then I'm set. I guarantee I'm the top of Roman's most-hated list."

"Then you'd be wrong. Because there's nobody Roman hates more than me."

I don't like the way Tristan talks around things, like he's testing me. He and Roman might not get along, but they both play mind games. "Why don't we quit the banter and just say what we mean. Have you been keeping Wren a prisoner to put pressure on Harper and her father? Yes or no."

"No," he says. Not a trace of deception.

"Then what's she doing here? Why has she been missing? Why hasn't Harper been allowed to talk to her?"

"I can answer those questions. But first, I want to know more about you." Tristan walks slowly to one side of the room. I mirror his movements, maintaining the same distance between us. "How involved are you in SunSpeed's business?"

"I'm a client. But I see the opportunity. Harper and Mason have worked hard to develop the business, and I know I can make them even more successful. Especially since Mason's health isn't good."

Translation: I'm happy to take control of my future wife's business and treat it as my own.

Tristan seems to like this answer. "And I assume you're aware of the nature of my family's business? The product Caldwell Enterprises distributes and how we're going to expand our operation using SunSpeed?"

I incline my head. *Yes, we understand each other. Get to the point.*

"Then you'd be interested to know that my father doesn't run Caldwell Enterprises. *I* do. Much like Harper is the real force behind SunSpeed. But like you, I see the opportunity to grow."

"Which means?" I ask.

Tristan shifts his position again, his back to the stairs, which blocks my access to Harper. Coincidence, I'm sure. "It means that I believe the Caldwell family needs a change in leadership sooner than expected. I was planning to speak to Harper about it as soon as the investor meeting was over. She's pushed that timeline forward by showing up here, but my proposal could be advantageous to us all."

"I'm listening."

"At the moment, Caldwell pays SunSpeed a percentage. Under my leadership, I'd make that number more generous." Tristan dives into a detailed discussion of profit margins and tables of increasing rates. I keep an interested, closed-mouth smile on my face. Like this is an intriguing business proposition. Like he's not discussing the distribution of drugs that kill people every single day.

But my inner DEA agent is far more than curious. I'm salivating for these details. He's giving me an insider look into the Caldwell crime ring. And this is just the prospectus, the general contours of an organization that he's offering to bring me into as a key player.

Agent Reyes would go wild for this. We've never had anyone placed this strategically within the Caldwells.

I came here to gather information on the investors, but what Tristan is promising me? It's the kind of access that would let me dismantle their entire operation from the inside out. And it could happen fast. No tedious flipping of one small piece after another. No, I'd go straight to the top. Help Tristan take control and then take him down.

Then I realize what I'm contemplating. If I keep playing Jake Worthington, Harper has to stay inside the organization too. I'd be forcing her to stay in a life that she hates. That she's desperate to escape.

But...that would mean I'd get to spend a lot more time with her, too.

And I *want* that. So much that the longing for her bounces around in my empty places, and I can hear the echoes. It's a crazy thought that couldn't possibly work. Right? Weeks or even longer undercover, with Harper by my side?

"Something bothering you?" Tristan asks.

Shit. This is why I should've stayed objective about Harper. I'm torn in two different directions, and that conflict is bleeding through the carefully constructed persona I'm supposed to be portraying.

I need to fix this. *Fast.*

"Just amazed by the possibilities. I can't believe Harper and Mason have been leaving so much money on the table."

"I'm glad you see what I'm getting at." He holds out his hand. "It sounds like you're up for working together? Can I count on you?"

Take down the Caldwells while getting to enjoy Harper at the same time?

Or save Harper now, tonight? Get her out before this family can shatter her any further? And then return to my own family and my regular life, where I belong. Without her.

I accept Tristan's hand. "Absolutely." But really, nothing's changed. Forget what Agent Reyes might prefer or what secret longings I might harbor.

Harper wants freedom. That's what I'll give her. Even if that includes setting her free from my selfish desires for more.

28

Harper

"*L*eave?"

Wren says this gently, as if I'm unstable and she's afraid of provoking me. "Where are you planning to go?"

I grasp her hands and cast another glance at the door. I keep having that nagging feeling that someone's listening. But this is the very risk that I came here to take.

"It doesn't matter where we go, as long as we're away from all of this," I whisper. "Amos and Tristan and Roman. Caldwell Enterprises. I've figured out a way for us to escape. For *good*."

A hundred different thoughts and emotions pass through Wren's face. Awe and confusion and fear and elation. So much that I can't keep track of it.

"How?"

"You asked about my fiancé. He's going to help us."

"You can trust him?"

"Yes. Completely. He's...someone special." I take a breath. "Someone you already know."

A smile teases her lips. "Really? Who? You sound happy."

I shake my head. She still doesn't get it. "I'm not really engaged to him. Our relationship is fake. It was a way to get him in here."

Her brow creases. "Who is he? Harper, what's going on?"

"He's Jake Shelborne."

At first, she doesn't recognize the name. But then she laughs. "Our *neighbor*? Your friend from high school? Are you kidding?"

"Not in the least. But you need to keep your voice down. Nobody can know."

"Okay, but *why*? Why is Jake Shelborne suddenly back in your life? Why is he pretending to be engaged to you? And why did you recruit him to help with this escape idea of yours?"

I whisper the next sentence so quietly she's reading my lips more than hearing it. "He works for the government. The DEA."

She sits back, letting go of my hands. "No. No way." Now it's Wren sending panicked glances at the door. "Harper, what are you *thinking*? What have you done? If anybody finds out—"

"They won't. Dad knows, but everyone else here thinks his name is Jake Worthington and that he's a SunSpeed client. Jake is going to get us out of here tonight. The feds will come and pick us up at a set location. As long as you can make it there."

"This is crazy. You're going to get yourself killed. I won't be a part of it." She gets up, turning away from me, and I grab for her hand.

"This is the only plan we've got."

She wrenches herself out of my grasp. "*No*," she shouts.

We both freeze. I wonder if someone's going to come running. But nobody does.

Wren advances on me, fury in her features. "You have no

idea what I've had to do the past few months. What I've gone through."

"You said they didn't hurt you."

"They didn't. Not exactly. But Harper... God." She sinks onto the couch, burying her face in her hands.

Tears sting my eyes. "What happened?" I ask. "Really?"

She's curling in on herself. Not looking at me. She holds her hand over her mouth for a solid minute. Then she speaks. "You remember I got into some trouble after college?"

"Yes."

Wren had a habit of getting involved with worthless men, drinking too much. In the past, I stepped in, told the loser boyfriends to get lost. Let her stay with me until she was back on her feet.

"About six months ago, things got bad again. My ex had spent all my money, and then some. There was no way I could pay it all back. What we owed."

"Why didn't you come to me?"

"Because you'd done enough! It turned out my ex was taking out loans from our uncle. Amos showed up and offered to wipe my slate clean. I knew what kind of deal I was making, but I accepted it anyway."

"Even knowing what he did to you?" I ask.

This is as close as I'll come to mentioning her parents' murder. Wren hates to talk about that. Once I brought up the anniversary of their deaths, and she didn't speak to me for weeks.

She swallows, and I see all the pain and guilt that she's trying to hold back. "I had to. He paid for me to go to rehab to stop drinking. Gave me a place to stay. It took me a while to realize that he wasn't going to let me leave. He said my debt was personal now, and I still had to pay it back. He sent me on dates with potential business contacts, people he wanted to influence or blackmail, that kind of thing. It could've been worse."

I might be sick. "Did you have to sleep with these business contacts?"

"It never came to that."

I'm not sure I believe her. But Wren has always tried to hide her pain from me. "I'm sorry I wasn't there," I say.

"I'm not. It forced me to be strong. For the first time in my life, I found my own way. Not relying on you or Dad to save me." She lifts her head. "I found a way to save *myself*."

There's a knock at the door. "Wren?"

It's Tristan. Instantly, her face closes off. I want to know what she was about to say. What exactly has she had to do to save herself?

Wren, I want to demand, *what did you do?*

But I'm not going to get the chance right now. She strides across the sitting room and opens the door.

Tristan and Jake are both standing there. The men walk into the room. Tristan goes straight to Wren and kisses her on the cheek. Then his arm goes around her waist. "I hope we're not interrupting?"

"Not at all," she says.

I rarely get a flicker of emotion from Tristan. But when he looks at Wren, I see warmth and affection in his eyes. The unease in my stomach quadruples.

I understand all at once.

They're together.

This is how Wren found a way out of her situation. She got Tristan to fall in love with her. My father adopted Wren as my sister, but technically she's not related to Tristan by blood.

He'd better be treating her well. If she even hints that he's not perfect to her, I'm going to rip his balls off.

"Harper," Tristan says, "didn't you want to introduce your fiancé?"

"Um." I'm still trying to process what I've learned. Then the picture gets even worse. Wren gently touches her stomach, and though she's not showing yet, I feel the truth in my bones.

She's pregnant.

I'm just standing there, choking on this knowledge. Jake comes to my rescue, as usual. He goes towards Wren and holds out his hand.

"Jake Worthington. Pleasure to meet Harper's sister."

I've messed up, haven't I? No wonder Wren got so upset at me. Tristan is her boyfriend. What's she going to say? Is she going to tell Tristan that this isn't Jake Worthington at all? Is she going to tell him everything I just confided in her? Just how badly have I fucked this up?

Wren accepts Jake's hand. "Harper's been telling me about you. What a love story." There's no sign of recognition in her tone. Nothing to betray that she knew him before.

I'm getting lightheaded. I stumble backward and have to sit on the couch. It's either that or end up on the floor. This is just too much.

Jake races over to me. "Harper?"

"I'm okay, just... Could I speak to Wren alone please?"

Tristan will probably think I'm upset about his relationship with Wren. Which is true. Hopefully that excuses my behavior.

"Alright," Tristan says. "We'll meet you downstairs. You'll need to be going soon. If you're gone too long, Roman's going to get nosy. He bothers me enough as it is."

Tristan heads to the door. Jake is more reluctant, hovering at my side, but I nod at him.

Then I'm alone with Wren once again. But nothing is the same.

Wren is Tristan's...what, girlfriend? Lover? *Wife*? Yet she didn't reveal Jake's identity.

What am I supposed to do with all of this?

She sits down beside me on the couch. "That's what I was trying to tell you," she murmurs.

"You made Tristan your protector."

"Amos wasn't happy about it, but once he found out I was pregnant and confirmed paternity, he relinquished any claim on me. Tristan is the eldest, and Amos has complete faith in him. Roman doesn't trust us, though. He thinks Tristan and I are plotting against him and Amos. Because we are."

"Roman was following his brother the other night."

"Roman knows where I am, but he can't touch me. He's been trying to find evidence of Tristan's betrayal to take to their father. But Tristan has been careful. He's been biding his time until he can take over Caldwell Enterprises and cut out Amos and Roman both."

Her smile is cruel. Not like my sister at all.

"And I won't cry to see Amos in the gutter," she says darkly. "You know that."

"But is this really the life you want for yourself? For your child?"

She flinches. "I'm surviving."

"But don't you want more than that?" I slide down from the couch and kneel in front of her. "Wren, please. Come with me."

"You don't have to fix everything for me."

"Then think of it as helping me. Because I can't leave here without you. I *won't*. Aside from Dad, and maybe Mia, you're the only family I have. You're my *sister*, in every way that counts. Stay with me. Please. Don't make me do this on my own."

Dad is dying. Mia will probably take the next flight to

some tropical paradise, or maybe the Peace Corps. Who knows?

And Jake? He's not mine, no matter how much I wish otherwise.

I need Wren. My sister.

"We can protect each other," I say.

All those different emotions are warring in her eyes again. But I force myself to wait. I'll wait all day here if I have to.

"Harper…"

"Please."

More silence.

Finally, she sighs. Her eyes fall closed. "Okay," she breathes. "You win. I'll go with you."

I hug her. *"Thank you."*

A single tear falls onto her cheek. "I'm doing this for you."

"I know. And I won't forget it."

ONE OF TRISTAN'S GUARDS DRIVES US BACK TO THE hotel, using the road that runs along the side of the resort property. He drops us off in front of the lobby. The moment that SUV turns around and we're by ourselves, I draw in a ragged breath.

Jake and I walk over to the fountain outside the lobby. The sound of the water will help mask our voices in case anyone's listening.

"What did she say?" Jake asks.

"Wren agreed to come with us tonight." I want to cry, I'm so relieved. Jake wraps me up in his arms. I tuck my head against his shoulder while I compose myself. But the rest of me is vibrating with pent-up energy.

"She's pregnant," I add, my voice muffled against his shirt.

Jake whistles. "Shit. Is the baby Tristan's?"

"Yep."

"I picked up on their connection, but not that."

"I doubt it was intentional." Jeez, at least I hope not. "She had to find a way to get away from my uncle. Amos was…" The words struggle to come out. "He was practically pimping her to his business contacts."

Jake's arms tighten around me. "No wonder Tristan looked like a good option by comparison. I'm sorry, Harper. It's despicable that she went through that."

And I wasn't there.

"How is Wren going to meet up with us?" Jake asks. "Did you talk to her about her security situation?"

I explain to Jake what Wren told me. Tristan's four guards take shifts at the cottage, but they have dinner every night at six. They bring Wren her food and don't bother her for another half hour at least while they eat downstairs.

"She thinks she can sneak away while they're distracted with dinner. She's planning to climb out a window on the first floor. She'll meet us at the villas, and from there we'll go to the extraction point together."

"It'll be daylight," Jake says. "We'll have to move fast, and it'll be dangerous. Especially if Tristan or his guards have realized Wren is gone. We'll have an extremely small window in which to move."

"I realize that. But Tristan doesn't keep her locked up. She said the guards are more for her protection than to keep her there."

"You're positive she doesn't feel conflicted about leaving him? Because if you have any doubts about Wren's loyalty…"

"*No*," I say emphatically. "She could've told Tristan who you really were when she saw you. But she didn't."

Jake runs his hand down my arm. "I'm not trying to upset you. I'm just nervous. I can't let anything happen to you."

"Then don't."

Besides, what else can I do? This whole time, I've had few options. All I can do now is follow through on what we've planned and let this play out until it's over.

But after today, I'll be with her. Somehow, we'll build a better life together. And I'll be an aunt. I'm still getting over the shock of that, yet it makes a new kind of hopefulness bubble up inside me.

A baby. A child we can raise away from this twisted family of ours.

I'm going to give Wren's child the fresh start that we almost had when we lived in West Oaks. Maybe I can find us a home near the water somewhere. Maybe not California, but Florida could be good. Or even New England, since I'm no stranger to harsh winters after my time in Chicago.

There's that disappointed twinge in my heart at knowing Jake won't be in my life. But I'll have a family of my own to care for. It's funny how the prospect of a child makes everything crystallize. All my preparations, the courage that I've had to gather drop by drop over the years—it all comes together in this moment. For this purpose.

"We'll be free of them," I say. "We'll live our own lives, and we'll finally be happy."

I wait for Jake to accuse me again of living in a fantasy. But he doesn't. He looks at me another long moment, softly kisses my temple, and says, "Then let's get ready."

WHEN WE REACH MY FATHER'S HOTEL ROOM, JAKE stops and checks his watch. "Two hours until the investor meeting. How do you want to spend it?"

"I know how I *wish* we could spend it," I murmur.

I could use some stress relief, and I'm already well acquainted with Jake's skills in that area. We could spend the next couple hours horizontal, getting lost in one another the way we did last night. I'd love to have my mouth on Jake again. To feel that moment when he loses control. I crave his weight on top of me, his body enveloping me and commanding me not to think about anything but him.

But that's what I tried to do that long ago afternoon fourteen years ago when I kissed Jake, undressed him, begged him in not so many words to help me forget the truth about my life. Even though it was the cruelest way of saying goodbye.

At least now, we both know the score. I'm not keeping anything from him. But getting naked with Jake won't change anything.

"I should check on my dad," I say.

Jake touches my cheek, longing clearly written across his face. "Good idea. And I need to call my friend. Make sure he knows what's coming."

He means Agent Reyes and the task force.

I lean in and whisper, "Where can you make the call?"

"I need to get my suitcase. I'll make the call in our original room. It's as good a place as any since they won't be listening. But I have no doubt Roman's keeping an eye on us, and maybe Tristan is too, so there's no hiding anymore. You'll be with your dad?"

"Yeah." I go onto my tiptoes and steal another kiss. "See you soon."

Jake heads down the hall, and I knock on my father's door.

"It's open," Dad says.

I find him and Mia bent over his small table playing cards.

Gin rummy, by the looks of it. My dad has old school tendencies like that.

"Want to play the winner?" Mia asks. "Your Pops is kicking my ass. We're killing time."

"Sure, why not?"

I sit on the bed, and Mia turns to me. "Okay, I'm trying to be low key and all, but could you fill us in? How'd it go with…you know…"

I think of what Jake said. That there's no hiding anymore. Of course, we can't say the wrong thing in front of the wrong person. But we'll be making our escape in just a few hours. Mia and my dad need to know what to do.

"Wren's coming with us. It's all settled."

My dad's shoulders slump as he exhales. Mia's fingers are tapping against the table top. "Shit. So that's it, then? We're doing this?"

"Yep. Wren's going to meet us just after six. We'll slip away after the investor meeting and just before dinner is supposed to begin in the ballroom. But we can't pack anything. We can't let anyone know that we're planning to leave."

Mia shrugs. "You got it. Where's your boy toy?"

My dad's face turns red as he makes a show of studying his cards.

"Jake's confirming things with his friends."

"Friends," she repeats, one eyebrow arching toward her hairline. "And where do these friends fit in? Where are they from?"

Mia still doesn't know that Jake is a federal agent, and I don't see the need to spell it out. She can think what she wants.

"They're the kind with resources. Who can send a boat and reinforcements to pick us up on short notice."

She holds my stare for a long beat. Then another. "Are we talking government resources?"

"Would that be a problem?"

"Not necessarily. But it would explain a few things." She sets her cards face-down. "If you trust Jake, then I will too."

"We'll all have to trust one another." I slide another chair in next to my dad and put my arm around him. "If we do, we'll make it through."

Mia nods, but she doesn't smile.

29

Jake

*L*aughter greets me as I walk down the hall toward Mason's room. I find the door cracked like they left it open for me.

Harper looks carefree and happy as she lays her hand of cards on the table. Mia's perched on the edge of the bed nearby, smiling.

"Gin," Harper says, and her dad groans.

"I never should've taught you."

"That was your mistake."

There's a brief moment when I absorb the good vibes they're giving off. I want Harper to be happy like this all the time. For nothing to ever bring her down.

But too quickly, their expressions sober as they look at me.

I nod at the phone in my hand, then stick it in my pocket. "Everything's in place. How about you three? Good to go?"

The others share glances. "Yep," Mia says. Harper and Mason nod.

I think we're all bracing ourselves in our own way for what's coming.

"Did your phone call go okay?" Harper asks.

"As well as can be expected."

Agent Reyes was concerned about my sudden need to leave. I had to tell him about the two dead bodies in the pool outside the villas. There's going to be all kinds of paperwork to do about that, and I'm not looking forward to it.

But Reyes was even less thrilled to hear that Harper's cousin and sister would be joining us. *The more people, the more likely something's going to go wrong*, he said. But I didn't give him any leeway. I just told him exactly what I needed and was quick to get off the phone as soon as possible.

So that's out of the way. One step closer.

"We have another hour until the investor meeting," I say. "Didn't mean to interrupt."

Harper and her father go back to playing cards, but the mood is more sober. Mia sits with her legs crossed, her foot bobbing as she thinks. And Mason keeps sneaking looks at me, as if he's confirming again and again that I'm still here. That I'll do what I said yesterday when he shared the news about his diagnosis.

I hope you'll take care of her. Protect her.

I said I would, and I meant it. Maybe Mason still has doubts. I guess I'll just have to prove it to him.

I watch Harper play cards, her hair falling across her cheek. My plans for this afternoon are already set, and all I can think about now is how much I'll miss her when this is over. After we're in government custody and safely away from here, my part will be finished. I won't be playing Harper's boyfriend anymore.

But I'll make sure she's okay and that the DEA does right by her. I'll make sure she gets the new beginning she's been hoping and dreaming of.

Even if that means I'll have to let her go.

Harper gathers up the cards and sets them aside. "I need

to change for the investor meeting. I'm supposed to get to the conference room a few minutes early to greet them when they arrive."

We confirm the next steps with Mia and Mason. Harper and I will leave from the pitch meeting and go straight to the villas while the other guests are prepping for dinner. Mason and Mia will meet us there, along with Wren. If all goes as I expect, we'll be at the extraction point by the time anyone, such as Roman or Tristan, realizes we're gone.

In our hotel room, Harper and I change quickly into business suits. She's wearing her knife under her skirt, and I've got my concealed holster. Our recording devices are stitched into the lapels of our blazers.

Harper opts for flats, since we'll need to hustle on our way to the meeting spot. She frowns at her belongings still filling out the closet. "My poor heels. I'm going to miss them."

All we're bringing is what we're carrying right now. Everything else will stay behind. "You can get more. Or not. Probably won't need heels as an art teacher."

She laughs slightly, though the humor doesn't lift the seriousness from her expression. "You're right." She takes a heavy breath, then blows it out.

I hold her by the shoulders. "You can do this."

"I can." She straightens my tie. "Let's go." Harper goes for the door, but I close my fingers around her wrist, stopping her.

"Wait."

She turns around, a look of confusion on her face. "What is it?"

I don't know yet what I'm going to say. Just that I need this moment. This might be one of the last chances I have to be alone with her. I made it fourteen years without that privilege, and now it's hard to imagine going back.

I pull Harper close to me, cradling her head as I tip her back for a tender kiss. I don't know the words to convey how important she is to me. No matter where the future takes us, I'll never forget what we've shared.

"I'm proud of you," I murmur against her lips. "Just wanted to make sure you knew."

She runs her fingers through my hair. "Jake…" Harper pulls me down for another kiss, and this time it's her turn to express things that are impossible to describe. "Thank you for what you've done."

"Don't thank me yet. Let's get through the next part."

"Do you think, when this is over… Will I be able to see you?"

I can't begin to answer that question. It depends on so many things. If I could, I'd bend reality to my will to make it conform to what I want. But the chances of that are slim.

"I hope so." That's the truth, and that's the best I can do.

On our way to the conference room, we pass the lobby bar, where Tristan is relaxing with the investors before the pitch meeting. He sees me and nods, lifting his glass. I tilt my head in acknowledgment. Roman's nowhere to be seen, probably because he prefers to spy on his brother while remaining out of sight. If Roman can stay focused on Tristan, so much the better for Harper and me.

In the conference room, a hotel staff member is setting out pitchers of water and snacks. There's a stack of pamphlets on SunSpeed waiting, and Harper flips through them.

"I requested a laptop for my presentation?" she asks.

"Yes, Miss Caldwell. It's on the podium."

"Thanks."

Tristan has already vetted the investors. They know what they're really getting into. While Harper's presentation will likely include tempting profit numbers, there won't be anything overtly incriminating. But who knows? Maybe we'll get lucky and our recording devices will snag something useful before we're on our way out of here. Agent Reyes might be less annoyed with me.

Business meetings, even ones about drug transport, aren't my usual scene when I'm undercover. My amped-up levels of adrenaline certainly don't match these surroundings.

Judging by the nervous way Harper keeps checking the pamphlets and the laptop, she's feeling the same levels of stress.

"Anything I should know for the presentation?" I ask.

"You're an expert bullshitter," Harper mutters. "I'm sure you can follow along. Besides, you're just here to make me look good."

I can't argue with that.

There's a clock on the wall on the opposite side of the room, and my eyes keep finding it as the minutes pass.

Just before the official start time, Amos strides into the room. "It looks like you've got everything prepped, Harper. Good. This is the moment we've all been waiting for, isn't it? The chance for you to shine."

Harper spins her diamond ring around and around on her finger. "I'll do my best not to disappoint you."

Her uncle's smile tightens. "I should hope so."

I see Harper's throat move as she swallows.

"I'm surprised Tristan hasn't arrived with the investors yet." Amos looks at his phone. "Is something holding them up?"

"Not that I know of," Harper says. "We passed them in the lobby bar a little while ago."

Amos grunts, conveying his annoyance.

I watch the second hand on the wall clock. With each passing moment, my unease grows.

Something's not right.

"Harper," I say, "maybe we should…"

The door bursts open, and Roman rushes in. "Dad! The security system just cut out. I can't get anything to work, and my team isn't answering my texts."

"Well, that's the least of our fucking worries," Amos hisses at him. He grabs the lapel of Roman's jacket. "Where the hell is your brother? Everyone should be here by now. The meeting should've started."

Harper slides her hand into mine and squeezes. I share a nervous glance with her. But Tristan and I are supposed to have a deal. He thinks I'm working with him, and that's the only thing that keeps me from charging for the door.

"Find Tristan and get him in here," Amos says to Roman. "*Now*."

"Not necessary, Dad. I'm here." Tristan pushes into the room with more people following behind him.

But these aren't the investors.

These are the four commandos that I saw with him at Wren's cottage earlier.

Amos is seething. "Where the hell are—"

"The investors aren't coming," Tristan says.

Harper looks at me with a panicked expression, but I shake my head. We can't freak out.

I rest my hand on her waist, subtly moving her so she's behind me, and wait to hear what Tristan says next.

"I want to know what the fuck is going on," Amos demands.

"So would I." Roman marches toward his brother. But one of the commandos steps forward and Roman stops in place.

Tristan holds up his hands. "Stay calm, and I'll be happy to explain. But if anyone makes a sudden movement, I'll have to have one of my men teach you a lesson. A lesson you might not be able to recover from."

Roman sneers at his brother. "Are you including me in

that? You fucked with the security system, didn't you? What have you been doing?"

Tristan's careful composure slips. "Shut your mouth, Roman. For once in your damn life."

Roman turns to their father. "Are you going to let him speak to us like this?"

Amos frowns at them both. "I want to hear what Tristan has to say. What's this about?"

"I was forced to send the investors away because I received some disturbing information. It seems we have an informant among us." Tristan turns, and his hard gaze lasers onto *me*. "I'm afraid your cover's blown, Worthington. Though that's not your real name, is it?"

Oh, *fuck*.

Panic is slightly more warranted now.

There are a variety of reactions around the room. Trembling from Harper, who grips my hand. Curses and shouts from Roman. And a silence so thick it's palpable from Amos.

But still, nobody has moved.

"He's an undercover agent sent by the DEA," Tristan says.

I huff. "That's absurd."

Wren told him. That's the only explanation. Harper's sister betrayed us. This is going to destroy Harper.

If she even manages to live through it, a cruel voice whispers in my head.

No, I won't even allow myself to think that. She'll make it through this because I'm going to make sure of it.

Any time I go under cover, I know this is a possibility. My cover has even been blown a time or two. I've always managed to find a way out of it.

"It's not true," Harper says sharply, but I just look at her and smile.

"There's been a mistake, but everything's going to be all right."

"Search him," Tristan says, lifting his chin in my direction.

I think about drawing my gun, but two giant guys with automatic weapons are approaching me. I'm not dumb enough to try firing on them now. All I can do is hope and strategize like mad to find some way out of this. For Harper and me both.

I put my hands slowly up. Then I add, "I'm armed, by the way. Lower back."

The first guard reaches beneath my jacket and pulls out my Sig Sauer.

"I *knew* something was up with that asshole." Roman is pacing the room like a caged tiger, practically spitting. "You see what I've been saying? He's a fucking narc. A *cop*."

"That's crazy." I'm busy coming up with stories to explain away the gun. A weapon alone doesn't prove I'm a cop.

Unfortunately, Tristan then goes a step further. "Strip search him."

Okay. This situation may have officially taken a turn for the worse.

Harper actually tries to put herself between me and Tristan's guard. "Uncle Amos, this is ridiculous. He's my fiancé. You can't treat him like this."

But the guard bats her aside like she's nothing more than a mosquito. Harper stumbles to the side, catching herself on the podium. The laptop falls and crashes onto the carpet.

Her uncle won't even look at her. "Do it," Amos says. "Search him."

Rough hands pull at my clothes. I try to help, but one commando orders me to stay still while another continues to hold a gun on me. They take off my blazer. My shirt. My pants. These guys are thorough. I'll give them that. Soon I'm standing in my skivvies and socks.

The first thug finds the recording device in my lapel and

rips open the seam. He tosses it onto a desk beside the stack of SunSpeed pamphlets.

Are they going to search Harper next? Will they find the bug that she's wearing?

The only person in the room who's loving this is Roman. "I knew it," he crows. "I fucking knew it. And it was *Harper* who brought him here." He points at her. "We should never have trusted her!"

"She didn't know," I say.

"You expect us to believe that?" Roman tries to get in my face, but a commando holds him back.

I look over at Harper. At her hazel eyes that are so full of terror and despair. She shakes her head.

No, she's saying to me. Don't you dare pull the hero card.

She should know me well enough now to realize what's coming.

"I've been lying to her," I say. "Harper had no idea. I'm sorry, darling. I wish it hadn't been necessary."

Tears streak down her face.

There's a terrible pause. Roman is seething, and Amos still looks unsure of what to think. But Tristan...

If Wren told him everything, she would've said Harper was in on it. That Harper wanted Wren to leave with them.

Tristan's sharp eyes pin me like a bug. Harper is completely at his mercy, and I can't do anything else to save her.

Not yet.

Then Tristan opens his mouth. "It's true. Harper had no idea." His eyes dart to his brother instead. "It was Roman who recruited Jake."

Roman actually laughs. "*Me*? Is this a joke? I sent Lars and Jimmy to kill that asswipe, and he offed them instead!"

Tristan smiles, and it's vicious enough to give even me a chill. "Lies. You arranged for Jake to kill Lars and Jimmy because they suspected you of working with the feds. They were going to report you to Dad."

"That's *crazy*."

Tristan lifts a finger, and two of his guards aim their weapons at Roman.

"Your turn, brother," Tristan says. "Search him."

They strip Roman to his underwear, like they did me. And to everyone's surprise, Roman's most of all, the guard produces another recording device.

Well, shit.

It's not one of mine. I have no idea where it came from. It might even be a bug that Roman planted somewhere in the hotel for regular security purposes. But I have no doubt that Tristan arranged for his guard to plant it on his brother.

I watch Tristan carefully, trying to puzzle this out, and the possible answers appear in my head. Because if I'd been in Tristan's place, I might've done the same thing.

Wren must have asked him to spare her sister. That's the only explanation. And Tristan decided to use the opportunity to destroy Roman instead. I've got to admire the move, actually. Even though it means I'm a dead man.

Because there's no way Amos and Tristan will let me leave this resort alive.

This is all part of some bigger plan of Tristan's. I'm sure he was telling me the truth earlier today about wanting to take over and get rid of his father. Who knows what else he has in store. I doubt I'll live long enough to see it.

But at least Harper will survive this.

It's Amos who finally speaks. *"Betrayer."*

Roman screams and protests that the recorder isn't his, while two thugs force him down on the ground.

Amos walks over, stands near his son's head, and spits on him. "My own blood. You disgust me."

"Dad, no!" Roman pleads. "It's him! Tristan is lying. He did this, and he's the one who's going to betray you!"

Amos grabs the submachine gun from one of Tristan's guards. He aims it at his younger son. I see the weight of his fingertip against the trigger. The whites of his bulging eyes. Gone is the smooth, charismatic patriarch. His face is a mask of uncontrolled rage.

Shit, I think. *He's going to murder Roman right in front of us.*

But he doesn't. Instead, Amos brings the butt of the weapon down on Roman's head, cutting off his son's pleading with a sharp blow. Roman's knocked out cold.

Which just leaves me.

Amos raises the weapon and walks toward me. I force myself to hold eye contact with him, ignoring the black circle of the gun's muzzle.

He presses it to my forehead.

"Uncle Amos, *no*," Harper cries. She tries to reach for me, but a guard keeps her back. "Please. *Please* don't hurt him."

"Dad," Tristan says. "It'll be easier to clean up if we do this elsewhere."

For nearly a minute, I don't breathe.

Then Amos lowers the gun. "Get this scum out of my sight. I'll deal with him and Roman later."

30

Harper

The guards drag Roman away and lead Jake through the door, his hands bound behind his back.

"Amos," I beg, *"please."*

He won't look at me. "Not another word." My uncle leaves the room. The guards are still holding me, and Tristan regards me with an unreadable expression.

No. This can't be happening. There's no way it can end like this.

I think of Jake's kids waiting for him to come home. If he gets hurt, if Jake—God, no, I can't even think it. My heart and soul rebel against it.

I *will not* let Jake die.

But when have I ever managed to save those I love? I tried with Wren. And look how that's turned out? I trusted her, and she chose Tristan over me. My heart wants to break, but I have to hold it together.

I lunge at my cousin while his men hold me back. These guys could be made of marble for all the emotion they're showing. They're like mercenary robots.

"What are you going to do with Jake?"

"He's a federal agent. What do you think we're going to do?"

"If you touch a hair on his head, I will blow *everything* up. I'll destroy you. I don't care what happens to me."

Tristan's smooth voice is far more sinister than Roman could ever be. "If you do that, I'll have to break my promise to your sister that I'd let you live. My father might not realize what you've done, but I do. You thought Wren would pick you over me? The father of her child?"

"You're toxic. Someday, Wren will see that."

"Don't misunderstand your position here, Harper. I'm granting you clemency. I hope you'll appreciate that for the gift that it is." He motions at his men. "Put her somewhere she won't cause trouble."

The guards lead me through the hotel. The hallways are deserted. I don't see any staff or guests, not even our extended family members, and doors stand ajar with suitcases half-packed. It's like everyone else has been evacuated. It must've happened fast.

I never should have brought Jake here. He should've followed his first instincts and walked away from me in Beverly Hills. Never looked back.

Are they hurting him right now? What about my dad and Mia? Where are they?

I'm so full of fury and agony that I can barely think. There's a freaking tornado in my brain.

But I cling to the few things I have left. Like the recording device underneath the lapel of my jacket. And the knife that's strapped to my thigh.

Why didn't Tristan search me? Does he not intend to let me leave, despite his promise? I don't know. But it's the tiniest hint that Tristan isn't all-knowing, all-seeing. He's not invincible. He thinks I can't hurt him. And that oversight is my advantage.

I'll get free and find Jake. I'll save him.

Somehow.

The guard marches me all the way back to a familiar hallway. It's my father's room. The guard unlocks the door and
pushes me in.

Mia and my dad are sitting on his bed, their heads
together, whispering intently. Mia jumps up the moment she
sees me and rushes over.

"Oh my God, Harper!"

"Jake. They've got him." I can't even get the words out.

We hug each other like we haven't seen each other in
years instead of just half an hour. "What's happened?" Mia
asks.

She pulls me further into the room, and we sit in a huddle
with my dad. He grabs for my hand and squeezes as hard as
he can, though that still isn't much. I'm worried about him.
It looks like he's barely hanging on.

But I have too many things to deal with right now. We all
need a way out of here. That's what I need to focus on.

"Tristan told your father that Jake is a federal agent. That
we've been working against the family and planned to betray
him."

Mia's curses are colorful enough to make a sailor blush.
Even my dad blanches, and he's lived his life around
mobsters.

"Was it Wren?" my father asks. "She did this?"

All I can do is nod.

Dad bows his head, a silent acknowledgment of the pain
we're both feeling. "You know what Amos will do to Jake."

"Of course I do," I say. "But Tristan claimed that *Roman*
recruited Jake, not me."

Mia's eyes go as wide as saucers. "So this is Tristan's big
move. He's going to get Roman killed."

"I'm sorry," I say. I know she's not fond of Roman, but

he's still her brother.

"I've been expecting something like this. And you know what? I'm done with these screwed-up people. Thank God you came along when you did, Harper. Because otherwise, I'd be all alone with this shit." She rubs her face.

"Me too," I say.

Except before, I thought I had Wren on my side.

But maybe that desire was selfish. I didn't want to be alone. I told myself I was saving my sister, but maybe I was just trying to save myself. Whatever the ugly truth behind my motives, it hardly matters now.

I've lost my sister for good.

Don't think about it, I tell myself. I can't afford to wallow in my broken heart.

"Tristan's guards took Jake and Roman somewhere," I say. "Tristan promised Wren he would give me clemency. I'm not sure if he suspects that the two of you were involved in this, but even if he did, I assume that he'll spare you too."

Mia waves her hand dismissively. "We're fine. A few minutes after you and Jake left for the investor meeting, things started to get wacky. We heard shouts, lots of foot-steps. I looked out into the hall and saw Roman's security team herding everybody out of their rooms and toward the exits. Barely even let people grab their stuff. They said it was an emergency, and we had to get out. All I could think of was trying to get to you and Jake and warn you, because I figured shit was going down. But then one of Roman's security guys grabbed us and shoved us back in here. Wouldn't let us out and wouldn't explain either."

"We were terrified," Dad says. "I thought for sure you'd been found out."

"Roman said he couldn't communicate with his security team," I tell them. "Tristan must've taken charge of them somehow." Perhaps his scary commandos waved their submachine guns around. "I don't know what Tristan plans to do with us, but I don't intend to sit here and wait around. I need to get to Jake. Before…"

Mia nods vigorously. "Hell, yeah. We're going to save him, right?"

My father nods as well.

"Do you realize what you're agreeing to?" They didn't see the look in Amos's eyes, or hear the thud when Amos brought the butt of that gun down on Roman's head. "Amos won't spare any of us. Not even you, Mia. And I doubt Tristan will step up to protect us if we defy him again, no matter what he promised to Wren. I'm the one who brought Jake here and got the DEA involved in the first place. I'm going to do whatever I can to help get Jake out of this, but you could accept Tristan's mercy and walk away."

I'm surprised by the strength in my dad's voice. "Absolutely not. Jake came here to help us. We're going to do the same for him in return. We owe him a hell of a lot more than he ever owed us."

Then we both look at Mia.

"Oh, me? I've been all-in this whole time. I didn't love the fact that Jake was a fed, but I'm coming to terms with it. We just need a plan. Sorry to say, that's never been where my talents lie. I'm devious, but you're going to have to play the general here. Give me some orders."

There's a knock at the door. I share a glance with Mia. I can't imagine our guard would be so polite. But at the moment, I can't discount anything.

"You both stay here," I say. "I'll see who it is." I walk over, my hand hovering near the bottom of my skirt. I'll grab my knife if I have to.

I peer through the peep hole. The face I see makes hurt and fury thicken in my throat.

It's Wren.

31

Jake

One of Tristan's beefy guards throws me into a featureless room. I land on my hands and knees, then jump right back up. "Where did you take Harper?"

My clothes sail in after me. "Get dressed, or I'll come in there and dress you myself." This commando has a scar across his eyebrow. "But you'll have to be unconscious first." He says this without any emotion whatsoever.

Okay, then. The guy isn't bluffing, and I'd much rather put my own clothes on, thank you very much.

I tug on my pants and undershirt. Could be worse. They could've left me here in my briefs. Or even naked.

Another guard drags in Roman a minute later. They've got him by the ankles, his head banging along the floor. That could've been me. So I manage to shut my mouth and slink into a corner, hoping to make myself uninteresting. It seems to work, because both thugs lumber out of the room and shut the door. I hear a lock twist.

They've left Roman and me in here together. I guess because they think we're co-conspirators. Or maybe Tristan is hoping that we'll kill each other and save him the trouble. For now, Roman is out cold.

I've had some ops go bad before. But never quite like this.

While I button my shirt, I strategize. First is a quick inventory of the room. Nothing I can lift or use as a weapon. The room is completely bare. No windows, no closets. There's a light overhead and the door to the hall. That's it. I'm guessing it's a storage space of some kind. There are indentations on the carpet like furniture was in here, but it got cleared out recently. I guess the resort didn't come with a prison cell, so Tristan had to improvise.

The guard didn't give me my belt. The guy even stripped the shoelaces from my shoes.

I glance over Roman as well, who's lying in his underwear with his own clothing balled on top of him. I pick up his shirt, then his jeans, but there's nothing useful here. Didn't think there would be, but I had to check.

So, now what?

I pace from one end of the small room to the other, my hands laced at the back of my neck.

I'm not dead yet. Which suggests there's something more that Tristan wants with me.

My only consolation is that Harper's safe. For whatever reason, Tristan protected her. I wonder if she could get word to the task force. But will Tristan give her free access to a phone? That's not damn likely. He's probably holding her somewhere, and I'll bet it's nicer than this makeshift cell, but there won't be any communications available.

What is Tristan plotting? He's got me here because he thinks he can use me. But for what?

I don't have to sit in suspense for long. The door opens, and the guard with the scarred eyebrow comes in, gun raised. "Stand back."

I retreat with my hands up. Tristan walks in, casually

lifting his jacket to show me he's armed. "Just in case you were thinking about doing anything foolish. I wouldn't recommend it."

"Maybe not, but from here it looks like I don't have anything to lose. Unless you're about to propose something else?"

He dismisses the guard and shuts the door, a curve at the corner of his mouth. "You catch on fast, Jake. I appreciate that. I'm less pleased that you're a fed and that I didn't realize it. But good on you. You had me fooled. I wasn't completely buying what you were selling, but I was still shocked when Wren told me who you really are."

I knew that Wren had to have snitched on us, but it's still hard to hear. "What about Harper? Where is she?"

"She won't be harmed. That's the promise I made to Wren, and I intend to keep it. You're a liar, but I get the impression that you didn't fake your feelings for Harper. So I think you can understand where I'm coming from. I'd rather not have to go back on my word and disappoint the woman I love."

"Sure. That's never a good look. How about this? You can let me go, and I'll escort Harper and her father out of here, and you'll never hear from them again. I'll tell the DEA I got nothing. That you were totally clean."

"A tempting offer. But unfortunately, I need to show my investors that I take security seriously. Both so that they have confidence in turning over their money to Caldwell Enterprises, and so that they don't consider stabbing us in the back."

"And what about Amos? You're still looking for a way to get rid of your father, I'm guessing."

Tristan's smile widens. "See, there's that cleverness I admire in you, Worthington. Sorry. I should say Shelborne.

It's too bad we couldn't have worked together, because I have the feeling it would've been a productive partnership."

"Peddling drugs so that desperate people can destroy themselves? Nah, that's not my idea of an attractive business proposition."

It feels really fucking good to be able to say that. One benefit to getting caught. No more having to pretend to be a lowlife like the rest of these assholes.

But I don't expect this opinion to faze Tristan, and it doesn't seem to. He tucks a hand into his pants pocket, looking thoughtful.

"Now, you're wondering what I intend to do with you. When Wren told me your real name, I looked you up. There's not much online about you. You aren't posting about your life all over social. But there are some things a good, law-abiding citizen like you can't hide. Like the fact that you have an ex-wife and two children."

My blood heats, and the primal rage in my veins goes from a simmer to a volcano. "Stay the hell away from my family," I growl.

He can taunt me all he wants, but Adrienne and the kids? That's crossing the line.

I take a step forward, and Tristan flashes his gun. "Careful."

With tremendous effort, I force myself back. My fists clench and unclench at my sides.

"I'm just reminding you that we have far more in common than our differences would suggest," Tristan says. "We have people in our lives that we want to protect."

"*And*?"

"And we're both killers."

That scalding heat continues to pump through my body. I don't say anything.

"I know you killed Lars and Jimmy. One of my men found

them in the pool outside the villas. It doesn't seem they gave you much trouble. In my experience, not all narcs are quite that efficient at killing. Where were you trained? Military?"

"You claim to have done your research. You didn't figure that out for yourself?"

He shrugs. "I didn't have as much time as I might like to speak with my contacts. I have friends in the government. People who give me information, do me favors in exchange for money. A lot of money. You could be one of them."

Is he forgetting I'm not Jake Worthington? He thinks he can buy me off? "I don't want your money."

"I assumed not, since you're settling for a public servant's salary. But what about the safety of your family?"

"If you go near them—"

"You won't be able to do a damn thing. Because you'll be dead. This is what I'm offering, and you can take it or leave it. Come to work for me and continue living your life as Jake Shelborne, DEA agent, but earning far more money on the side. Or, die today not knowing what I might do to Adrienne and Riley and Hudson. Or Madison. Your parents... You have a lot of people to lose."

I bite the inside of my cheek so hard I taste salt and metal. It takes every ounce of control inside me not to launch myself at him. Tear him limb from limb.

And Tristan knows it. He's got his hand on the butt of his gun.

"Think about it. You have an hour or two to decide." He spares a single glance for his brother, who's just now stirring on the ground. "This is better than the deal I'm offering my brother. Don't be an idiot, Shelborne. Take it. It would be a shame to see talents like yours go to waste."

He leaves the room, and the door slams to punctuate his exit.

Roman drags himself into a sitting position. "Was that my traitor brother? Get him back here. I'm going to kill him."

I lean against the opposite wall. "Something tells me that wouldn't go well."

Roman rubs his forehead, then winces when he touches the raised red lump that's there. Courtesy of his father. "Then I'll settle for killing you."

"You're welcome to try," I mutter. "But could you put some pants on first?" I look at the closed door instead of him. Roman curses and grabs his clothes.

32

Harper

"Wren." My voice sounds like broken glass being raked over asphalt. "How could you?"

She presses her lips together, eyes pleading. "Can I come in? I need to talk to you."

"Why do you bother to ask? You could just have one of your goons shove his gun in my face."

"It's not—" Wren glances behind her, not finishing her sentence. Then she walks inside the hotel room and shuts the door. "Mia. And *Dad*. It's so good to see you."

Wren starts toward him, but Dad flinches away from her. He hasn't seen her for months, but because of her, Jake's being held somewhere and won't live long unless we find him.

If my sister was hoping for a positive reception, she might've rethought some of her choices.

But I still can't manage to hate her. The anger just bleeds out of me as soon as it appears. Instead, all I feel is scooped out and empty.

How could she have done this? And how could I have been stupid enough not to see it coming?

"Why?" I whisper.

Wren takes a step toward me, and I move back an equal distance.

"I didn't see any other way. You were going to get yourself killed."

"So you decided to sacrifice Jake instead?" My voice breaks and burning tears fill my eyes. "He has children. He's your *friend,* and he only wanted to help you." Because *I asked.* He put himself at risk for *me.*

She looks stricken and tries to take my hands, but I pull away from her.

"Harper, listen. Tristan was going to catch on to what you were doing. You really think I could've gotten away without anyone noticing? It was impossible. But I know you. If I'd told you how things really are, you'd just dig in your heels and insist on saving me. So I decided I was going to *save you.*"

"But what about Jake?" I choke out. I scratch my nail into the skin at my hairline, wondering what Tristan could be doing to him even now. I can't stand it. Somehow, I convinced myself that Jake was invincible. That he could face any danger and come out unscathed. But I should've known better. I should've done *more.*

"I had to give Tristan something," Wren says. "Okay? I had to tell him the truth about Jake. But then I told him how he could use it to his advantage. Tristan's been looking for a way to make a move against Amos and Roman. This is the perfect opportunity. I bought your freedom in the process. The same with Dad and Mia. But do you really think I would let Jake die? I would never do that to him. Or to you."

I allow myself the tiniest sliver of hope. "Then what do you propose? Because Tristan has Jake with a bunch of armed guards around him, and Amos looked like he was one breath away from shooting Jake and Roman himself."

There's no possible way that Tristan will let Jake go free.

Not after finding out that he's with the DEA. And even if I tried to buy Jake's freedom—with what money, I don't know —I doubt that would be enough for Tristan either.

Wren glances behind her at the door and herds the rest of us to the opposite side of the room. "Here's what's going to happen. Tristan won't do anything to Roman or Jake here at the resort. He's planning to drive them out to the wildlife refuge south of town where it's more isolated. Easier to, you know…dump a body and make sure it's never found."

I gag and cover my mouth. There are miles of coastline in the refuge. I went there a few times with Jake when we were teenagers. And Wren is right. It's extremely isolated. If Tristan tried to get rid of Jake off a cliffside here, the DEA would be combing the shores looking for its agent. It would be too easy for them to connect the dots.

No, Tristan would be much smarter than that.

"But you're assuming that Uncle Amos won't decide to lash out and dispense judgment before then," I say.

"We're not going to let that happen. I know where Tristan is holding Jake. We can get to him and get him out of there. Then you can go to your meeting point and Jake's agency can come get you like you were planning before."

"And how the hell is that supposed to work? You must've told Tristan the rest of what we were planning. He'll head us off."

She shakes her head. "I didn't say you were leaving by the water. I said you were going on foot to the main road and a car would pick you up. I'll distract Tristan and his guards and then help you make your escape across the resort to the water."

Mia finally speaks up. "That's nice and subtle."

"Your mistake was thinking that you could ever go unnoticed," Wren says. "Tristan has missed plenty of things, but he knew that Roman had been following him around, and he knew that you were getting close to Harper, Mia. I know Tristan, and I know his team. The best way to move against them is to strike as hard as you can and get out fast."

This new scenario takes shape in my brain. We could activate the beacon and contact the DEA. Jake mentioned an emergency raft, so maybe we could get out on the water right away. The task force would hopefully respond within minutes. Maybe even with helicopters in the air and speedboats racing toward us. It sounds like an action movie, but the feds have deep pockets for things like that. Right?

But there's a far simpler solution.

"Why don't you just call up the DEA right now?" I ask. "We can't because Tristan took all of our phones, but if he trusts you so much, you must have yours. Call for someone to get us out of here."

My tone is harsh and accusatory. I'd be a fool to trust Wren after what she did. What if she's leading us into some new trap?

If she wants to help, why doesn't she use the most straightforward solution?

Then she tilts her head and gives me a *look*, and I feel like I'm staring into a mirror.

"If the police show up here and surround the resort, what do you think is going to happen?" Wren asks. "I told you this is the only way, and I meant it."

That's a decent point. I guess she's thought this through.

It seems my sister is all grown up. The last few months have changed her in ways I couldn't imagine. But maybe I've always seen her as that vulnerable teenager, the girl who had just lost her parents.

I'm not sure I can forgive her for the way she's handled this. Blowing Jake's cover, putting him in mortal danger. But can I understand her desperation? The realization she must've had that only the boldest move might be able to make a difference when you're facing impossible odds?

"And what about you?" our father asks her softly. "You expect us to leave you behind?"

She goes to sit down beside him. "I wish I could go with you. If we had more time…" Wren closes her eyes and shakes off that thought. We all know time is exactly what we don't have. "Dad, Harper told me you were sick. I'm so sorry. But this is my life now. I know it's hard to believe, but Tristan isn't so bad."

"The man who would murder your friend *isn't so bad*?" I spit out.

"Tristan is good to me. He's been useful. The world isn't black and white. You know that as well as anyone."

I bite my lip, holding back my response. Because I do know. As much as I hate it.

"Amos won't be in charge anymore," Wren says. "Tristan's men are going to turn on Amos at the wildlife refuge. He won't walk out of there alive, and all of you will be safe. That's worth it to me."

"And you'll go off with Tristan to live happily ever after at the head of Caldwell Enterprises?"

She shrugs. "Leave Tristan to me. He's my concern, not yours. I don't need you to look out for me anymore, Harper."

What else is there to say?

Wren and Dad sit hand-in-hand, talking quietly. These could be our last few minutes together. If we somehow make it out of this alive, by no means guaranteed given the shoddy plans we're working with, our father doesn't have long because of his diagnosis. And Wren will have taken her place beside Tristan at the head of the Caldwell family.

I'll probably never meet my niece or nephew. Never see my sister again.

Yet I can't bring myself to join their bittersweet moment.

I'm already too full of emotion. Any more and I'll spill over and everything I'm feeling will drown me.

I walk over to the window, and Mia comes over beside me. "If Wren's going to get us out of here, we need to move. We don't know how long we have before Tristan packs up Jake and leaves. Once they're gone?"

She doesn't need to say it. Jake will be as good as dead.

"Still sure you're up for this battle?" I ask.

Mia already knew that Roman was done for. Now, she's heard that Tristan will kill their father too. This can't be easy for her, no matter how much she says she's expected it.

She smiles ruefully. "I'm dealing. Same thing I've done for a long time. I try to get through my day and not think too much about the rest. And definitely not *feel* too much."

Exactly where I'm at. *Survive*. Get us through this. Exactly what Jake would do if he were here.

I have to get to him.

"Wren," I say, interrupting her conversation with our dad. "How will you cause a distraction?"

She waves us closer and drops her voice again to a whisper. "Thought I'd keep it simple. You have two guards outside your room. I'll scream and get them in here. We disarm them, take their weapons. That's two of Tristan's guys down and our path cleared out of here. The only other guards are outside the room where they've got Jake and Roman, and I can lead them away. As for Roman's security team, most of them have left with the other guests, and the remaining ones are packing up the SUVs."

I stare at her.

"Right. So simple. Except you just assume we can get the guns away from *two trained commandos* without getting shot first."

"At least there's four of us," Mia says, suddenly playing the optimist. "Only two of them."

Then a light seems to go on in my father's eyes. "Oh, I have this." He gets up and sticks his hand underneath his mattress. "Remember, Harper? You told me to hold on to this earlier." He pulls out the pistol I stole from Jimmy at the villas. "The guards didn't bother to search the room. They must've underestimated the sick guy. Which is fair, because I practically forgot I had this thing."

Dad holds the gun out to me.

Wow. This is a crack team I'm working with. A pregnant woman, my ailing father, my petite cousin, and me. The four of us against Tristan's mercenaries.

This is going to be *great*.

I check the barrel of the gun. It's still fully loaded. "They didn't search me either. I've got my knife. For whatever that's worth."

Mia scowls dramatically. "And I have my *very* intense glare."

"Then let's do this," I say. "Before we all realize how stupid it is."

~

THIS PLAN IS CRAZY. WE'RE ALL AWARE OF THAT fact. But the craziest part? It actually works.

Sort of.

We're all in position. I'm right behind the door with the pistol. Mia's hiding nearby with the knife. My dad is...staying out of the way.

I nod at Wren. *Go.*

She screams.

The first guy comes bursting through the door. "Miss Caldwell!" he shouts.

The moment he steps into the room, I push the barrel of

the pistol against his head. I don't get a word out before his elbow flies at me. I duck, almost dropping the pistol.

I don't know how Jake made this shit look so easy, because I am a mess.

But just as the second guard comes through the doorway, Mia lunges out from behind the dresser and stabs the first one in the leg. He shouts, arm flailing, and his gun goes off, spraying the wall with gunfire.

The second guard steps right into the path of the bullets.

Ugh. I turn away from the blood spatter. But that worked even better than we'd anticipated.

My dad runs out from his hiding spot in the bathroom. He and Mia jump on the first guard's back and manage to topple him like a tree. Dad grabs the submachine gun away. We both hold our weapons on the first guard while Mia uses Dad's belt to secure the guy's hands behind his back.

"This is not going to end well for you," Tristan's thug says.

But I don't have time to exchange action movie lines with this guy. We just need to get out of here. I raise the pistol and bring it down on the back of the guy's head, knocking him out.

Wren is crouching in the far corner.

"You okay?" I ask her, thinking of the baby.

"Fine." She gets up, leading the way to the door. "Come on. We need to hurry. Somebody will have heard those gunshots."

The halls of the hotel are just as deserted as they were before. Only a single guard comes running, one of Roman's team. He stops when he sees Wren and Mia. And he clearly has no clue what's going on.

"Is everything—"

I step out from behind them, raising the pistol.

The guy's hands fly up to surrender so fast, I can feel a breeze go through the hallway.

We get him into the nearest hotel room and tie his hands and feet with cords from the blinds. A pair of abandoned socks goes into his mouth as a gag.

We continue on, Wren leading the way, followed by me, with Dad and Mia bringing up the rear.

I've got a submachine gun in my arms, carefully pointed away from my sister. An extra handgun tucked into the pocket of my skirt. And my knife is back in its holster. I've never been so heavily armed in my life.

We take a shortcut through the abandoned kitchens. There are cutting boards full of half-chopped produce, pots of soup still simmering on the stove tops. As if the cooks were just here and fled. It's an eerie feeling, this hotel being so empty when it was busy just hours ago.

"Shouldn't there be more guards?" I ask. "Why aren't more of them coming for us?"

"I don't know," Wren murmurs. She carefully checks around a blind corner. "This way. Jake's in a storage room down here."

"*Wait.*" I touch Wren's shoulder. "I'll go first."

My sister frowns, but she lets me take the lead. I want to see exactly where we're going.

We enter a long hallway. This is where the security room is located, and I pass the *No Admittance* door. I've got the master keycard with me, another item Tristan failed to take away. I swipe it across the lock.

Then I twist the handle and point my gun inside. Nobody's here. All the camera feeds are dark.

We move on.

I hear Dad taking labored breaths. Aside from that, it's just the beating of my heart and the rushing in my ears. This place is way too quiet.

There are no guards here. *Nothing.*

Wren tugs my shirt. "It's around the next corner," she whispers. "End of the hall."

I press myself to the wall, doing my best super-spy impression. Then I dart out, my gun raised.

There's an open door. I run forward and find an empty room.

We're too late. Jake is already gone.

33

Jake

"Tristan!" Roman screams, banging on the closed door. "Let me out of here!"

"You've been at it for ten solid minutes," I say. I've got my arms crossed, leaning against the wall. "I don't think anyone's coming."

While I can understand his frustration, I don't see the point in wasting my energy on a tantrum. But that's Roman. He doesn't think carefully or bide his time.

Unsurprisingly, he snarls and comes at me. "Should I take my anger out on you, then? Since this is your fucking fault?"

I almost want him to do it. It would feel so good to split my knuckles against his face.

I lift a single finger, and that's enough to make him stop. "You want to try, go ahead. But has that gone well for you in the past?"

If Roman had a gun right now, he would pull the trigger on me without a second thought. *If* I didn't manage to disarm him first. But he doesn't. And self-preservation wins out.

"How did Tristan find out who you really are?" Roman asks.

"Bad luck." I'm not going to tell him all about Wren double-crossing her sister.

"But Harper knew. She had to."

"Why? I was sleeping with her. You know that for a fact. I made her believe what I wanted."

"I don't trust a damn thing you say."

I shrug. "That's irrelevant now. But it might be the smartest thing I've heard come out of your mouth."

Sneering, Roman goes back to banging on the door.

Finally, the door unlocks and pushes open. A gun points in at us. "Step away from the door."

Roman obeys, and the two guards from earlier come inside, including the guy with the scar on his eyebrow. "Where's Tristan?" Roman asks. "I want to talk to my brother."

"He's waiting." The guard with the scarred eyebrow throws us each a heavy-duty zip tie. "Put those on each other."

"No," Roman spits out.

"Other option is to die."

Grumbling, Roman puts a tie around my wrists, and I do him. He shoves me away from him as soon as I'm done.

Scarred Eyebrow gestures at me and Roman with his submachine gun. "Let's go. It's time."

"Where?" Roman asks.

"Don't you get it?" I mutter. "They're going to kill us."

Tristan's commandos don't even blink.

We enter the hallway, a guard on each of us. Roman is ahead of me, and he keeps slowing down.

"I'll double what Tristan is paying you. Triple."

No answer from the commandos. The guard on Roman prods his back to keep him moving.

"My father will figure out what Tristan's doing, and then

you'll all be dead meat. Every single one of you who helped my brother."

The guards ignore him.

Then Scarred Eyebrow, who's behind me, says, "Have you considered Tristan's offer?"

I remember something Harper said to me a long time ago. *Don't do anything stupid, army.*

I've been assessing everything I see. The guards' placement, their weapons. Looking for some small glimpse of weakness. Haven't found it yet. But I'm adaptable. That's what makes me so good as an undercover officer.

"Still pondering my options," I say.

"Time's running out."

Give me something to work with, I think. I don't need much. Just an inch.

A moment.

We reach the lobby. Amos and Tristan stand just outside the glass doors, waiting. They're banked by five guys I recognize from Roman's security team. These guards look antsy and unsettled, nowhere near the hard-edged confidence of Tristan's personal commandos.

Behind the men, two shiny SUVs are parked beneath the porte-cochère, with the grand stone fountain as a backdrop.

The glass doors slide automatically open. We go outside.

"Dad, don't do this," Roman says. "He'll betray you the moment he gets a chance."

Tristan crosses the space to his brother and pats Roman on the cheek. "Dad knows the truth. You realized you'd never rule Caldwell Enterprises, so you decided to destroy us instead."

"I would *never* betray our father."

Tristan turns to me. "Time to decide, Shelborne. What'll it be?"

"Where's Harper?"

"My men will keep her and Wren safe. Enough stalling. What's your answer to my offer?"

"I'll decline."

"Too bad."

"Why did he get offered a deal?" Roman asks. "What about me?"

Tristan leans in close to whisper into his brother's ear. But I'm standing right beside them, so I hear every word. "You could've played nice, but you didn't," Tristan says quietly. "This is what Dad has always taught us. Not to turn your back on anyone who has the strength to take you down. So consider this a compliment, Roman. I'm going through a lot of effort to get rid of you."

Tristan backs away, a smug smile on his face, and Roman absolutely loses it.

He drops to his knees, raises his hands. Babbles and begs and pleads. "Dad, *no*. He's lying! Please!"

Amos walks slowly toward us, hatred radiating from his every move, from every pore of his body.

"You can't believe I'd do this," Roman goes on. "*Everything* I've done is for you. Tristan is the one who's going to stab you in the back."

Amos grabs Roman beneath the arm and hauls him upright. Then throws him to the ground near the SUVs. Roman lands hard, catching himself on his bound hands.

"You're no son of mine. Tristan is my only son."

I guess that's the ultimate irony. Amos sees himself when he looks at Tristan. But he doesn't see the problem in that. Tristan is just as treacherous as Amos. Just as bloodthirsty. And now, Wren is pregnant with Tristan's child. Maybe this sad, twisted narrative will repeat all over again.

I believe there are all kinds of ways to form a family, but a father can make or break a person. The evidence is right before me. I'm not a perfect father to Riley and Hudson, but at least I love them and care for them.

I have to get out of here. I have to see them again.

For several seconds, I'm consumed with these thoughts. Until the hairs on my arms raise.

That's the only warning I get before chaos erupts.

There's the snap of automatic weapons fire. Heads duck. Roman is already down, but Tristan and Amos dive for the ground as well, along with half the security team, covering their heads in self-preservation.

But I do the opposite.

I tackle Scarred Eyebrow and knock him to the concrete.

We roll back and forth as gunfire continues to roar in my ears. My opponent is strong and knows what he's doing, but I've got pure rage and desperation on my side.

I get control of his submachine gun and shove the muzzle underneath his chin. He's splayed flat on his back on the ground, holding out his hands, his eyes bulging, the scar white against his pale skin.

He hasn't done much to me, so I won't kill him if I don't have to. But he makes the decision for me.

In a blink, he draws a hidden knife from his sleeve and swipes it at me, cutting a gash in my sleeve.

I shoot him and roll away, dipping behind the valet stand. Meanwhile, more gunfire continues to snap through the air.

Only now do I consider what's happening. Is it possible the DEA figured out I was in trouble and sent reinforcements? Did Harper somehow get word to them?

The gunfire is coming from behind the fountain. Are they friends of mine? Enemies of the Caldwells? Either one is good news for me.

I glance out. Tristan's other commando, the only other one here, barrels toward me while he continues to shoot over his shoulder. Like he can't decide who's the worse threat, me or whoever else is shooting.

I take him out with a burst to his chest.

Did I mention my hands are still tied together?

Roman pops up next and starts to run, but Tristan grabs him around the legs and sends him sprawling across the concrete. Amos has just drawn a gun from his jacket and is shooting at the fountain along with the remaining guards, who've fanned out into a defensive formation. No one else is paying attention to me. They've got their hands full.

Then I hear a familiar voice right behind me.

"*Jake.*"

I whirl around and find Harper crouched there. She's just emerged from the lobby doors. I quickly drop the aim of my gun. She's the last person I'd have expected to sneak up on me right now. But damn, I'm happy to see her.

Not a fan that she's shown up in the middle of a gun battle, but still happy.

She draws her knife and slices through my restraints.

"Who's shooting from behind the fountain?" I ask.

"Mia and my dad. We disarmed some of the guards. We need to get to the west side of the hotel. That's where our ride will be waiting."

I can't believe what I'm hearing. "This is an insane risk for you to take."

She smirks. "You can say thank you later. I figured if we got this started, you'd know what to do."

"Counting on my superhero skills?"

"The security team has Mia and Dad pinned down. *You're* our exit strategy. Any time you want to get started."

Good point.

I burst out from behind the valet stand, already shooting.

I take out two security team guys with a couple of bursts. Amos sees me coming and dives behind between the SUVs.

Roman and Tristan are still fighting each other on the ground. Roman's managed to get free of his bindings and has his hands around his brother's throat.

My finger itches on the trigger as I consider taking the brothers out. But I fire on two more security guys instead. I run for the fountain.

"Come on," I shout, and lay down cover fire while Mason and Mia run toward Harper and the lobby.

Amos pokes out behind an SUV and takes a couple of shots at me with his handgun, but they go wide. I fire again, the bullets pinging off the metal of the SUV, and Amos crawls away.

"Go, go."

Still aiming the submachine gun toward the SUVs, I push Harper, Mason, and Mia behind me into the lobby. Mason is nursing a wound on his arm. One of the guards must have managed to graze him. But we're all still alive, which is pretty damn miraculous.

We run through the lobby, then out the west side entrance onto the deck.

"Where is this ride you promised?" I ask.

"There." Harper points.

A golf cart pulls up with Wren in the driver's seat.

I skid to a stop. "No way. Are you kidding?"

"She's been helping us." Harper waves me on. "We couldn't have gotten to you otherwise. Jake, *please*."

The others pile onto the cart. Wren gives me a closed-mouth, apologetic smile. But there's no time for discussion or debate.

We need to get out of here *now*. Before Tristan or Amos catches up to us.

I jump into the back of the cart, and Wren takes off. I have to grab onto the canopy as she swerves along the path. I'm facing the direction we came from, ready to shoot down anyone who appears. But no one seems to be following us. Not yet.

Mia is next to me, while Harper's up front with her dad and Wren. Harper shouts directions to the extraction point. I take over as we get closer, since I'm the only one who's been there before.

"Get as close as you can," I say, "and we'll have to go on foot the rest of the way."

Once we reach the cliffside, we all get out of the cart and start down the stairs to reach the water's edge. Wren is staying with us, but I don't comment on it. We've got another half mile along the coastline to go. "It's down there." I point out the spot where the rocks jut out into the water, and the brush gets thicker.

I grab Harper's hand as we go.

"Thank you," I say. "You saved my life."

"I owed you one, army. But let's not make it a habit."

She's got a pistol in one hand, another handgun tucked into her waist, hair streaming behind her as she runs. And the woman's still wearing the skirt and silky top from the investor meeting. Talk about impressive.

The sun is sinking, turning the sky fiery colors and shining in her eyes. Long shadows trail to our sides.

Harper has never looked so beautiful. Or so fucking sexy.

But I have to let go of her when Mason starts to fall behind.

"I'll catch up," he says.

"Nope. Not leaving any of my rescuers behind." I put an arm around him to support him. Mason has still managed to hold on to his submachine gun. It's more than I ever expected from him.

"You decided to turn into an action hero today?" I ask.

He just smiles and pushes onward.

The beach is strewn with rocks here instead of sand, and we have to slow down, picking our way.

Finally we reach the brush where my dry bag is hidden. This is the gear Agent Reyes left here days ago.

"Mia, Harper, you keep watch."

They nod, Harper trading her pistol for her dad's submachine gun. Wren stands with her, looking over at me, but I haven't got the time or patience for that conversation at the moment.

I start the emergency raft inflating. It'll only take a couple of minutes. Meanwhile, I set up the emergency beacon that will contact the DEA and the task force, letting them know I need a quick exit. Then I turn on the emergency radio, set it to the pre-planned frequency, and call for help over the encrypted channel.

As the boat inflates, I stow the other gear and the beacon inside.

Wren appears at my shoulder. "Need any help?"

"No," I say sharply.

She's just standing there. And I've run out of tasks.

"Harper told me I have you to thank for that dramatic rescue," I say.

"I had to tell Tristan who you really were. But I wasn't choosing him over Harper, or even you."

"Damn well felt like you chose Tristan."

She chews her lip. "Did you shoot him when you were escaping?"

I glare at her. She holds my gaze. I can't tell if she'd be upset if I said yes or not. "No. I didn't."

She nods, giving away nothing.

I move around the raft, checking it, then heft the heavy motor into place. "You coming with us?" I ask.

"I can't. I just wanted to thank you for what you've done

for Harper and my dad. And I hope I've managed to repay a small bit of that."

"If I can get them out of here in one piece, then yeah. I'd say you've done your part. But you should be talking this over with them, not me. They're the ones who are going to miss you." I lift my eyes to hers, and I see the sorrow and regret there. She still feels something after all.

Wren walks away. I notice Mason sitting on a rock nearby. He heard all of that.

Mason struggles to stand, bracing himself against a spindly tree to push up. "Wren already said goodbye. She knows I probably won't live long enough to see her again. Harper is the one who's going to feel the loss of her sister. Because once I'm gone, she'll barely have anyone left."

I slam the top of the motor a little too hard as I secure it into place. "She'll have me."

And I mean it. Whatever happens after this, whatever Harper needs, I'll find a way to deliver. I can't even begin to wrap my head around what that will be. This entire mission has gotten so fucked. But if I can get out of here without anything else going wrong, then I'll be counting my lucky stars. The rest I'll sort out later.

Mason nods, holding my gaze. "Then I guess I don't have anything to worry about."

The radio beeps, and I grab for it.

It's the captain of a Coast Guard ship. It's being sent to intercept us. Agent Reyes already had them in the area after my warning this afternoon. ETA about ten minutes. So we'd better get the hell out on the water.

"Everyone," I call out, "the boat's ready. Let's go."

Harper and Mia jog over. I push the raft partway into the surf and secure the rope to keep it in place. The inflatable rocks gently in the waves. Mia climbs on first.

Wren is hugging Harper and their father goodbye. Tears

streak down Wren's face. Harper's eyes are bloodshot, and I know how hard it must be for her to hold back what she's feeling.

Movement draws my attention.

My hand goes to the small of my back as if reaching for my holster. But I haven't got my gun. The submachine gun I was using earlier lies useless inside the boat.

And Roman has just stepped out into the open a couple of yards away on the beach.

He's aiming a gun, finger on the trigger.

The next few moments unfold in slow motion before my eyes. There's no way I could see the bullet. It hasn't even been fired yet. But I can see its trajectory in my mind.

Harper and Wren are in the line of fire.

I shout a warning. My muscles tense and push as I run toward them, but there's no way I'll reach them in time.

Mason is closer. He lunges in front of the women, moving faster than I would've thought him capable of.

The sound of the gunshot echoes against the cliffs. Seagulls scream.

And Mason lands heavily on the rocks.

I sprint at Roman. Which is suicidal, considering that he's still aiming that gun. He squeezes off another shot. I feel the bullet fly past me so close that I'd swear it brushes my jawline.

I barrel into him, slamming him into the rocks.

I grab the wrist that's holding the gun and twist. Roman's finger pulls down on the trigger again. The sound is so loud that I can't hear anything but my ears ringing. Roman kicks and bucks beneath me as we struggle for the gun. Feral rage shines from his eyes.

But that's nothing compared to the fury blasting through my veins.

He meant to kill Harper. I'm pretty sure he hit Mason. Not to mention the fact that he's tried to kill me.

My mind goes dark. Like there's an eclipse of the rational, humane sides of my brain, and all that's left is a bloodthirsty craving for vengeance.

Holding Roman's wrist, I bend his arm until the muzzle of the gun points against his chest. He does everything in his power to fight me. His snarl turns to fear. Then shock. But he can't stop me.

I force his finger down on the trigger.

His body jerks, then goes still.

My ears are still ringing.

I push away from him and stagger back toward the others. Mia and Harper are carrying Mason toward the boat. Wren is sobbing.

"I've got him," I try to say, though I can barely hear the words. I pick up Mason and set him down gently between the seats of the raft. "We need to go. They'll have doctors on the Coast Guard ship."

Though I'm not sure what doctors can do for Mason now. He's wounded in the stomach, and he's losing blood fast.

Mia climbs in right behind me. She presses her hands to Mason's wound. But Harper has turned to her sister, and I don't need to hear what she's saying to realize what she's trying to do.

Harper's taking one last chance to convince Wren to escape with us. But Wren shakes her head, backing away. Who knows what she'll be returning to. Tristan could be dead. I have no doubt Roman tried his best.

But Wren has made her choice. It's over, and we have to go.

"Please!" Harper's lips form the word. She's still reaching out for her sister. I jump out of the boat, circle my arms around her waist, and carry her. She tries to fight me, but it's instinct. I don't think Harper knows anymore what she's fighting. She's shell-shocked.

I gently set her down beside Mia and Mason. Then I fire up the motor and get us the hell out of there. Harper's facing backward, and I know she's watching as her sister's form disappears.

34

Harper

etective Angela Murphy walks into the interview room and sets a cup of fresh coffee in front of me. I mumble a thanks.

"You look like you could use a break," she says.

She's just interrupted Agent Reyes, who's been questioning me for…a century?

I can't keep track.

Agent Reyes sits back in his seat, frowning with disapproval at the detective. We're at West Oaks PD headquarters. I haven't seen Jake in ages. Or Mia or…

I swallow. Tears burn in my eyes, and I force them down.

"I just have a few more questions on this list," Reyes says.

But Detective Murphy shakes her head. "Nope. I don't think you do."

"Uh, pretty sure I—"

Murphy grabs his notepaper and tears it in half.

"What the *hell*, Angela?"

"Don't act like this isn't being recorded. Or like you don't have underlings watching and taking copious notes of their own. Miss Caldwell needs a break, so she's getting one. She can't answer questions effectively if she can't sit upright."

"This is not your decision."

"And yet…" Murphy puts a hand on my shoulder, helping me stand and steering me toward the door.

"Wait." The chair scrapes as Reyes stands. "Miss Caldwell, try one more time. When was the last time you saw your jacket with the recording device in the lapel? Was it at the resort? The golf cart as you fled? We've got agents on site, and they haven't recovered it."

"I'm sorry. I don't remember."

Murphy opens the door for me. Reyes is still protesting, and I can't blame him. I haven't exactly been forthcoming. There's been a lot of *I-can't-recall*. A lot of *I'm-not-sures*. The names of the investors have vanished from my head. It makes sense that Reyes is pissed.

But I can't do anything about that. This is the deal I made with Wren to keep Jake and his family safe from Tristan.

Murphy walks me down a hallway. She's carrying my coffee. "Do you need a bathroom visit?"

"No, thanks."

"Then how about a quiet place to relax for a bit." She takes me to a room where there's a comfy couch and a water dispenser. I sit, and she tucks the coffee into my hands. "I'll be back in a few. Holler if you need anything."

"Okay." My voice is hoarse. From talking or crying, I don't know.

I sit quietly until I zone out, and numbness spreads through my body. But I can't fall asleep. I see images from our escape instead.

The crash of the waves and spray of the ocean as we raced away from the shore. My father, lying in my arms as he took his last breaths.

I finally got the chance to protect my daughters, he said as I held him. *I had to go out anyway, Harper. This is a far better way.*

I try to take a sip of coffee, but it won't go down.

The door to the hall opens, and Jake steps inside. "Hey. Murphy said you were in here."

I set aside the coffee and stand up. I walk straight into his arms. He catches me up on what's been happening. Mia is around here somewhere, and she's okay. Jake has been answering questions, too, and his bosses aren't much happier with him than with me. Though for different reasons.

"Reyes is furious that I blew my cover with Wren, and that led to everything going sideways. Nice big mess for the DEA to clean up."

"It was my fault."

"I was right there with you. I made my choices." He holds my face in his hands. "Harper, I'm so sorry about your dad."

I nod and avert my gaze.

A Coast Guard ship intercepted our raft and brought us on board. They rushed my father to their infirmary, but he was already beyond help. I can't remember what happened between there and ending up here at the police station. It's all a blur. But I know I changed out of my bloody clothes, which Agent Reyes took as evidence. I'm wearing sweatpants and a shirt that the police provided me.

Jake hugs me for a while, and I zone out again. The next thing I know, Detective Murphy has joined us and she's holding out a small bag to me. "These are for you and your cousin. Shelborne said you had to leave all your belongings."

She's right. I don't even have my phone. I have *nothing*. "Thank you. Where are we going?"

Jake trails his fingers down my hair. "I'm taking you home. Same with Mia. You both need to sleep. If Agent Reyes has more questions, he can ask them tomorrow."

Murphy drives us there. Jake sits in the front seat, while

Mia sits beside me in the back, squeezing my hand. She hasn't said much.

I lost my father and my sister. But Mia's lost so much, too. From the hints Reyes and Jake have dropped, it sounds like the DEA swarmed the resort. But there was no trace of Tristan, Amos, or Wren.

Murphy glances at Jake. "Are you sure you want to go to your house? That'll be the first place people will look for you."

"I don't care. I'll handle it. But I'm going on vacation after this. For a year, maybe."

Murphy chuckles. "You've earned it. I'll arrange for a West Oaks PD car to sit outside your place and keep an eye on things for a few days."

"I'd appreciate that."

We reach Jake's house. It's a one-story with blue siding and colorful wind chimes hanging from the porch. Inside, it's exactly what I would've expected. Simple with lots of light. Homey touches, toys scattered in corners. And it smells like him. The real Jake, not the expensive cologne that's worn away from his skin.

I'm just standing in the living room. No clue what to do. And so many awful memories and emotions trying to rise up inside me.

"Make yourselves at home," he says. "My kids are with my sister on Catalina Island for a couple more days. My fridge isn't stocked, but I can place an order. Hungry for anything in particular?"

Mia rubs her eyes. "I don't want to think about food. I just want to shower and pass out for at least the next day. Should I take the couch?"

"You can stay in the kids' room." He walks her to a nearby doorway. "Take either bed."

Mia looks in. "The one covered in stuffed animals looks

like the best spot in the world. You sure your kid won't mind?"

"That's Riley's bed, and she's not so good at sharing. It can be our secret."

Mia puts a hand over her heart, pretending to gasp. "You lie to your kids? Shocking."

I don't know how Mia can do that. Joke around when we've just lost everything. Maybe that's how she copes. But I'm too exhausted. My soul has been wrung out of me.

I didn't even cry when… When I knew Dad was gone. I wouldn't let myself. I feel cold. As cold as my dad's fingers as he tried to grab my hand.

Jake's hand rests on my shoulder. "Harper?" He's speaking with infinite patience, but I get the feeling it's not the first time he's said my name.

"Yeah?" My voice doesn't sound like mine.

"What can I do for you?"

"I…don't know."

"Come with me." He takes my hand. Leads me down a hall and to his room. In the on-suite bathroom, he warms up the water in the shower, helps me undress. There's no trace of desire in his touch or his gaze. Just kindness.

But I wish he'd kiss me. Get undressed and press his body against me so I feel something *good*.

The water is hot, but it does little to warm me on the inside. When I get out, Jake wraps a towel around me.

"Did you need to clean up?" I ask.

"I did at the station. I'm sorry we were separated for so long. Reyes wouldn't let me see you."

I'm nodding along, though I'm barely listening.

He leads me over to his bed and tucks me into the covers. Brushes the hair back from my forehead as he sits beside me.

Jake says there's a manhunt for Amos and Tristan. But at this point, the DEA doesn't have much evidence against the

Caldwells beyond what they had before. Kidnapping against Jake, sure, maybe even attempted murder for the plan to kill him. If we can prove it. But not the actionable intelligence the DEA wanted about the organization and investors.

I curl up against Jake's side. "We can't go after Tristan. That was the deal I made with Wren on the beach, right before we got away. I told her I'd stay quiet in exchange for Tristan leaving you alone."

"Harper," Jake says on a sigh.

"I gave her the recording device, too, with everything about the investors. I had to do it. Are you angry?"

"It's in the past." He's been brushing his fingers gently along my hairline. But his hand stops, his eyes shining, and I see the pain that I *should* be feeling. That I can't let myself feel.

"Harper, I can't express to you how sorry I am. I told you I'd get Wren and your dad out of there, and—"

I can't talk about my father.

"Jake," I say, interrupting him. "I want you to kiss me."

He leans forward and softly presses his lips to mine. I wrap my arms around his neck to hold him to me as I deepen the kiss. He's slow to respond. He moves his mouth to kiss my jaw and neck instead.

But there's no passion there. This isn't what I want.

With Jake, I used to be able to weave a fantasy of something better. That's what I need right now. An escape. I need him to sweep me away and pretend that everything's all right.

I slip my hand into the waistband of his pants. His cock responds, starting to fill as I stroke him.

"Make love to me," I beg. "*Please*. Make me forget."

He gently takes my hand away. He tangles our fingers together instead. "I can't do that. You need to feel whatever you're feeling."

"But I can't stand this. It's too much."

"You can take it. You are so strong. So brave. But you won't be alone, okay? I'll be right here with you."

He keeps kissing me and touching me, but chastely. Sweetly. I wish he wouldn't because this *hurts*. I can't keep up my defenses. Everything I don't want to think about, don't want to feel, is rushing at me. Unstoppable.

Finally, I bury my head against his chest and muffle a scream against his heart.

He doesn't flinch. Only cinches his arms tighter. "I'm here," he murmurs. "I'm here."

Jake holds me as I fall, completely and utterly, apart.

35

Jake

I'm in my kitchen staring into a cup of orange juice when Madison arrives the next morning. She unlocks the door with her key and steps inside. "Jake?"

"In here." I clear my throat, embarrassed at the way my voice cracked.

She walks in and takes one look at me. "Shit, it was a bad one, huh?"

I called Madison last night to ask her to come back early from Catalina. I hated cutting her vacation short, but I need my family. I need to see my kids, and I need my little sis.

And...God, I need help figuring out what to do for Harper. Because she's not all right.

Madison hugs me, and I return her embrace. "Riley and Hudson?" I ask.

"Emma and Nash took them to the park, like you asked."

I wanted her to come alone first so I could explain. I'd rather not discuss any of this while my kids are in the same house. And I don't want them to see me like this. Battered and bruised and letting too much of what I keep on the inside hang out for all to see.

"The op got all kinds of fucked."

She pulls up a chair next to me. "I guessed that. But the CI? Your friend?"

"She's here. Staying with me for now, along with her cousin. They're both asleep." There's no any good way to ease Madison into this, so I just say it. "It's Harper. From across the street when we were growing up."

"Wait a minute. Harper Kendrick? *That* Harper?"

"Yeah. But her real name is Caldwell."

Before I can explain, Madison jumps up. "Hold that thought. I can already tell I'm going to need a fresh pot of coffee for this conversation."

While the coffee brews, I start spilling my guts. I tell her absolutely everything, letting the words run from my mouth in whatever order they occur to me. I shouldn't be telling her all of this. It relates to an ongoing investigation. But there's just no way I can keep it in. Madison is the only person in the world I can share this with right now.

My sister gives me a lot of confused looks and knitted eyebrows. But eventually, she starts to get the gist.

When I tell her about my cover being blown, how close I came to never coming back, she takes a deep breath.

"So Harper got you out."

"Yeah, she did. Her father died because of it."

"The gun wasn't in your hand."

"I know that." Madison's in law enforcement, and she knows just as well as I do that it's fruitless to blame ourselves for the choices of others. Yet we still do it.

My sister gets up to freshen her coffee. "So, what's really eating at you?" she asks.

I push my orange juice and my coffee mug away from me. I haven't touched a drop.

"I left a lot of dead bodies behind me. I have before, not

like that's new, but this time... The things Harper saw me do..."

"From what you said, she's not a stranger to violence. She knew when she brought in the DEA what it might lead to."

"She did. But the thing is, I'm not sorry for any of the deaths I caused. Not even Roman's, and I could've theoretically wounded him instead of killing him. But I didn't want to. In fact, I wish I'd ended him earlier so he couldn't have killed Mason." I press my hand flat against the table, imagining I see red on my skin. "When Roman went limp and the light died from his eyes, all I felt was satisfaction. I'll never admit this to my bosses, but I acted out of *vengeance*. What kind of man does that make me? What kind of father?"

I say all of this in a whisper. It feels like I'm dragging it from the depths of my soul. I've never confessed anything like this to my sister before. Madison's been through some rough situations, but she's got a nurturing side a mile wide.

Now that she's heard me say these things, I don't know if she'll be able to look at me the same way again.

My sister cups the back of my neck and meets my gaze. She has almost the same eyes that I see when I look in the mirror.

"Jake, it makes you human. And a damn good human, at that. Your kids don't need you to be an ideal good-guy superhero. To them, you're the person who loves them and protects them. That's who you've *always* been. That's who you are. Nothing you feel in the heat of battle will ever change that."

There's a weight pressing down on me. I thought telling Madison would help, but it hasn't. "Feels like the only good thing about me is the people who love me."

She smiles and hooks her arm around my neck. "Then you must be doing something right."

I want to do right by my kids. I'm taking a leave of

absence from work, and I intend to spend a lot of quality time with them as soon as a few things are sorted out. But there's someone else who needs me, too. Needs more than I can possibly give her.

I exhale and rub my hands over my face.

"I don't know what to do for Harper. She's lost everything. She planned to start over after leaving Caldwell Enterprises behind, but she thought she'd have her dad and sister with her. She's got Mia, but from the hints Mia gave, she's not going to stick around here long. Mia has friends and a life at her university. But I don't think Harper has anyone."

"She has you."

That's true. But right now, that doesn't seem like enough.

"And she has the rest of the Shelbornes, too," Madison says. "We'll do whatever we can. I'll call Mom, she'll tell Aiden to start cooking, and she'll inundate you with more food and love than you can handle. That's what Shelbornes do."

"But Harper needs more than that. She's so messed up over this, and I don't think... I don't know if being around me is actually the best thing for her."

Last night, I held her until she'd cried herself out and fell headlong into sleep. I would do the same every night if that's what she needs.

But I'm also the guy who made a lot of promises he couldn't deliver. What if I'm a never-ending reminder of the worst moments of her life?

"Plus, my kids need me too," I add. "I have no idea how to navigate this."

Madison finishes her coffee and sets her mug on the counter. "Then here's what we're going to do. Harper is going to stay with me and Nash. We have the guestroom. It's quiet and calm. I know firsthand that it's a great place to recover. Nash and Emma and I will be there for her if anything comes up. We've all been through some shit."

That's for sure. "Quiet will be good. That won't be what she gets around here. Not when the kids are staying with me. I'll see how Harper feels about it, but I think that could be good. Thank you."

She gives me another hug around the neck. "I have a hunch that Harper will want to see a lot of you, too. That's what it was like for me and Nash after what we went through together. We needed each other that much more."

I'm skeptical that Harper will feel that way. Maybe the separation will make her realize we're better off apart because the memories are too much. But we'll just have to wait and see.

"It'll be okay, big brother. I promise. We can get Harper settled today. And I know Riley and Hudson are excited to see you."

"Give me another half hour? Then you can bring the kids."

When I go into my room, Harper is awake. She's got the puffy, blurry-eyed look of someone who cried herself to sleep. But she's still so beautiful that my chest goes tight. I sit down beside her and reach for her hand.

"Hey, how are you doing?"

Before she can answer, there's a knock behind us. "Hope I'm not interrupting?" Mia asks.

Harper tugs her hand out of my grasp. "No," she says. "Come in."

I scoot over so there's room for Mia. She puts her arm around Harper, and Harper leans into her.

"I can give you both a minute." I start to get up.

But Mia shakes her head. "No, you should hear this too. I have a friend in LA, and she's on her way to come pick me up. I'm going to stay with her a few days, then go back home to Berkeley. I have classes, tests. I could probably get more time if I spoke to the dean, but..."

Harper smiles at her, though it's forced. "You don't have to explain. You want to get back to your life."

"Yeah. I need to focus on that, you know? I was all set to give it up, just run away if that's what I had to do to escape our family, but now I want my friends. My apartment. I want to finish my degree. Does that make sense?"

"It does." Harper gives her a squeeze. "Completely."

"But I wanted to say goodbye. And you can call me anytime, Harper. Trust me, I'll be calling you plenty. You're going to stay here with Jake, right?"

They both look over at me.

My heart twangs with guilt, knowing I'll be sending Harper to Madison instead. Even though I think it's for the best.

"She's got a place to stay in West Oaks for as long as she wants it," I say. Nice and vague because I just don't know how this will go. I don't think I've *ever* been this uncertain. Not even when my marriage was ending.

Harper says she wants to get dressed, so I walk with Mia to the living room. I offer coffee and breakfast, but she wants to get out on the road as soon as her friend arrives.

"I probably seem like a jerk for bailing so soon," she says. "But this is the only way I can maintain my sanity."

"Harper understands. So do I."

I'm amazed that Mia is standing here at all when I'm the man who killed her brother in front of her. Not that I'm going to bring up *that* subject. She doesn't either.

"Let me know the details of Mason's funeral?" she asks. "I want to be there."

"I will. And I'd like to let the task force know your location. I can arrange for protection for you, even when you go back up north."

She crosses her arms over her middle. "I'll consider it. But Tristan's not going to mess with me. He's probably glad to be rid of me. And as for my father? I've never warranted much attention. My guess is that he'll have his hands full with Tristan."

"I imagine so." All I know is that we didn't deal Caldwell Enterprises a death blow. If anything, we helped clear the way for Tristan's takeover.

If Amos survives his son, it'll be as a useless figurehead unless Amos finds some way to fight back. I'm sure the DEA is going to continue pursuing the remaining Caldwells, but they'll have to bring in other agents for that. I'm going to stay out of it.

Harper emerges from my room in time to say goodbye to Mia. The two hug and promise to talk soon. With another apologetic glance, Mia runs out to her ride.

Harper's wearing jeans and a T-shirt, her hair down around her shoulders, not a trace of makeup. A scrap of memory appears in my mind: Harper when we were teenagers. When she was my best friend, and I had no idea how much she really needed me.

"Are you hungry?" I ask.

She shakes her head. "Can we sit down? I guess...we should talk."

Harper and I go outside and sit on the back porch. The sun is warm, high in the sky. A perfect Southern California summer day. I hear a lawnmower running. Sprinklers with kids laughing and running through them. This place feels a million miles away from the golf resort, even though it's a fifteen minute drive.

Is that far enough for Harper? Is this distance still too close to what happened?

I last mowed a week ago, but already the yard is overgrown. Harper picks some long stalks of grass and twists them between her fingers.

"I want you to stay here in West Oaks," I say. "At least for a while. To get on your feet."

"Still bossing me around, I see." Her joke is half-hearted.

"I'm speaking as your friend. But…" Here's the hard part. I don't want her to take this the wrong way. "Madison would love to have you stay in her and Nash's guestroom."

Harper's eyes widen.

"It's just a few minutes from here," I rush to say. "They have a really nice place. Quiet. And they're laid-back. You can come and go as you please."

Harper nods, twisting the grass stalks again. "I'd appreciate that. I'm short on options at the moment. SunSpeed is dead. My savings are questionable. And the last of my family just walked out the door."

"I'm not pushing you away. That's not what this is."

"No, I know. I need to figure out what I'm going to do with myself." She smiles sheepishly. "And we've already proven that sharing a bed is too much temptation for us. I threw myself at you last night."

"I didn't want to say no."

"But it was better that you did."

I should be glad she sees it that way. Yet somehow, having her acknowledge that we're better apart disappoints me instead of reassuring me that I'm doing what's best.

"Madison's on her way with Riley and Hudson. Would you like to meet them?"

Her eyes light up. A small glimpse of the vibrant Harper I know is still inside her somewhere. "I would love to."

A short time later, Madison and Nash arrive with the twins in tow. They're each holding one of Emma's hands, and the poor girl looks exhausted. But she smiles when she sees me, and the kids race each other toward me. Buster runs through the door too, brushing past them.

"Daddy! Daddy!"

I kneel and scoop them both into my arms while Buster's tail thumps into everyone. For a couple minutes, it's just hugs and kisses, questions that they don't pause to hear the answers to, and the inevitable bickering. But I've never been so happy to be near them. I've missed their wiggles and their laughs and even complaints about how Hudson ate all the french fries at lunch yesterday and how Riley wouldn't let him color in her coloring book.

Then Hudson asks, "Who is she?"

I set them both on the ground and turn around. Harper's standing in the living room, petting Buster, who's already getting to know the newcomer. He went straight to her after greeting me.

Harper gives them a small smile. "Hi."

"This is Harper," I say. "She's very special to me. A really good friend."

Her eyes fly to me, blinking fast.

The kids walk over to her. Hudson is first, because he's always excited to meet new people. Riley is slower, not because she's shy, but because she likes to get a feel for someone before deciding her opinion. Harper kneels on the ground and greets them both.

Then she pulls something out of her pocket. A couple of woven circles made of grass, studded with tiny flowers. She must have made these while we were sitting in the backyard.

She holds out the tiny wreaths. Hudson takes his and holds it up to show me, beaming. Riley examines hers closely. "Can you show me how to make my own?"

"I'd be happy to. Any time you like."

"It looks hard, though."

"It's a little hard. But I bet you can do it."

Madison strides over. "Okay, munchkins. I think Harper might like a rest, and I know I could use one. Let's get your bags out of the car, and then you can show your dad all the seashells you collected."

There's a mad dash to unpack bags. I walk Harper to the door. Madison's already told Nash and Emma that they'll have a guest, and they're waiting in the car outside.

"Can I give you a hug?" I ask.

"You'd better." She sinks into my arms, cheek to my chest. "Thank you," she whispers.

I kiss her on the forehead. "I'll see you soon."

"Promise?"

"I promise."

After Harper's off with my sister and her family, I sit at the kitchen table and learn every detail about the seashells Riley and Hudson found on the island. They argue about which one is better and want me to pick a winner. I tell them they've found an equally diverse yet ideal assortment of shells. Which is an answer that neither kid likes.

When that's done, Hudson says, "That lady was nice. But she seems sad."

"Harper?" I turn one of the scallop shells over in my fingers. "You're right. Her father passed away."

"That *is* sad," Riley says, rearranging her shells on the table.

Hudson's nose scrunches up. "Can we make her happy?"

"Yeah, can we?" his sister parrots. It's a rare moment when the two of them agree on something.

I love them so much that I don't see how I can fit the feeling inside me.

"I'd like to try. If you'll help me."

∾

THAT NIGHT, WHILE I'M TUCKING RILEY IN, SHE grabs my face and pulls me close. Hudson already passed out during bedtime stories.

"Daddy, I saved what you gave me." She holds out her hand, palm up, but there's nothing there. Then I remember.

"You mean my heart?"

She nods. "Don't you need it back?"

I carefully fold her fingers over her palm. "Nope. That one is yours to keep. Always."

After I close the kids' door, I go to my room and wash my face in the sink. I study the reflection in the mirror.

You're the guy who loves them and protects them. That's who you've always been.

Sometimes, I'm not sure. But that's who I want to be.

36

Harper

adison and Nash's house is adorable. It's a mid-century bungalow with the cutest retro kitchen. Madison shows me to an office that they use as a guestroom. It's bright and airy. The kind of place that makes me want to curl up and relax.

"This is perfect," I say. "Thank you."

She leans into the doorway. "Nash let me stay here when I was recovering from an injury. Well, we were both recovering. We were helping each other. And then we totally fell for each other, and here we are."

"You'll have to tell me the rest of that story."

"When you have a few hours and nothing else going on, I will. But my point was that I know what it's like to recover from something traumatic. Being surrounded by people who understand and care really helps. And we *do* care."

"Not sure I deserve that. But it means a lot."

I sit on the bed. I'm grateful to Madison for letting me stay here, but I already miss Jake.

It stung that he asked me to stay here instead of with him. Yet it's also a relief. Does that make sense? I don't know anymore how I'm supposed to act around him, especially with his children there. But Riley and Hudson are the cutest things ever. So sweet. And they look just like Jake. I wanted to cover each of them in a thousand kisses. Which would've been weird coming from a woman they've never met before.

Just yesterday, I was imagining that Jake could somehow be a part of my future. Right now, the thought of trying for any kind of relationship is far beyond what I'm capable of.

My heart is rubbed raw.

So yeah, this arrangement makes more sense. Space to sort myself out. I need to figure out what the heck I'm going to do with the rest of my life.

No big deal.

Luckily, Madison has her mind on the more practical aspects of my situation. "Make a list of the things you need. What about a phone? Do you still have yours?"

I shake my head. "I lost it somewhere. Agent Reyes said they'd return my belongings to me if they find them. The DEA is all over the hotel right now, from what they said. But I don't know if they'll find my phone."

"Then I'll make that a top priority. I might even have an old phone around here that you could use for a while. I've got some bath stuff, but we'll need to get the stuff you like, new clothes, all the basics..." Madison taps a finger against her lips, thinking. "You know, I hate to say this, but we need an expert. We need my mother."

"Your mother?" *Jake's* mother?

"Is that okay?"

"Um, sure. But she'll probably remember the last time she saw me. Jake and I were..."

Madison cracks up. "Yeah, Jake told me that story. Mom caught you two in the buff?"

"He *told you*?"

"Not when I was a kid! Like, six months ago. But don't

worry about our mother. She's intense, but it's all from love. Might as well get used to it. You'll be an honorary Shelborne in no time. That's just how this family rolls."

There's a bubbly feeling in my chest, much like I felt when I met Riley and Hudson.

I stop Madison before she can leave the room. "You're a police officer. You know Jake was undercover with me, right? I was informing on my family. Do you know the kinds of things the Caldwells did? What *I* was a part of?"

Her expression sobers, and she holds my hands in hers. "Jake told me everything, and it makes no difference. You're important to my brother, and that means you're welcome here. We take care of each other."

I thought I cried enough tears for a lifetime last night. But somehow, I find more. I wipe them away from my cheeks as they fall. And Madison just sits with me and holds my hand as I cry, as if this kind of generosity is the most natural thing in the world.

I guess in the Shelborne family, it is.

As each day passes, my lungs fill a little deeper. My heart beats a little lighter. And the memories get easier to bear.

Through all of it, Jake and his family are right there beside me.

Madison's predictions prove correct on all counts when it comes to Mrs. Shelborne. The moment Jake's parents hear about my troubles, Heather charges in with supplies and food. She's far too polite to mention that awkward moment when Jake and I were teenagers. Instead, she reminisces with me about my dad, sharing stories about the two years that she and her husband were friends with my parents.

Jake's brother Aiden brings delicious meals over. He's matured into a gruff, handsome man, though far less talkative than his siblings. Madison takes long walks with me. We go all over West Oaks, and day by day, the good memories of the time I've spent here start to overwhelm the bad.

Emma's starting to look at colleges, so I tag along with her when she visits campuses and learn more about the art education courses and financial aid available. I get back into my art too, setting up an easel in Madison's backyard to paint. I draw so much that my fingers cramp. Whenever Riley and Hudson come over, we do arts and crafts together, and I'm always laughing at the things they say.

Nash is great about hanging out when I just need quiet but can't stomach being alone. He has this gravitas about him that makes me feel completely safe and at ease. A little like Jake, except whenever Jake's in the vicinity, every cell in my body seems to reach out to have him closer. Nash is like my long-lost, silent older brother. And the way he adores Madison and Emma? It's such a beautiful dynamic to see.

The best part of every day is seeing Jake. He drops by Madison's house to say hi, or invites me and the rest of his family over for dinner or outings to the boardwalk and the beach. We talk and text on the phone. Spend hours getting to know each other again, sharing book recommendations and watching TV shows the other missed. If I give in to the temptation to draw him on occasion, I never let anyone see the results.

We're friends. Close friends, which is exactly what I need.

Slowly, I try to tackle the collapsed layers of my life.

First is my mother, who barely reacts on the phone when I tell her Dad has died. Even before the divorce, Mom never had much to do with SunSpeed or the rest of the Caldwell family except for the pills she could get through Caldwell suppliers. And sadly, that's all she cares about now. I even offer to buy her a ticket to Southern California and pay for a treatment center, but she refuses. Just as I expected she would.

I can't save someone who doesn't want to be saved, and though I'm not ready to stop trying with my mother yet, I have to let go of the hope that she'll ever accept it.

As for my apartment in Chicago, it was a month-to-month lease, nice and temporary. No issues there. I decide to donate just about everything in my bank account to charity. I'm not proud of where that money came from, even if most of SunSpeed's business was legitimate.

My dad's condo and accounts will require more work to tie up. He left everything to me and Wren in his will, with me as the executor, so I'll deal with it as soon as I'm able. In the meantime, I'm earning money by working for the Shelbornes' catering company. Heather's got me doing the financials, and I'm glad all those years with SunSpeed taught me a few things about running a business.

I finish all of my interviews with the DEA. Agent Reyes seems to know I've held things back, but he can't force me to talk. I suppose he could turn over my case to a prosecutor. But Jake would fight back against that. So the DEA lets me go.

I wait and I wait to hear something more about Tristan or Amos. I assume that Wren will have kept up her end of our deal. But she has no sway over Tristan's father. Maybe Tristan has convinced Amos not to seek revenge. Or maybe Amos is dead, as Tristan planned.

I'm hoping for the latter.

Before I know it, two months have passed since Dad's death. And I find that I'm smiling and laughing a lot more than I'm sad.

I'm ready for what's next, but I'm not yet sure what that is.

ONE SATURDAY AFTERNOON WHEN THE SHELBORNES descend on the beach for a barbecue, Jake's ex-wife Adrienne pulls me aside. "How was the memorial service? I'm sorry I couldn't make it."

We're standing a little ways from the kids, who are making sandcastles. Jake is out on the waves teaching Emma how to surf, all his muscles glistening with sun and seawater.

"It was good. Peaceful. I think my dad would've liked it."

Dad was cremated, and I decided to wait on holding the memorial until Mia could make it. No other Caldwells showed, but everyone from Jake's family aside from Adrienne and the kids came. Mia stayed the night, and the next day Jake took us out on a rented boat to scatter my father's ashes off the coast according to his wishes.

"Have you sent in your school applications yet?"

It takes me a moment to register Adrienne's question. I was getting distracted watching Jake maneuver his surfboard. "Not yet. I haven't decided if I should apply to schools near West Oaks or up in the Bay Area where my cousin lives."

Mia expects to graduate at the end of the next semester. She offered to be my roommate if I wanted to relocate. It would be a new place, a fresh beginning.

I'd be lying if I said I wasn't tempted.

Adrienne's eyebrows crease. "I didn't know you were considering the Bay Area. I thought you were staying in West Oaks."

"Just weighing my options."

"Does Jake know that?"

I bite my lip. "I haven't brought it up with him."

Adrienne and I have become good friends these past two months. She asked me to lunch, and from there, we clicked. She's told me about her marriage to Jake and why it didn't work out. I've shared my story with her in turn. I can see why he fell for her and why they're still so close. I might be jealous, as if I had any right to be. But Adrienne leaves no doubt that she has only platonic feelings for him.

Plus, she's Riley and Hudson's mom, and I adore those kids. She and Jake have done an amazing job.

"It would be hard to leave all of you because you've been wonderful," I say. "I don't want you to think I'm ungrateful. But it might be easier for me to start over somewhere else."

She's quiet for a moment. "Maybe this isn't my place, but I assumed that you and Jake are, you know, in love. The way you look at each other..." She trails off. "I just figured you were keeping it quiet for the kids' sakes. Is that not the case?"

All the blood rushes to the surface of my skin. "Jake and I aren't... I mean, we were something, but at the moment we're just...friends. Maybe best friends, I think, but not more than that." I close my mouth so I'll stop babbling.

"Do you *want* to be with him?" Adrienne asks. "Romantically?"

It should be hard to talk about this with Jake's ex. But there's something about Adrienne that makes me want to be honest. Maybe because she's been so open with me.

"I do. I really do. But Jake hasn't given any indication that he feels the same."

Jake shows me affection every day, but as a friend. We haven't kissed since the first night I arrived at his house. Jake and I see each other all the time, yet we've avoided the subject of the future.

For a while after Dad's death, I wasn't ready to think about relationships. But now, I'm not sure what Jake wants from *me*. I think the physical attraction is still there. But we had a fling. That doesn't add up to a love story. Jake has given me so much, and I don't know how I'd ever repay him or his family for what they've done.

But as much as he means to me, I'm not sure I can stay in West Oaks if I'll never be more than his friend.

"That's the thing about Jake," Adrienne says. "He's very passionate, but he's also the most patient man I've ever met. Maybe he's waiting for *you* to be ready."

I look over at him in the water. His golden skin and hair. Even brighter smile. The blue-green ink of his tattoos and the kind way he shows Emma how to get up onto the surfboard.

I want to believe that Adrienne is right, but it hurts to hope.

Yet it hurts even worse not to.

"Would you be okay with that?" I ask. "Jake and me together?"

Adrienne smiles. "I'd be thrilled. And so would the kids. We all want to see Jake head over heels. But only if it's right for you. Decide what you want and then be honest with him. He's one of the best people. I wasn't his perfect match, but maybe that can be you."

My heart takes off like an eager puppy. I want Jake so badly. *All* of him. And I want to give him all of me too.

Is it really possible?

Adrienne squeezes my hand. "He was yours before he was ever mine. Let him make you happy, and do the same for him. I wouldn't settle for anything less."

Later that day, after we're all sunburned and full of barbecued hamburgers, I walk down to the water's edge. Jake is standing ankle-deep in the surf, staring at the horizon. He looks over, already grinning like he's not surprised to find me there.

"Hi," he says softly.

He's been stealing glances at me for the last couple hours,

ever since I spotted him and Adrienne chatting with their heads together. It makes me wonder what she told him.

"Did you have a good day?" he asks.

"Almost perfect."

"Almost? What would've made it better?"

I can't explain all the fluttering in my stomach. The shyness I suddenly feel. Jake knows me inside and out, literally. And that's how well I know him. Except for this one subject that we've been avoiding—*us*.

"I could've used more of you," I say.

"That can be arranged." He holds out his hand and tangles his fingers with mine.

The look in his green eyes nearly undoes me, right there. Desire and longing and desperate hope. Everything that I'm feeling, too.

"Wanna get out of here?" he asks.

"Can we?"

"Adrienne's got the kids tonight. We can sneak away. Everyone will notice, but who cares about them?" He lifts my hand and kisses the back of it. Shivers cascade over my skin. "Would you go on a date with me?"

I grin. "A date?"

"Yeah. We've never been on one."

"Should we get cleaned up?" I'm in my bikini and a translucent cover-up. Jake's wearing just his swim trunks. His hair has dried in this messy, tousled way that somehow looks even better than when he styles it. I wouldn't change a thing about how he looks right now, but we're both covered in salt and sand.

"I'll put on a shirt, but aside from that, there's no dress code where we're going. You look great."

"Already have a plan for where we're going?"

"Of course I do. I've wanted to take you there for a while."

"Why haven't you?"

"I'm not sure. Maybe I was waiting for the right moment."

We walk to Ocean Lane, the main boulevard that's full of shops and restaurants. I figure it out when I see the neon sign up ahead. "Ice cream?" It's the place we used to go when we were teenagers.

He gives me a sweet, mischievous smile. "I want to see if I can remember your order, so don't tell me."

"Oh, I definitely remember yours."

We reach the ice cream parlor and wait in the line, hand in hand. *Please say this is really happening*, I think. Because it's everything I've dreamed of. For most of my life, people have accused me of being rebellious. But my fantasies are ridiculously tame. It's just a moment like this with the boy I like, and no dark secrets hanging over us.

When we get to the front, I order Jake a double scoop of triple chocolate ice cream with fudge and chocolate chips on top. Then I give him a smug grin.

"Your turn," I say.

He rubs his chin. "Okay. Challenge accepted." He orders me two scoops of vanilla with raspberries, caramel sauce, and extra whipped cream. "And two cherries," he finishes.

I laugh. "How am I going to eat all that? I don't burn as many calories as I did at seventeen."

"I'll eat what's left after I'm done with mine."

"Because you're still a pig?"

"Hey!" He tugs me closer, grinning, and plants a kiss on my temple. "You got my order exactly right. I'm impressed."

"And you got mine right, too. Except for the caramel. It sounds good, but that wasn't part of my order."

"The caramel was my extra touch. I didn't want to give you the same old thing. I want it to be better than before."

The air in the ice cream parlor is brisk, but I'm melting

into a swoony puddle at his feet. Good thing he's got an arm slung around my waist to hold me up.

We sit on the seawall to eat, pressed together from our shoulders to our hips to our knees. We take turns feeding each other ice cream. Jake keeps giving me looks that are hot enough to liquify an ice cap, let alone two scoops. Electricity lights up my nerve endings and pools in my belly, as vivid as neon.

He swipes a bit of caramel from the corner of my mouth. I lick it off the end of his finger. "Good?" he asks, all husky and low.

"The best."

"I was right about the caramel, huh?" He's leaning in. His nose brushes my forehead. My temple.

"Yeah. But I wasn't talking about that."

I want you to kiss me, I think.

But instead of asking, this time I make the move myself. I tilt my head and close that inch of distance. Our lips fit together, separate slightly, then meet again. His arms snake around me. His tongue slides past my lips, and I open up for him. Jake tastes like chocolate and salt and everything I could ever want.

"Don't want to cut our date short," he murmurs, "but I'd like to take you back to my place."

"I'm surprised at you, army. I thought you were a Boy Scout."

"You saying no?" He gives me another smoldering kiss before I can answer.

"I'm saying, hell yes. Does that make me seem easy?"

"I'm not judging."

We kiss more while we're waiting for the Uber. Then trade teasing kisses and play footsie in the driver's backseat, barely able to contain our eagerness.

The minute his front door is closed, Jake lifts me by the hips and fuses his mouth to mine. I wrap my legs around his waist. We only make it to the living room, where we collapse onto the couch with me straddling him. Jake pulls me as close as we can get while still wearing clothing—way too much clothing—and we both gasp when his erection presses against my core.

I dig my fingers into his hair and lick the ocean flavor from his skin. We manage to get his rash guard off, then my cover-up. He groans and cups my breasts in their bikini top. "Fuck, you look sexy in this."

"Then I'll leave it on. But I need you inside me. Right now."

I dive in to kiss him again. My fingers trace down his torso, following his happy trail to where it dips inside his waistband. My fingers close around his hot, hard length, and I give him a stroke. His cock jumps in my hand and he moans, but this time he sounds uncertain.

"Wait. Wait. I need to…"

I let go of him and sit back. "Something wrong?"

"*No*. Not even close. But I need to tell you this before we go any further." He touches my face. Drags his thumb over my lips. Searches my eyes. "I want you to stay."

"Stay tonight? Or…"

He tugs me forward until our foreheads touch. His hand goes to the back of my head, holding me there.

"Stay forever. With me."

All the emotions I've been keeping at bay roar straight into my throat, making it impossible for me to speak. All I can do is nod.

I want to be with you. I want to stay. Forever and ever.

"But I need you to be sure about what you're getting," he says. "You know…the things I've done. You've seen. I have stains on my soul that will never wash out."

I get my voice to work. "So do I. Different kinds, but still."

"That's not what I see in you."

"Then you know exactly how I feel when I look at you. You're the man who makes me whole again."

He swallows, and tiny droplets coat his lashes when he blinks. "Is a first date too soon to say I love you?"

I laugh, and that's the only reason I'm not crying right now. "Not if the other person says it back."

"I love you," he whispers against my lips.

"I love you too. And I *really* need you inside of me now."

Then it's hungry mouths and tongues and hands trying to get past our clothes. Jake rips the seam of my swim bottoms as he pulls them over my hips. We only get his trunks partway down his thighs before I start to sink down onto his cock. He hisses and grabs two handfuls of my ass cheeks. I have to go slow because we haven't had much foreplay. But I've been waiting long enough for this.

I want to feel every inch of him spreading me apart.

And he's so damn patient. I know he wants to take over. Jake loves his control. But he waits for me, watching my face as I impale myself inch by inch. "I love you."

I smile and lean forward to kiss him, nibbling on his lower lip. "I love you."

Finally, I bottom out. I feel him so deep inside of me. In every way.

We rock and roll our hips. Suck each other's tongues and lips and necks. Jake hooks his fingers in my bikini top and tugs the triangles down over my pert nipples. He bends forward and lavishes each bud with attention while I ride him. It's a little dirty but mostly sweet, which is exactly what I need. This intimate moment with him, kissing and sighing into each other's mouths, our bodies growing slick with sweat and arousal and delicious heat. Love. So much love.

My heart calls out to him. I feel his answering back. We come at the same time, on the same breath, staring into each other's eyes. This beautiful, wonderful man who I trust with every piece of me.

We stay there on the couch and hold each other, saying *I love you* so many times I lose count.

But we're making a mess, so finally Jake picks me up, kicking off his swim trunks the rest of the way, and carries me into his bedroom. We shower off together. Then we tumble into his bed and crawl under the covers.

"Did Adrienne say something to you at the beach?" I ask.

He's trailing his fingers down my backbone. "She told me to get off my ass and tell you how I feel before you leave. I realized I was doing the same thing as when we were kids. Letting you slip away in the name of giving you space. I couldn't let that happen."

"I was repeating the past, too. Thinking I couldn't have you."

"Guess we're both dense sometimes," he says.

"Yeah." I cuddle against him. "Good thing Adrienne's not."

Jake turns onto his side so he can meet my gaze. "I don't want to relive the past or be who we were before. I want to be so much more than that for you."

"You already are."

37

Jake

I feel like I cheated Harper out of a real first date. Ice cream was a nice start, but shouldn't I have done more?

Then again, from the look of pure bliss on her face and the *I-love-yous* falling from her lips, maybe not.

We don't move from my bed as the sun goes down and the house goes dark around us.

And I can't stop smiling. Everything feels right with the world. This moment between us has been a long time coming. We've both fought for it in so many ways. Watching Harper and her agony the past two months was difficult, but hearing her laughter return, seeing her bond with my family —it's made me happier than I can possibly explain.

I've always said I would do anything for her. I wanted to give back what the Caldwells had taken. I know the hard work was on Harper's part, but if I helped her along, then I'm honored and grateful that she trusted me enough to lean on me.

For me, the most difficult part of the last two months was stepping back and letting other people help her too.

After taking a solid month off of work, I went back to the office. I haven't returned to the field, but I've been keeping a close eye on the Caldwell investigation. Last I heard, Tristan had a team of lawyers defending him and there weren't going to be any charges against him. He managed to slide by, just like I thought he would.

Harper already knows that SunSpeed's assets have been seized by the government for running drugs, based on the evidence Harper previously provided. But the proof connecting those activities to Caldwell Enterprises was simply too tenuous. Harper wouldn't testify to keep her deal with Wren, and we didn't get the proof we needed, so the DEA decided not to pursue it for now. Sometimes, that's how it goes. That battle was lost, but the war goes on.

I still wonder about Amos Caldwell, though. Harper's uncle. It seems like he's disappeared from the face of the earth. I hope his bones are rotting in some barren wasteland. Soon to be forgotten.

But I'd feel better if they'd found his body.

If seeing Harper hurting made me feel that pain in my own heart, seeing her joy with my kids and family filled me with an equal measure of happiness. Day after day, thoughts of her took up more space in my mind. I longed to have her near me. If we weren't together, I wanted to know what she was thinking and doing. And whenever I saw her again? Damn, it was like my own personal fireworks show going off in my chest.

Add that to the insane levels of lust coursing through me whenever I look at her? Sounds like being in love to me. Feels like it too.

But of course, because I don't know when to quit, I didn't realize Harper was ready for a bigger declaration from me until Adrienne clued me in.

And she loves me back. She wants to stay. *Finally*. Some

part of me has been waiting for Harper to come back into my life for fourteen years.

My patience paid off after all.

"I got an email from Wren," Harper says.

We've been kissing and talking in my bed for at least an hour. I prop my head against my hand to see her better. My other hand draws circles against her bare arm. Our legs overlap beneath the blankets.

"When was that?" I ask.

"About a week ago. I wanted to tell you, but I've been trying to figure out how I feel about it first. She said she's doing well. She's back in Chicago, and she's seen our mom. She said..." Harper pauses, eyes shining, and I draw her closer. "She said she misses me and she wished she could be there for Dad's memorial service. I haven't written her back."

"You don't have to if you don't want to."

"I just don't know what to say. If she's reaching out to me, is it wrong for me not to answer?"

I slide my hand up her body and rest my palm on her cheek. "You risked everything to help her. You don't owe her anything more. If you want to talk to her, you can. But if you choose not to, you're not allowed to feel guilty about it."

Her lips twitch. "Is that an order?"

"Yep. I won't allow any guilty feelings. Only good stuff for you from now on."

"Because you command it?"

"You're getting the idea."

"I love you. Even if you're annoyingly bossy."

"I love you, too. Even when you don't listen."

She laces her hands behind my neck and pulls me down to kiss her. My tongue licks into her mouth, and she sucks on it. In seconds, my cock swells against her thigh.

We make out for a while until we're both panting and

she's on her back beneath me. My tip smears precome on her stomach as I rut gently against her, showing her what I want.

"You ready for me again?" I dip my hand between her legs to massage her clit. She gasps and moans. "You sound ready."

"I am. But I want you rougher this time."

My cock jerks. Adrenaline surges in my veins. I kiss the quivering pulse point at her neck. "Do you? Making demands?"

"Just saying, I know how raw and filthy you can get. That's what I want." She drags me to her and puts her lips to my ear. "Fuck me like you own me."

I grasp her jaw and squeeze oh-so-gently until her lips part. "You want me to own you?"

"You can try." She's got a wicked gleam in her hazel eyes. A naughty little smirk.

God, I love this woman.

"You're mine." I gather up her long hair and wrap it around my fist. My mouth trails hot kisses and bites over her neck and shoulders. "Mine to love," I murmur. "Mine to fuck."

"Prove it."

"I will. I'll show you so you won't ever forget it."

I pin her arms with my hands, then push her legs apart with my thighs and hold her there. The head of my cock meets her opening and slowly slides in. It even infuriates me, I'm moving at such a glacial pace.

"Still a tease, army?" she says with a smirk.

"Still got that bad-girl attitude?"

"I'm irrepressible."

"Wouldn't have it any other way."

She's wet from my come and her arousal, wiggling beneath me, testing me, and it takes all my willpower not to drive into her.

But once I'm all the way inside, I don't move my hips. Instead, I keep her there as I caress her face and cover her with soft, tender kisses. To her nose, her eyelids, her chin. I take my time connecting the freckles on her cheeks with my fingertips. Trying not to miss a single detail.

She's rolling her eyes at first. Then confused. And then...awed.

"I remember the first moment I saw you," I murmur. "So fierce and so beautiful. You had my heart, and there was nothing I could do about it."

This is what I mean when I say she's mine. That I own her when we're like this. I'm going to take care of her, even when she doesn't want me to. This is what she needs. So that's what I'll provide.

"I love you," I say. "I love you so much. Forever." I've told her fifty times that I love her in the past hour, but she still has shock in her expression when I look down at her.

"Jake," she whispers. A tear slips onto her cheek, and I kiss it away.

She's gone limp under me. Trembling slightly.

"Now," I growl, "I'm going to fuck you."

After more kisses and caresses, each more intense than the last, I pull out of her and flip her onto her belly, then grab her hips and tug them up until she bends at the knees. She arches her spine, her sex exposed, offering herself to me.

I'll take all of that and more.

Mine.

My cock slides into her pussy. Harper whimpers and whines as I thrust, withdraw, thrust. My shaft is bright red, shiny with wetness. Lust turns my brain fuzzy. It's a high like nothing else. Getting down and dirty with the woman who owns my heart.

"You're shameless for my cock, aren't you? Love watching you take it. You can't get enough."

"More," she whines, "more."

I hold on to her hair with one hand, my other pressing between her shoulder blades. I rest more of my weight against her, and Harper flattens out onto her stomach. Legs spread. I fuck her hard into the mattress.

The noises she's making are driving me wild.

She throws her head back as she convulses and cries out my name.

My orgasm overtakes me like a high-speed train. It slams into me, starting in my balls and my lower spine, then running rampant through every part of me. Blacking out my vision with hot, liquid pleasure. Jets of come spurt out of my cock into her. Marking her. *Property of.* Damn right.

I curl over her protectively, another possessive growl rumbling from my chest. For several minutes, neither of us moves except to breathe. My mind is completely blank. Just peaceful. Tamed.

After, I turn her over and tuck her into my side, my arms surrounding her. Her breasts rise and fall against me as she catches her breath. "That was...wow."

I laugh and bury my face in her hair. I feel just as wrecked as she does. Just as satisfied. From my perspective, forever doesn't seem like long enough. Not when it comes to Harper and me.

38

Harper

The next few weeks are some of the happiest I've ever spent. So I can't explain why a part of me still feels unsettled. Maybe I'm not used to so much goodness in my life. Like my heart can't believe this perfection could be permanent, even though Jake tells me every day with his words and actions that this is forever.

I want to believe it.

The morning after our ice cream date, Jake takes me with him to pick up the kids from Adrienne's. We walk inside, and two sets of little eyes zero-in on the spot where Jake and I are holding hands.

Hudson jumps up and down excitedly. "Did you make her happy, Daddy?"

Jake raises his eyebrows at me, and Adrienne smiles knowingly. All three adults crack up, and the twins frown in confusion.

Jake lets go of my hand to hug both kids. "Harper is my girlfriend. She's part of our family, and we can *all* make each other happy."

Riley looks up at me. "Are you going to live with us now?" She doesn't seem thrilled by the idea.

"Not yet," I say. I know what I want, but I'm hesitant to rush the kids.

"But someday," Jake adds firmly. "Soon." His eyes are full of love and hope and forever-feelings, and my heart does backflips in my chest.

Whenever the kids are at Adrienne's, Jake and I screw like bunnies in his bed. Or maybe like horny teenagers, except the way Jake fucks is all-man and very much eighteen-plus.

He's an intensely physical being, affectionate and generous with touch with all his family and friends. But he loves to express his physicality through sex, and that hot, dirty version of Jake is just for me. We say things through our bodies that I couldn't begin to form into words. And afterward, his relief is obvious. We connect on all kinds of levels, of course, but sex? It's a top contender for my favorite.

I send in my application to West Oaks College. It's the closest by distance, and a lot of the classes are online. While I don't need another degree since I've got my bachelor's in business, I need to complete enough education courses to qualify for the state exams, and once I pass, I can apply for my teaching credential.

While I continue living with Madison and Nash, I start spending more time with just Riley and Hudson. Art is the perfect medium for us to grow closer. We've made dozens of projects weaving grass and flowers together, drawing with pastels, paper mache. I love seeing their pride in their work. Of course, everyone in the Shelborne family oohs and aahs over each new project. We have family dinners almost every night, sometimes Jake, Adrienne, me and the kids, other times with Madison's crew. On Sunday nights, it's the entire Shelborne clan.

Everything is *perfect*.

And yet…there's that prickle of unease inside me. Something unfinished. Something *wrong*. And it's been growing instead of fading.

I tell Jake my fears, and he asks if I've seen anything specific near his or Madison's houses that worries me. But I haven't. It's just this feeling I can't shake. Madison asks her colleagues at West Oaks PD to step up patrols in the neighborhood in an abundance of caution.

But aside from that, I try to move past it. I'm seeing a therapist, and I'm living my new life. My wonderful, amazing life.

Even if I'm also carrying around the knife Jake gave me.

Today, I'm taking Riley and Hudson to a nearby art museum. It's a small collection of mostly watercolors, but the kids love it. They can't wait to get home to try painting some of their own. Jake is leading some sort of training with West Oaks PD's undercover officers today, and the kids had an early dismissal from kindergarten.

It's a gorgeous day, all blue sky and sea breezes, and we walk back to Jake's house. Riley and Hudson are on either side of me, holding my hands.

We stop at a park to eat the lunch I packed. I spread out peanut butter sandwiches, carrot sticks, and applesauce packets on a picnic table. Hudson scarfs a couple of bites before running off to climb and swing on each part of the equipment as fast as possible, but Riley likes to take her time. Usually, she'll eat what she wants, then choose her favored section of the playground and hang out there the whole time.

But today, she stays at the picnic table even after she's done eating. She's always thoughtful, but today she's extra quiet. Hudson makes space-battle noises in the background as he crosses the monkey bars.

"Harper?" Riley asks.

I set down my sandwich. "Yeah?"

She takes my hand and flattens it on the table, palm up. Then she draws a heart shape on my palm. Happy tingles race up my arm.

"That's lovely," I say. "Thank you. What's it for?"

"My daddy gave me his heart, and he said I could keep it. But...it would be okay with me if you borrow it. Sometimes."

I will not cry. I *will not*.

"Thank you," I whisper, with a lot more feeling this time. "I'd like that."

"Daddy said love doesn't run out. No matter how much you give, there's still more."

I've never loved Jake more than this moment, and he's not even here. "Your dad's right." I take her hand and draw a heart there. "You can have my heart, too. To keep."

She stares at her palm. "Do I have to share it with Hudson?"

"There's always more, remember? I'll give him one of his own."

And that's what I do, as soon as he returns to the table. Hudson grins and hugs me. Riley joins him. I circle my arms around them in our first group hug. Every day lately has been nearly perfect, but this one's a little more perfect than most.

"My watercolor painting is going to have a heart in it," Hudson announces on our way home.

"No, *mine* is," Riley says.

I squeeze their hands. "Remember? There are enough hearts for everyone."

We're almost to the house. I let go of the kids' hands and dig into my backpack for the keys.

Hudson tugs at my shirt. "Harper, look. The window looks funny."

I glance up. We're standing at an angle to the house, and

from here we can see a window on the side. There's a pane near the bottom that's broken.

I never would've noticed it if Hudson hadn't pointed it out.

Plenty of innocent explanations jump to my mind. Like the neighbor kids hitting a baseball the wrong direction, which they sometimes do. Or maybe the handyman who helped Jake fix the roof knocked into it and didn't say anything.

But I know in my gut it's not any of those things.

Primal terror claws its way up my throat.

I grab Riley and Hudson's arms and march them across the street, then down a few houses, where I pull us into the neighbors' backyard.

"What's wrong?" Riley asks. "I wanna go home."

My hands are shaking as I dig my phone out of the backpack. "I want you to wait at Mrs. Robinson's." She's retired. Never leaves the house. She loves when the kids come to visit and always gives them sugar cookies. "Ask Mrs. Robinson to call the police if I'm not back in five minutes."

"You mean Aunt Madison?" Hudson asks.

"I mean 911. It's a secret mission. Okay? Can I count on you?"

They both nod. I send them off on their way, through the gate that connects this yard with the Robinson house. I wait until the neighbor answers and lets them in.

I know they'll do what I asked.

The most cautious, self-preserving side of me is screaming that I should go with them. That I'm crazy to do what I'm about to do. And Jake would be furious if he knew.

But if someone came to Jake's house to hurt the people I love, came there because of *me*, I can't run and hide. What if the person leaves and comes back? Continues to haunt me like a ghost, making it impossible for me to move on with my life?

I told Jake I would stay with him, and that's what I'm going to do. But If I'm bringing danger to his door, I have to be the one to fix it. I won't let anyone hurt the people I love ever again.

This is my past coming back for me. Refusing to go away.

I have to fight it.

I walk back toward Jake's house. At the same time, I call his number on my cell and leave a voicemail. Then a text.

With every step, the fear recedes, replaced by a steady determination.

I circle around to approach the house from the back, going through some of the neighbors' yards. I take the knife from my backpack and hold it in one hand. My keys are in the other. I leave the pack by the fence.

My heart throbs as I approach the back entrance to Jake's house. *Thump thump thump.* I mount the steps.

Then, I just stare at the door for what feels like ages.

In my heart, I know it. He's here.

Enough, I tell myself. *This has to end.*

I try the knob, and it turns. Unlocked. Like he was waiting for me. Like he knew I'd come.

I step inside, grip tightening on the knife.

"Where are you?" I ask. My voice is thin with anger, yet hard, like the blade in my hand. "I know you're here."

My uncle steps into view.

Amos has lost at least thirty pounds since the last time I saw him. His salt-and-pepper hair has gone nearly white. There are sunken wrinkles around his face, as if all his years of cruelty have finally caught up to him. There's no trace of handsomeness or charisma about him now. He looks like the walking dead.

He holds a gun loosely in his fingers.

"It was all because of you," he says, sneering. "I know that now. You and Tristan, working against me. Did you really think I wouldn't make you pay for your betrayal?"

I widen my stance, shifting my weight from foot to foot. "No, I knew," I say, and it's the truth. Even if I've been trying to deny it since the moment we fled from the resort. Deep down, I knew this moment would come. "I figured you'd try."

He starts to open his mouth. Amos probably has some big, scary speech planned, all about how I'm nothing and I never should've had the audacity to think I could topple him from his throne.

Etcetera, etcetera.

But I have no interest in his monologue.

So instead, I lunge as a primal scream roars out of me. Like some Amazonian warrior.

I knock him onto his back. He loses his grip on the gun and it skitters across the floor, hitting a wall. I bring my knife up to his throat.

"The police are on their way. Give up, and I won't have to use this."

But my uncle's not done yet. With a sudden burst of viciousness, he knocks the knife aside and rolls us both over. He's taller than me. And even though he's much weaker than he used to be, he has no hesitation about hurting others. He smacks me across the face. His hands close around my throat and squeeze.

Suddenly, Amos flies backward. He hits the wall and slides to the ground.

Jake is here.

He's snarling, head down and fists clenched. Murder in his eyes. "Harper, go," he says through gritted teeth. "I'll handle this."

I hear sirens getting louder in the distance.

Before my uncle can get up, Jake is on him. Slamming his fist into my uncle's face. Again. Again.

Amos looks woozy, like he's barely conscious. He's not fighting back.

But Jake isn't stopping.

"Jake." I grab his shoulder. "*Jake.*"

His arm pulls back to hit Amos again, but he stops. His whole body hums with energy, and I can feel how much he wants to unleash it.

But instead, Jake's arm drops to his side. The fire of bloodlust dims from his eyes. "Amos Caldwell, you're under arrest. And if I have anything to say about it, you're going away for a long damn time."

Then he gets up and we hold each other until the local police come. Jake presses his face to my hair. "Thank you," he whispers.

It might seem strange for him to say it, since he's the one who showed up just when I needed him. But I understand exactly what he means.

∿

WE'RE BACK AT THE POLICE STATION. I KNOW NASH and Madison work here, and Jake spends time here, too. But if I never see this place again, it'll be too soon.

Thank goodness Jake was leading that training here today, because it meant he could get home to me lightning fast.

Jake hasn't left my side for a moment, even when Detective Murphy said she needed to speak to us each separately. He refused, and she let it slide. She's tough, but she's got a soft heart underneath. Like several other people I know.

The rest of Jake's family snapped into action just as quick. Riley and Hudson are at their grandmother's house now, and Madison is here at the station with me and Jake.

As expected, Jake wasn't happy that I chose to go into the house without waiting. But mostly, he's just relieved, like me. Riley and Hudson did exactly what I asked and had Mrs. Robinson call the police. Aside from that, they have no idea what a close call we had.

If Hudson hadn't noticed that broken window, I don't know how the story would've ended. It scares me to think of it. I know I would've fought until my last breath to protect the twins. No doubts there. But I'm just glad they didn't have to witness it.

"We found the car that your uncle's been living in," Detective Murphy says. "We think he's been hiding from the authorities for the last two months."

"And hiding from Tristan," I add.

I have no idea what happened. Whether Tristan tried to kill his father, and Amos escaped. Or if Amos realized Tristan's treachery beforehand. Regardless, I'm guessing that Amos saw me as an easier target for revenge than Tristan.

I'll bet he's been watching me for weeks.

It doesn't matter. The police have him now. Even if they can't pin anything drug-related on him, ridiculous as that seems given all I know to be true, they've got him on battery charges against me. Maybe even attempted murder, not to mention the whole breaking and entering part.

When we get a moment alone, Jake pulls me into a quiet meeting room at the station. He holds me so tightly it's a struggle to breathe, but I hug him back with equal force.

"Are you okay?" he asks.

"I am now. I'm sorry, Jake. I'm so sorry. Amos could've hurt your kids because of me."

"No," he insists. "Don't ever think of it like that. You belong with us. You're part of this family, and no one's *ever* going to take that away from us."

That night, all the Shelbornes end up at Jake's parents'

house. Madison says it's not the first time that's happened after a crisis.

Jake and I spend time with Riley and Hudson, giving them as many hugs and kisses as they can tolerate. They ask lots of questions, but all they know is that a bad guy came near their house and that Jake and I stopped him. Then they both want to play superheroes and get into an argument over the rules of this new game.

My family, I keep repeating in my head. *No one is going to take that away from me.*

But the ache in my heart doesn't go away until I hear the news a few days later: Amos is dead. One of the other inmates in the county lockup attacked him.

The picture becomes clearer when I get a greeting card in the mail. It's addressed to me at Jake's house, where I've been spending every night since Amos's reappearance. The front of the card has a photo of a sunset over the ocean.

The inside has two sentences. *I took care of it. You have nothing to fear.* It's not signed, and there's no return address. But I know the hand-writing. It's from Wren.

I'm not sure what it means. Did she ask Tristan to arrange Amos's death? That couldn't have been too difficult. Yet her phrasing is strange.

Is *Wren* in charge of the Caldwell family now?

An even bigger shock arrives a month later. That's when Jake comes home from work and tells me about the massive break in the DEA's investigation against Tristan. The agency has just received a data dump of insider information about Caldwell Enterprises from an anonymous informant. Tristan's lawyers won't be able to squeeze him out of this one. He's going down.

And Wren? I get another card, this one stamped from Tahiti.

You started this, and you gave me the courage to finish it. I think

we made a good team. I love you, Harper. You will always be my sister.
Be free and be happy. That's what I'm going to do.

I show the postcard to Jake. "Wow," he breathes. "She came through. I never saw that coming."

"Me neither. But I'm proud of her." I hope I get the chance to tell her.

No matter what, I'm going to spend the rest of my days with my beautiful family, showing them how much I love them.

EPILOGUE

Jake

"*I* pronounce you husband and wife," the officiant says.

Nash and Madison kiss, and the audience cheers. Harper claps beside me, and I let out a loud whoop. I've been to a lot of weddings, and this one might just be the best—so far, anyway.

I put an arm around Harper and tilt my head against hers.

Nash and my sister opted for a backyard ceremony at my parents' house. They really did this place up right, with flowers and greenery everywhere and summer jasmine in the air.

We toss confetti at Nash and Madison as they dash together down the aisle, and people start getting up. But Harper leans over to me. "Where did you go just before the ceremony started? You disappeared."

"Nash just needed a little pep talk." He was having wedding-day jitters about his second marriage, not wanting to mess it up. I assured him that he'd found the right person and he's where he's supposed to be. Anyone who sees Nash, Madison, and Emma together would think that's obvious.

Finding your true family doesn't always happen right away. I'm in the same boat. Harper is my forever, even if it took a while for us to get here.

I've been with Harper for a year now. She's my best friend, my partner in everything, and she's also the gorgeous woman who can't get enough of my cock. Can it get better than that?

Probably not. But that doesn't mean I won't try.

My work life has definitely improved in the last year. I've stopped doing undercover work, and now I train undercover officers for the task force. Otherwise, I work on DEA investigations from behind a desk. When I go home to my family, I have no conflict about who I am. Loving Riley and Hudson and Harper is always my top priority.

But at work? I still fight bad guys. If I didn't, I wouldn't be me.

Tristan Caldwell is serving a ten-year sentence in federal prison on a racketeering conviction. He got a reduced sentence for providing information on some of his business associates, including the government agents who were on his payroll. Somehow, I got a lot of the credit for the destruction of Caldwell Enterprises, even though it was Harper and Wren who made it possible. In the end, the info Wren provided was enough to seal Tristan's fate.

Harper has spoken to her sister a few times. Wren had her baby, and she's continued living out of the country. Whether she's afraid of running into the remnants of the Caldwell family, or if she just needed to get as far away from her old life as possible, I don't know. But she and Harper have made their peace. They lead separate lives now. But they each know that the other is thriving.

The only remaining Caldwell in Harper's life is Mia, her cousin, though Mia isn't technically a Caldwell after changing her name. She's graduated with her social work degree, and she's busy being an advocate for crime victims. Earlier this year, Harper and I took a road trip with the kids up to Northern California and stopped to see her. Mia's living with a ton of friends in San Francisco and loves every second of it.

"Want to get out of here?" I ask Harper, dropping my voice and giving her my best smolder.

"We're not bailing on your sister's reception to get naked."

"But the kids are playing with Emma. We can slip away, and they won't even know we're gone."

"Don't tempt me." Harper tugs at my hand. "Come on, let's get some champagne. I feel like celebrating."

"Wait," I say, pulling her back to me. "Kiss me?"

I want to bask in the moment a little longer. Plus, I know that the minute we join the crowd, they'll start asking questions about when Harper and I are going to tie the knot. I could put them out of their misery and say, *I'm working on it*, but that would just make them more demanding. Especially my mother. She hates being the last to know anything, but on this particular subject? Sorry, Mom. I'm keeping my secrets.

Harper smiles up at me. She cups my face, pulls me down, and our mouths fit together. I nudge my tongue along the seam of her lips, my hands wandering along her side to her ass, but she pulls back.

"We're going to scandalize your grandparents," she says. "Don't you have a good-boy reputation to uphold?"

I shrug. "I don't think they're buying that anymore. Not after what happened at Christmas."

She snorts a laugh, cheeks turning red. "Your *grandparents* know about that?"

"Are you kidding? *Everyone* knows about that."

At Christmas, right after Nash proposed to Madison, my mother realized that Harper and I weren't in the room. We'd missed the happy moment. So she went looking for us, and…

Let's just say, my mother will never again open a closed door without knocking first. You'd think she would've learned after that first incident way back when Harper and I were teenagers, but nope. I'm equally to blame because I failed to lock the door to my childhood bedroom, where I'd sneaked away with Harper halfway through Christmas morning's festivities. I just couldn't wait to get my hands on her. At least we were mostly clothed that time. But my mothers yelp of surprise brought everyone else running. Aiden and Madison ragged on me for the rest of the holidays about my lack of self control.

I give Harper another kiss, keeping my lips closed this time. "Looking at you, I don't see how anyone could fault me. I have extremely good taste."

Harper's grown her hair a bit longer, and she's got tiny gold rings lining her ear cartilage like when we were teenagers. Gone are the business suits and heels she wore as a SunSpeed executive. Now, she's all about the ripped jeans and T-shirts with designs she makes herself. At the moment, she's wearing a long blue sundress that clings to her ample curves.

My girl finished her certification, and she's an art teacher at the elementary where Riley and Hudson go to school. Their favorite thing in the world is going to art class, though there was an issue with them arguing over who got to sit closest to Harper's desk. She had to banish both of them to the back of the class for their misbehavior. Adrienne helped them make cards to apologize.

Harper's been working on her own projects as well. I built her a small studio in the backyard, and recently she had her first showing here in West Oaks. A guy named Nic Anderson owns the gallery. He's a friend of a friend of Madison's. I was wary at first because Nic Anderson wasn't always his name. I knew him as the mobster Dominic Crane, and he's got a checkered past that's far worse than Harper's. But he seems like a nice enough guy these days. He's living proof of second chances.

At Harper's show, I was both embarrassed and proud to find out that one of her drawings was of *me*. The kids loved seeing it framed in the gallery. Adrienne bought it and presented it to me wrapped in a bow. And trust me, my siblings aren't going to let me live it down either. They keep sending me listings about modeling gigs. The dumbasses.

Harper and I grab our champagne glasses and avoid my relatives' nosy questions. I take her for a spin around the dancefloor as soon as the official dances are over.

"Do you think you'd want a party like this for a wedding?" I ask. "Or something smaller?" There's a slow song playing, and I've got Harper pulled as close as I dare without edging into dirty-dancing territory.

She smirks. "Why, is this a prelude to a bigger question?"

"I'm just curious. Nash and Madison's ceremony was beautiful, but I'd rather skip the fuss altogether."

"Same here. Quiet is good."

"Like...just you, me, Riley, and Hudson?"

"That could be nice. Someday."

"What about tomorrow?" I ask.

Her eyes flare. She stops dancing.

I lean into her and whisper in her ear, "Marry me?"

And then, she goes and laughs. "You're the worst tease, Shelborne." But I just smile softly at her, and her eyes widen even more. "Wait. Are you serious?"

"I am. But it's a bad sign if you don't believe me. I could ask Detective Murphy if West Oaks PD has any more diamond rings in the evidence room, but—"

"That is *not* the kind of proposal I want." She looks up at me, those green irises studying me. "Jake. Do you mean it?"

I nuzzle my nose against hers. "Yeah. I looked it up.

There's no waiting period, and the county clerk's office is open tomorrow. We could take the kids and make this legal. If you really do want the diamond ring and the white dress and the big party, I'll give that to you. But—"

"*No*. I mean, crap, *yes*. I'm saying yes. I don't need all that stuff. Just you and the kids." She laughs and bites her lip. "Will your mom forgive us if we don't tell her first?"

"My mom loves you. She'll forgive you anything. Besides, she just got the big wedding. She's set for a while."

"Okay. I'd do it for the last name change alone. Save some time on the paperwork. Mia complained about it."

I bark a laugh. "Glad to be of service."

We giggle and kiss and sway to the music, and it's disgustingly romantic. Somebody clinks a fork against a champagne glass, calling for Nash and Madison to kiss, but I've only got eyes for Harper.

"You're already a Shelborne," I murmur to her. "This will just make it official."

"That part will be nice. But the best part will be knowing I'm yours."

"You know I'd do anything for you."

"Just love me. That's all I need."

"I've got you covered, then. You're making this easy." I kiss her again. "I love you," I whisper. "Always."

"I love you too, army."

I'll never get tired of hearing that.

The End.

ALSO BY HANNAH SHIELD

THE WEST OAKS HEROES SERIES

THE SIX NIGHT TRUCE (Janie & Sean)
THE FIVE MINUTE MISTAKE (Madison & Nash)
THE FOUR DAY FAKEOUT (Jake & Harper)

THE BENNETT SECURITY SERIES

HANDS OFF (Aurora & Devon)
HEAD FIRST (Lana & Max)
HARD WIRED (Sylvie & Dominic)
HOLD TIGHT (Faith & Tanner)
HUNG UP (Danica & Noah)
HAVE MERCY (Ruby & Chase)

ABOUT THE AUTHOR

Hannah Shield once worked as an attorney. Now, she loves thrilling readers on the page—in every possible way.

She writes steamy, suspenseful romance with feisty heroines, brooding heroes, and heart-pounding action. Visit her website at www.hannahshield.com.

Made in the USA
Coppell, TX
06 February 2024